*no place I'd
rather be*

Books by Cathy Lamb

JULIA'S CHOCOLATES

THE LAST TIME I WAS ME

HENRY'S SISTERS

SUCH A PRETTY FACE

THE FIRST DAY OF THE REST OF MY LIFE

A DIFFERENT KIND OF NORMAL

IF YOU COULD SEE WHAT I SEE

WHAT I REMEMBER MOST

MY VERY BEST FRIEND

THE LANGUAGE OF SISTERS

NO PLACE I'D RATHER BE

Published by Kensington Publishing Corporation

no place I'd rather be

CATHY LAMB

KENSINGTON BOOKS
www.kensingtonbooks.com

KENSINGTON BOOKS are published by

Kensington Publishing Corp.
119 West 40th Street
New York, NY 10018

All Kensington titles, imprints, and distributed lines are available at special quantity discounts for bulk purchases for sales promotion, premiums, fund-raising, educational, or institutional use.

Special book excerpts or customized printings can also be created to fit specific needs. For details, write or phone the office of the Kensington Sales Manager: Kensington Publishing Corp., 119 West 40th Street, New York, NY 10018. Attn. Sales Department. Phone: 1-800-221-2647.

Kensington and the K logo Reg. U.S. Pat. & TM Off.

eISBN-13: 978-1-4967-0982-0
eISBN-10: 1-4967-0982-9
First Kensington Electronic Edition: September 2017

ISBN-13: 978-1-4967-0981-3
ISBN-10: 1-4967-0981-0
First Kensington Trade Paperback Printing: September 2017

10 9 8 7 6 5 4 3 2 1

Printed in the United States of America

For Dr. Karen Straight

and Marcus and Nancy Sassaman

with love, always

Prologue

〜

November 1945
Kalulell, Montana
Gisela Martindale, future grandmother of Olivia Martindale

Her hands shook as she held the cookbook. It was old, the leather cover cracked, the pages blackened by fire around the edges. Blood stains were splattered on more than one recipe, words smeared by tears and tea on others. The pink ribbon that tied it together, once bright and clean, was ragged and worn.

The recipes within it had been handed down through five generations of women, starting with her great-great-grandmother. They were written in four languages, across three countries.

Inside was her family's history, with hand-drawn pictures of family members, old and young, some who lived a long time, others who didn't, whose deaths were a crime. There were pictures of a village in a far-off, distant land, people on horseback, donkeys pulling carts, women with kerchiefs and shawls in the middle of a town square, city homes with red doors and lush gardens, herbs and vegetables, red geraniums, sumptuous cakes and cookies. There were recipes written in the midst of tragedy and stifling fear, and recipes written with a light and joyous heart. She knew the stories behind every one of them.

Between the pages, she had left the pressed and dried pink rose; two heart-shaped, gold lockets; a charm in the shape of a sun; a white feather; red ribbons; recipes taped onto back pages; the photographs and the poems.

One day, she would cook from it again. One day. When the book itself didn't make her feel like crying, breaking down, dying. She pressed the ancient cookbook to her chest, the tears racing from her green eyes down her cheeks, light streaming in from the only window in the attic.

She tucked it into the bottom of a cardboard box. On top of it she folded a simple, white lace wedding dress and veil; a dark blue dress and matching blue hat with flowers on the brim and a white ribbon, which she would never wear again; and a white nurse's uniform, also stained with blood.

She added a tin box, on its lid an old-fashioned picture of ladies in fancy dresses dancing at a ball, that had been hidden beneath the floorboards in another country for many dangerous years. Inside were two red and purple butterfly clips, two charm bracelets, the lost letters from lost people, colored pencils, and a small silver treasure that had survived two attacks. She brought the treasure to her mouth and kissed it.

She pushed everything down, gently, her tears soaking into the nurse's uniform, the cookbook, the blue hat. She taped and sealed the box, extra tight, too much tape, way too much tape, as if the grief and terror of her past life would stay locked inside if she could cover it in enough tape.

When she was done, she pushed the box to the far corner, the darkest corner. The rest of the attic was empty. They didn't have much. She, certainly, did not have much. In fact, she had next to nothing.

But the log home that they had built together was finished. It had a view of the winding Telena River and the snowcapped Dove Mountains. When he had asked her what she wanted in their new home, she had cried when she told him why she always needed to see in all directions, why she needed many windows. He had held her hand and told her he understood. Their home was filled with far more windows than a traditional log cabin would have.

She had also told him why she needed a red door and why she would always plant red geraniums in the summer. He had painted the door red and built flower boxes at every window for her red geraniums.

He told her he would build her a gazebo in the summer, and he told her why. Dear man, he knew her well.

It was a new life she had now in Montana, thousands of miles away from where she had been, from what she had seen, from what she knew.

She bent over the box, her thick, brown hair falling forward, and cried until she could cry no more. Then she dried her tears, pushed her clawing, scraping nightmares back into a far corner of her mind, as she had pushed the cardboard box back into the far corner of the attic, and went downstairs. She put a smile on her face for her new husband. She loved him so.

The taped box, and the old cookbook, stayed right where she left them for decades.

Until it rained one winter day.

Chapter 1

∽

January 2010
Kalulell, Montana
Olivia Martindale

Do not drive in blizzards.

Especially in Montana, at night.

It will make your heart pound as if it's trying to escape from your chest, your foot on the accelerator shake, and your mind leap in a thousand panicked directions. It's dangerous, it's life-threatening.

It's stupid.

I am stupid.

We left Oregon early this morning. To be honest, I rushed us out of Oregon. I had my reasons. The reasons scared me to my bones and made them rattle. Suffice it to say: We needed out. Immediately. As soon as I had written permission, we left.

It was cool in Oregon, raining and misting, sweater weather only. We drove east, then north, and all was well, until we had a flat outside of Coeur d'Alene, Idaho. I hauled out the jack and changed the tire, but we got behind. It started snowing lightly when we started up the mountains; became worse at the top; and, coming into Kalulell, the snow turned into a blizzard. My phone was dead, so that added to my teeth-grinding anxiety.

But I was close to home, close to the log cabin with the red door that my granddad and grandma had built together, in 1945.

I saw a familiar sign announcing Kalulell. It was almost covered with snow, but I knew I had only a few miles to go. The snow fell faster, thicker, and my wiper blades could not keep up with it. My tires, even with chains on, slid sporadically over the ice. The wind that whistled around my car as if taunting me, the sideways snow that made me feel upside-down, and the fact that I could hardly see ten feet in front of my face yanked my fear up to stratospheric levels.

I gripped the steering wheel with tight hands and tried not to have a panic attack. I breathed deeply, then panicked when I couldn't breathe deeply again. I tried to breathe shallowly, then panicked when I thought I wasn't getting enough air. Maybe I was having a heart attack. Oh dear, oh no, I could not have a heart attack now. Not now.

I had to fix things first. I had to protect them.

Growing up here in Montana, I learned how to do a lot of things. I can break a horse, no matter how rebellious. I can work outside all day on our property. I can chop wood for hours, I can milk cows, and I can ski on one foot. One time I faced down a bull because I knew I couldn't sprint to the fence fast enough. He turned away.

But I don't drive in blizzards. Call it a personal hysteria button.

I reclenched the steering wheel, my black cowgirl boot shaking on the accelerator, and saw another sign. I looked away. I knew what lay beyond that particular sign, in a place where the grass was green in the summer, the buttercups a golden blanket. I also knew what was on top of that hill, way across the meadow, with a view of magical sunsets. I felt a thump in my heart and wanted to cry.

"Stop it," I whispered to myself. "Stop it now, you baby. Buck up."

But I didn't buck up. I couldn't. And that's the problem when you return to a place, a place you called home, and things happened that were shattering and you leave and it's easier because you don't have to be reminded of the things you don't want to think about when you're gone, but then you come back, and there it all is, like mini lightning strikes to your soul.

Through the swirling snow I could see the outline of a familiar white fence, which meant that the river was now on my other side. Fence on the left, river on the right. The river would be filled with snow and ice, dangerous and fast, a gray, slithering snake.

I had driven alongside this fence more times than I could count, and it was a comfort to me in some ways. I knew where I was. And yet seeing it made breathing hard and I tried to inhale and the air seemed to get stuck in my lungs.

The wind hit my car with a howl out of hell itself, and I felt it shift, snow covering my windshield. Through my silly tears the white twirled all around me, like a snow tornado. It was then that I hit a patch of ice. We skidded, like a marble across a wood floor, careening to the right, then the left, back to the right. I thought of the raging river snake below us.

I braked, we spun in a final circle, I screamed.

They woke up and screamed along with me. They had had more than their share of screams in their young lives, and this was not fair. They did not deserve any more screams.

We tipped, a horrible jerk over the edge of the road, the front of my car pointing down toward the broken ice in the churning river, a skinny tree trunk smashed into my right side.

We were going to die.

Oh no. We were going to die.

I had left my job as a sous-chef two weeks ago, after I threw a chicken at my boss.

"What are you doing, Olivia?" Carter shrieked, turning toward me in his state-of-the-art, cold and sterile stainless steel kitchen.

It wasn't a live chicken—that would not have been kind to the chicken—but a whole, plucked chicken. Clearly I was losing my mind. Probably because of the phone calls I had been getting. The underlying threats. "Stop yelling at Brayonna, Carter."

"What?" His face, sweaty and flushed, scrunched up in fury. "What?"

"She burned the crème brûlée, Carter. That's it. It's a dessert. Only a dessert. No one was hurt. No one was in danger. She doesn't deserve to be yelled at."

That I interfered in the middle of his swearing tantrum enflamed him and his ego. "It's not just a *dessert,* Olivia. It's my famous crème brûlée." He stabbed his finger at me. "This is my restaurant and everything must be done flawlessly, perfectly. If she can't do perfect, she's out."

All of the other chefs were suddenly quiet, standing still over bubbling pots, gas-fired stoves, bowls full of cake batter and soups, thick steaks and shrimp, fresh fruits and vegetables ready to be sliced. Outside the double doors we had customers waiting, people who had sat on waiting lists for weeks, tonight a special event for them.

"You yelled at Ethan tonight, too, Carter, because you said his sauce wasn't creamy enough. You berated him until he cried and left."

"It *wasn't* creamy enough," he seethed, then slammed down a wooden spoon. "Not. Creamy. Enough!"

"It's sauce. It's not life." Of all the things to get upset about. Crème brûlée. Sauce. It made me want to cry. These are not things in life to melt down over. "You knocked Georgia's hat off her head tonight because you said she didn't add enough butter. It's butter. That's all it is. Chill out."

"No, Olivia!" His voice spiked as he charged over to me. "It's not. Butter makes or breaks my recipes, so it makes or breaks my reputation. No one can blemish my reputation!" He threw a dish towel to the floor. "And stay out of this! Who asked you what you thought?"

"I always say what I think, and what I think is that it's only butter. From a cow." I had had it. I knew it at that moment. Carter demeaned people constantly. Everyone hated him, except his henchman, Ralphie, who smirked at me. Every dictator has a right-hand henchman who doesn't think for himself. I don't hate anyone, but Carter was one of the meanest people I have ever met. I think that's why I picked up an egg and threw it at him. He ducked and I missed, which was disappointing. I take pride in my aim—being a Montana girl I knew how to shoot a gun and a bow and arrow—so I threw a second one. Got him. He dodged to the left, then to the right. I pelted an egg at the smirking, nonthinking Ralphie, too. Target hit.

"What the hell, Olivia?" Carter lurched left. I got him again.

I wasn't angry. Some part of my mind couldn't believe what I was doing. The other part thought that a man who could actually turn into a frothing Tasmanian devil over crème brûlée deserved to have eggs thrown at him. Did he not read the newspaper? Did he not see what happened to people? Now, that was worth melting down over. I myself had had a total meltdown two years ago. It had had nothing to do with crème brûlée.

"You need to stop yelling at people, Carter. You need to treat people like humans. Don't be a frightening prick."

He gasped. "I do treat them like humans unless they're screwing up my restaurant! What? Ethan can't make sauce right after I've shown him twice? Brayonna still can't make crème brûlée without burning it? Are they stupid?"

"No." For some reason I thought I should throw a potato at him, so I did, and he ducked and swore, but I had anticipated the duck, so the potato smacked him. I chucked one at smirking Ralphie, too. Dead center. He said, "Ooph."

Carter's was now a popular restaurant in Portland. I had worked for him as his sous-chef since I left Montana, two years ago. I was in charge of the kitchen when Carter wasn't there. I was in charge of the menu, including all of the specials, and often worked twelve-hour shifts. Carter would not admit it, but his restaurant was not doing well when I arrived on the scene. In fact, he was close to going belly-up.

He and I sat down and revamped the menu. We cooked together. I showed him my recipes. We made them and he loved them. I had the restaurant remodeled. We had an excellent review in the paper, then another one, and it was word of mouth from then on out.

I think of it as American fine dining, elegant and plentiful, with a splash of Italian and the colors and spices of Mexico. I needed the job when Carter hired me. I had nothing. He gave it to me and I was grateful, but he was a temperamental and explosive chef, and my frayed nerves couldn't take him anymore.

"I'm out." I turned to the other people, my coworkers, who were equally fed up with crazy Carter, and said, "I'm sorry."

Two people closest to me reached over and gave me a hug, then more came. "Please don't go," they whispered. "I can't handle Carter without you . . . don't do this . . . Leave now, come back tomorrow, please, Olivia . . . I can't take his screaming with you gone. . . ."

"Olivia!" Carter yelled at me, his finger waving, egg dripping down his white chef's coat. "If you leave here, you can never come back! If you come back tomorrow, I will close the door. If you come back in a week, probably I will keep the door shut. If you come crawling back in a month, I will think about letting you back in, so do not leave. I have made you the chef you are. You owe me!"

I laughed. So did a bunch of other people. It was so patently false that in response I picked up an onion and pitched it at him, and then, my finale, because he had yelled and yelled at me for months, carrots. He dodged and ducked and swore as one after another hit. Ralphie was hiding behind the island. I managed to land an onion on him anyhow. Again: I take pride in my aim.

I heard the other chefs smothering their laughter.

I took off my hat, and the net, my brown hair tumbling down my back. I grabbed my bag, all of my recipes that I'd collected in a notebook, and my knives, and I walked out through the front door, waving at the waitstaff, their faces confused.

I went home to my small, one-bedroom apartment in downtown Portland. The girls, six and seven years old, were in bed, my bed, as I was now on the couch in the family room, and I paid the babysitter. She has tattoos and piercings and is sweet and loves to do crafts with the girls.

I took a shower, unfolded the couch into a bed, piled on the blankets, and opened my computer. I had some savings. Not a lot. The attorney had cost a bucket of money. My car had broken down, too, which was expensive. I missed the truck I had had in Montana. I had to sell it to pay the attorney. I made another payment to the hospital. A few months ago I had had to spend four days there for a bleeding ulcer that hit an artery. My deductible was $6,800. I would be making payments for months.

I was a single mother. It was still hard for me to grasp that after six months. But I might not be their mother forever. There were complications, problems, issues. Terrifying things. And now I had no job. Fear, strangling and tight, curled around my entire being.

The next morning, early, I got another call. The woman's words terrorized me.

And that's when I knew we had to leave, to escape, immediately.

The car teetered on the edge of the icy road, as if we were on a multi-ton seesaw.

"What's happening?" Stephi yelled.

"Aunt Olivia, what's going on?" Lucy said.

The car wobbled, up and down, again. My windshield wipers were still on, but they were hardly making a dent in the snow coming down like a white, cold blanket, ready to smother anyone who stood too long in one place.

I knew what was below us. I knew what would happen when the car tilted down a few inches in the wrong direction. "Don't move," I choked out. "Don't move." The car stopped, the engine growling.

"Don't move?" Stephi said. "Oh no oh no. Oh no."

"Right. Stay still."

"I'm scared," Lucy said. "So scared. Help, Aunt Olivia! Help me!"

"I know, baby. But don't move."

I could hardly see. The wind battered the car. I didn't want to open the door, because I didn't know if I would drop down the side, between the road and the car, and disappear. But I couldn't stay in the car with them and risk plunging down the cliff into the river. I had a vivid image of the car filling with freezing water and ice as I struggled to yank the girls through a window. I shoved down bubbling hysteria, knowing hysteria would not help this situation.

We teetered again, and I jammed my teeth together so I didn't let loose a bloodcurdling scream. I opened the door to the car, slowly, so slowly, to see if my half of the car was still on the highway. If it was, I would carefully climb over the seat and haul the girls out. I would not think about how the three of us would survive in a blizzard once we were out. At least we would have a chance. The river offered no chances; the river snake would drown us.

Snow flew in when I opened the door, and the girls whimpered. I wanted to whimper, too. How far over the edge were we? How much pavement was on my side? Should I have the girls climb out on their own and stay where I was to balance the car out?

The wind whooshed through the car and the girls screamed, the noises blending together. Then the car rocked up and down. We were going down the cliff and into the river. At that cataclysmic moment, between life and death, I thought of *her.*

She had breathed into the phone the morning after I'd quit my job. Heavy. Deliberate. She lowered her voice. "I have a surprise for you, Olivia."

I would not like the surprise, I knew that.

"Want to know what the surprise is?"

"No." I hated her calls. I gripped the lid of the blender. I was making the girls a fruit smoothie with raspberries, bananas, and strawberries.

She giggled. "Surprises are fun." She sang the word *fun.* "Fun and exciting."

I waited, my throat tight.

"You're going to lose, Olivia."

I closed my eyes.

"You lose," she singsonged. "I win, win, win."

"Don't call me again."

"Why? I like talking to you."

"I don't like talking to you."

She laughed and laughed. "Olivia, you have no idea what's going to happen soon. None. But I know and I like it. You won't like it. You won't like it at all."

"What are you talking about?" I walked away from the blender, passing a mirror I have in the nook. My green eyes, cat eyes I'm told, that tilt up at the corners, looked stricken.

"It's a secret. I like secrets."

"Last time, what are you talking about?" I felt my whole body clench, as if waiting for a blow.

"What am I talking about?" she whispered. "What am I talking about? That's easy." She giggled again. "Revenge, Olivia. I'm talking about revenge."

I hung up on her laughter. She thinks she's so funny.

I don't find her funny at all.

Her sick rage echoed in my ear.

Her harsh words cut through my heart.

Her hissed threats clogged my throat until I could hardly breathe.

I gripped the counter in front of me, the silence a sickening contrast to the evil conversation I'd had. Outside my apartment the gray clouds rolled, the rain pouring down, blurring everything.

I had to get out of Oregon.

I had to go where she could not find me, find us.

I knew exactly where to go.

I called my attorney.

In two weeks, with permission, with hands that trembled, I began to pack. Then I gave away our furniture.

I would keep them safe. I would hold them close.

I would never let her come near them again.

That's why I had to survive this car accident. Because of her. For them.

Through the open door, I could see that my car, on my side,

was still on the pavement. How much pavement I didn't know, the snow near blinding. It couldn't be much, as we were rocking back and forth. "Unlock your seat belts, Lucy and Stephi. I'm coming to get you."

The car tilted forward again. "Stop! Don't move. Wait!" The car leveled out.

"Aunt Olivia!"

"Wait . . . wait . . . okay. Do it now! Unstrap." My voice was sharp. They unbuckled, and I started to crawl over the seat. "Wrap your arms around my neck. Stephi, over here. Lucy here. Hold on. Do you hear me? Hold on as tight as you can."

They sobbed, but they did it, brave girls, their blond curls in my face. "Don't move!" I snapped as the car moved again. I closed my eyes. When we stopped moving, I swung them onto my lap and opened the back door. The door opened so easily, too easily. The snow blew in, cold prickles on my face.

"Give them to me."

I jumped at the man's voice, not two feet from me. Through the blur of white I saw him. A tall man, huge shoulders, thick black jacket. He reached in and grabbed us, all of us, his arms long and strong.

Our eyes met, now inches away, over the girls' blond heads, and for a second, only a second, as we had no more time than that, I saw his utter shock. I felt the same shock. I knew him. Knew that body. Knew that voice.

"Let's go." He lifted us up.

I put a boot down on the icy pavement, then the other one, as he pulled us out of the car, away from the edge of the road, the blizzard whipping around us. My car groaned behind us, shifting forward, then back, then toward the river. The girls screamed as the car tumbled over the side, smashing into the roiling river snake below.

I let him pull the girls from my arms.

"Put your arms around my neck," he told them.

"Aunt Olivia!" They reached for me, their expressions scared as this huge man took them away.

"Hold on to him! I'm coming with you."

"Grab my jacket, Olivia." We bent against the snow and headed toward his truck, his lights on. He opened the back door and dropped the girls in, shut the door, then opened the driver's door and pushed me in, gently. I scrambled over to the passenger seat as he got into the driver's seat and shut the door against the blizzard. The warmth, the feeling of safety, was immediate for me. I was with him. All would be fine. We would be fine. I collapsed against the seat and tried to breathe. That was a miracle. He was a miracle. He returned my gaze, calm, reserved.

"Who is that?" Stephi whispered to me, but loudly, staring at him with her huge, dark eyes.

"What's going on?" Lucy said, pushing her blond curls back. Her eyes were the same as her sister's: chocolate brown.

"Strap in. Everything's okay, girls." I reached my hand over the seat and held their hands. Tears of utter relief rolled down my cheeks as I looked at their sweet faces. I turned back around to face him, wiping my tears off. "Thank you. Thank you so much."

"You're welcome." He put his hand out, and I held it with my other hand, all of us now linked. "You okay?"

"Yes, I'm fine." So not fine. I was horrible. I was in shock. We had almost plunged into a river, in a blizzard. We had almost died. "I'm fine."

"Aunt Olivia. That man. Who is that?" Lucy asked, pointing.

"Is he a stranger? Is he stranger danger?" Stephi said. "We're not supposed to get into cars with people we don't know, Aunt Olivia."

"No, it's bad." Lucy leaned forward. "Are you a bad guy?"

He turned around and smiled at the girls. "No, I'm not a bad guy. I'm Jace Rivera."

Yes. He was.

Jace Rivera.

Definitely a good guy.

He smiled. I smiled back. I tried to catch my breath, tried to stop trembling and envisioning my girls drowning in the life-sucking river snake.

Hello, Jace.

* * *

"Thank you again, Jace. It's not enough to say thank you, I know it isn't."

"No problem. Glad I was there."

"Me too." I shivered, one of those whole-body shivers. A shock shiver. I knew I was probably as white as a ghost. A ghost who had almost pitched forward down a cliff into a river filled with snow and ice.

He looked slightly pale, too, in his jeans, cowboy boots, and black sweater.

Jace and I sat in front of the two-story fireplace in my grand-parents' log cabin. I had been so happy to see that red door and my granddad's lasso wrapped around one of the wood beams, so happy the girls and I were alive, that I made a strangled sound in my throat when we arrived.

My grandma had moved in with my mother to our two-story blue farmhouse, which also had a red door, where I was raised, about a half mile away, after my beloved, smart, brave grand-dad died two and a half years ago of multiple strokes.

Jace and I both clenched coffee mugs between our hands, a fire roaring. Rock from our property had been used for the façade so it had a true Montana-y look. We sat across from each other, in the wood furniture my grandparents built, the cushions wrapped in light blue denim, thick and comfy. We used the black trunk with gold buckles, which belonged to my grandparents' grandparents, between us as a coffee table.

We'd brought the girls in, fed them, and I put them to bed with a hug, a kiss, and an "I love you." I was grateful my mother and grandma had stocked the fridge for us. They had gone right to sleep after Lucy said, "He looks like a giant. Is he a giant?" and Stephi said, "Is he a superhero? I always knew they were real. But he doesn't have a cape, only cowboy boots. He needs a cape."

"You saved all three of us, Jace. I couldn't have gotten them out of the car if we hit the river, and even if we didn't go all the way in and I did get them out, we would have frozen out there."

A muscle was moving along his jaw, and he became whiter.

"Are you okay, Jace?"

"Olivia, unless you want me to have a heart attack, I don't want to talk about what happened."

"Right. Okay. Please do not have a heart attack."

"It's going to give me a nightmare tonight. In fact, I'll probably have nightmares for weeks, so let's let it go."

"Are you sure I can't get you a drink? I, personally, feel like having eight drinks. I feel like swimming in scotch."

"No, thank you." Those dark eyes held mine. Jace had a hard face. Hard jawline. Thick, black hair. You wouldn't look at him and say he was handsome in a model-like sense. He had a scar on his left temple. He had another small scar on his chin. He'd spent years outside in Montana. His face showed the weather, the sun, the snow, the wind. He was solid, strong, brave. Jace was sexy. He was huge. Six four, built like a tractor, strong shoulders, grippable and muscled. He didn't talk a lot, but he always had interesting things to say.

He smiled at me, a small smile, filled with what wasn't being said between us, and I could feel myself tumbling backward into that familiar despair. The guilt rushed in. I was ashamed of myself for what I'd done to him. He hadn't deserved it.

I was an awful person.

He saw me tumble, I knew it. He knew me so well. Too well.

"How have you been, Olivia?" His voice was low, quiet.

How had I been? Pretty much all over the spectrum, from floundering around on the bottom of life to finding hope and joy and love in Stephi and Lucy, then back to numbing grief, then to absolute terror from the calls I was getting from her and what the future would hold. "I'm . . . I'm fine. I'm good and fine. Good." All lies. "How are you?"

He stared back at me for long seconds. He knew I was lying. "I've been fine, Olivia."

"I'm . . . yes, I'm . . ." Gall. I could hardly concentrate around Jace. He had always done that to me. "I'm . . . uh . . . er . . . happy and glad." *What?*

He nodded, and I studied my hands. The fire crackled and we listened, waiting for the other to talk. Jace had been driving home when he saw my car ping across the road like a pinball, then watched it spin and crash. He hadn't known it was me, as I'd sold the truck I'd had when I was here.

"So. Lucy and Stephi," he said. "They are?"

"My daughters. I'm in the process of adopting them." I wrung my hands. "That sounded too hopeful. I want to adopt them, but things aren't going well."

I saw his colliding emotions fly across his face before he shut down: Shock. Pain. Disbelief. Acceptance. We sat in that silence, then he cleared his throat.

"You want to adopt them from foster care?"

"I want to adopt them through the state, but I can only if their mother's and father's rights are terminated, which they have not been. The girls were living with their grandma. She passed away. Annabelle and I were friends." I wrung my hands. We were still friends. It was as if Annabelle was still with me. She was in that place in your soul where friends go who die but you still love them and talk to them and think of them.

"I'm sorry about your friend, Annabelle, Olivia. I really am."

"Thank you."

"Why would their parents' rights be terminated?"

"It's a long story." It's a miserable and chilling story.

"I'd like to hear it when you want to tell it."

"Okay."

"Too much for tonight?"

"Yes. It's complicated." It's an epic disaster.

"They seem like nice kids."

"They are. They are such nice kids. I adore them."

"You've always had a big heart."

"Big heart." I tapped my head. "Screwed up here, but I'm trying."

"You're not screwed up, Olivia."

"Oh, yes, I am."

I could tell what I said upset him, but his eyes stayed steady on mine. "How long are you here for?"

"I don't know." I'm hiding. Holing up. Escaping. And seeing you is breaking me in half.

"You're not staying, then?"

"No." Probably not. Maybe. I don't think so. How could I? Yes. I loved it here. But it wasn't possible. No.

He was waiting for more information. Evaluating. Listening. Patient. Kind.

"Okay." He sighed. I wanted to cry. The fire crackled again, sparks flying.

He stood up. I stood up, too.

"Jace—"

"Yes?"

I didn't know what to say. So I said what I'd already said before, many times. "Thank you so much."

"You're welcome, Olivia." He pushed his black hair back, then ran his hand over his face. "I cannot believe that happened."

"Me either."

"I may not sleep for years."

"I may be up for years, too."

He had aged a little, not much. It was in the creases by his eyes, the older expression that he wore, the reserve. He was even tougher, that I saw with no doubt.

"Call me when you want to talk," he said.

"I will." He should have been furious at me. He had every right.

"Should I expect a call?" Jace towered over me. He stood too close. I wanted to reach out and hug him. Wrap my arms around him and squeeze and feel safe and warm. It wouldn't be fair to him, so I didn't.

"I don't know." Voice weak, small. I am such a mess, and he makes me messier. We have an insurmountable problem.

"Whenever you want to talk, I'm here, Olivia."

I couldn't say anything else because my tears were tight in my throat and throttling me. He turned, broad and tall, black haired and harshly handsome, all man.

" 'Night, Olivia."

I couldn't say it. It reminded me of too many nights when he had said the same thing to me.

The door closed behind him, and I collapsed on the couch.

I should have apologized to him. Again. I should have. I couldn't. I'd done it already, but another apology was due, and I knew it. I felt lower than a slug for what I did to him. I always would.

After Jace left, I crawled into the king-sized bed in my grandparents' bedroom on the first floor. My granddad, Oliver Martindale, was six three and needed a large bed. He used to say all he ever wanted was a twin-sized bed so he could be close to my grandma, Gisela, all night long.

I smiled, tearfully, at the memory, then burrowed deeper into the quilts and blankets, my body and brain now in post-shock from what had nearly happened to my girls. It was pitch dark, the moonbeams glowing through the tall windows.

My grandparents' two-story log cabin is charming and homey and I love it. I told myself to concentrate on the cabin, not the almost-disaster, so I could sleep. The cabin, along with our blue farmhouse, sits on one hundred acres.

My grandparents stayed in a trailer, on their land, while they built their log cabin. Luckily it did not take too long with the help they had. The trailer did not have electricity or plumbing, which my grandma said was a real "romance killer. You don't know how much you love a toilet until you don't have one."

They built the cabin together with the help of my granddad's parents, and other friends and neighbors, some of whom are still around and close friends of our family. In fact, the Martindales go generations back, in terms of friendships, with many people in Kalulell. My grandparents, for example, were friends with Jace's grandparents.

It's a medium-sized cabin, with windows all over, far more than what you would see in other log cabins. It's like the logs are there to prop up the windows. The windows let in the huge, blue Montana sky in all directions; the Dove Mountains; and the Telena River, which is about thirty yards from the house.

The ceiling in the family room is two stories high. Upstairs there's a loft, which opens to the downstairs, separated by a hand-carved wood rail. There is also a bedroom, which was my mother's as a girl, and the bedroom my sister, Chloe, and I slept in when we had sleepovers with our grandparents. There is also a separate den, and a bathroom, all with oversized windows. The den was where my granddad, the town doctor, worked after hours. We have kept his medical journals and books. There's a small attic above the den with one window.

On the main floor is the kitchen, which has been remodeled more than once, most recently five years ago. The cabinets are white, the backsplash is white beadboard, the counters are all butcher block. A huge window over the white apron sink looks straight out at the snowy mountains.

The dining room table, which seats ten, was made by my granddad with wood from trees on our land. The dents and scratches come from sixty-five years of Martindale family dinners; patients who were laid flat on it for medical care, including stitches and tourniquets; and the baking prep my grandma did there. As a teenager my mother carved her name beneath the table when she was forced to help my grandma cook a Thanksgiving dinner one afternoon, when she really wanted to help my granddad at his medical clinic instead.

The family area, dining area, and kitchen are essentially one room. Another full bathroom and the master bedroom look toward the river.

The front door is red, and in all seasons but winter, two red Adirondack chairs are out front on the deck and four others are on the back deck. Red is my grandma's favorite color, so my granddad painted the door red. The red door and the red Adirondack chairs match the red geraniums my mother, grandma, sister, and I plant each summer.

Red geraniums are the "family" flower, so to speak, that all the women in my family grow, so it's important it's *that* flower on the deck and in the window boxes.

When as a young girl I asked my grandma why red geraniums are the family flower, she said, "Because, dear Olivia, they are." Her face tightened, saddened.

"But why? Why not tulips or daffodils?"

"It's a long story." She pushed her hair back. It was thick, and brown then, like my mother's, like mine and my sister Chloe's, but mixed with white.

"I love stories! Will you tell me?"

"No, dear." She put a hand on my shoulder. I didn't understand why it shook. I didn't understand why her eyes flooded. I still don't. "It's not a story I want to talk about now."

"Okay, Grandma." I was so sad that I had made her cry that I cried. She held me close. "This has nothing to do with you, my precious, Olivia, my dear Cinnamon. Only things I don't talk about anymore."

And that was it. We went horseback riding an hour later, and she talked to me about how to survive in the wilderness if I was ever lost. She also told me what to do if a bear charged me. So I don't know why red geraniums are the family flower, they simply are.

An old wagon wheel leans against the cabin because my granddad's relatives came west on the wagon train from Missouri, and that's what's left of that journey. Two cowboy hats— one my granddad's and one my grandma's—are nailed to the right of the door, and there's a weather vane with a sun on top of the roof.

My granddad always said my grandma was his sun, hence the sun weather vane.

Near the river is a gazebo my granddad built, with benches and a wooden picnic table inside. When I was a child I would often see my grandma at the table, gazing at the mountains, seeming to be far, far away from Montana. One time I went to sit with her, but my granddad, gently, held me back. "Not now, Olivia," he said. "Wait."

I learned then to leave her alone when she was in the gazebo unless she invited me over.

One time, when I was a teenager, I said to her, "What do you think about when you're in the gazebo, Grandma?"

She said, "I think about things I don't want to think about. If I don't think about them now and then they come and get me and force me to think about them."

"I don't understand, Grandma."

"There are many things I do not understand, either." She kissed my forehead. "Let's go shoot some arrows, shall we? It's important for you to have precise aim." She was an excellent shot.

I asked my mother about my grandma when I was about ten. Where was she born? Does she have sisters and brothers? What happened to her parents? My mother's face became drawn and serious. "I don't know, Olivia. She refuses to talk about it. But I know that whatever happened to her was bad." She paused and ran her hands over her eyes. "Very, very bad."

I knew my grandma was from Germany. She speaks English with a British accent, a tinge of German, and a heavy dose of American English. There's another language mixed up in there, too, but I can't place it. I didn't know if she left Germany as a child or as a young woman. We know nothing of my grandma's life before she was in England, working as a nurse in a hospital during World War II where she met my granddad, a U.S. fighter pilot.

It was as if she were born at the age of twenty-two, in 1944, in London, when she met my granddad, and there was nothing to her before that. No family. No relatives. No friends. She had never talked to my mother about it, but my mother said that my granddad knew. He wouldn't share, either, my mother told me. "When I asked him about Mom, he told me that her past was for her to tell me about, not him."

The truth is that my grandma is the kindest person I know. But always, starting when I was a child, I sensed her grief, her loss, an emptiness. I sensed her secrets, which I knew hurt her.

I lay back in the huge bed of their master bedroom. I would see my grandma tomorrow. She reminded me of cinnamon rolls, which is ironic, as she calls me Cinnamon. I would see my mother, too. She reminded me of tough steak. She sometimes calls me Rebel Child because I didn't become a doctor, like her, to her eternal disappointment.

I snuggled under the quilts and I wondered what Jace would feel like in this bed. I knew he'd like it. He would also like the view and watching it change through Montana's colorful seasons. I tried to push that thought out of my mind, but I couldn't, so I relived one of the times we'd been naked, on his property, outside, on a picnic blanket, in the woods, until I cried and my face swelled up and I was a sniveling and pathetic mess with tired, green cat eyes and I finally went to sleep.

Then I had a nightmare about what happened that day and woke up with a scream stuck in my throat as if an icy, slithering snake had crawled down it.

"My cooking partner has returned." My grandma pulled me into a hug, her white hair, pulled into a loose ball, blending with my brown waves. She is five three, with light green eyes—a striking woman—and her face reflects courage, wisdom, and beauty. Grandma always wears flowered scarves because "We humans need more beauty." She calls me Cinnamon because I loved cinnamon as a little girl. She calls my sister Nutmeg. Same reason. Chloe loved nutmeg. She calls my mother, now and then, The Fire Breather. My mother has a fiery personality. "Hello, Cinnamon! I am so glad you're here."

"Give me a hug, Rebel Child." My mother, Mary Beth Martindale, reached for me and hugged me close, too. She went back to her maiden name after my father left us, and when we hadn't heard from The Deserter in a year, my sister and I changed our names to 'Martindale, too. He abandoned us, and we abandoned his last name. At eighteen, we did it legally.

Earlier that morning my mother walked over to say hello at the log cabin. I told her what had happened last night, and she stomped herself over to the windows and glared at me. She crossed her arms, tapped her cowgirl boot, and said, "Irresponsible. Careless. Reckless behavior. I raised you better than that. Montana women aren't *stupid,* Olivia. Even *I* wouldn't have been out in that blizzard."

This was her way of telling me she loved me. When I was younger we went head-to-head sometimes because of her bluntness and my stubbornness. Then I left for years, mellowed out, missed her, had new realizations about that tough-talking mother of mine, and accepted her butt-kicking Montana ways.

"If Jace wasn't there to haul your skinny butt out of the car . . ." She'd stalked back, still glaring at me, and I hugged her while she said a bad word, told me I was "deranged," then we'd both lain flat on the floor and tried to breathe. "Think of an operation," she murmured to herself. She thinks of operating on people when she needs to relax. "Take the scalpel, cut into the stomach . . ."

"Mom," I'd said. "Please."

"What? Thinking of operating on people calms me down." She cleared her throat and continued her one-way conversation. "Think of opening the rib cage, Mary Beth . . . your hand on the heart . . ."

My mother is a family doctor and has her own clinic. Her hair is brown, thick, and shot through with gray. She wears it up in a loose ball, like my grandma.

She has huge green eyes—everyone in my family has some shade of green in their eyes, and they have wisdom and experience and sharpness in them. She is a straight shooter. She is not afraid of anyone or anything, and she will tell you what she thinks, to your face, no matter if you want to hear it or not, including telling you that "your brain is full of rocks."

Mary Beth Martindale can shoot a deer, clean it, and cook it; wrestle down a calf and keep it there; lasso a cow; and brand any animal's behind. Grandma taught her how to shoot a bow and arrow, and her aim is true. We Martindales pride ourselves on our archery skills. I've also seen her lay more people than I can count up on our farmhouse kitchen table—built solid by my granddad when my mother first had this house built on our family's property, before we were born—and treat/sew them up.

"Give me those whippersnappers," my grandma said, reaching for Stephi and Lucy. She hugged the girls, then kissed both of their cheeks as they hugged her back. "I'm so glad you're here."

"My turn next," my mother said, grabbing the girls, lifting them off their feet, and giving them a twirl. They giggled. "Let me gaze upon these future doctors and hunters. I am so pleased you're here. Now we can continue your medical education. What do you know about sutures?"

Lucy and Stephi loved my grandma and my mother, especially when my mother said to them about four months ago, when we came to visit because we needed a break, "You two girls must be tough-ass women after what you've been through, and I like tough-ass women. Never stop being a tough-ass woman, and welcome to the family. We're all half-crazy, so if you've got some problems, don't worry. We all have problems, and the women in this family like to deal with them with archery. Think you'd like to shoot a bow and arrow?" Oh, they did.

My grandma and mother took them horseback riding because "All brave women need to know how to handle a horse."

On another visit, they took them skiing several times because "You've gotta be comfortable with speed. Who wants to ski fast?"

They took them fishing because "You will see God while you fish. You only have to look for him here in the river."

My mother showed them photos and videos of operations, "to prepare them for life as a surgeon." The girls loved them. When I saw the photos, I shut the folder. "You did that to me when I was a kid, showing me all those cut-open people, and photos of the heart, and diseased kidneys and sick lungs and blown ligaments and broken bones and everything else, and it gave me nightmares, Mom."

"That's because you didn't want to be a doctor, Olivia." My mother was quite self-righteous as she snatched the photos back from me. How dare I interfere with her lesson on how to put a balloon in someone's artery to open it up! How dare I take away the photo of the man's leg split to the bone! How dare I not allow the girls to study photos of what advanced diabetes does to limbs!

"You wanted to spend all your time in the kitchen cooking, but these girls want to be doctors." She turned again to the girls and whispered, "Who wants to see a photo of what happens to your lungs when you smoke?" Oh boy! Did they! And "Who wants to see photos of kidneys, both healthy and sick, so you can make contrasts and comparisons?" More excitement!

"Cinnamon," Grandma said. "I heard you and the girls were in that blizzard. That makes me scared even thinking about it." She moved to the kitchen island and stirred a buttermilk pancake mixture. A strawberry syrup was gently boiling on the stove. The kitchen island, about eight feet long, was partially made, five years ago, when they remodeled the kitchen, from an oak tree that was split in half by lightning. It was my mother's favorite tree. She grew up climbing on it. The oak tree island has a long, white marble counter, perfect for my grandma because she loves to cook and bake.

"It was not my best night."

My mother rolled her eyes. "Not your best night? That's how you would describe it? You never should have been out in that. I should take you out to the back shed and whip your butt, Olivia."

"You never did that when I was a kid, I bet you wouldn't do it now." I kissed her cheek.

"I would, too. Don't push it, kid. Check the weather in Montana before you come. You know better. Never drive in a blizzard in Montana. Best to live with a working brain, Olivia, not rocks. Get the rocks out of your brain." She tapped her head. "It will keep you out of trouble."

"I'm glad you made it safely," my grandma said. She shuddered, walked back around the island, hugged me again, then went back to the stove. "Had I known you three were out in it I would have shaken in my cowgirl boots."

We Martindale women take our cowgirl boots seriously. My mother has a collection. Over forty pairs at last count. She dresses in jeans and sweaters, but those cowgirl boots, different colors, different designs, they make her statement, yes, they do. Today she was in black with silver star cutouts.

"Thanks to Jace they're all safe," my mother said, hands on her hips. "Prince Charming came roaring on in in his black truck."

"I don't like the rescuing prince image," I said. "As if I was a damsel in distress."

"You were more than a damsel in distress," my mother snapped. "You were almost a river rat, along with my girls. Dang, Olivia."

"What's this about Jace?" my grandma said.

"Jace grabbed Olivia and the girls out of the car before it careened into the river," my mother said.

My grandma's head snapped up. "What?"

I tried to downplay it, so as not to scare my grandma, but it was hard to do so when my mother said, "And where is your car now, young lady? The river. Nose down. After flying back and forth across the highway. All avoidable! Damsels should not get themselves in situations where they need to be rescued by princes."

My grandma tilted her head back to the ceiling and closed her eyes. "My. Oh my. Cinnamon!" She left the syrup and hugged me once again, then hugged the girls.

"Ruthie Teal saw Jace driving you home, and she already called and asked if you and Jace were getting back together," my mother said. "She was cleaning her gun. She wants to know if he spent the night. She couldn't stay up late enough to see if he left, because this morning she had to leave early for ice fishing with her boyfriend."

"Ruthie has a boyfriend?" I asked, ignoring the other question. Ruthie is eighty. She lives about a mile down the road.

"You bet she does. She's getting some action," my mother said. "He's twelve years younger. Name is Sam. She's riding him like a horse."

"Mom? The girls are sitting right here."

"Ruthie rides a man like a horse?" Lucy's brow furrowed. "Does she put a saddle on him?"

"What do you mean she's getting action?" Stephi said. "Like exercise?"

"Getting some action means that they do cartwheels together," I said.

"Yes, indeed," my mother said. "Cartwheels. And it also

means they ride horses. Like you two girls will do when the weather is better here."

"I want to ride a horse!" Stephi and Lucy yelled.

"A brave woman needs to know how to handle a horse," Lucy said, raising a finger in the air.

"Can we go skiing so we can get comfortable with speeding?" Stephi asked. "I want to go fast."

"What about fishing? We can see God hiding in the river then," Lucy said.

I leaned back and drank more coffee and enjoyed the peace of being home. Our farmhouse kitchen has light blue cabinets, matching the light blue of the exterior of the house. The other counters are a white marble, too, with a tile backsplash. My mother let a friend of hers go "flower crazy" on the backsplash. Dina is a semi-wild-eyed artist who painted this flowing, colorful swirl of red geraniums, yellow lilies, white daisies, and blue irises and delphiniums.

The downstairs of the farmhouse is one open room, like the log cabin, lots of windows, with our enormous brick fireplace rising two stories. The walls are all butter yellow. "I sure as heck didn't want any red walls," my mother announced. "I've got enough blood in my life at work."

Books, cookbooks, piles of medical journals, and oversized, unmatched, colorful furniture and quilts fill out the room. The two couches are red and two soft chairs are purple, with embroidered pillows all over. The quilts, two hung on walls, are all gifts from patients.

There are four bedrooms upstairs—master bedroom for my grandma and second largest bedroom for my mother, at my mother's insistence. When my grandma moved into our farmhouse after my granddad died, my mother shifted everything out of the master bedroom. "I could not sleep at night unless I gave my mother the best. If I didn't, God in his infinite wisdom would punish me by making my butt grow to the size of a hippo's."

We commissioned two paintings/collages from our favorite

artist, Grenadine Scotch Wild, of both my grandma and grand-dad's log home, and of our blue farmhouse, both red doors prominent. They were about five foot by five foot, hanging on a wall in the family room.

On the log cabin she had added the wagon wheel, the lasso wrapped around the post on the deck, Grandma and Grand-dad's cowboy hats, and the sun weather vane. Grenadine even remembered the red geraniums in flower boxes on both houses, the gazebo outside the log cabin, and the collection of bird houses my mother has hanging on the white front porch of our farmhouse.

Not only had she painted the homes perfectly, at Grenadine's request we sent her bark from trees off our properties, tiny pinecones, sticks, swatches of our favorite fabrics, and dried flowers, and she incorporated them into the collages.

"Girls," my mother said. "Let me tell you about a patient I saw on Wednesday. So, the patient had to have part of a leg amputated because of—"

At that moment our red front door flew open and banged into the wall, and snowflakes flew in.

"Mary Beth!" a man in his sixties yelled at my mother. "Mrs. Gisela, help me!" He was gray haired, nose like a turnip. His name is Jeffy Rochs. I've known him since I was a kid. He owns five plumbing stores in western Montana. Toilets are lucrative. Jeffy was holding up one of our neighbors, who was bleeding profusely from a wound in his shin. "Terry had a fight with a horse. As you can see, the horse won round one."

"Go upstairs," I told my daughters, giving them a little shove. The girls didn't move, staring, transfixed.

"They can stay," my mother said, moving toward Jeffy. "This isn't too bad, and I can show them how to sew someone up."

The girls squealed in delight. "Oh, good," Lucy said. "This is gonna be fun."

"Finally," Stephi said with relief. "We can play doctor for real."

I shot them a baffled look, then my mother and grandma and I sprang into action. Grandma and I cleared off the kitchen table, and we flipped a plastic covering over it that we keep in a wooden chest. My mother grabbed her black medical bag, which my granddad owned before her, and got her supplies ready. She tossed my grandma and me gloves, and I immediately cut off Terry's pant leg. We manhandled Terry, moaning and teeth clenched, up onto the table. My grandma grabbed clean cloths we keep in a drawer for this type of thing.

"Sorry to intrude, Mary Beth, Mrs. Gisela, and hello, Olivia, heard you were back in town." Terry sucked in air, then groaned. "Heard it from Ruthie. She was up late last night cleaning her gun. She said you were with Jace. Hope you two can get yourselves back together."

I tried not to roll my eyes. I rolled them anyhow.

"Did you know that Ruthie has a boyfriend now?" Terry went on, panting from pain, white around the edges of his face. "He's younger. Gotta respect that lady. Dang this hurts." He groaned again, sagged.

"Close your eyes, Terry, and quit yakking," my mother ordered as she pulled on gloves. I held him down to keep him from wriggling, as did Jeffy, as my mother put pressure on the wound, a deep one, I could tell.

Terry stifled a ragged moan as more blood gushed.

"Hang in there, Terry," I said. "Now you'll have a scar and a story to tell."

"I don't need any stories," Terry groaned. "Hildy says she's tired of my stories and she's going to be madder than a hot cat stuck in a box when she sees what I did today, getting myself bashed by a horse."

"She doesn't like it when you make her nervous," Jeffy said, clicking his tongue. "Says it gives her hives. You really gotta keep that in mind, friend."

"It does give her hives," my grandma confirmed, deftly handling the bloody cloths. "I've seen them. When you get hurt or sick, she gets hives. Tell her I said to get in a milk and oatmeal bath. You make her worry, Terry. She's going to be upset with you, honey. You must prepare yourself and sincerely apologize for what you've done to yourself here today."

"I'll tell her, Mrs. Gisela. And I feel awful about this. Right awful. My poor Hildy." Terry teared up. "She's going to be covered in those darn hives."

"You should feel awful," my mother snapped. "Hildy's hives spread all over her body. When you got double pneumonia, when you broke your ankle, when you were hospitalized with that heart attack, all of that upset her and she broke out as if an alien had attacked and lay her bare with red spots."

"Horrible!" Terry moaned. "It was horrible!"

"All this blood is making me sick," Jeffy said, leaning over, hands on his knees.

"Hold still," my mother said, perfectly calm, as was my grandma. Nothing rattled those two. Nothing. "Now, girls, watch what we're doing." She kept the pressure on. My grandma stood beside her, assisting my mother.

Lucy and Stephi crammed in close to my mother, two blond heads leaning over a bleeding man.

"Step back a bit, girls," I said.

"It's all right," my mother said. "They need to learn by being close up."

They were fascinated.

"Look at all that blood," Stephi gushed. "Boy! He's got it all over the place."

"Can I sew him up, Grandma Mary Beth?" Lucy asked. "Please! Grandma Annabelle taught me how to sew."

"No, me, Grandma Mary Beth!" Stephi said. "I want to."

Jeffy stood back up, eyed the damage, then leaned back over, pale. "I'm not gonna faint. Don't worry, Mrs. Gisela. But if I do, I know you can bring me back around with herbs or something. I'm going to need the healing you do in the natural way."

"No sewing today, girls," my mother said. "You will love medical school, though. You'll want to be assigned to an inner-city hospital. You'll get action there."

"You have blood coming out all over," Stephi said, in admiration, to Terry. She had a few of her rocks from her collection in her pocket, and I saw her fiddling with them. Stephi loves her rocks. "This is so cool."

"I can see almost all the way down to your bone!" Lucy smiled at Terry and pointed her finger in the air. She likes to point her finger in the air to make her point. "That's pretty cool."

Stephi turned to Lucy. "Mr. Terry is getting all sewn up like Aunt Olivia sews up a turkey. Remember that, Lucy? She used string to tie the turkey's legs together last Thanksgiving."

"Are you going to tie his legs together, too, Grandma Mary Beth?" Lucy asked.

"No, I'm going to sew this man up like I'd sew a new dress for you two," my mother said.

"Are you going to sew us dresses?" Stephi asked.

My mother snorted. "I have no idea how to sew. It was in reference to other people sewing. Not me."

"She never wanted to learn," my grandma told Terry and Jeffy, who had stood up, then leaned back over once again, rather green around the gills. My grandma shook her head in deep disappointment. "I could barely get Mary Beth to cook. She was always more interested in blood and guts and diseases, like her father."

"I cook," my mother said. "It's called takeout food."

When the blood slowed a bit, and the numbing agent started to work, my mother cleaned the wound, quite deep I saw, then dug out a surgical suture and sewed him up. In the clinic she used a vacuum-like thing to clean and reheal, but this was good enough for today. She was tight and quick with her stitches. She dug out bandages as my grandma cleaned up around the stitches.

"Nice job, Mom and Grandma," I said.

"Yeah, nice job, Grandma Mary Beth and Grandma Gisela," Stephi said. "He was in two pieces on his leg and now he's back to one."

"You're a skin sewer!" Lucy said.

"A skin sewer," Jeffy muttered, crouching down now on his heels, hand to head, back against the wall. "Get ready to treat me in the natural way, Mrs. Gisela."

"I will, Jeffy," Grandma called. "Hang on. Head down."

"Now, Terry," my mother said, so competent. "Don't forget to duck if Hildy throws something at you for this. For heaven's sakes, though, tell her not to aim for this leg. Last time you got yourself in a poorly condition, the hives got on her butt and she was more pissed off than a bear woken up in winter."

"You go home and apologize to Hildy, Terry, honey," my grandma said. "Those hives are awfully hard on her."

Terry groaned. "She'll be in bed for a week with this one."

Jeffy said, still pale, "This isn't going to play out right for you, man."

Later, Terry said, "Thank you, Mary Beth, Mrs. Gisela, Olivia." He leaned heavily on Jeffy and me as we moved him back out to his truck. "You saved me a thousand dollar bill at the emergency room. Send the bill, Mary Beth."

My mother would not send a bill. Terry would send her part of a dead deer as a venison gift.

She thought it a fair exchange.

Chapter 2

❧

My mother's and grandma's patients, and their downtown Kalulell clinic, are their life. Their practice, which my grandma and granddad launched when they arrived here in Montana after the war, and which my mother was skipping around in as a kid, and working in as a teenager as an assistant, takes up most of their time.

They have a two-story brick building on Fifth and Mountainside Drive, two blocks from the center of town. In honor of the past, there are three old-fashioned medical bottles painted in black, six feet high, on the side of the building. Inside, the furniture is Montana lodge. Leather couches and chairs, wood tables, fishing poles and skis on the walls for décor, along with cowgirl and cowboy hats, donated by their patients. Coffee and cookies, all the time.

"People get nervous coming to the doctor, so we want to make them comfortable and settle out their nerves," my grandma said. "But we do not serve whiskey unless it's a desperate circumstance. One shot is our limit."

"Some people don't get nervous coming to see us, Mom," my mother said to Grandma. "They love coming. They like to visit with us and with everyone else there. They come and yak." That was true. People were known to come two hours ahead of their appointments, have coffee, eat cookies, and chat with their neighbors. "By God. Do I look like I'm running a social hour in there?"

"No, Fire Breather," my grandma said. "No one would ever accuse you of being socially friendly."

The clinic has four other various doctors, four physician's assistants, eight nurses, and support staff. People come from all over the state to see my mother and Grandma. My mother is very popular, blunt as she is she gets you fixed up right, but so is Grandma. Patients will often call to make an appointment and say, "I want to see the mother, Mrs. Gisela." Or, if they're younger, "I want to see the grandma, Mrs. Gisela."

When my grandma tells them what to do to get better that has nothing to do with modern medicine, and everything to do with "natural healing," and herbs, and old-fashioned wisdom like chicken soup, salted poached eggs, and steak "to build the blood back up," they jump and do what she says. "You are to drink a full cup of carrot juice a day, Peter. Here. I made you a jar with my juicer this morning to get you started."

Or, "Your smoking is killing you, Stanley. Every time you want a cigarette I want you to nibble on these mint leaves I brought for you out of my garden. It'll work."

She extorts the wisdom of papaya, to kill bacteria in the stomach; broccoli, to clean the colon; bananas—"Let me tell you, Sylvia, it will help with your depression if you eat two a day, one dipped in melted chocolate chips"—plenty of water to flush out the system, and garlic cloves, eaten raw, to boost the immune system.

When my mother tells her patients to do something, for example, taking traditional medicines or treatments, or undergoing an operation, they usually do it, but not always. Many of my mother's patients, especially the older ones, have looked at my mother with great skepticism when she tells them about the modern treatments they need to abide by. "Have you checked with Mrs. Gisela about this, Mary Beth? What does she think? We'd prefer to do this naturally."

My mother will roll her eyes, then call my grandma in. My grandma will tell them to take the medicine, and then she'll give them her old-fashioned wisdom about the merits of onions because they "kill the germs inside of you," or Saint-John's-wort or, dear me, you're having trouble sleeping? One shot of vodka. One.

There! Now everyone is happy. Traditional medicine mixed with Mrs. Gisela's trusted wisdom.

My mother and Grandma are both talented at treating the whole person. As my mother said, "I can diagnose an illness or injury by observation, by feel, by blood test, by MRI, but I have to treat the whole person, not simply the sickness or no one gets better and they droop around until they die like dead ducks."

Some of their patients have been with them forever, since my grandparents started their clinic. My grandma has a number of patients whom she has known since they were babies, and they have adult children of their own who have children.

The Martindale Clinic treats whole families . . . and their grandchildren.

There are many people who are treated who can hardly pay my mother because they're sick or disabled. She treats them anyhow. They pay her in homemade goods. She's also been the recipient of an intricately hand-carved bow and arrow. Dead rabbits for rabbit stew. A gun from World War I. Baskets of cookies and treats. A kitten. A painting, twenty years ago, by a broke and unknown artist named Cleever Daniels, who was suffering from gastroenteritis, who is now famous and the painting is worth about $250,000. It hangs in the waiting room.

What is difficult for my mother and grandma to manage sometimes is the huge amount of invitations they get to baptisms, weddings, and birthday parties. If they don't go, their patients come in hurt. Sometimes they have three events on one Saturday. They are flying.

And now and then the patients end up on our kitchen table in the blue farmhouse, exactly as patients sometimes ended up on my grandma and granddad's dining room table in their log cabin. Good thing my granddad knew how to make an unbreakable table. When you can get 350-pound Alphy Knickerbocker on that table and it doesn't snap in half, you know it's built to last.

*   *   *

Alphonse D'Ellieni, who owned D'Ellieni's Tow Truck Services, brought all of my and the girls' suitcases, boxes, and my purse to my home. Interestingly, our suitcases and boxes in the trunk weren't soaked as the car was nose down in the river, the back leaning against the embankment. My purse was soaked, phone shot. I shivered. The thought of what almost happened was snatching my sleep away like a snake snatches a bite out of your belly.

"Got your car out of the river, Olivia," Alphonse said, "but it's blitzed. Totaled. Smashed. Kerplopped. Left it at the shop." He shook his head. "Man, you are lucky that Jace came along. Hey! You two getting back together? Ruthie said she was cleaning her gun and saw him driving you home. You know that gal's got a boyfriend? He's younger."

I washed and dried my clothes. I'm a skirt sort of woman. If I can wear one, I do. When it's snowing in Montana, I'm in jeans and my cowgirl boots. But if it's only moderately freezing, I'll pull on a warm skirt, and a couple of pairs of leggings. I also like wearing things from my travels around the world. Dangling gold earrings from Thailand, silk scarves from Cambodia, embroidered shirts from street vendors in Mexico, bangle bracelets from China. All so cheap, but I love 'em.

I like to wear the world.

On Sunday it rained. It was unexpected. It shouldn't have rained; it was supposed to snow. My grandma and mother had taken the girls to the clinic to "further their medical educations." I knew my mother was going to show the girls all of her equipment and what it was used for and, probably, videos of surgeries. Hopefully they would not have nightmares.

I was making tomato bisque soup and homemade croutons when I heard water dripping. I looked up and couldn't see a leak, but I know a leak when I hear it. I went to the loft, the girls' bedroom, and my granddad's den and couldn't see anything. I opened the door to the attic. The attic was small with one window and one lightbulb in the center.

My grandparents were both very organized people, as is my mother. You've heard of hoarders? We're the opposite. We're throwers. So the attic wasn't crammed, only a few old cardboard boxes piled up on one side near the window in the corner. I looked up and found the leak right above one of the boxes.

"Dang." I moved the box, then ran downstairs and out to the barn and got a huge metal pan we used to feed animals when we had them. I ran back up and put it under the dripping water. I could see straight up through a hole in the roof. My granddad would not be happy. He was kind, efficient, and liked everything in working order.

I knew I had to fix the roof, or our log cabin would be swimming in water. I ran back out to the barn to a shelf labeled ROOFING MATERIALS. I put on my granddad's spiked roofing shoes and the tool belt, and I climbed up on the ladder with extra shingles tucked into the belt. Luckily the leak was close to the edge. I knew I'd have to make several trips up and down the ladder. I nailed down a small piece of plywood first to cover the hole, added the roofing felt, then used the nail gun on the new shingles.

When I was done, I put the roofing supplies and shoes away, washed my hands, grabbed paper towels and cloth towels for drying whatever was in the box, and headed back up to the attic. There was so much tape wrapped around the box that had gotten wet, I had to go back downstairs to get a knife. It was as if whoever put the box up there never wanted anyone to get at the contents.

I paused. Should I open it? Should I leave it and tell my grandma? Was it private? I put my hand on the top of the box. It was soaked, and my grandma was at the clinic. It was probably old photographs of my mother and me and Chloe or our school artwork or gifts made out of clay or papier-mâché we'd given Grandma and Granddad. I would lay whatever was in it out, up here in the attic or downstairs, so it could dry.

I used the knife and cut through the layers of tape, then opened the top. I sat back on my heels when I saw what was in there, stunned. For long seconds, I couldn't move.

I carefully pulled out Grandma's white wedding dress and veil. My grandparents had a photo of themselves on their wedding day in their bedroom, but I had never seen the dress. The dress was white, lacy, straight. The veil was made of the same lace. It was elegant, delicate, stylish. We asked her about her wedding dress one time and she had waved her hand and said, "I don't know where it is anymore," which was odd, but it was one more thing she didn't want to talk about, and we had left it at that.

I found an old, white nurse's uniform. Forties? Was that dried blood? Not surprising. Grandma had been a nurse during the war. I found a dark blue dress, too. High style in the mid-1940s and a classic. Straight lines for the skirt, a jacket with a vee and blue buttons, a belt to cinch in the waist. A matching hat with dark blue flowers and a white ribbon completed the absolutely darling outfit.

I found a tin box with an old-fashioned picture on the lid of ladies dancing in fancy ball gowns, their dresses filled with lace, flounce, buttons, and bows. Inside I found two hair clips, one shiny red butterfly, one purple. I picked up two charm bracelets, each with a red pomegranate, a Star of David, a faux-blue stone heart, a lion, a tree of life inside a circle, a four-leaf clover, a cat, a dog, and a key. There were colored pencils, old photos, and letters addressed to Gisela and Renata Gobenko in London.

At the bottom of the box I found a small, silver menorah, maybe six inches high.

A menorah. She had saved a menorah.

And there it was. Part of Grandma's truth: Grandma was Jewish.

This was not surprising. We knew that Grandma had lived in Germany, and we knew when the attacks began on Jews. We suspected she was Jewish, but as she didn't talk about her past, we didn't know.

At the bottom I found an old, thick, heavy book, the leather cover cracked, a pink ribbon, fraying and stained, tying it together. I untied the pink ribbon carefully, afraid I would tear it. I could not read the inscription on the inside front cover as it

was in another language . . . what was it? Yiddish. I recognized
it from when I took a class on Jewish history in college.

The pages were burned around the edges. Some had clearly
sustained water damage. There were recipes, pages and pages of
recipes, some in Yiddish, some in . . . was it Ukrainian? German,
for sure, and English. Some of the recipes were taped to the
back pages. "It's a cookbook." I laughed out loud. A cookbook!
What a treasure! What a beautiful find!

Pictures were drawn around the edges of the recipes, below
them, and on the pages facing each one. The early pictures were
drawn with pencil—exquisite, detailed pictures of a handsome
smiling man with a beard, riding a horse, working on a saddle
with a tool, on a farm with a rake, and in a garden. There were
pictures of a family, children, grandparents. In one picture they
were all gathered around a long table eating, Shabbat candlesticks lit, a fire in the hearth. The women and girls were in long
skirts and kerchiefs, black boots. The men were in suspenders,
fur hats, beards.

A small home, made from stone and wood, with a brick chimney, took up another page. In other drawings there were chickens
and lambs outside, and sometime inside the home. There were
benches, chairs, and several tables, all solidly made, reminding
me of the tables that Granddad had made us. There were
shelves on a wall with baskets and pots, dried flowers hanging
from the rafters, pillows on the backs of chairs, and drawings of
herbs and a vegetable garden.

On other pages there were pictures of a village—late 1800s?
Stone homes. In the distance there appeared to be a city. There
were men holding two silver pails attached to a stick over their
shoulders, women with shawls and kerchiefs on their heads,
people riding horses, donkeys pulling carts, sheep being herded
in the street, a rooster, cats, cobblestone streets. There was a
menorah in a windowsill. I picked up the menorah I'd found.
Could it be the same one?

I turned the page, then turned back. The author had changed.
The previous recipes were in Ukrainian and Yiddish, these were
in German and the handwriting was different. But this artist

drew herbs and flowers. Some were tracings, clearly drawn with a flower or leaf underneath the paper, and a colored pencil over the top. There were recipes named "Esther's . . ." or "Alexander's . . ." in German. I also recognized the words, Isaac, Gisela, and Renata over other recipes, as if those recipes had been named after those people. *Gisela.* There was Grandma's name in this old, old cookbook.

There were stains in the cookbook. I peered closer. A few pages looked like they had dried blood on them. That couldn't be. Could it?

Within the pages I saw the fragile flakes of a pressed rose; two thin, heart-shaped gold lockets with a hook on top for a chain; a white feather; a charm in the shape of a sun; red ribbons; a few old photographs; and what looked like poems in Yiddish and German.

I could hardly breathe. I stared at the cookbook.

And there it was. Finally.

My grandma's past. Her history. Her family.

Her tragedy. I sniffled. I bent over and hugged the battered cookbook close to me. I cried for my grandma, for what she had been through, and my tears soaked into the leather. I cried for what she had lost that we didn't know she had lost but had sensed, had known, had always known. When I was done crying, I opened the book again.

I went back to the first signature, on the first page.

Ida Zaslavsky

Who was Ida Zaslavsky?

December 1904
Odessa, the Russian Empire
Ida Zaslavsky, great-great-grandmother of Olivia Martindale

Ida Zaslavsky finished her drawing of her family at the dinner table. She had only a pencil and a flickering candle. She had started drawing to calm her nerves, to still her racing, fearful thoughts.

Her own mother, Sarrah Tolstonog, had given her the thick, leather bound book, with blank pages when Ida was married six years ago. "Fill it with your thoughts and drawings. Put your recipes in there, and mine and Grandma Tsilia's, so you'll always have them. You are an artist, Ida. You have true talent." Sarrah had written, "To Ida Zaslavsky, Love Mother," in Yiddish on the inside front cover.

Sarrah had gotten it from a man she worked for as a maid. He made books for the wealthy but had seen her interest in them and had put together the leather cover and the pages for her. She had wrapped it in a pink ribbon to hold the book together.

Ida had decided that she would write her recipes on the right-hand side and that she would draw pictures of her family, her farm and garden, and her neighborhood, which felt like a village, poor and on the outskirts of Odessa, on the left-hand side and around the edges of her recipes. She wrote down the recipes that she and her mother made together, and the recipes that she had from her grandma, Tsilia Bezkrovny. Beet root soup with pepper and onions. Braided egg bread. Fish from the sea with garlic, but never sturgeon. Jews did not eat sturgeon.

She wrote down her husband's favorite recipes, including fried fish with ginger and garlic, and drew him, careful with every detail. Boris was so handsome with his beard and broad shoulders, and his smile. She loved his smile. She drew him working on the saddles he made and sold. She drew him working on their patch of land, their garden, though the soil and weather were often unforgiving. She drew him with their children at the table, a fire in their hearth, and giving the blessing, the light from their Shabbat candles flickering in front of him.

She drew her parents, Sarrah and Efim, and her grandfather and grandmother, Aron and Tsilia Bezkrovny. She drew her five siblings, even Iosif, who had died at the age of two.

Her parents had wanted her to marry Boris when she turned

eighteen. He was a fine young man, they told her. Strong, healthy, gentle. His parents had wanted him to marry her. He was twenty-two, time to settle down. Their parents were friends. She had known Boris since she was a child, but she couldn't imagine marrying him. In fact, Ida had her eye on another young man.

Boris and Ida finally acquiesced because they loved their parents, but both had been resentful, angry . . . until they had fallen madly and passionately in love. She smiled. That was why they had so many children already, she thought. They could not stay away from each other at night, when the children were asleep. She giggled, then told herself to stop giggling.

She would give birth again within a week or two, and that made her happy, so laughter was at the tip of her lips. The baby would join his sweet siblings, Esther, Moishe, and Zino.

Ida drew her home, so drafty in winter, but it was filled with their love. It was made of wood and stone. She and Boris had done much of it themselves. It had two rooms, and she was grateful for both and her brick fireplace. She drew their chickens and lambs, which were brought into their home in colder months so they didn't freeze.

Inside, Boris had built her a long, strong table for dinner and two shorter tables so she could cook. He had also built three chairs and two benches. He had built three long shelves and attached them to a wall so she could store their food, baskets, pails, and pots. He had even built a bed in the corner for the children. Boris could build anything she wanted; he was so smart. She hung dried flowers from the rafters to add color during their long and harsh winters and sewed pillows with whatever scraps of fabric she could find.

She drew their garden, and their herbs, the countryside and their village. She drew people on horseback on the cobblestone road; men holding silver pails attached to a stick over their shoulders; donkeys pulling carts; the women shopping with their shawls, kerchiefs, and long skirts; the men going off to work at factories or at the port. She drew sheep being herded, a rooster, cats, and their silver menorah on the windowsill that her grandfather had made for her when she married Boris. She drew her lace head covering that had been passed down from her grandmother.

She did not draw the times when she thought they all might starve or be murdered in their sleep by an angry mob or when the snow was so incessant she thought it might bury them alive if they didn't freeze to death first.

That night she decided to write another recipe in the book, this time in Yiddish. If it was a recipe from her mother or from her grandmother, it was in Yiddish. If it was her recipe, she wrote in Ukrainian. This recipe was for cheese dumplings, from Tsilia, so it was in Yiddish.

Ida loved her family first, her recipes and cooking second. She chastised herself. She should have said she loved God first. But where had God been lately? Why had he not protected the Jews from the pogroms? There had been attack after attack over the years. The government had looked away or endorsed it. They hated the Jews, their money, their success, their religion.

Homes and buildings and businesses were burned. People beaten and killed. Women raped. Homes robbed. Jews were fleeing. She, too, would escape with Boris and their children soon. They had to or they would die, even though the government tried to prevent them from leaving.

They would leave soon. They were all in danger. Even her parents, who had lived through a pogrom here in Odessa when they were children, told them to go. They were not healthy enough to make the journey, but they wanted their children and grandchildren saved. Ida would not leave her parents if she was not so desperate to save her own children.

They would go to Germany and have a new life.

She felt the baby move and put a protective hand on her stomach. It was a boy, she knew it. They would name him Liev.

Boris came to her. They smiled at each other. He held out a hand. She placed her hand in his and he kissed it. Such a romantic man.

* * *

When I returned home from the grocery store there was an envelope underneath the mat in front of my front door. It was a check from Jace. He had attached a note: "You are half owner of Martindale Ranch. This is your share of the profits."

It was a huge check. I wanted that money, I did. Mostly so that I wouldn't have to worry about making payments to my attorney, Claudine Wren, and to pay off the hospital, but I couldn't take it. I had not worked for this money. Jace had. I didn't deserve that check, for many reasons, and that was the honest truth.

I ripped it up.

My phone rang the next morning.

I saw the number.

I didn't answer.

Later, I listened to her message.

I listened to her swear at me. I listened to her tell me how manipulative I was, how greedy, how hateful.

I listened to her tell me that she would make me regret this for the rest of my life. Every. Single. Shitty. Day. You bitch.

I closed my eyes.

"I'm going to put the kids in school tomorrow and find a job."

My mother nodded. "Those girls need to be in school so they can master basic skills as I move them toward biology, anatomy, and chemistry."

I laughed, she winked at me, and I handed her a piece of pumpkin cheesecake. We were on my deck that night at the log cabin, in jackets and hats, admiring the snow-topped Dove Mountains. We could hear the Telena River rushing through the darkness, constant and smooth, soothing.

"Thanks, Mom, for being so great with the girls."

"I love them." She crossed her legs and leaned against the railing. She was wearing beige cowgirl boots with silver trimmings. "They're my granddaughters now. They've got grit." She raised a fist in the air and shook it, her brown/gray hair slipping out of her bun. "They'll both feel comfortable digging bullets out of people, as I am. And gushing blood they will see as a fountain that must stop, not someone bleeding out."

"They'll be the doctor-daughters you didn't get with me."

"Don't remind me of my ongoing hell, Rebel Child," she grumbled. My mother had so wanted me to be a doctor. Preferably a surgeon. "Tell me what happened, Olivia."

I told her about Carter and how I felt compelled to throw a chicken at him, not a live one, and maybe an egg or two, then I told her about the calls and what my attorney had said, and why my bones were almost frozen together in abject fear.

When I was done she was quiet for a while, then said, "What a dang mess. You have many things going wrong in your life. One . . ." She started holding up her fingers. She is a very precise woman. "The girls are endangered. Two, you have no job because you threw a chicken, not a live one, I'll give you that, and eggs, at Carter, I hope your aim was true, and three, you're almost broke because of the attorney's fees and your adventure at the hospital."

"That about sums it up."

"I will give you money."

"I would not accept a penny."

"Olivia, don't make my estrogen rise. Get your head out of your mule's butt. You are so stubborn. It is not endearing, it's irritating."

"No. And I am paying you and Grandma rent for the cabin."

"Hell's bells, you are not," my mother said. "Your grandma would never accept it, either. Don't you upset her with this inane drivel."

"Mom, yes, I am."

"Olivia. You've been through a heckuva hard time. Let me help you. For the girls, not for your sorry nondoctor self. Oh! Will I ever stop my mourning at your career choice? No. I won't. The torture continues. Please stop arguing with me. You're giving me a headache. I have to see twenty patients tomorrow and I do not need your sass."

"Mom, I can't accept help."

"Why, ridiculous daughter?"

"Because of how you raised me."

"And how did I raise you?"

"To be independent."

"You are independent."

"I'm paying rent, Mom, or I'm leaving and I'll pay rent somewhere else."

She knew I meant it. She knew I could not move into my grandparents' log cabin and feel like I was mooching off of her and my sweet Grandma.

"You are like a bullet out of a gun. Unstoppable."

"Got it from you."

"Take the truck until you get a new one, as you demolished your car when you made a poor choice in a blizzard. What were you thinking? Must have been rocks in your brain that day."

"Now, that I'll take you up on."

We ate the pumpkin cheesecake in peace for a while and watched two falling stars take their last dive through space. The river rolled, and the snow shone in the dark on the mountain peaks.

"You're going to apply to be a chef in Kalulell, then?"

"Yes. I thought I'd look for temporary chef positions until I figure out what to do. We had to get out of Portland quick until things are settled, and I know the girls will be safe there in the future."

"Jace is looking for a chef."

That hurt. "It won't be me."

"That's a dang shame."

I knew what she was talking about.

She held my hand. "I love you, Olivia. Lord knows you have given me a run for my money with your wildness in high school with Chloe, the pranks, still talked about today in town, and your unwillingness to be a doctor, but I forgive you for it because you make delicious desserts."

"I love you, too. I enjoyed being wild. The pranks were fun. Sorry about the doctor part. I wanted to mix sugar and flour and eggs. Not medicine."

She sighed. "Disappointing. But I've gotten over it, Olivia."

We sat in the dark silence as another falling star soared through the night.

"No, you haven't." I laughed.

"You're right." She stabbed her cheesecake with a fork. "I haven't."

"Hello, I'm Olivia Martindale."

"Yep, yep, yep. I know, honey." The tall, beefy man with a fat chest, stubby legs like sausages, and a brown, scraggly beard under a balding, shiny head shook my hand. Larry Harrison's eyes traveled from my head to toe like a slithery eel, and I wanted to smack him.

I didn't because I needed a job and this was his restaurant, Larry's Diner, a semi-dive in the center of Kalulell. He could have called it Disease And Bacteria On A Plate. It had blue leather seats not more than thirty hard years old, a bunch of brown tables, ugly dirty carpet, and an old menu. Rumor had it he was still in business because his mother owned the building and didn't charge him rent. But I was desperate, and when you're desperate you can't be picky.

Plus, this was the fifteenth restaurant/café I'd hit up for a job, and there were no openings for a chef. It wasn't a big city. I knew who Larry Harrison was. He was about fifteen years older than me and moved back to Kalulell to live with his mommy about four years ago. When I lived here I avoided him like I would avoid a rattler.

Kalulell is charming. I had loved living here. It's a tourist destination between mountains and rivers, with a blue sky that goes on forever. We have delicious restaurants, art galleries, boutiques, cafes, bakeries, and gift shops. People come to fish and ski and hike and to attend our festivals. Downtown Kalulell has about three streets, and is decorated with twinkling lights during the holidays. There's a town parade on Fourth of July, a Skinny-Dip Day in the middle of winter where everyone jumps in the lake, and a Halloween parade down Main Street that can be absolutely freezing if the weather doesn't cooperate.

There aren't a lot of jobs out here for chefs, and I had run out of options. There were a few bars I did not want to work in, though I have a bartending license; but I was going to those next if Larry, whose reputation was pig boar, didn't hire me.

"I know your mother and grandma, Olivia girl. Your mother took a splinter the size of a small tree out of my arm a few months ago when I got drunk and landed myself in my wood-pile. Smashed on down like a bowling pin, ya know? Ha-ha. Had too much whiskey that time. Or beer. Can't remember. Ha-ha. Another time I crashed my tractor into my barn. Had too much Jim Bean, I remember that for sure. You know him, right? Jim Bean. Hurt my noggin'." He pointed to his head so I could find it. "Bam. Fixed me right up, your mom, did. Put me in the hospital."

My mother was the one who had described this restaurant to me in graphic terms. "Smells like fried goat in there. And the goat was bathed in a fart before it was fried."

"I'm glad you're better." I'm glad you're still alive so I can apply for a job. I tried not to breathe in. He smelled like onions and whiskey.

"Look here." Larry pointed to a scar on his arm. "I actually like this scar from the woodpile incident. Looks like a snake. I like snakes. Not afraid of them buggers at all. I got my gun on me all the time, anyhow. Got a right to protect myself and my women." He winked at me.

I had to keep my eyes straight so I didn't roll them back into my head. What an idiot. I felt a wave of depression. This was what it had come to. After graduating from college, traveling the world for years and working in many restaurants, culinary school, and more years of hard work, I was now asking for a job from a man who reminded me of gonorrhea.

I reminded myself that I was now responsible for two little girls. That prevented me from turning on my burgundy cowgirl boots and heading straight out the door.

I had dropped Stephi and Lucy off at school and registered them before hitting the restaurants and cafés in town on my first day of job hunting. It was the same elementary school I had gone to. My friend from high school, Mattie Shoemaker, was the secretary, and another friend from high school, Sheryl Lalonski, was the principal.

When I saw them I could not help but remember the glorious night that they, along with my sister and I, decided it would be a fabulous idea to go drag racing outside of town, in my mother's truck, with everyone else in the back in bikinis. We threw in a plastic kiddie pool filled with a mixture of water and beer. Another time the four of us got drunk on the football field's fifty-yard line. We decided to strip and run around naked. Worked until someone turned the lights on.

No, we were all professional, but we hugged and laughed, and Sheryl winked at me and said, "Can you believe this? I'm a principal of a school."

And I said three words to them. "Fifty-yard line," and we all cracked up.

Stephi and Lucy gave me long, somewhat tearful hugs before heading to their new classrooms, Sheryl holding their hands. I hugged them back, sent them on their way. I did not know how long I would be here, but I did know they were not going to miss school. Then I started my job search.

It took four days, going door to door. I thought of going to other towns, but that would be a lengthy commute driving in winter conditions, which meant less time with the girls.

On the fifth morning I arrived, with black dread, at Larry's doorstep. It took all I had to open the door, pride crushed, hopelessness hopping around my heels.

"I saw your sign outside that you're looking for a chef." I pulled on my blue scarf. It had a charming English village on it. I had picked it up in, wait for it, an English village. It felt like it was strangling me. My gold hummingbird earrings were from Laos.

"You're hired."

"What?"

"You're hired. Get in there and start cooking." He smiled. It was more of a leer than a smile as his eyes dropped to my chest.

He was missing two teeth. He had a tattoo of a mermaid on his arm. The mermaid's boobs were probably the only boobs he ever saw.

Could I even do this? I thought of my checkbook. I thought of the money I owed my attorney and the hospital. Frightening. "We need to discuss my salary."

"Your salary? I'll pay you minimum wage."

"Plus five dollars."

"No."

"Okay." I started to walk away. I could go into a different field. Different job. Maybe I'd haul rock. Maybe I'd work in a salt mine. Do we have salt mines anymore?

"Okay. Plus four dollars."

I kept walking.

"Five. You win. You get yourself and your little ass on in here."

I whipped around. I have a no-tolerance rule for harassment from men. "Do not talk about my ass again, Larry, as comments like that make me feel like vomiting." I didn't smile when I said it.

He seemed surprised. "I don't take any of that back talk from my employees. You work for me now, missy."

"And I don't take sexual harassment. Your choice. You don't make any comments about my ass and I won't make any comments about how your body reminds me of gray Play-Doh infused with chicken pox."

His jaw went slack. "What? No, it don't look like that. Okay. I won't say anything about that . . . that your ass."

"Good."

And that was it. I was employed.

The kitchen was gross. The dining room wasn't clean. How had this restaurant passed inspection?

Two of the line cooks, Joey and Garrett, looked like they would sooner be out back shooting possums. Two others, Justin and Earl, seemed nice. The waitress, Dinah, platinum hair, dark make up, early twenties probably, looked interesting and hopeful. She probably wanted another woman among these testosterone-driven hyenas. Larry told me they all worked part time.

I had a moment of blackness. I did not want to come back to my hometown and work in a dive. I didn't want to come back here after my mother and grandma told everyone I was a chef in a "fancy-pancy" place in Portland and start flipping burgers. I didn't want to work for Larry, whom no one liked, in his grease-filled slop of a kitchen and have people I've known since I was a baby see me in the back of this squalid, virus-laden hole. I didn't want Jace to see me here most of all. Not Jace.

My shoulders sunk. I was broke, but my pride was gone in favor of two little girls with blond curls and beautiful smiles whom I loved and adored. *Buck up, Olivia,* I told myself. *You are making me ill with your pity party. No whining. No complaining, you pathetic, wretched creature. Get to work.*

I pulled a fairly clean apron off the hooks and introduced myself to everyone, smiled, was friendly and firm. I told the potential possum killers, Joey and Garrett; Larry; and the other three what we needed to do.

The possum killers and Larry balked at first at my long list of things to get done. I could feel the "I'm not taking orders from no woman" mentality. I started sharpening the knives. "Larry, I'm not arguing with you. You and your two tongue-wagging friends here either do what I say to get this place cleaned up before the state Department of Health shuts you down, or I'm leaving and you'll have no money."

The no-money part moved Larry.

He brought himself up. It was like watching a drunk grizzly finally standing on two feet. "I got money. We been here for years."

"Hardly anyone comes here, Larry, and you know it. Let's clean it up. Now."

"You drive a hard bargain, Olivia. You're feisty"—he winked—"and I like that."

"Gross, Larry. Stop."

"In fact"—he swirled a finger in the air—"that's what I'm going to call you from now on. Chef Feisty."

The two possum-killing young men snickered.

I turned to them. "Do you need a tissue for your noses? I'm hearing sounds come out of them I don't like."

"Nothin', nothin'." They exchanged a smirk. Larry saw it. He belched, grinned, hit his chest with his fist.

"You can respect me as the chef, or you're out," I said. "Yes. You two. Respect me as the chef or find another job sweeping gum off the streets with your teeth."

One of them had big teeth, which prompted that comment. He closed his mouth. He knew he had beaver teeth.

"Hey, you two," Larry said, slamming a hand on the counter. "Do what she says, or I'll knock your stupid heads together and you'll be stupider than you were before."

I caught Dinah's grin. I knew she was loving that they were finally getting their due.

I looked around. "Close this place down, Larry."

"What? No. I'm stayin' open."

"Don't. This place needs help. It's not like you're flooded with customers, anyhow, right?"

Larry mumbled. Something about a "slow day."

"We're remodeling and we're cleaning. I need to go shopping with your credit card for new décor and for ingredients. We'll reopen when this place doesn't look like a disease anymore." I opened a menu. "Breakfast and lunch."

"You think you know what you're doin', do ya?" Larry said, hands on his hips.

"You clearly don't."

"Now, that ain't nice, hon. I'm in business."

"Barely. And my name is not Hon. My name is Olivia. Close down. Now. It's disgusting in here. I will not cook in this wreck. Are we ready to get this place back together?"

The possum killers, Earl and Justin, Dinah, and Larry the Lazy nodded.

The possum killers took a break after an hour of semiwork to smoke a cigarette.

An hour later they took a break to smoke pot out in the back alley by the trash cans.

I fired them.

One of them threw his joint at me, and it hit my chest.

I picked up a piece of wood about five feet long and swung it at both of their heads. I knew they would duck, and they did. Then I chased them out of the alley and to the street. They were shocked that a female had fought back.

No one should mess with a Montana woman.

On the way home, I drove by the white fence, out into the country, away from town, and got out of my mother's truck. The blue sky was clear, the silence peaceful, the wind a soft puff, the branches of the trees holding snow with gentle hands. I stared across the property toward a hill in the distance.

I would go there soon. It would bring me to my knees, but I'd do it.

The insurance company called. They acknowledged that my car was totaled.

They offered a horrible amount of money for it. They always do that. All those years of paying monthly premiums and they stiff you when you need them.

"It's worth far more than that."

They did not think so. We had an argument. I was unhappy.

I had my attorney call. She got me a thousand dollars more. "There were 120,000 miles on your car, Olivia. That's all I can do."

I took it.

That night I thought about Jace and tried not to cry. That proved impossible, so I tried not to cry about him for very long.

Chapter 3

〜

"I think I'm going to get a boob job."

My eyes dropped to my sister, Chloe Razolli's, boobs. She is . . . fully endowed. Chloe's about five foot five and two hundred proud pounds. Says she's got a 'whole lotta body to love,' and she is "proud to be a woman of physical substance. My body is a temple of lush."

My mother, grandma, Chloe, and I were making Carefree Cowgirl Coconut Chocolate Cake together at the farmhouse. When we bake cakes together we call it Martindale Cake Therapy because we all feel better when we're done.

"Is your back still bothering you?" I asked.

"Yep. It's like I've got jumping watermelons pulling on my spine all day long." She wrapped her fingers around the ends of her brown ponytail.

"Then do it." I used a wooden spoon to stir cake batter away from the edges of the bowl.

Chloe spent six years in the army. She works in Kalulell as a paramedic and, when needed, flies a search and rescue helicopter up into the mountains of Montana. Talk about a badass. When she's not being a badass, she is hanging out with her son, Kyle, who is fifteen, brilliant, and has Asperger's.

Her husband, Teddy Razolli, died mountain climbing eight years ago. He was as much of a daredevil as she was, and had also been in the army, as a Ranger, which is where they met. Teddy was a kind, loud, brave man who adored Chloe. After he died Chloe said, "I am knocked down but not out. I will honor my husband by not being a wuss." She said this while she was semi-hysterical, my mother preparing to give her a pill to calm her down before she hyperventilated.

Teddy's death had been an enormous blow to our families, it had knocked Chloe flat, and she had eaten her grief away to the tune of an additional sixty-five pounds, but now Chloe was dating. Or, trying to get up the courage to date.

"Those udders get in the way of her paramedic work," my mother said, sweetly tactful as always. "Can you imagine Chloe leaning over you after you've had a heart attack and those huge boobs bearing down on you like moons?"

"Exactly, Mom," Chloe said, not offended, pointing at her boobs, both fingers, nodding her head. "But I'll tell you, these bamboozas get the men's heartbeats going real quick. I had one man, on the ground, waking up from a heart attack after I'd revived him, and he actually reached out his hands to grab them."

"What did you do, Nutmeg?" my grandma asked. She was wearing a white silk scarf with pink zinnias. Bringing beauty to the world. "I swatted his hands away and told him if he touched my knockers I'd hit him so hard his heart would stop again but this time I wouldn't revive him." She grabbed a beer.

"I bet that got his hands back down." I looked at Stephi and Lucy, dozing on the couch in front of the fire, probably trying to sleep off a crash in a blizzard, the loneliness of starting a new school, and their ever-present grief from missing their beloved grandmother, Annabelle.

"Sure did. He knew I meant it, too. I said it in a calming voice, soothing, because that's my job: Stay calm. But I don't want the girls squished by some old man with vampire hands."

"No to vampire hands," I said.

"Always no," my grandma said. "And if he doesn't take no, you take action. The Fire Breather and I taught you girls how to protect yourself."

My mother nodded proudly and tapped her red cowgirl boot. They had done their duty: knee, punch, kick with the cowgirl boot, claw, hit. Begin again.

"Chloe, will you pass me the cocoa powder?" I asked. I winked at my mother.

Instead of passing me the cocoa powder Chloe turned, opened the fridge, and handed me cream. When my sister is talking in the kitchen, she gets easily confused. We ask her for stuff to see what she'll do. My mother clipped her laughter. My grandma smiled. I got the cocoa powder.

The four of us have been making cakes together since I was little, although my grandma and I do most of the work, as we share an adoration of baking. My earliest memory is sitting at my grandparents' solid wood dining room table in the log cabin and watching her add pink dye to a ballerina cake she was making me for my birthday. The ballerina had a fluffy pink tutu with silver candy sparkles. A baker was born on that day.

The women in our family don't make normal cakes, though, like a simple three-layer white cake. Every cake has to be special. For example, take Feminist Fun Caramel and Chocolate Cake with Pecans. Six layers. We each took turns writing our names along the sides in pink icing because we are feminists, then we had a straight shot of vodka with the cake.

Kick-Ass Carrot Cake is one of my favorites. We make carrots with orange and green icing but stick a giant real carrot in the center because we think we're funny. It was Grandma who taught us that carrot cake should be served with a carrot.

We love using fondant, so our cakes sometimes come out wild and crazy. We name those cakes Martindale Chicks Crazy Cakes. In the past we've made cakes in the shape of a drunken-looking turkey for Thanksgiving holding a bottle of wine; a stack of four fancy hats with lace and candied baubles, one by each of us; a purple dragon because we needed to laugh, badly, that day; intricate wild flowers with faces; and four slinky, sexy, funky bras.

Some families watch movies together. Some families drink together. Some families camp. We bake cakes. And eat them. The eating is the best part.

"Chloe," I said, "would you hand me the buttermilk?"

She handed me pepper. My grandma couldn't hide her laugh

as she added marshmallows and coconut to a mixture. Chloe seemed confused by Grandma's laughter.

"Anyhow, I'm thinking about getting a boob job to get littler knockers. Look how mongo these suckers are." She lifted up her shirt. I have seen her girls before. They are impressive. "They hurt. I can't run because my boobs will hit me in the face and knock me out. I can't golf because the girls get in the way of my swing. Last time I tried to golf I was afraid my boobs were coming off with the ball. I've got porn star boobs and I don't want porn star boobs."

"Then have them reduced, Nutmeg," my grandma said. "Can you hand me a fork, Chloe?"

Chloe opened a drawer, pulled out a carrot peeler, and gave it to my grandma. My grandma said, "Thank you, dear," and Chloe said, "You're welcome, Grandma."

"There's a problem with reduction." My sister sat down on a stool. "I don't like the idea of a knife on my girls."

"Don't think about knives," my mother said, "think about how freeing it'll feel to get the udders reduced."

"Right," Chloe said. "Not so cowlike then." She tapped her beer bottle on each boob.

The cake batter was done, and my grandma and I poured it into four pans, as it would be four layers. I handed two of the pans to Chloe. "Can you put these in the oven?"

"Sure, Olivia." She took the pans and put them on the kitchen table. Grandma laughed. Chloe seemed confused, once again, by the laughter. I went behind her back and put them into one of my mother's two ovens.

"Yeah. I might have to take the girls down a notch," Chloe said, holding her boobs up with both hands and staring down at them. "I mean, the men go crazy when they see them. Crazy. They lose it. I don't blame them. Look at these. If I were a man I'd lose it, too."

"They're eyeball catchers," I said.

My grandma said, "But you do a nice job of not flaunting them around and about."

Chloe always wore high-collar shirts and sweaters.

"Drives them crazier still, Grandma. They can't see 'em, they can't touch 'em, they can only envision what's underneath. The men." She waved her beer around. "They can't stay sane."

We laughed, even though Chloe was semi-serious.

We cleaned up. Then we had wine and waited for the cake to bake. Later we'd ice it and drop the coconut and chocolate chips on the top layer with the girls. Our tradition with this cake was to yell, "Giddyap, cowgirl! Get that carefree cow!" and clink our milk glasses together before we ate it. It was going to be delicious. The smell of Carefree Cowgirl Coconut Chocolate Cake wafted through our home.

Measure. Mix. Stir. Whip. Bake.

There's something comforting about good old fashioned cake.

I walked Chloe out to her car that evening.

"Chloe, I have to talk to you."

"I know." She turned and put a hand on my shoulder.

"You know?"

"Yes. You have to talk to me about how you shut me out of your life when you lived here that last year, and when you moved to Portland, and how that banged up my heart and my head and hurt my feelings and made me feel sad and lonely."

"Yes." That was exactly it. "Chloe, I am sorry. I was so depressed here, for so long. I could hardly get up. I lost it."

"I know, but you had me. I'm your sister. I'm your best friend, and you cut me out like you'd cut the fat off a steak. You cut me out like you'd cut a sausage out of an apple pie because I know you don't like sausage. You cut me out like you'd cut a rat out of a bag of caramel morsels."

I paused on the graphicness of her rant. She is creative. "I did. I had nothing in me, Chloe. I am so sorry." I put my hands to my face, so ashamed of what I'd done, so guilty for the pain I'd caused her, and she pulled them away and we went nose to nose, like when we were kids, and held hands.

"I'm sorry, too, Olivia. We've both been through bad times. Like moths trapped in bottles and the bottles are being shaken up and down. Like we used to do when we were kids. Those moths had a bad time getting all shook up, and we had bad times."

"Yes." I sniffled and snorted. "We did." I told her I was sorry, again.

"Hey, hey. It's okay." She cupped my face with her hands. "I know what happened to you, and one apology is more than enough. Let's bake a cake together, you and me, all right? You and me. A healing cake. Something with layers and layers of icing. I have to feed this two-hundred-pound proud woman. Men like stuff to hold, which is what you don't have, skinny chicken. We'll bake a cake together again and fatten you right up so you can curve like me." She tapped my nose with hers.

"I think that's a sweet idea, sister."

"Me too. Love you, Olivia, you bow-and-arrow-shooting warrior woman."

"Love you, too, Chloe, you tough-talkin', hip-rockin' Montana woman heroine."

Chloe is a heroine. She saves people all the time as a paramedic and a search and rescue helicopter pilot. She has people who have seriously said they would die for her because she saved their son/daughter/wife/husband.

They mean it.

I had arranged for painters to come immediately to Larry's. Larry would pay time-and-a-half to get them working into the night. I had new floors, toilets, and sinks put in the staff and customer bathrooms. The old ones were cesspools of goopy germs. Larry whined about the cost until I told him that his restaurant was so off the charts for a lack of sanitation it was surprising no one had died eating his food. Undoubtedly he got the money from his mommy, but that was not my business.

I had the carpet ripped out and new fake wood put in. I had new lights hung over each table and bought tablecloths to cover the ugly brown. I bought candles and vases for flowers for each table. I ripped down all the dusty curtains. The new décor was now Montana cowboy. I hung cowboy hats and huge photos of Montana and cowgirls and cowboys. I hired a cleaning service.

Most important, I revamped the menu. I made it smaller, better.

I made Earl, Justin, Dinah, and Larry a meal. Tossed salad with a strawberry vinaigrette, chicken sandwiches with avocado and a secret sauce I concocted, and crisp onion rings stacked up into a tower. Montana mountain food with elegance, which is how they like it here.

"Best food I've ever had," Earl said.

"Me too, ma'am," Justin said.

Dinah said, "This is dang tasty." Dinah is twenty-three and named after her grandma, a showgirl in Vegas. Today she had a purple streak through her platinum-colored hair and a lot of black makeup. She went to school at the local university and was studying engineering.

"I needed a job and that's why I'm here," she whispered to me when the men weren't listening. "Glad you're here. We need sanity to balance out the dick." She pointed to Larry.

We laughed.

Larry smacked his sausage lips over the sandwich. I've never liked sausage. "Not bad, Chef Feisty. I'll keep you on for another day."

Larry's a jerk, but I had a paycheck. I would move on as soon as I could. But first I had to keep Larry in business so I could keep myself in business.

"How was school today?" I poured Lucy and Stephi glasses of chocolate milk when we got home early Tuesday evening. Lucy accidentally knocked her glass over and started crying. The milk spilled onto my red cotton shirt with embroidered flowers I'd bought in Mexico, my black skirt, my wool leggings, and down into my red cowgirl boots.

"I don't have any friends," Lucy said. She put her hands to her face, her blond curls all over.

"I don't think anyone likes me," Stephi said, those deep

brown eyes despairing. She took a few rocks out of her pocket and fiddled with them. They're like her worry beads.

"I sat by myself at lunch." Lucy cried into her new glass of chocolate milk. "Someone said my sandwich smelled like poop and they didn't want to sit with poop."

That sandwich was one of her favorites: egg salad with celery. It did not smell like poop. I ached for her. Sitting all alone with a poopy-smelling sandwich.

I had arranged for the girls to go to after-school classes when school got out at three o'clock. I knew they would rather come home, but it is what it is. I work. I'm a single mother. We can't all do what we want.

Monday they had art, Tuesday and Thursday they had indoor soccer, and Wednesday was science class. On Friday my grandma said she would leave the clinic early and pick them up for Grandma Gisela and Granddaughter time. They were thrilled. They knew that meant cooking treats with Grandma Gisela in her kitchen at the farmhouse.

But a new school is tough stuff for kids.

"I sat by a boy at lunch who flipped up my skirt and I hit him and he told the teacher I hit him and she said, 'Violence is never the way, Stephi' and I said, 'If he doesn't flip up my skirt, then I won't have to be a violent girl,' and she gave me a mean look and seemed confused and I said is he getting in trouble for flipping up my skirt and she said yes. I told him not to do it again, but everyone likes Damon so now no one likes me."

"It takes time, girls." I reached out and held their hands. "You'll make friends. Smile. Say hello. Be kind. Ask kids questions about themselves. Do they have pets? Do they have sisters or brothers? Then you can ask if they want to come over here and play."

"I think I want to move back to Portland, Aunt Olivia," Stephi said. "Where I had friends who wanted to eat lunch with me and didn't treat me like I'm invisible."

"I do, too, Aunt Olivia. A girl named Bella said I look like a blond doll. I think it means I look weird. Do you think I look weird?"

"I don't think anyone liked my rock collection, but I like my rocks." Stephi took more rocks out of her pockets.

They both burst into tears, and I pulled them into my lap. I knew they were upset about school, and friends, and I knew they still, every day, missed their grandmother, Annabelle.

The part about parenting that I didn't know, but have learned quickly, is how your heart can break when your children are sad/lost/lonely/left out.

Even after being their mom for only six months, my heart felt bigger with love, but definitely beat up and battered.

I dropped the girls off at my mother's two nights later at her request. She was going to crack open an anatomy book so they could get a "head start" on medical school. "I couldn't get my daughters to become doctors, maybe I can with my grand-daughters. It's like I'm being given a second chance at medical fulfillment. Do you think the girls will want to take over the clinic when they're older?"

Larry had few customers when we reopened a week later. One was drunk, one was homeless, one was a friend of his who made weird grunts and squeaked, as if he were swallowing mice as he ate.

I knew I wouldn't have a job if Larry didn't have more cus-tomers. I whipped up some omelets with mushrooms, a mix of cheeses, chives, avocados, diced tomatoes, and a few shakes of salt, pepper, and paprika. I put the samples in tiny plastic con-tainers and added a plastic fork to each one.

I grabbed my red ski jacket and gave away the samples out-side, from a tray, the sky blue, the air freezing cold, the snow piled up. I saw tons of people whom I knew from childhood, from school, and as my mother's and grandparents' friends. They hugged me, and we laughed. They did express some sur-prise, quickly covered, that I was working for Larry. It was de-moralizing. It was humiliating. It was my reality.

No, I didn't like coming home and working at a dive like Larry's. But I needed the job, needed the money, and it was what it was. My grandma taught me this: When things aren't going your way, smile harder. It will get better.

I smiled harder. Several people said, "Are you and Jace getting back together, honey? Ruthie Teal told Hank and Hank told his cousin Lou Lou, and Lou Lou told me that you two were together one night when she was cleaning her gun."

I told them no, and they said, "That's a shame . . . That makes me sad in my heart . . . I wish you two would try again . . ."

And "Olivia, did you know that Ruthie has a boyfriend? He's younger."

I smiled harder and handed them another sample. Put something in their mouth, maybe they will shut it.

Larry finally waddled his bulky self outside and bellowed, "What are you doing, little lady, giving away my food for free? You think I've got money up my behind?"

"That is a disgusting image, Larry. Don't ever talk to me in a way that gives me a disgusting image."

Larry continued to be surprised when I pushed back. He, with his bullying ways and his momma's money, was used to dominating people. "Who works for who here?"

"I work for you. When your mother comes down from her mansion and tastes the food that I'm making, she'll be glad that you're making money. Maybe you can start paying her rent."

Larry's eyes bulged. "I pay rent."

"No, you don't." I saw the truth in his eyes. "I'm giving away food to show people there's a new chef here and that you're not serving the usual slop crap. You want business, you have to show people you've changed." I handed him a sample. "Here."

He liked it. He dragged his grunting anteater self back inside.

So I stood outside Larry's Diner and handed out samples. Wasn't long before we had more people inside the restaurant. Justin and Larry and I were cooking, and Earl and Dinah were waiting tables. I sent Justin out now and then to help with coffee and water and trips back and forth for condiments. Larry actually could move quick when yelled at.

We stayed open for breakfast and lunch and closed at three o'clock.

"We stay open for dinner," Larry said.

"I already told you we don't. We need to build a clientele for breakfast and lunch, and I have to figure out a dinner meal that won't make people sick. That's why you don't have customers at dinner time. Your food makes them sick."

"My dinners don't make people sick. That wasn't even my fault last year. I had a bum-ass waiter and he was a bum-ass hand washer. And the second time . . ." He seemed confused, so he burped, thumped his chest. "It happened without my knowledge. Three people that time. No one died."

"Your dinners are slop. You have to be better. Want to know how much we made?"

He did. I showed him. His eyes widened.

I tipped Dinah and Justin and Earl in front of him.

Their mouths fell open.

"Thank you, ma'am."

"What the hell?" Larry said.

"You're welcome. Thank you. And be quiet, Larry. They deserve it."

Larry was thrilled, but threatened. Threatened by me, as a woman. He likes to control, he likes to make sure that women obey him.

"Don't make my decisions for me again, Olivia."

I stared at him until he turned away. But first he had to run his creepy gaze over my body, head to foot. It was deliberate, demeaning. He wanted me to know he saw me as a body and he had the right to evaluate it. He was the boss and I should remember that. He was the man, I was the woman. He could look if he wanted to. He wanted me to know he was envisioning me naked. He liked that power, the sick sexuality behind it, liked infuriating me.

I seethed. The worst thing about working for pig boars is that you need the money and the job, so you can't always say what you want and you can't walk out. Stuck, stuck, stuck. I hated that, too.

* * *

Jace had never treated me like that when we worked together. Never. We ran Martindale Ranch as a couple. We laughed all the time. We laughed until all the laughter stopped and went straight up the hill to a quiet place with magical sunsets and there it stayed.

I kept wondering if I should say anything to my grandma about the cookbook, the old-fashioned tin box, the charm bracelets and butterfly clips, the gold lockets and the nurse's uniform, the blue dress and her wedding dress, and the silver menorah. Should I let it be? What right did I have to bring it up, to force the conversation, to invade her privacy? Would it hurt her? Yes, I answered that question myself. It would hurt her. It was her past. Her past was painful. Probably wretched. That's why she hid it.

I didn't want to bring up something that she wanted to forget.

But she was eighty-eight years old. Would she want to see these things again? Especially the cookbook? She had written recipes in it herself, I recognized her handwriting. But the other recipes were written by other people who were probably no longer alive. Would it pain her to see those recipes, or would she feel relieved to talk about her family, to remember the happy memories?

I decided to bake red velvet cookies with a cream center and think about it. Cooking is soothing, so helpful thinking can take place.

Jace loved my red velvet cookies.

I bit my lips. Measure. Mix. Stir. Whip. Bake.

I saw Jace in town the next week when I was leaving work, so I skittered behind a building. It was freezing out, snowing lightly, but I felt sweaty from bending over the gas stoves and hustling for eight hours in a hot kitchen. My hair was falling out of my bun, and I knew all semblance of makeup was gone.

At least I had showered that morning. Dang. Had I showered? Had I put makeup on? Had I put on deodorant? Shoot. *I hadn't.* We'd overslept. I'd yanked on jeans and a red sweatshirt, made eggs for the girls, and shuttled them out the door. They were miserable about school and having no friends, so they moved at about the same speed as lazy porcupines. Stephi insisted on running back into the log cabin to load her pockets with part of her rock collection, while Lucy pointed her finger in the air and said, "I'm moving back to Portland tonight."

I was gross.

I leaned against the wall of the brick building, crossed my arms over my chest, and scrunched down into my jacket. I could not see Jace now. I swallowed hard. No, I couldn't do it. I looked like pancake batter and felt like rotten tomatoes. Plus, it felt wretched to think about him. Probably always would.

I tipped my face up to the snowflakes, hoping they would make me feel cleaner and freeze the tears in my eyes. When I was sure Jace would be gone, I slunk back around the building like a sneaky coyote, and there he was.

"Hey, Olivia."

"Jace." Shoot, shoot, shoot.

"It's probably not necessary to hide from me."

I could lie. I wouldn't. "I didn't think it would be much of a wait until you were down the street, so it was no problem."

His mouth tilted up in a smile. I used to kiss that smile. His black hair ruffled in the wind.

"Maybe we should talk."

"No, thank you." He was so tall. Heckuva manly man.

"No? Never?"

"I don't think we need to right now." My breath caught and I made this awkward, high-pitched sound.

"I do. But, Olivia, we don't need to talk about anything"—he looked away for a second—"stressful. We don't need to talk about us. I'd like to hear about your girls. Your job in Portland. Your family. Easy stuff."

"You think we can do easy?"

He smiled. "I think we can do anything, but maybe we need to start easy."

"No."

"How come?"

"What's the point, Jace?" I tried to get control of the tears that I could feel welling up in my heart. "I'm here for a while, probably not long, and then I'm going back to Portland." No, I wasn't. Not if she was there. Not if the threat wasn't smashed down. Heck no. I felt scared to my toes thinking about her. I refocused on the cowboy in front of me.

"For me, the point would be to spend time with you again."

"Why would you want to do that?" I could think of many reasons why he wouldn't want to. I didn't blame him at all. He had every reason to be furious with me. I deserved it.

"Because I like being with you."

How could he like being with me after what I did to him? How could he stand there and be nice and friendly? Why didn't he hate me? "Why, Jace? Why would you want to be with me?"

"A hundred reasons, Olivia." He kept smiling.

I about melted. "Jace—"

"Lunch? Coffee? Want to see the ranch?"

I thought about it. I was so tempted. I was also tempted to take off his clothes. "No. No. And no."

I did not miss the hurt in his dark eyes before he covered it up.

"When do you think that might be a yes?"

"I can't do a yes with you, Jace." A whisper. It was all I could do.

"I wish you would."

"I can't." I turned to walk away. I think I swayed. The tears got me off balance. The memories almost brought me to my knees.

Because I was the temporary guardian of Lucy and Stephi, Children's Services in Oregon would regularly send one of their caseworkers to see us at my apartment in Portland. The case worker would talk to the three of us together, then he would talk to me alone, and to the girls alone, to get all the different perspectives. His name was Dameon. He was dour, serious, had little personality, and never smiled. The girls were a tiny bit afraid of him.

He wrote me glowing reviews. "Girls are thriving . . . Olivia Martindale is an outstanding mother to Lucy and Stephi . . . Family activities are numerous . . . Girls learning how to cook . . . Many books and crafts . . . A patient and caring woman . . ."

When I moved to Montana, I had a new caseworker, who would report back to Children's Services in Oregon.

I was nervous for her visit. By the time she arrived at the log cabin my hands were shaking. After all, the caseworkers have the control. If she didn't like me, that was going to be an enormous problem.

Joan was about forty, lots of frizzy red hair, huge smile.

She loved the log cabin, the gazebo, the lasso around the deck. She loved making ice-cream sandwich chocolate chip cookies with us. The girls made her play Candy Land with them. On the way out she said, "That game drives me out of my head."

I knew we'd get along.

Jace's Martindale Ranch was on the front page of the newspaper the following week. The newspaper was highlighting companies that hired local people. Jace hired many local people to work at the ranch that had been in his family for three generations, and he hired another group of employees for Martindale Ranch, and more again in the summer and fall when tourists poured in. It was also highlighted because when people are staying on the ranch, they wander into town and spend money there, and attend the art, theater, and symphony festivals.

There was a photo of him and a photo of the ranch from the top of a hill, which showed the charming guest cabins, the dining hall where all meals were served, the game room, the towering mountains, and the lake. The ranch was perfect, so perfect. I remembered all of our happy planning, watching the buildings grow from the ground up, the marketing, the menu planning, the activities we scheduled for the guests, the opening . . .

Jace was quoted as saying a number of interesting things but one was, "When we opened we had an outstanding chef in Olivia Martindale. A huge part of the reason we were successful early on was because people were coming to eat the best food in Montana."

I must stop being so emotional.

I received a check from my car insurance company. I used all the cash, plus another $500 from my account that I desperately needed, and I bought a truck from an older neighbor. It had 160,000 miles on it. It was light blue. Fifteen years old. Two rows, open cab in back.

I hoped it wouldn't fall apart. I waved at Sherman when I left. He waved back, then gave me a thumbs-up.

Yes, I needed a thumbs-up. The truck growled. I liked the growl.

We heard three knocks on the door of the log cabin. It was Kyle, Chloe's son. He always knocks three times.

I hugged him when he walked in. I adore Kyle. He hugged me back. He was stiff, patted my back three times. Chloe had had to teach him how to hug. "Who knew I'd have to teach my own son how to hug? Like he's a shark or something and has to figure out how to get his flippers around someone. Like he's a robot and has to program a hug in. This Asperger's is a tricky one, but I am wrestling with it and I will win."

"I like your outfit, Aunt Olivia, because I like a cacophony of color."

"Thank you." I was wearing a pink kimono-type jacket with dragons—so comfortable—from Japan and purple jeans.

Kyle is over six feet tall. Brown hair cut short, same green eyes as his mother, with some blue thrown in. Glasses, black rims. Gangly. He stands as if he doesn't know what to do with those long legs and arms, as if they are appendages he has to manage. Sometimes his hands flap around, as if caught by air.

For six months after his father died, he didn't speak. Later he said that he had not had anything to say because his father had left a hole in his life and that hole held no words.

"Your log cabin is two point four miles from my house, Aunt

Olivia. The average speed of cars traveling along the roads through town is twenty-four miles an hour. Out here in the country, it's forty-eight. Today the average temperature is expected to be thirty-five degrees, snow expected tonight, accumulation of one inch."

"Glad to know it. How are you, Kyle?"

"Fine." His gaze met mine, then slid away. His hands flapped, then stopped in midflap. "How are you, Aunt Olivia, birthday February twenty-seven."

Kyle knows everyone's birthday. Truly. Everyone's. If you give him your phone number, he will have that memorized, too. And any previous phone numbers. "I'm better now that you're here, Kyle. Would you like to come in and have cookies? I made snickerdoodles."

"Snickerdoodles. Made with cinnamon, cream of tartar, salt, other ingredients. Are they still warm?"

"I can warm them up."

He thought about that. "I can have three snickerdoodles. Warmed up." He cleared his throat. "Mother says it is appropriate to say please when offered food, and I did not say it. She says people without manners are rude like baboons that slobber, her words, not mine. I apologize. Please."

I smiled at him. "Super. Come on in."

He stopped in the entry. The girls were standing in the middle of the family room, holding hands. They were unsure about Kyle. He had come to visit me twice in Portland, with the rest of the family, but they didn't know what to do with someone who spoke formally of extremely complicated topics like the origin of black holes, what Saturn's rings were made of, and the full history of the beginning of the universe, including basic information on evolution.

"Hello, Lucy, oldest sister, birthday July one. Hello, Stephi, birthday November twelve."

His tone was, as always, formal.

"It's a pleasure to see you once again."

"Hi, Kyle." They had been making a tent out of blankets. The blankets kept falling off the chairs and table.

"Are you constructing a tent?" he asked.

"Yes." They were hesitant, shy. They are afraid of men, but Kyle was a teenager, so maybe he was safe. "Do you want to play?"

Kyle studied the tent, the blankets in a pile. "I believe I can be of assistance to provide a better structural foundation for the tent."

The girls were confused. "What?" they both said.

"We don't always understand you, Kyle," Lucy said, pointing her finger up in the air to make her point.

"You're confusing," Stephi said.

"I'm afraid many people hold this unfortunate opinion about me. It is something that I must continue to work on with diligence, and with the help of my mother. She has told me that my ability to understand social situations and people's emotions is, and I quote her, 'Poor.' I agree with her. However. If I apply my limited knowledge of home construction, weight-bearing walls, and the most effective way to adhere blankets to poles, I'll be able to design a tent that you can play in." He turned to me. "Do you have a drill? Where is your spare wood?"

A drill? Spare wood? I saw the hopeful expressions on Lucy and Stephi's face. "I do."

We all trooped out to get wood from the barn and the drill. We also brought in a hammer and nails. Kyle drew a rough draft, in detail. The girls were fascinated. In the loft upstairs, he went to work and the girls received their first construction engineering lesson.

He was at our house for three hours. I served him the snickerdoodles and a snack. Kyle's food must be separate. I was careful that his sandwich, fruit, and salad not touch one another.

In the end, the girls had their tent. It had a wood floor, studs in each corner; a roof in which he sawed a hole for a skylight; and a pole in the center for the blankets to hang on. Both girls could stand up in it.

They hugged him and he patted their backs, three times. They jumped up and down, then brought their books and games into it. It was perfect.

"We love it, Kyle." They jumped up and down again.

Kyle nodded, gave them a slight bow. "I think this will give you an area for creative play, to use your imaginations, and hopefully a quiet place to read and reflect upon scientific topics."

He took out a small black notebook. It was his Questions Notebook. That was actually the title of it. He wrote things down in there that he didn't understand so he could ask my sister about it later. "I am writing down a question for Mother, which is, 'As a conversation starter with peers my own age would it be appropriate to tell them that I built a tent fort, including the dimensions of the wood, number of nails, and structural integrity, or would that constitute boring conversation?" He closed the notebook. "I'm leaving now." He started out.

I hugged him. He let me. Patted my back. Three times. "Thank you so much, Kyle. That was so kind."

He was puzzled. "Kind? Stephi and Lucy needed a tent to play in, and because they are my new cousins I provided it. Mother says that our family is the most important thing and must come first. Hence, the tent. She told me this after she told me that I needed to quit flapping my hands like a 'damn bird,' her words, not mine. I endeavor not to swear. I am trying not to flap my hands so much. I do not want to resemble a bird, as I am human. Good-bye, Aunt Olivia. I am two hours and twelve minutes late."

"Late for what?"

"My studies."

"What are you studying now?"

"The works of Michelangelo. He is a fascinating man. I am studying his paintings now, then will move on to his sculptures."

And out he went.

When Kyle was a baby and then a toddler he wouldn't make eye contact. He would cry and pull away from being touched or hugged, except from Chloe. He would kick off a yellow blanket but not the blue knitted one. He would wear one of two T-shirts and throw a fit if Chloe tried to put him in something else. He would wear his pajama pants with galaxies on them or red cotton pants, not the black ones. His fits were impressive, his distress acute, when he was dressed in anything else.

He had hardly any expression on his face unless he was throwing a fit. As my sister said, "His face is a blank slate. What the hell happened to his emotions? Did they slide out of my placenta when I was pregnant?" His first word wasn't *Mama* or *Dada,* or *bird,* it was *paramedic,* followed by *Dove Mountain Range, cirrus cloud,* and *weather vane.* He had seen the sun weather vane on top of the log cabin that my granddad put up for my grandma.

As a toddler he was soon fascinated by weather, and my sister brought home piles of books from the library on weather and clouds.

He had to listen to classical music or he couldn't sleep. He played with LEGOs for hours and built intricate houses within neighborhoods. He collected pens and grouped them by color. As he grew, he developed this loose-limbed, almost on his tiptoes walk, and his fingers were constantly tapping the insides of his palms.

The brilliance came early. In kindergarten he did a report on Mozart. He wrote about him, and he drew his picture. This was followed by piano lessons, which he continues to excel at today. He was doing complex multiplication at the age of six and reading at an eighth-grade level. He started studying biology, the universe, and animals in depth. Books and charts all over.

He has all As and is currently taking calculus, chemistry, and physics, but he hates the physical act of writing and his letters are a scrawl. He wants to type everything. He does calculus for fun and is even in an online calculus group with other brilliant people. He is a whiz at computers. Truly genius.

"It's like raising Einstein," Chloe said with total exasperation. "The way he talks, Olivia. Big, complicated freaking words, all said so precisely. I mean, does he think he's from the sixteenth century? The other night I told him he sounded like a prince from a castle in England, and he thought about that and then said that could not be true because modern syntax, American-accented English, and twenty-first-century cadence would rule out the possibility."

He loves to draw and paint and has for years. He studies how to draw people, and he studies the great masters.

The painful problem is social. Kyle doesn't get it. He can't read people's expressions, doesn't get sarcasm or jokes, and can't pick up verbal and nonverbal cues. He sometimes will laugh at inappropriate times and smiles when he shouldn't, for example, when something sad or embarrassing happens to someone else.

He talks at kids, not with them, in a monotone, and doesn't understand when they're bored straight out of their minds. He will appear unempathetic to other people and difficult situations. He can come across as a know-it-all. He doesn't mean to be either, though my sister has told him, "Look, Kyle. Restrain your brain. You come off like you know everything on the planet, so knock it off. It's irritating." His response? Surprise. "Mother, I know only a tiny fraction about the planet Earth, its inhabitants, history, mathematics, and science, which is why my studies are ongoing. My knowledge is extremely limited."

The worst thing is that he's sometimes picked on and bullied in school. Most kids are nice, or flat-out ignore him, but there are always a few, and a few boys now—Eric, Jason, and Juan—who are particularly mean to him. Those three are knuckle-scraping idiots who will amount to nothing, but for now they constantly try to bring Kyle down. He does get hurt; he knows he doesn't fit in. He realizes he doesn't have friends, like other kids do.

If only everyone could see Kyle's heart. He is one of the kindest people I know, he simply shows it in a different way. My sister works with him all the time. Kyle told me that she has said the following things to him: "Look, Kyle. You come off odd, okay? Strange. So you have to accept it and change some of this shit you do."

My sister has also told him, "Don't ever rock back and forth in your chair like that at school, Kyle. You look like a dying turkey. Sit straight and don't fiddle and for God's sakes if your food touches other food in the school cafeteria don't look at it like the freakin' world has come to an end" and "Kyle, smile. Okay? No. Not like that. You look like you want to fart. Smile normal. Oh, my God. Are we going to have to practice smiling? Yes, smile like that. In a friendly way, not like you're a robot."

And, most important, "Kyle, I love you so much."

Kyle told me once that with his mother's help, "I am learning to act in a more normalized manner, socially speaking, within the educational construct of my high school, which has many perplexing and changing cultural dynamics. Each day Mother and I address my questions in the Questions Notebook. Mother is extremely wise."

My phone rang.

The number hit me in the gut, as usual.

I didn't answer, also as usual. It made me shake.

She told me that what I was doing was illegal. She was going to sue me. She would see me in court.

I was a whole slew of terrible words, including a bitch, a slut, and a whore.

The words didn't bother me.

It was what was behind them that did.

It was that kernel of truth, the fact that she might be right. Not the part about me being a bitch but that she would win and I would lose and then all the rest of the years of my life would be utterly and completely miserable.

Chapter 4

〜

"I'm not going to the hospital, Mary Beth."

"Mr. Giles, I am not here to argue with a crotchety old man. It will only be for a few days, so get your feathers settled back on down." My mother held Mr. Giles's hand, gnarled from arthritis and eight decades of working outdoors. "While you're there I'll come and harangue you every day. That will be a benefit to you. My pleasing company."

I sat beside my mother in a chair at Mr. Giles's bedside in his Kalulell home. He was propped up on pillows, a table full of medicine beside him. He had a fever and labored breathing and looked pale. He was eighty-six years old with a full head of white hair. Mr. Giles was a successful rancher and farmer, and I'd known him all my life. He and his wife were close friends of my grandparents. His wife, Mellie, was on the other side of his bed smiling vacantly and swaying, as if she had a song in her head.

"And that would be right kind of you, Mary Beth, to take time out of your day to harangue me, but no thank you."

"You're so pale you look like a dead ghost." My mother impatiently tapped both cowgirl boots. Today they were turquoise with gold stars. "You're so weak you're like paper. I'm surprised you can stand up to piss. Your chest sounds so cluttered I feel like I'm listening to tar boil. You are going to the hospital, Mr. Giles."

"Isn't my mother kind?" I asked. "Isn't her bedside manner soothing and comforting, so gentle."

My mother snorted and said, "I do not coddle my patients, Olivia."

"But you should go to the hospital, Mr. Giles," I said, "if I can weigh in here."

"Hell no, Olivia, and I apologize for swearing in front of you ladies, and you are both ladies except for how all the women in your family handle guns, including Gisela. You're all as quick at the draw as the boys I served with in the military, but a hospital trip is not gonna happen."

His wife giggled. Then she put her hand to her mouth, in a flirty way, and blew him a kiss. She giggled again. He smiled at her, such a gentleman. I did not miss the worry when he did so.

"The hospital will send me a bill larger than the state of Montana, Mary Beth. They'll charge me fifty bucks for an aspirin. They'll charge me if I pee too long. They'll charge me if I breathe heavy. You go to the hospital, and if you're not careful they'll take your kidneys out and sell them on the black market and send you a bill for that, too."

"Mr. Giles, you have pneumonia and heart disease," my mother said. "And I promise you that no one will take your kidneys and sell them on the black market. Your kidneys aren't anything to be proud of. You're way too old, and no one wants them. I'm being honest with you."

"I always appreciate your honesty, Mary Beth, even when you told me the last time I saw you that I was more stubborn than a mule with a stick up its ass. But I got my woman here with me. She's taking care of me plenty fine, isn't that right, Mellie?"

Mellie, eighty-five years old, white curls, climbed up on the bed and bent down and kissed Mr. Giles's head and whispered, "I think the aliens are coming tonight, my darling. They'll take us away like they did last night." She giggled. "I wonder if they'll do that same thing to us again." She giggled once again, then patted his crotch beneath the blanket.

"She's a mite confused," Mr. Giles whispered, grabbing her hand. Mellie smiled, sitting cross-legged on the bed. She was wearing a silky pink dress, tennis shoes, and a black witch's hat she must have saved from Halloween. Mellie had always been kind and creative, and she still was.

"And who is taking care of Mellie?" my mother asked.

Now that question upset Mr. Giles. He was a true Montana man. He provided for and protected his wife. He sniffled. His nose turned red. He blinked rapidly. "I'm doin' my best, Mary Beth. This here pneumonia has only gotten me down like a frozen cat for the last couple of weeks. I can get up now and then, and I make sure she turns the stove off. Forgot again yesterday, that she did. She put a frozen turkey on the stove and turned it on high." He wheezed. "And she did try to leave yesterday. I found her all dressed up in her Sunday best in the driveway. She said she was waiting for the aliens."

"And how did you feel after you had to get up and convince her the aliens weren't coming?"

"The aliens are coming, dear," Mellie said, looking at my mother, smiling. She swayed with that song in her head then readjusted her witch's hat. "Soon. But they're nice. And they let me sleep with my cougar." She pointed at Mr. Giles. "He's a cougar in bed." She growled, a sexy growl.

Mr. Giles cleared his throat. "I had to be in bed the rest of the day, but I was able to move a table in front of the door. Mellie don't like to push things aside, and that seemed to do the trick."

Mellie got up, skipped to the kitchen, and came back with a beer. She reached over to give it to Mr. Giles, then snatched it back, sat down, and started drinking it. When their white cat jumped on the bed, she put some beer in the palm of her hand and said, "Here kitty, kitty. Have your cream."

My mother and I waited for Mr. Giles to speak. He wheezed again.

"Mary Beth, I can't leave Mellie."

"She can go into Morningside Heights for elderly care. I already called Sylvio Martinez, and I have it arranged—"

"No. She would be scared. She wouldn't like it."

"Mr. Giles, you have got to start thinking here, for Mellie's sake." My mother tapped those cowgirl boots again, with force. "I'm getting irritated."

"Mellie!" Mellie said, as if she was cheering. She threw the beer in the air. "Gooo, Mellie!"

"Denial is never an effective choice for wise living, so quit doing it," my mother said. "If you don't get better, she's going to Morningside Heights forever. Do you not understand that? You die, and you will if you don't go to the hospital, you will lie in that bed and suffocate, and she's there. Alone."

His face crumbled. "Mellie and I agreed years ago that neither of us would put the other in a home. We didn't let our parents go in homes, either. We took care of all four of them when it was their time, right here, in our guest room, and her mother went batty and used to dress like a princess and carry a wand. I love my Mellie and we are staying together."

"I wish I had a screwdriver, because I'd give you a lobotomy myself." My mother exhaled.

"Once again," I said, "my mother shows her gentle, soft side. Very impressive, Mother."

She glared at me for half a second. "You don't have a choice, Mr. Giles. You. Are. Going."

"I will take care of my woman here. I've got the medicines you gave me."

"I have known you my whole life, you stubborn old coot, and I've tried very hard to be as polite as I can be today, which was hard for me, but we're doing this my way or you're going to die, and instead of calling an ambulance Mellie will put a witch's hat on your head and get the cat drunk."

Mellie giggled. "Drunk cat! Here, kitty, kitty, have your cream." Mellie put more beer in her hand. She held it out to the cat, who backed away, then Mellie lapped it out of her palm with her tongue, like a cat. She meowed, then turned to Mr. Giles, leaned in close, and growled once again. In a sexy way.

"It's my way or the highway." My mother glared at him. "Don't take the highway."

"Mary Beth—" Mr. Giles stopped arguing when Mellie stood

up on the bed and took off her witch's hat, then the silky pink dress, while humming some kind of stripper song. She was wearing a red bra and red underwear. Very pretty. She wriggled her hips, then climbed under the covers with Mr. Giles, rolled on top of him, and kissed him as if we weren't even there. "Want to see my pussy, darling? She wants to meet your cougar. Meow!"

He kissed her back, then pulled away, as Mellie started working her way down his body.

"Okay, Mary Beth." He sighed, resigned, so sick, exhausted. "I'll do it."

"Meow, meow!"

I had eleven dollars.

I was broke.

I hate being broke. When I was younger and broke, traveling the world after college, working in restaurants in different countries, it didn't bother me so much. It was only me. But now I have two kids.

And a legal fight baring down on me like a tiger showing its fangs.

This wasn't working. I was cooking eight hours a day at Larry's, and I was planning menus and recipes at night, but it wasn't enough. I had payments due to my attorney and the hospital. I had already started using my credit card to survive.

I put my head on my granddad's scratched and dented, sixty-five-year-old dining room table and tried not to cry, then I decided to buck up and make a pineapple upside-down cake with the girls, and that's what we did.

I was teaching them about the Martindale family code: When life gets bleak, start baking a cake.

Measure. Mix. Stir. Whip. Bake.

Martindale Cake Therapy always works.

"Grandma, the other day, in the attic, there was a leak through the roof." I put my teacup down on the dining room table in my, *her,* log cabin.

"Did you go out to the shelf in the garage that says Roofing Supplies? You did. Good. Your granddad was so organized. Is it fixed now?"

"Yes. Grandma, I patched things up but afterward I opened a box that had gotten wet." Okay, Grandma. Are you ready for this? I still fought with myself. Was I being selfish because I was curious? Because I wanted to know about her past? Maybe I shouldn't say anything. Was it even my place to say anything? Was it a violation of her privacy? Was it forcing her to talk about things she didn't want to remember or talk about? I didn't want to hurt her. But would she want to, finally, talk about her life? Her life before England? Her family? Her cookbook?

"I took the things out so I could dry them." My voice wavered, the fire crackled. I took her hand. "Grandma, I found your wedding dress. Your elegant, lacy wedding dress and veil. I found the butterfly clips, the blue dress and the hat with the white ribbon, the nurse's uniform, the tin box with the charm bracelets. The menorah. And I found this." I turned to a shelf and brought the cookbook to her with the cracked leather cover, the pages that had been singed by fire around the edges, the stained pink ribbon tying it together. I had dried it out, sometimes using a hair dryer on it, at a low speed.

My grandma paled, becoming whiter and whiter.

"Oh, Grandma," I cried. I am an awful, awful person! I am so awful! "I am so sorry. I kept arguing with myself, wondering if I should even show it to you—"

She held out shaky hands, and I gave the cookbook to her. She held it gently, and two tears slipped out of her eyes and down her cheeks and soaked into the battered leather cover.

"Grandma," I said so gently, begging. "I didn't mean to hurt you. I am brainless. I am thoughtless. I am an idiot."

"You didn't hurt me, darling Cinnamon." Her voice wavered. "They did. They hurt me, not you, never you, sweet girl." She drew a finger down the cracked leather, over the pink ribbon. "So, you are here again," she whispered to the cookbook. "We have found one another."

"I hope you don't mind, Grandma. I looked at the recipes, the pictures. I found flakes of a rose, a sun charm, two gold lockets, red ribbons, a white feather, poems..."

She nodded and dabbed her eyes with a napkin. "You see, Cinnamon, my mother, my grandma, my great-grandma, we all loved to cook." Her head wobbled, her white hair swaying, as if what happened had affected the strength of her neck. "Our favorite recipes have been written in this book."

"It must be very old."

"Yes. It's very old. Much older than me. You see, we had to save this, save our history, when we escaped, and this is what my mother chose for us to save. It's what she hurriedly gave to me before..." She stopped, her mouth tightened, twitched. She closed her eyes, and I knew she wouldn't finish what she started to say. "But this is more than a cookbook. This is my family line, it's your family line. It's us. You saw the drawings." I nodded. "We've been through terrible times, and so many didn't survive. But I did. I should not have. I was less deserving than all of them. The guilt has followed me my whole life. Why me? Why did I live and not them? It shouldn't have been me."

Who was she talking about? What happened?

She opened the cookbook and touched the drawings of a smiling family on a bench, in front of a fireplace, in what must have been the late 1890s or early 1900s, judging by the long skirts of the girl and the mother, the shawls and kerchiefs, and the boots and suspenders of the boys and the father. There were two smiling boys; one girl, who looked to be the oldest; and a baby boy. They were all holding a bowl in one hand and a slice of bread in the other.

She turned to the pictures of the small stone and wood home with geraniums in front, a village with cobblestone streets, a handsome man working on a saddle, the inside of a home with flowers hanging from the rafters, shelves holding pans and baskets.

One of the pictures was of tall fir trees, the sun peeking through the branches, a meadow with flowers, and two deer. Peaceful. But somehow it seemed lonely to me. Sad. Dark.

"I couldn't bear to use this cookbook, Olivia." Her voice cracked. "I couldn't handle that pain, that loss. All of them gone." She wiped tears from her cheeks.

All of them gone. How many had she lost? How many had died? How had they died? Where? I had not forgotten the menorah.

"If I cooked their recipes, I would be cooking without them. I would have to remember what happened, what they went through, and I..." She cried harder, and I got up and put my arms around her. Why did I do this? I had made my grandma cry. What kind of woman does that to her grandma?

"It still hurts. Decades later. I never expected it to stop hurting, though." She turned the pages as I let go and wiped the tears from my cheeks. She touched the recipes, in different languages, written in different hands, with her fingers. "But maybe..." She took a deep breath. "Maybe it's time. I'm an old woman. I will join them soon. I feel them, sometimes, around me, in the gazebo."

"Please don't say that you'll join your family soon, Grandma. I love you so much." *I will miss you when you're not here.*

"I love you, too, Cinnamon, but it's always best to be realistic, dear." She took a long, long breath, then exhaled, as if she was releasing some of that pain. "Maybe it's time I cooked their recipes, and showed you and your sister how to make our family's recipes. Maybe it's time I show Kyle and Stephi and Lucy their heritage. Who their ancestors were and how they baked."

"I would love that. We would love that."

"You would?"

"Yes. Definitely yes."

She nodded. "Then let's do it." She brushed away her tears and turned the pages of the cookbook. When the recipe was in Yiddish, she said a few words in Yiddish, reading from the page. Then Ukrainian, German, and English—but English with a British accent. More tears poured out onto the recipes in the book, from both of us. Finally she said something in Yiddish again.

"What did you say, Grandma?"

"I said, 'Beloved family, you are here again.'" She brought

the cookbook to her lips and kissed it. "We saved this cookbook from hate. From Sarrah Tolstonog to Ida Zaslavsky to my mother, Esther Gobenko, to me. The love of our family. From Odessa in the Russian Empire to Germany to England to Montana. We saved it time and time again."

October 1905
Odessa, the Russian Empire
Ida Zaslavsky, great-great-grandmother of Olivia Martindale

Outside Ida Zaslavsky's small home, on the far edges of the city of Odessa, in what felt like a village, all was black and quiet. Too quiet. It didn't feel right to Ida. Something was off, something was wrong. She opened the leather-bound cookbook her mother, Sarrah, had given her, hoping it would calm her nerves.

Ida adjusted her skirt, beige and hanging to her ankles, and took off her blue kerchief. Her long, thick brown hair tumbled down. Boris loved her hair. He was a good man. Perhaps too much good in the bedroom now and then. He told her that her green eyes slanted like a cat's. He joked that it was helpful that he liked cats.

She was pregnant again. Three months, maybe four. It was a girl, she knew it. They would name her Talia. Talia would join her sweet siblings, Esther, Moishe, Zino, and baby Liev.

She had written down recipes from Sarrah, and from her grandmother, Tsilia Bezkrovny, and tonight she would write down a recipe for beet borsch, but first she drew a picture of their children, all sitting in front of the fireplace, including herself and Boris, on the bench Boris made, laughing and holding wooden bowls of borsch and a chunk of bread.

Ida wrote the recipe on the right side. When she was finished, she put the cookbook on the windowsill, then picked up her knitting. She would darn Boris's socks. The man worked so hard he was always getting holes in his socks. Her hands shook, and she took a deep breath in the silence.

Odessa felt dangerous now. It was a modern city. People from all over the world lived there. The French, Greeks, Italians, Russians, and many Jews. It seemed as though every language on Earth was spoken. The port was thriving. Businesses were growing. But more people moved into their city on the Black Sea every year, straining employment and jobs, creating competition and strife for work.

Odessa was on edge. It was a frightening, tense time. The hatred against Jews was rising. There were shootings at the docks, strikes, chaos, demonstrations, and barricades. There were military patrols, and many schools and shops were closed. Police were attacked, and they attacked others, including shooting student demonstrators. Jews were insisting that they be treated as equals in all areas of life, and the clashes were fierce, deadly. There were rumors of revolution, a conspiracy, an upcoming attack.

Ida heard horses neighing but thought nothing of it. She didn't think anything of a crackling sound, either. Perhaps it was a neighbor starting a fire. But it made her nervous, those sounds, all the same.

It was when she smelled smoke, and heard the screams, that she flew from the table and ran to her window, her hand leaning on her cookbook. Men. Men in military and police uniforms with guns who did not belong here and men in regular street clothes. Men with torches, setting her neighbors' homes on fire, their roofs soon in flames. She heard them yelling, "Die Jews! Die Dogs!"

She saw the Feldmans running from their home, her friend Raisa screaming as she carried her youngest son, Pyotr. Ida stared in shock as her friend was shot and then tumbled to the ground. Pyotr crawled to his mother and he was shot, too. Ida thought she might faint.

"What is it?" Boris ran toward her, grabbed her. The second he reached her, she heard a whoosh and a boom as their bedroom went up in flames, straw and wood flying, black smoke filling the room.

Their three oldest children, curled up in bed by the fireplace, woke up and started crying when they saw the circling black smoke, the leaping flames.

"Get out!" Boris yelled at them, running toward the bedroom, to the baby Liev, in a crib. "Get out, now!"

Ida grabbed Esther, Moishe, and Zino and shoved them out the door as sparks flew, flames climbed up the walls, and the roof started to smolder.

"Run for the woods," she yelled at them. "Stay together. Hide. We will come for you. Go Esther, take your brothers. Go!"

They were hysterical, crying, but Ida did what she had to do. The flames were spreading, a hot roar, singing her hair and filling her lungs with heat and smoke. She shoved them, hard, out the door before they burned to death. "Now, now!" They turned and ran.

"Get the baby!" Ida screeched to Boris. "Get Liev!" But she had already seen the blazing fire that had engulfed their bedroom. Boris had already tried to get Liev, but it was too late, too late, too late. Ida thought she heard the baby scream and on instinct she stumbled for him through the smoke, prepared to run through that wall of fire. Boris caught her and she struggled against him, her lungs burning. "Let me go! We have to get Liev, let me go!"

"Ida, no, no." Boris held on to his fighting, clawing wife, using all of his strength. "He's gone. We can't save him."

Ida was sure she could hear the baby crying as the roof over the bedroom made a whooshing sound and collapsed, wood chips flying. Boris forcibly hauled her out the door and into the chaotic night, her hands scratching, feet kicking. When she continued to fight him, hysterical, he threw her over his shoulder and ran. Ida looked back in horror as the rest of the roof of their home caved in, the fire leaping toward the sky, their neighbors' homes suffering the same fate. She saw panicked horses bucking, children screeching for their mothers, and men going from home to home, torches in hand, burning them to the ground. Gunshots tore through the night.

The black smoke, churning from a crime against humanity,

hid Ida and Boris as he stumbled toward the woods. He dropped her from his shoulder behind a tree. "Liev," she cried out, straining against Boris. "Oh, Liev. My son. Liev!" But she knew the truth: Liev was gone, gone in an oven made by evil men. Boris yanked at her, and they ran through the shifting shadows of the trees, panting, terrified they would not be able to find their other children, devastated beyond belief.

They found Esther, Moishe, and Zino an hour later, hidden inside a log, crying. The five of them did not go home for two days, foraging in the woods for food, making sure the invaders were gone. Ida didn't speak, staring straight ahead. All she could do was hold her children and rock back and forth. They had lost a baby. They had lost Liev. Their lives were ruined.

When they finally returned to their home, smoke still rising from the rubble of their neighborhood, most of the other families were gone or dead. They heard from a wandering man, shell-shocked, who had hidden under his home in the muck that there were attacks in the city, too. Jews in Odessa were mercilessly beaten and killed, thrown out windows, women raped, even children and babies murdered. Homes and businesses were robbed.

Even their water tanks, where they collected rainwater, their water supply too mineralized coming from wells so close to the ocean, had been destroyed. Ida and Boris could find few things that had survived the fire in their home. They had never had much, eking out a living, poverty at their door every day, but now . . . nothing. Ida couldn't even find the crib where her baby had been sleeping, but she did find fragments of bones, which she held in trembling hands, her body racked with a pain she knew would never leave her.

When Ida moved again, it was only because she saw her cookbook, the pink ribbon a beacon amidst the blackened destruction. She crawled toward it through the soot. Unbelievably, miraculously, it had survived. Perhaps it had been blown through the window when the house caught fire. The pages, along the edges, were singed, black and brown. The leather was dirty, the pink ribbon stained, but it was still there. Ida fell to her knees, clutching it to her chest, rocking back and forth, her tears soaking into the leather. The Shabbat candlesticks, however, were nowhere to be found. They were gone, too. Gone like Liev.

Boris knelt with her, crying, too, along with their children. Then he said they had to leave immediately. Who knew when the invaders would be back to kill more Jews, to rape, to pillage and destroy. They buried the bones in the forest. She and Boris made a tear in their clothes, they prayed, Boris recited from Psalms. But they could not stay and mourn for seven days. They would be dead if the attackers came again.

Boris blamed himself. They should have left earlier. He had seen the signs. But his business was here. He had six mouths to feed. He would live with the guilt of his mistake forever.

Boris managed to find some of his tools for making saddles and bridles, and he slung them into a sac over his shoulder. On their way out Ida saw something shiny. It was their silver menorah, made for them by her grandfather, Aron Bezkrovny, as a wedding gift. She cried over that, too, her tears spilling from the menorah to her cookbook.

The family walked for miles and miles, holding each other, hiding in the woods when they could, a barn one night when they thought they might freeze, in the back of a home of a rabbi who took pity on them. Two months later, on a pitch black night, Ida gave birth on the side of a dirt road. It was way too early. The baby, a girl, who they would have named Talia, was dead. Ida was too shattered to cry.

The next day they buried her in the forest, as they had buried her brother's bones, and then they moved on. They had to. It was move on or be caught back up in another pogrom. That night Ida drew a picture of the burial grounds of her daughter in the cookbook, the sun shining through the fir trees. She added a meadow, with flowers, and two deer, off in the distance. One deer for Liev, one for the baby, Talia. Her grief was crushing her.

By train, now and then, but mostly on foot, sometimes by hiding in the back of a wagon, covered in hay, by begging, by starvation, by literally running for their lives, they headed to Germany. They had heard that life was easier there for Jews. It took them fourteen months to get to Munich, as they had to stop and let Boris work sometimes so they would have money for food and shoes, and time to rest.

They never returned to Odessa, but Ida and Boris never forgot the beloved children they left behind.

School was not getting better for the girls. When we arrived each morning in the parking lot I dried tears and told them they were brave and courageous Montana women. I watched them walk into school, gripping each other's hand like they were holding a lifeline.

Lucy got in a fight with a boy who said she resembled an ant with that "huge head." The huge-headed ant stomped on his right foot, then his left, and said, which I thought was quite clever, her finger pointed up to the sky, "Now you know what it feels like to get stepped on like an ant, you stupid boy."

Stephi was sent to the principal's office for letting the frogs out of the fish tank saying they needed to "be free." She was not popular with that move, as the class loved Herbert and Crazy Ellen. Two girls and one boy cried when they realized that Herbert and Crazy Ellen were gone for good. She was called Frog Freak, and someone told her she should go to frog jail with her "weird rock collection." She was still crying at bedtime. "I didn't like seeing Herbert and Crazy Ellen trapped!"

They were grieving, too, these poor girls. They missed their grandmother. They missed their school and friends in Portland.

And I'd moved them. New home, new family, new school, and, as Lucy cried one day, "No friends," and Stephi said, "No one likes me or my rocks."

I watched them walk in the front door of the school, my heart clogging my whole throat, then I raced to Larry's Diner.

That night I heard a cough and I looked out my window. My grandma was in the doorway of the gazebo, wrapped in her coat and her blue scarf with white magnolia flowers on it, her head tilted back toward the shimmering stars. She smiled, then lifted a hand up and waved toward the sky.

The next week at work I handed out samples whenever I had a free minute. Small cups of blueberry cinnamon muffins, banana bread, scrambled eggs with cheese and sautéed mushrooms. I even handed out orange smoothies with a hint of vanilla, ice, and ice cream. That was popular.

Kalulell is a small town, and it wasn't long before word got out the food wasn't slop-crap anymore, and we had a lot more customers. We needed more employees.

"You need to hire more people, Larry."

"Hell no. I'm not a money machine. I got Dinah and Justin out front. They can do it."

"They can't. The customers are waiting too long. Earl and I are cooking as fast as we can, and you're not cooking half as fast as either of us."

His mouth dropped. I swear his gut had grown since I came to work there. He heaved himself up. "This is my restaurant and ya ain't gonna talk to me like that, Chef Feisty, though I like 'em feisty. Ha-ha."

Some things I had to ignore or I'd clonk him. "I need to be honest with you, as the chef here, about how things are going, Larry."

"I'll tell you when we're hiring people, Olivia. You get your pretty self back in the kitchen where a woman belongs."

I thought I would lose it. I did. Every day Larry was worse. If I wasn't broke I wouldn't have stayed. I had gone from Carter to Larry. I had worked for so many chefs—men and women—who might have been temperamental and overly picky about what was produced in their kitchens, but they were kind people at heart, at least when nothing was burning on the stoves. But I'd had two strikeouts in a row.

I didn't like the way Larry yelled at Justin and Earl. "Move your butt . . . Justin, you take a shower this week? You smell like monkey breath. . . . Earl, your momma must have been surprised when she had you. I bet she felt those elephant ears when you were coming out of her privates . . . Your momma's still single, right? I think I'll pay her another visit." Earl turned red and balled his fists.

"What the heck kind of comment is that, Larry?" I'd said, slamming a pan down.

"My momma doesn't want you to pay her a visit," Earl said, voice so low.

"Oh, I bet she does. She's a fine woman."

"She doesn't want you to come over. She told me if you ever came over again, she'd call the police."

"No, she wouldn't," Larry drawled, but his face flushed. He was embarrassed. "Her son will be out of a job if she does that."

"That's illegal," I said, slamming the pan down again so I didn't slam Larry's face. "That's a threat. You take that back, you oversized baboon. No woman wants you to come and visit. You apologize to Earl."

Earl stood right in front of Larry. He was ready to hit him.

Larry smirked. He's a tall, hulking, blubbery man. Fat, arms like beefsteaks. Earl is tall and thin, a kid. But no one insults someone's momma in Montana and gets away with it.

"Whaddya got, kid?" Larry said, his voice low, provocative. "I can't say your momma is hot?"

"No." Earl said. "You can't. You are disrespecting her, and me." He punched Larry so hard and so fast in the chin Larry flipped up in the air and landed on his back, where he lay like a stuck pig, groaning.

Earl stormed out after calling Larry a name he deserved to be called.

Larry couldn't get up. Blood gushed from his nose. None of us helped him. I leaned over Larry and told him, "You are obnoxious. You get your fat butt up and go home. Tomorrow you call Earl. Do not go to his home, or I will inform his mother, Carly Mae, whom I have known since second grade, to shoot you. You will give Earl a raise."

"I'm not givin' him a raise," he sputtered, blood spurting. "I'm calling the police and he's going to the slammer."

"No, you won't," I said. "Because what I saw was you shoving Earl, hard, right here in this kitchen, against the wall, after you insulted his mother. Then you raised your fist and swung at Earl and Earl ducked."

"That's what I saw," Dinah said. She flicked her hair back. She had dyed the ends lime green. "You attacked Earl."

"I saw it, clear as day," Justin said, crossing his arms. "It was self-defense. Earl should call the police on you. In fact, I think I will. That was assault."

Larry kept panting. He was cornered. His nose was broken. He swore.

"You will give Earl a raise. I need him here. Did you hear me, Larry?"

He grunted. He tried to get up, lay back down. We didn't help him.

"Get out. You're getting blood in my kitchen. And do not go to my mother to fix you up. I am calling her right now and telling her to refuse."

He glowered at me. "You're not always goin' to win, Olivia."

"I don't want to win. I want you to treat people with respect and stop trying to club them into the ground with your boot because for some inane reason you think you can smash people."

He lumbered out, cloth to his smashed face.

We cooked.

Earl came back the next day. He got a raise. He hugged me. "My mother says hello."

Larry didn't say anything about Earl's mother again.

I hired six more people, some part time. Two single mothers, four college students. We were humming right along.

On Tuesday, Chloe ended up on the front page of the state's newspaper. A car had flipped completely over, the engine was burning, and she'd hauled out two kids, one under each arm. I saw a video of it made by a bystander. She was a hero but she was pissed because the driver, the kids' father, was drunk. Her comment, "Dumb (expletive) people who drive drunk with kids in the car should go to jail. That's it. Lock that (expletive) up. He could have killed those two kids."

There was unilateral agreement.

Chloe is popular in Kalulell. She tells it like it is.

On Sunday night Stephi got the flu. I was up all night with her and drove Lucy to school. I brought Stephi with us because I didn't want her alone at home. Lucy did not want to go to school without Stephi, so she cried. Stephi threw up in the truck on the way home. I got Stephi to the bathroom, washed her up, got her on the couch, and went to clean up my light blue truck. It was snowing.

The school called. Lucy threw up in her classroom. I packed Stephi back up and we went to get Lucy. I brought the girls home. They both threw up.

It was going to be a long day. I made them chicken soup. We read stories and played Candy Land and Chutes and Ladders. I hate Chutes and Ladders. It's enough to make a mother lose her mind. As soon as you think the game is finally over, no, you're zapped back to the beginning.

We all took a nap in the afternoon. When they woke up they wanted to talk about their grandma, Annabelle, and how she used to make them brownies when they were sick. I made them brownies.

I was up most of the night with Lucy hanging out by the toilet.

No one can prepare you for parenthood.

I met Annabelle, Stephi and Lucy's maternal grandmother, when I moved into an apartment building in Portland after leaving Montana in my truck, my mind a shattered mass of pain.

It was a pre-war building, all brick, the awnings green. It needed updating. It needed new floors, new lighting, a new entry. It had an old-world, traditional charm, though. It had a cool Portland vibe. It was clean.

There was one apartment available, top floor, fourth floor, corner, and I jumped at it. I unloaded my truck and moved in.

The apartment building, with sixteen apartments, had a mix of people. Some seemed pretty affluent, a couple of attorneys, two doctors starting out, a few businesspeople. But the building also had "affordable housing," which meant there were some people there who were struggling. We were all colors, all faiths and no faiths, with one family newly arrived from Ethiopia and one from Iran.

Being in Portland, but not in the busy part of downtown, made it a peaceful, but interesting, place to live. I knew the area because of the years I had spent in culinary school there.

The apartment building was up on a slight hill, one block off a street filled with restaurants and shops. I could catch the streetcar, the light rail, and go anywhere.

Not that I wanted to go anywhere.

What I *wanted* to do was to crawl into bed and not come out for several years. Maybe I'd get a pile of cats and stay inside all day forever.

My apartment was a one bedroom. It was flooded with light and had a view over the top of the city to the river. Through French doors, a small balcony fit two chairs.

The kitchen cabinets were light gray and new. I heard that the previous renter was mad at the landlord because he wouldn't allow him to keep his three dogs there, barking all day, so he'd ripped the cabinets down when he was evicted. The laminate counters were a darker gray but new, too, with a white subway tile backsplash. The renter had taken an ax to the old ones.

The wood floors were scuffed up, but original, as was the wide, white trim and baseboards. The beige walls would do. I didn't have the energy to paint them.

I had a small breakfast nook with an old-fashioned arc separating it from the kitchen, and a family room with another arc. My bedroom, in the corner, had two large windows and a window seat.

The first week I arrived I slept a lot, in my sleeping bag, on the floor of the family room. When I was not sleeping, I was lying in that sleeping bag like it was my coffin, staring. I stared out at the sunshine, out at the rain, and at the hail. Sometimes I slept on my balcony.

I heard people outside my door, specifically two little girls. It hurt to hear their sweet kid voices, and I pulled the pillow over my face.

When I could finally get out of my sleeping bag/coffin for more than three hours at a time, two months later, and I was near broke, I went to work for Carter. I was screamed at like everyone else, and I screamed at him sometimes, which he seemed to respect because he was half devil. I was on edge, my nerves shot.

On my days off I drove to the beach and walked for hours. I drove into the mountains and walked around and around a sparkling lake with a view of Mt. Hood for hours, too. I hiked in a nearby forest. Now and then, I started to see a tiny, flickering light. I clung to that light as hard as I could so the darkness wouldn't drown me.

Two months after that, sick of sleeping on the floor and leaning against a wall to eat breakfast, I went to a funky used furniture store and sat on a couch. The couch was in the shop window overlooking a busy Portland street. I sat in it for so long I decided to buy it. I couldn't remember what color it was. I was glad when it arrived that it was blue and in an L shape. It was actually much bigger than I remembered. I bought four wood chairs and a wood circular table at an antique shop in the country. I bought a comfy red chair at a garage sale for a corner of the room and an ottoman with red flowers from Goodwill.

I knew pretty pillows would help the couch. I stood in the pillow aisle of a big-box store and cried. I could not decide which pillows to get, which upset me. I started grabbing a mismatch of them and headed out. I bought a bed. I lay on a whole bunch of mattresses in one shop and started to cry because the last bed I had was bouncy but firm, a perfect bed with a warm man in it, and I was not in that bed anymore and I'd left the man.

The saleswoman was sympathetic enough to lie down on the bed with me and hold my hand while I cried. "Bad time, huh, honey?"

I nodded.

"I'm sorry," she said. "I hate men."

It wasn't the man that was the problem, but I didn't say that.

I found a huge, old traveling chest at a secondhand store and used that as a coffee table. I found two bookshelves at a garage sale and painted them white. I found an old church pew and put it in my bedroom. I bought an assortment of dishes, many of them china, from Goodwill, and I bought pans, and pictures for the walls from a variety of places and called it good.

Good, as in good enough for now.

Then I became friends with Annabelle Lacey and two miserable, frightened, reeling children.

Chapter 5

On Saturday my mother and grandma volunteered to take the girls skiing. My mother thought the ski lift would be an "appropriate educational setting" to talk to the girls about what the life of an orthopedic surgeon would be like, and how exciting it would be to put bones back together with screws and plates. "They need to understand the choices available to them in the medical world. My next talk will be about the benefits of being a heart surgeon."

I rushed on over to Goodwill to buy them the ski stuff they needed and, thankfully, found ski pants in about their size. Lucy's was a bit too big, Stephi's a bit too small, but whatever. I also found them ski gloves, thick socks, and helmets that looked brand-new. I zipped them into their jackets, made sure they had their hats, and off they went, thrilled.

"We've got to be comfortable with speed," Lucy said, finger pointed in the air.

"I'm bringing my rocks. We're going to ski fast," Stephi said.

My grandma and mother would take them for pizza afterward.

I cleaned the house, then took a shower and finally washed my hair. I needed color, so I pulled on red jeans and my red cowgirl boots, a purple sweater, and a flowered scarf in red, purple, and yellow, shot through with gold thread that I bought in Italy. I added dangly silver frog earrings from Laos, then grabbed my red coat.

I drove to the grocery store so that we would not all starve. The snow was coming down, but light and fluffy. I headed down the aisles, with my coupons, comparing prices. My account was anemic. I would get paid on Monday, but much of it had to go to my attorney and my monthly "bleeding ulcer" payment to the hospital. Minimum wage plus five dollars an hour does not go far at all.

I counted up the costs of the groceries in my head, minus the coupons. I had just enough to cover it. I'd probably have about ten dollars left. We would have the staples: spaghetti, tacos, burritos, lasagna, and crock pot chicken dinners. Luckily, I knew how to make bland, cheap food taste a lot better, and sometimes I was able to bring home leftovers from Larry's.

The cash register lady was sullen. When she saw my stack of coupons she cracked her gum, rolled her eyes, and glared at me as if I were algae scum. "All these coupons yours?"

"No. They belong to a green space alien. He dropped them into my hands then skedaddled back up to his spaceship."

For a second, I thought that gum-cracking idiot believed me. She grunted. "Whatever."

She rang up my groceries, moving like an annoyed anteater, and started in on the coupons, running them over the scanner. She sighed again. She made impatient noises. She said, "Hope these things don't take too long."

There was no one in line, so I said, "With the mob behind me I hope not, too." That's when Jace turned the corner with a small hand basket and got in line behind me. He was in a dark blue sweater and beige jacket. Jeans. Cowboy boots. Black hair had a few snowflakes in it. Gall. It was like looking at a seductive cowboy gangster.

The cashier actually stopped gnawing on her gum to ogle him. "Hey, Jace. Hi, Jace. Do you remember me? I'm Bailey. Like the drink."

"Hello, Bailey."

After more ogling she studied the coupons in her hands and grunted again. Lovely. I had a mean cashier making impatient grunts with my desperately needed coupons and Jace the seductive cowboy gangster behind me.

Jace would be shocked to know I was this broke.

I hate being broke, I do, but it is what it is and I'm trying.

"Hello, Olivia."

"Hi, Jace." I felt my face redden as the cracking gum girl slowly scanned each coupon as if every coupon was taking a day off of her miserable life.

"How are you?"

"Fine." I looked at his hand basket. He was buying sandwiches, fruit, salad stuff. I used to make him the best sandwiches. He loved my steak sandwiches with blue cheese. Loved my chicken tomato sandwiches with finely cut onions and my special sauce with vinaigrette. "Looks like lunch."

Cracking Gum Idiot bit out, "This one doesn't work, wrong store . . . you bought the wrong size on this can of corn . . ."

"Okay," I said to her. I wanted to drop through the floor, via an earthquake crack and disappear.

"This coupon is expired," she said it as if I were trying to rob the store. "You have to buy two of these to get a dollar off and you *didn't* . . . This cereal box is twenty-six ounces and the coupon is for the *fifteen*-ounce size . . ."

"That's fine," I told her. "A crime was committed and I accept responsibility."

She cracked her gum yet again and smirked. "Looks like your space alien didn't collect the right coupons."

"Looks like you have enough gum in your cheeks to turn you into a chipmunk."

"Very funny." She looked at Jace and rolled her eyes. Then ogled/grinned at him.

He glared back. She stopped grinning.

When she was finally done, breathing heavily from coupon-caused exertion, I ran my debit card and . . . the card was rejected.

"Rejected!" Cracking Gum Idiot said, smiling with victory. "Insufficient funds!"

Shoot. I pulled out my wallet. I had eight dollars.

"If you don't have enough money you need to put something back." She raised her eyebrows and tightened her squirrely mouth as in, "Gotcha now!"

Humiliating. I didn't have enough money for groceries. Wanting to disappear, as Jace was a witness to my personal economic collapse, I started pushing the bread back, and the pasta . . .

"She has enough money," Jace said. He ran his card through.

"Please, don't," I automatically protested.

"I got it, Olivia, no problem." Jace winked at me. He has dark, gentle eyes.

My face was on fire. Flames of shame were probably leaping from my ears. "Thank you."

"Do you want your coupons back?" the cashier asked. She was disappointed Jace had come to my rescue. He had ruined her fun! She liked making fun of poor people! "The ones that didn't work? Took me a lot of time to run them. You need to check them more carefully next time so there's no holdup in the line."

"No, thank you. You can eat them. Or chew on them. Like your gum." I grabbed the receipt. "Thanks, Jace."

"You're welcome." I saw him shoot the cashier a withering stare that said, "*That's enough.*"

The problem with trying to make a hasty exit after a mortifying moment is that you never can. It's like the universe conspires against you. I was trying to steer the cart and get out of there quick, but I rushed and the creaky wheel in front turned and hit a stack of cans. The whole can pyramid tumbled down with a crash. I said a bad word, chased after the rolling ones, and started stacking them, along with Jace, my total embarrassment complete. A manager rushed over and helped. The gum cracker snickered and snorted.

When we were done, I thanked them both, again, truly wanting to cry, and headed out. I saw Jace turn and hand the gum cracker cash for his food, then he followed me out. This time, in my scramble to escape, I stumbled on the mat by the door and had to lean heavily on the handle of the cart to catch me so I didn't face plant. I whispered another bad word.

Jace moved quick and steadied me. "You okay?"

"I'm fine." I struggled back up to my feet and searched for my truck so I could dive in it and hide forever. I was so rattled I couldn't remember where I parked. Ah. There it was. Jace's huge black truck was near my blue one. "I'll pay you back, Jace." I didn't even try to tell him that there was a problem with my account, or that the bank must have messed up, because I don't like to lie and he wouldn't believe me anyhow. I was flat dead broke.

"I will not take a dime."

"You have to." I felt my throat tighten up, loss stuck in there like a pinecone, because Jace and I were not going out to the parking lot together, to one truck, we were going to separate trucks. "If you don't, I'll feel like I'm taking charity and you know I'd rather shoot myself in the foot with my granddad's rifle than take charity."

"Please don't shoot yourself in the foot. You have nice feet. And you're not taking charity. It's money you already earned from being a half owner of Martindale Ranch, which you have refused to take for over two years."

"I am not a half owner."

"You are a half owner. Your money is in a separate account. I will send you yet another check, and I hope this time you will cash it."

After I left him Jace started to send me checks each month for my half of the profits on Martindale Ranch. I wouldn't cash them. I couldn't. It was Jace's land, his family's ranch, and his money that launched the business.

I hadn't put any money into the ranch, only my work. Like an employee. I returned the checks and they finally stopped coming, even though he called, and e-mailed, and told me to take the checks.

I started to unpack my groceries into the truck. He said, "Let me do this," and I said, "I can," and we did it together. "Thanks, Jace."

I turned and hauled myself and my deep embarrassment into my old light blue truck. I turned the key. Nothing. Turned it again. Nothing.

It wouldn't start.

Naturally.

I leaned my poor head against the seat and tried to avoid Jace's sympathetic gaze. When I did turn toward him he was already on the phone calling Alphonse D'Ellieni for a tow truck.

This was Jace in action. He solved problems. He provided and protected. He was loyal and faithful.

And I'd left him.

"Thanks for the ride home, Jace."

"My pleasure."

We were at my log cabin, we'd unloaded the groceries, and I'd made Jace lunch to thank him for paying for my groceries, having my car towed, and then driving me home. He loved my turkey avocado tomato sandwiches, and I made one for him. I also made him a salad with chopped walnuts and cranberries and blue cheese.

"Ah, Olivia. You're making me The Gobble Turkey Tomato sandwich?"

"I am." My words came out tight so they wouldn't wobble over The Gobble Turkey Tomato sandwich.

I could tell that Jace, grinning and sitting on one of the stools in front of the butcher block kitchen island, was thrilled and grateful. "Thank you."

"And I'm making you peanut butter chocolate chip cookies."

"This is the best day I've had in a long, long time, Olivia. In fact, for over two years." He was a low-voiced cowboy stud. "Thank you."

I felt all warm and . . . hot. There was something about that cowboy praising my food that made me want to take off my clothes. Jace and food blended together equaled an aphrodisiac.

"I've always liked it here." He glanced around my grandparents' log cabin, taking in all the windows, the three-hundred-sixty-degree views, the colorful quilts, the fire he had started for me. "Homey. Cheerful. Happy."

"Thank you. I think a lot of it is the windows. With the mountains and the river you feel like you're standing in a post-card, but you have a roof over your head." I'd draped some quilts over both couches, thrown a red knotty blanket over the handle of a chair, tossed around the colorful assortment of pil-lows I'd had in Portland, and added some of my pictures and the girls' framed art. In the kitchen I had put out my red mixing bowls, my small kitchen appliances, and a red teapot.

"One of the finest views in Montana," he said.

"And yours is the other finest," I said.

"Come and see it." He smiled. I froze. "I'll have Max and Joe bring you my gray SUV today. You can use it until your truck is fixed."

"Oh, no. But thank you." I couldn't take anything from him. "My mother has her old truck. I'll drive that."

"I'd like you to drive mine. I know the truck you're talking about, and it's pretty old."

"Jace, that's nice, but no."

We sat in the silence. I could tell that he wasn't happy because I'd hurt him by rejecting his offer of assistance. Jace was old-fashioned in some ways. I knew it when we were dating, knew it when we were married. He wanted to provide and protect. It was instinct. Pure instinct. His father and grandfather were like that, too. I was not allowing him to do that, which made him unhappy. He stared out the window. The snow had slowed con-siderably, as if it was tired of snowing that hard.

"So, what's going on, Olivia? Why didn't you have enough money for the groceries?"

I went and sat by him on a stool while we ate the sandwiches and salad. "I'm broke."

His head snapped back as if I'd slugged him one. "But you had a job in Portland, I thought, as a chef?"

"I did. I was fired when I threw a chicken at my boss."

"You threw a chicken at him?"

"Yes, but the chicken was dead."

"That says something." He laughed.

"I also lobbed a few eggs. There may have been a potato. I clearly lost my mind yet again."

"I bet he deserved to get hit with a chicken."

"Carter's got a temper, he says terrible things to people, and he let loose on a few younger chefs one time too many. Chefs will yell, it's a given. You have to put up with some of it, but it was relentless." I thought about the other expensive problem. "I am the temporary guardian of Lucy and Stephi, but I've had to hire an attorney. I'm trying to adopt them and I ran into problems with their biological mother, who is currently . . ." How should I say it?

"Currently . . ." he prodded.

"She's in jail. She wants them back when she's out. Her parental rights have not been terminated. There are a few other complications." I paused, I didn't even want to think about the complications.

"What about the father?"

"He's in jail, too. They robbed a liquor store together. He's in for a longer amount of time because of prior arrests. They broke in at night when it was closed, no weapon, no assault. They ended up stealing only five hundred dollars. The girls . . ." I took a deep breath. I have to breathe deep whenever I think about what happened to Stephi and Lucy. "The girls were taken from their parents by Children's Services when the police came to arrest their parents. There were cameras in the liquor store, so they were identified from previous arrests. They're drug addicts. Their home was dangerous and chaotic. CSD found a bunch of other drug addicts living there, no food, needles and trash everywhere.

"The girls came to live with Annabelle, their grandma and my friend, about two weeks before I arrived in Portland. Annabelle said they had bruises, flea bites, cigarette burns, and scars on their fingers, face, and bottoms when they arrived at her place. I noticed they were way too skinny, and later Annabelle told me that they were two years behind in weight and height from where they should have been."

"That makes me sick." Jace put his sandwich down and closed his eyes for a minute, his face drawn and tight. That man had a gangster face but a compassionate heart.

"Me too."

"That's a brutal childhood. Addicts for parents. Neglect and abuse. Mother and father in jail, and their grandma dies."

"Yes."

"I'm glad they have you."

"I'm glad I have them. I'm sure it was a surprise to hear that I have children."

"It was. I see your mother and grandma now and then. They didn't say anything. Or your sister."

"Martindale Cowgirl Clan secrets," I joked. But it was true. The Martindales stuck together. "I love them so much and I'm hoping to formally adopt them." If I won custody. If I didn't, which I didn't even want to talk about, I would be crushed to the ground and would not be able to get up and live my life, because I wouldn't be able to breathe.

"Didn't your being married come up with Children's Services, with the state, when they were reviewing your request to adopt?"

"Yes, it did."

"And they didn't ask what your husband thought of it? What I thought of adopting two girls? What I thought of becoming a father to two girls?"

My husband.

My smart husband, my calm and reserved husband, my husband who was warm and snuggly and seductive in bed who I could hardly sleep without. Yes, the husband in front of me.

"Olivia? You all right?"

No. Not at all. I am not all right.

"Olivia?"

I need to buck up. "I've only been able to file a motion to adopt, but I can't adopt because the parents' rights haven't been terminated, they might never be, and they haven't signed over their rights. I was the person closest to the girls, and I wanted to take care of them, so they came to live with me. I had to get written permission from the courts, through my attorney, to come here. But in that process I told Children's Services we were separated and would divorce."

He flinched, then covered it up. "I don't like that word, babe."

I didn't know what to say, so I sat there in that heavy and sad silence.

"Even though their parents are addicts, Olivia, and were living with their young daughters with other addicts, and the girls were malnourished and too skinny and had rat and flea bites, they might go back to living with their mother when she's out of jail?"

"It's ridiculous, I know. But the courts heavily favor the biological parents, almost regardless of circumstance. The father won't get out in time to be a father to the girls—they'll be teenagers when he's released—but the mother will be out. She could get out of jail, go to parenting classes, stay clean, not get into trouble, find a job and a home, and then the girls could go back to her, despite how bad of a mother she was to them in the past.

"When Annabelle wrote her will, she included a letter asking that I be the girls' guardian, even though she had had only temporary legal custody. She knew her request in the will wasn't legally binding—she had custody only when her daughter was in jail—but she wrote it anyhow, to be clear about where she thought the girls should go, in case it was ever needed in court. She couldn't give the girls to me—they weren't legally hers, though she wanted to. There are no other relatives on the mother's or father's side able to take them." I sniffled and wiped my eyes with shaky hands. I am scared to death I will lose those girls to their loser mother.

Jace put a warm hand on the side of my face and brushed my tears away. I closed my eyes and more tears fell out. I thought my heart would shatter at his touch. Crack, break, crumble.

This was the pain and the love I'd run away from, all the way to Portland. This was the pain I could not handle. This was what made me feel like I was losing my mind. I had barely gotten a smidgen of my confidence back in Portland, gotten myself back, and now I could feel myself sliding back into Jace and our impossible, wrenching problem.

If confidence was a bottle of cinnamon, I had one shake of it.

"You are the smartest, most giving, toughest woman I have ever met."

I wanted to turn my face into his palm. I wanted to look up and have his mouth come down on mine. I wanted to be against that chest, warm and snug, and I wanted to hug him all night like I used to.

Instead I pulled away and we were silent in that log cabin my grandparents built, with love, with a red door, as my grandma wanted, and a weather vane with a sun above us because grandma was the sun to my granddad. And here I was, in a broken marriage in their home, but Jace was still my sun. He would always be my sun.

"Come back to work on the ranch, Olivia. Please."

"No."

"I need you there. I'll give you space, I promise." He put his palms up. "You're the best chef in Montana."

"No."

"Why?"

"Because, Jace."

"Because you like working for Larry?"

Jace couldn't stand Larry. "No." I wrung my hands together. "Maybe we should talk about...about..." Could I even say it? It made me feel like splitting in half. "The divorce."

"The divorce?" His expression said he wanted to talk about a divorce about as much as he wanted to talk about leprosy on his cows. "No. I don't want to talk about that at all."

"Okay." Relief. Sweet relief rushed through me. He didn't want to talk about divorce even after what I'd done to him! I smiled at him, couldn't help it. I am a mass of confusing, confounding, crazy contradictions, I know this, I do.

His dark gaze shifted toward the windows. My mother and grandma were dropping the girls off.

My spirits lifted as they always did when I saw my sweet girls. "Do you want to say hello to them?"

"Yes."

"They're noisy," I said.

"I like noise."

"They say odd things sometimes."

"I like odd."

"They are blunt and honest."

"Always the best way to live."

"Now and then they'll talk about their past. It comes from out of the blue. Most of the time it's shocking."

"I had the shock of my life when you left me. I'm sure I can handle this shock, too."

The door flew open and my little tornadoes flew into the cabin. My mother and grandma pointed at Jace's truck, then gave me the thumbs-up and drove to the farmhouse.

"Are you a giant?" Stephi asked Jace while she twirled her parmesan spaghetti around her fork.

"Yes."

Stephi gasped and put her fork down on my granddad's table next to a few rocks from her rock collection. She had already shown Jace her rocks. He liked them. "You are?"

"Yes."

"Wow." Stephi whispered, awed. "I've never met a giant before."

"He's not a real giant," Lucy said, the older sister who knew everything. She narrowed her eyes, unsure. Jace *was* extremely tall. "Are you?"

"I'm a real giant." Jace's hands were clasped in front of him. My! What those hands used to do to me in bed. "My last name is Giant."

"It is?" Lucy and Stephi said at the same time. Not surprisingly, they didn't remember his last name from the night of the blizzard.

He nodded. "I eat all day long to get stronger, but none of the stuff I eat is as delicious as what your aunt Olivia makes me."

"Yep! Aunt Olivia is super-duper at cooking," Lucy said. "She makes the best brownies. Extra chocolate chips in them." She pointed her finger up to make her point. "That's the secret. She tells us the secrets, to me and Stephi, because we keep her cooking secrets and don't tell anyone."

"And another secret is," Stephi said, "when she makes lasagna she makes her own red sauce with tomatoes and a lot of spices and that's why it's extra yummy in my tummy tum tum, and when she makes pancakes she puts in a cup of buttermilk. That's another secret that we don't tell anyone."

I could tell Jace was trying not to laugh as Lucy and Stephi proclaimed themselves to be such super secret keepers.

"And she makes the best banana bread in the world," Stephi said. "She cooks with love. She puts love in our food, that's why it tastes so good." Stephi said this in all seriousness. "It's the love."

"If you cook with love, food tastes better," Lucy said.

"I agree," Jace said. "Your aunt is the best cook in the state of Montana because of the love she puts in her food."

"Yep," Stephi said. "She's delicious!" She put her fork in the air and waved it around, the spaghetti flailing.

"Mr. Giant, can you wrestle a cow?" Lucy asked.

"Yes," Jace said. "If she's agreeable to it."

I tried not to laugh.

"What do you mean?" Lucy asked.

"If the cow wants to wrestle, I'll wrestle it. But first she has to ask."

"How does she ask you?" Stephi asked, eyes wide, leaning across the table toward him.

"She says, 'Mr. Giant, do you want to wrestle?' and I say, 'Yes, I do.' Then we wrestle."

"Who wins?" Stephi asked.

"Usually me. Unless she's an extra-large cow."

The girls stared at him, mouths gaping. Then Lucy giggled. Stephi did, too, finally. "You don't wrestle cows!"

He arched his eyebrows as in, "Maybe I do, maybe I don't."

"Do you?" Stephi said.

"I can catch bat monsters, too."

"What's that?" Stephi and Lucy said at the same time. "What's a bat monster?"

So Jace, right in front of me, created this scary story about how there are bat monsters living in the trees. Bats with green monster faces. It was like a bat monster ghost story. The girls loved it so much, they stopped eating their parmesan spaghetti, hanging on his every word.

"And then—" Jace abruptly raised his hands in the air, quick, like wings taking flight. Both girls startled and semi-screamed. "Those brave girls chased the bat monsters out of the woods forever."

"Wow," Lucy said, panting. "That was scary! Those girls had a lot of bravery in them."

"That was a fright story, that's what I call it," Stephi whispered, clutching her rocks, still with the bat monsters. "It gave me a fright. I think I peed my pants a little bit but that's okay, right Jace?"

"You bet. Sometimes that happens to all of us."

I stood up and went to the kitchen so the girls wouldn't see me cracking up.

And that's how the afternoon went. The four of us. As if we were a family, when I knew we weren't. In fact, I didn't even know if I'd be the girls' mother at this time next year, which would take away the family's children, and the father would go home to his house and eventually we'd have to sign divorce papers and end this misery in which we had an unsolvable problem.

I swallowed all those fearsome, bone-rattling thoughts down, then brought everyone a plate full of peanut butter chocolate chip cookies.

"See?" Lucy slid out of her chair and stood close to Jace, holding the cookie in her hand. "Aunt Olivia cooked this with love. You want a bite?" She held the cookie out toward his mouth.

Jace winked at me.

Seductive cowboy gangster would be an excellent cowboy gangster daddy.

I waved at Jace from the deck when he left, the girls beside me. They scampered back inside and I walked down the drive, then stood staring at the log cabin, the red door, the wagon wheel, the lasso, my grandparents' cowboy hats, and the sun weather vane. They had been through so much, those two, especially my grandma. My grandparents were brave and strong.

I needed some of that bravery, that strength. I needed to find them within myself. At the moment, it felt like my bravery and strength were hiding and cowering behind my kidneys.

I chopped wood on Saturday for our fireplace. I got up on the roof and replaced six more shingles on Sunday afternoon. I saw a bear in the distance and got my shotgun out. It was too early for him to be out. It was still winter, moving toward spring, but still. What in the heck? I would never try to hit or kill a bear, unless it was barreling down at me, but I don't need bears on our property, especially with my girls around. I put two shots pretty close to him and he turned and lumbered off, back into the woods.

Later that night the girls and I watched a Disney movie. I've watched it so many times with them I know all the words to the songs. The girls and I sang together.

It's another form of torture to go to bed and have all the Disney songs rattling around in your head when you try to sleep.

"Grandma Gisela, I have a question for you," Lucy said Tuesday night at a family dinner. My grandma was kneading bread on the kitchen island in the farmhouse. Lucy was on a stool, as was Stephi. The stools had wrought iron steel backs in the shapes of cowboy hats. The girls looked pretty cute up there, as they had both decided to wear their faux raccoon hats. "Aunt Olivia is mine and Stephi's mommy now, and Grandma Mary Beth is our grandma and you are our great-grandma, but who is your mommy and who is your grandma?"

My mother, Chloe, Kyle, and I all stopped what we were doing.

Kyle said, "Interesting. Out of respect for Mother and her threat to 'box my butt,' her words, not mine, I have refrained from asking the same queries. It's curious that you have not been told the same thing, Lucy." He took out his Questions Notebook and started writing.

At the same time, Chloe said, "Holy cow and horses."

My mother put a hand on her mother's hand, then said to Stephi and Lucy, "Let me tell you about the long-term effects of diabetes and amputated limbs—"

I said, "Lucy, honey, we don't talk about that—"

Surprisingly, shockingly, my grandma said, "Lucy, that's a smart question to ask. My mother's name was Esther Gobenko, my grandmother's name was Ida Zaslavsky, my great-grand-mother's name was Sarrah Tolstonog, and her mother was Tsilia Bezkrovny."

Stunned silence from my mother, whose mouth dropped. Chloe said, "I'll be danged." Kyle scribbled something in his Questions Notebook, then looked up. "What are their birthdays?"

"My mother's birthday was December 2, 1899. Her mother, Ida's, was May 16, 1880. Sarrah was born in 1857 and Tsilia in 1836, but I don't remember the months."

"I like those names," Lucy said, adjusting her raccoon hat as it fell over her eyes. "My favorite name is Ida."

"They are beautiful names," my grandma said. "They were beautiful women."

"What happened to them?" Stephi asked.

"Let's talk about that land mine another time," my mother said. "Let me tell you what can cause arteries to clog."

"Lucy, Stephi—" I said.

My grandma stopped all of us, an elegant hand raised. "It's all right. Perhaps it's time." She blinked rapidly. "Yes. Perhaps it is."

"It is?" Chloe asked.

"Are you sure, Mom?" my mother asked.

"Yes." My grandma kept kneading the bread, flour covering her hands. "I used to make bread with my mother and my grandma."

"Like we're doing with you!" Stephi said, smiling.

"Exactly."

"So what happened to them?" Lucy asked.

"All of them are dead. They died a long time ago."

"That's sad," Lucy said. She reached over and patted my grandma's hand. "I'm sorry, Grandma Gisela."

"You mean they died like Grandma Annabelle?" Stephi said, her chin quivering.

"Yes, but they died in different ways," Grandma said. "Some of my relatives died when they were very old."

Lucy's brow furrowed. "Did some die when they were very young?"

My grandma's face paled around her cheeks. "Yes. Some died when they were young."

"Oh no!" Stephi said, and burst into tears. "Here. Have a rock, Grandma!"

"I'm sorry, Grandma Gisela!" Lucy said.

"I was sorry, too." She thanked Stephi for the rock, then pushed the dough down again.

"How did it happen?" Lucy asked.

Whew. We all stared at my grandma. She had kept this part of her life secret for so long. Decades. Would she talk? Would she say what we always thought had happened to her family? Were we right? Were we wrong?

"A very bad man decided that he did not like my family or millions of other families. Many more millions of people agreed with him."

And we were right. I didn't want to be right. None of us wanted to be right on this one.

"Why did he not like you, Grandma Gisela?" Stephi asked, squishing a finger into the dough.

My grandma paused. "Because we're Jewish."

My mother was not surprised, neither were my sister and I. We know history. We knew she was German. But it still felt like being kicked in the teeth. She was Jewish. Her family was Jewish. And they were nowhere to be found.

"What's Jewish?" Stephi said.

"It's like our friends Benjamin and Gabriel back home," Lucy said. "They're Jewish. It means you get to have all this food at dinner on Friday night, with twisted-up bread, and blessings and singing, and they don't eat bacon, and you have eight candles on a candlestick, and it means the boys wear a little black hat."

"Judaism," Kyle said, then went into a lengthy and complete description. "If you are Jewish, Grandma Gisela, and Granddad Oliver wasn't, that makes Grandma half Jewish. It makes my mother one-quarter Jewish. I am one-eighth Jewish. This is news to be proud of. Many excellent scientists and artists were, and are, Jewish."

My grandma smiled, a sad and tight smile. Then two tears slipped down her cheek and into the dough.

My mother, my sister, and I put our arms around her as two more tears slipped in, too.

"Oh no, Grandma Gisela!" Lucy said, crawling over the counter and hugging Grandma. "Don't cry!"

"Grandma Gisela!" Stephi emptied her pockets. "Here. You can have all my rocks."

Kyle said, "I am not understanding this situation, but I do understand that when someone you love cries, you give them a hug." He hugged Grandma. Patted her back. Three times. Then he wrote something in his Questions Notebook and said to Chloe, "I have a lot of troubling and confusing questions here, Mother, for which I will need your wise counsel."

"I know, brainiac, I can tell," she said. "It'll set your neurons on fire, but we'll talk later."

My grandma patted Kyle's cheek, leaving flour there, then went back to kneading the bread, her white hair swaying, her tears adding the salt we needed. "One thing you all need to remember, though," she said, "I love you. I love you all so much."

My grandma didn't say more that night. It was enough. We talked and laughed and ate the chicken tortilla soup with sour cream and chips that I made. Chloe brought salad in a bag. She's not a fanatic about cooking like me, and neither is my mother. I definitely get my semi-obsession with cooking from my grandma's genes.

Chloe said, "I made an appointment to get these knockers taken down a notch. Also, I'm going to start dating. I know there's a lot of love in this two-hundred-pound woman and I, as a tough-talkin', hip-rockin' Montana woman, want to share it with someone." She indicated her boobs with her pointer fingers. "They're ready to get on out there again, but I have questions."

Kyle reached for his Questions Notebook again and adjusted his glasses, waiting.

"How do you date?" She threw her arms out. Kyle scribbled. "How do I get asked out on a date? Why do I have to wait to get asked out? Why put the power in the man's hands? Why does he get to control the relationship from the start? I don't have to prove myself to him or hope that he likes what I've got, or be good enough. He has to prove to me that he's good enough. None of this, am I woman enough for him? It's 'Is he man enough for me?'

"I'm going to ask men out if I think they'll be able to handle me as I need to be handled, and see what they say. Hell, Teddy and I met in Iraq. Talk about not romantic. Sand. Guns. Bombs. But love bloomed like an explosion, and we heard enough of those. We didn't date in a traditional sense. Too many AK-47s around. But he acted like a total man when I told him I wanted to have dinner with him in the cafeteria and then, if he had time, I wouldn't mind slipping myself into his bunk for some bunking."

Kyle scribbled away. I don't think my sister even noticed.

"I saw a man who I thought could handle all of my womanliness when I was up in Telena, and I walked straight up to him after seeing this tall drink of Montana water and I said to him, "My name is Chloe and I think someone like yourself can handle someone like me. How about dinner?"

My grandma sighed. "Oh, my dear Nutmeg."

My mother said, "Way to take charge."

"And he said..." I prompted.

"He said, 'Lady, are you asking me out?' and I said, 'I sure am. I'm a feminist and I don't think men need to have the power in this dating game anymore so I'm taking the power,' and he said he right liked that idea but he was married and had five kids."

"And then you said . . ." my mother prompted.

"I said to him, 'I don't mow other women's grass, so I'm going to continue on and get myself a few straight shots at the bar,' and he said, 'Thank you for asking me out. You made me feel better. I've got a stressful job, my mother's ill, and the five little ones need a lot of attention and I'm flattered, ma'am. I am. If I was single, I would have said yes,' and I said, 'Thank you, too, you tall drink of Montana water,' and I went to the bar and had a cry into my vodka. Dating is not going to be fun. I'll probably meet a lot of donkey men, but I'm a shootin' woman with love to give." She shimmied her top half, and we laughed.

My mother talked about a patient of hers who came in with worms, which was fascinating to Stephi and Lucy but not appetizing, as there was chicken in the soup, which made me think of flesh.

"Fire Breather knows how to eradicate worms," my grandma drawled, patting my mother's hand.

I talked about my job as a chef and how I might serve Larry up one day on a platter.

Kyle discussed astronomical physics until his mother said, "Kyle. I think that's enough for our brains tonight. Remember don't yak on and on for long periods of time."

"Thank you, Mother. I forgot. I apologize." We told him he didn't need to apologize at all, his knowledge was impressive, but he opened his Questions Notebook and made a note about not yakking on and on.

Lucy talked about how she found herself in another fight at school, and Stephi said she was wearing her raccoon hat to school tomorrow and she was going to wear a tutu over her favorite cat sweatpants and if a boy bugged her she would throw her "throwing rock" from her rock collection at him.

Then we ate brownie sundaes and hugged and went to our separate homes.

I stood on the log cabin deck that night and looked toward the towering, snow-covered Dove Mountains. The night was clear but freezing, so I had on two jackets and my boots over my pajamas. My pajamas were at least ten years old, but I liked the little white lambs on them. Chloe had given them to me.

A star shot through the night. Falling stars are one of the many things I love about being in the country. The city lights cover stars up, but when you're out in the country, no lights on, you can see the full glory of the universe. When someone tells you there are billions of stars out there, you believe them, because you can imagine it.

The stars had been especially bright and twinkly on Jace's ranch. It was peaceful. So peaceful. Until.

Monday I took the girls to school, volunteered in their classrooms with an art lesson, and met several of the other mothers. I smiled, chatted, liked them. I had had to promise the pig boar, Larry, that I would work Saturday morning in exchange.

I volunteered so that my girls could have play dates with their girls. I don't know much about parenting, but I do know, from Chloe and Annabelle, that you have to meet the other mothers and there's a whole tricky social dynamic at school. I did know a number of the parents at the school, as I went to school with them, or they or their family members were patients of my mother and grandma, or I knew them from town, so that helped a ton. They didn't know at first that Lucy and Stephi were mine, because they had a different last name, McDaniel.

The girls still felt they had "no friends," and thought the other kids thought they were "weird and dumb," but I was hoping that when the other mothers realized they were my kids and I was unlikely to abduct their precious children to Siberia, they would encourage their sons and daughters to play with Lucy and Stephi.

It's what a helicopter parent does, tries to engineer social stuff at school for their kids, but I was broken by the girls' tears and abject loneliness, and if I had to helicopter around for a while I would.

So there.

I had a bit of time before I had to be at Larry's, so I drove alongside Jace's white fence into the country. I stopped and got out of my truck, the sky blue and wide, a cold, white blanket over the countryside. In the distance was the hill with the view of magical sunsets that will make you feel like you're in a painting.

Maybe I would go there soon.

She called me.

When I listened to her voice mail, all I heard was laughing for about a minute. This twisted, high-pitched laughter that made my spine tingle and my fear skyrocket.

Her words were short. "Hello, Olivia. I'll see you soon. Won't that be lovely?"

I can be overly emotional, and I cry too easily now and then, but I also deal with a latent anger that claws itself out of me at times.

My anger is one of my many faults.

My first experience with true fury came after my father left us when I was ten, Chloe eleven. He was an emotionally absent man when we were growing up. He worked as a pharmacist and had no idea how to be a father. One morning we had breakfast with him in our blue farmhouse, scrambled eggs and toast, and the next morning, a Saturday, he was gone.

He walked out of our lives. There was another woman.

His leaving was devastating. No hug, no good-bye. He was simply gone. It was a blow, as if he had hit us with his treasured red sports car, a ridiculous car to have in Montana because of our winters.

I remember peeking in at my mother, sitting on their bed, reading a letter, which I later learned was the letter he left her. She read it, stood up, walked to the window, and stared out, her arms crossed. After a couple of minutes, she shredded the letter and sent it down the toilet. There were no tears.

My mother told us the truth that morning in my and Chloe's bedroom in our farmhouse. It was summer, sunny and warm. My father's desertion brought ice into our home that day.

"He's not coming back?" Chloe asked.

"He will come back to visit with you two, but he won't live here again," our mother said, an arm wrapped around each of our shoulders. "He's divorcing me, but he's not divorcing you, that's important to remember. He's your father, he'll always be your father, and he loves you both very much."

"But why did he leave?" I asked.

And there my mother hesitated. She was careful not to talk much behind my father's back when we were growing up, but she also believed in the truth, as she told us later. Was she to lie to us? Was she to make up some fairy tale that our father was helping orphans in Africa and that's why he wasn't here?

And why, she asked herself, should she lie to protect him and his egregious, selfish actions? Why was the burden on her to soften this up and make our father appear better than he was? Plus, we would find out the truth when we were older, and then we would know she had lied. We would have one parent who abruptly abandoned us and another parent who fogged and deceived our perceptions of our own reality, and she knew it. She would also not downplay or minimalize what he'd done, which would not validate our pain. Mary Beth believed in honesty. She believed we were better off knowing the truth. So she told us the truth.

"Your father has a girlfriend. He is going to marry her. She lives in Las Vegas. He has been seeing her on his business trips when he's not here."

I remember the silence in our bedroom. That silence shook, intense and suffocating, as I stared out at that bright, bright sun. I sat absolutely still, my mother's words penetrating, one letter at time, then the full word, then the sentences and the meaning behind it. When I finally understood the enormity of what happened, I stood up and threw a framed picture of him and me across the room. It made a hole in the wall. Chloe stood up, put her hands on her hips, and yelled, "Damn him!"

I picked up a jewelry box he had bought me on one of his trips to Vegas. Showgirls were dancing on it. I lifted it high above my head and smashed it. I threw a blue and pink paperweight he had given me straight through the window. Luckily the window was open.

I turned and ran out of our blue farmhouse. I ran and ran and ran until I couldn't run anymore, and a neighbor, Mr. Buckley, who lives seven miles out of town, drove me home. He found me sitting on his fence.

That's where the anger started.

My mother, grandma, Chloe, and I had always baked cakes together for Martindale Cake Therapy, and the night my father left I made a simple chocolate fudge cake. The next night I made a white cake with pink peppermint frosting. The third night I made a lemon cheesecake.

Later, when I was a teenager, often rebellious and wild, surely because of the abandonment and anger issues I had, after I snuck out at night, to drink beer or party, I came home and baked. When I missed my father and I thought the hurt and rejection would explode inside of me, I baked. When he missed Christmas and my birthday and Chloe's birthday, I baked. When he never came to visit, I baked. Baking occupied my mind, my hands, and I could forget.

I branched out to cooking. My mother gave me cookbooks. I went through an Italian stage. For weeks, all we ate was Italian. Then a Japanese stage, French, Hawaiian, Mexican, Spanish. For some reason I had to cook my way around the world. It was as if sifting flour, stirring batter, dumping berries in a pie, rolling out a crust, watching bread rise, and boiling noodles took some of the anger away from me. It was art, in a culinary sense, and art is always healing.

I finally made it back to traditional American food. My mother loved that I cooked, so did my granddad and grandma. The three of them were always busy at the clinic, helping people, so to have dinner made at night, well, they were thrilled, especially my hard-working, compassionate granddad, who was more of a father to me than my father had ever been. He said, "Olivia. You are making heaven in that oven. Can't wait to eat that heaven tonight."

When my father did return, five years later, he came back for a day with a new wife, not the woman he left my mother for, my mother told us, and two kids—one three years old, one four. They were our half brothers. It felt like we were getting kicked in the teeth. Chloe and I met him at a restaurant.

His wife, much younger than him, was from the city and wore pancake makeup with blue eye shadow. Her perfume had rotted. She wore fancy/slutty clothes, and her shirt was unbuttoned so low her boobs were half out. Our father was wearing a suit.

He hugged us, smiling, motioning for us to sit in the booth with them. "So great to see you two again. How are you?"

He was trying to be the proper pharmacist. Pompous. Proud of himself. As if he hadn't deserted his children. It hurt to see him. Hurt like we were being stabbed in the chest.

"This is your new mother, Pam."

"She's not our new mother," I said.

"We have a mother," Chloe said.

Awkward. New Wife frowned at us.

Our dad reprimanded us. "Please show better manners." He turned to New Wife and muttered, "Their mother..." and shook his head, as if our disgrace of a mother was responsible for our poor manners. "I'm sorry I haven't seen you girls much over the last two years."

"Five," Chloe and I corrected him.

"You haven't seen us in five years."

New Wife frowned again, this time at our father.

He waved his hand as in, *whatever*. "Your mother didn't let me see you. She told me I couldn't come. She took custody of you."

"That's a lie, Barney," Chloe and I corrected him, together. We called him Barney, not "Dad." He had not acted like a dad, so he didn't get the title. Our granddad was our dad.

"She never said that to you," I said.

"I heard her telling you, on the phone, to come and see us anytime," Chloe said. "Many times. And you didn't."

"You walked out on us," I said.

"You didn't even say good-bye." Chloe gave him a disgusted look. "Barney."

"You didn't say good-bye?" New Wife said. "You didn't tell the girls you were leaving their mother? You said that their mother was verbally and physically abusive to you and that your girls agreed you had to leave for your own safety."

"Never," I said. "Our mother is a doctor. He was the one who would have temper tantrums like a baby and stomp out and slam the door. Do you still stomp, Barney?"

"Nope, Second Wife," Chloe drawled. "That's another lie."

"Yes . . . yes! I said good-bye to the girls," Barney stuttered to New Wife. Our half brothers started crawling into their mom's lap. "Their mother was . . . was . . ." He couldn't meet our eyes.

"Our mother is the best mother on the planet Earth," Chloe said, stabbing a fork into the table. "Don't criticize her, or I'm going to use my karate skills on you."

"There was no good-bye when Barney left," I said to New Wife. "None. Here one day, gone the next. Off to see his girl-friend in Vegas." I turned to Barney. "Was she a hooker?"

New Wife glared at him. "What girlfriend? I met you five years ago. You said I was the first after your marriage."

"There was no girlfriend," my father said, flushed. "Only you. I left my marriage because I couldn't stay with my ex-wife, who is crazy and is mentally . . . disturbed, that which . . . uh . . . she hides from everyone else. Hides it. She's disturbed."

Chloe and I laughed.

"Try another lie, Barney," Chloe said, still stabbing that fork but edging closer to his hand.

"Barney, you didn't even send Mom money for us, either. Ever." I gave him a disgusted look, too.

"I did!" He pulled on his tie.

"You didn't," Chloe and I said together.

"You said, Barney," New Wife said, impatient now, suspicious, "that you make huge child support payments to their mother and that's why you don't have much money." Her eyes narrowed.

"I do make payments," he said, his voice faltering, but that pompous note still rang through. "When I can."

"No, you don't," Chloe and I said together.

"Mom said the girlfriend's name was Bambi," I said. "Like the deer."

"Bambi Nugent?" New Wife leaned toward him, her face scrunched in anger. "You said you had only met her *twice*."

"Barney didn't call us on our birthdays, and neither did Bambi," I said.

"Or Christmas," Chloe said.

"You said"—New Wife was getting more and more angry—"that you called the girls all the time."

"He's gonna lie to you, too," Chloe said to New Wife. "He lied to my mother. He took a lot of trips when he was married to her. He said it was for work. It wasn't for work. He was visiting his Las Vegas girlfriend."

"I want to ask you again. Was Bambi a hooker?" I asked.

"No!" my father snapped. "She was not a hooker."

New Wife was pissed. We'd hit a nerve.

"Chloe Rossbach, Olivia Rossbach—" he started, trying to reprimand us. "Don't you talk to me like that—"

"My name isn't Rossbach anymore," I said.

"Neither is mine," Chloe said, that stabbing fork edging closer to him. He moved his hands. "I'm Chloe Martindale now."

I stretched out my hand to my father to shake it. "I'm Olivia Martindale."

The boys started to wriggle around in their seats. One got out and climbed between Chloe and me. He was cute.

The waitress came by, smiling. Chloe and I ordered lemon meringue pie. "Can we get whip cream on top?" We could. "A lot?" Yes.

When she brought it, Chloe and I knew what to do. We both

picked up the pie with our fingers and tossed it at him. We had admirable aim because of target practice and our archery skills.

He was spluttering and swearing when we left, New Wife steaming mad.

Three years later he came back with another new wife and a baby. For one day. We had no use for him. We met them for lunch again. This time it was cherry pie. Guaranteed to stain.

His phone calls, over the years, have been sporadic. I never called him. I have currently not spoken to my father for three years. He called to tell me he was getting married for the fourth time and said he was sorry he couldn't invite me, but they were going to get married in Hawaii.

"Barney," I said, "I don't care that you're getting married. Why should I? You deserted and abandoned Mom, me, and Chloe. You walked out. You didn't pay any child support. You didn't call. You've abandoned two other women and your other children. If I had children I would sooner cut off my own feet and walk on my knees the rest of my life than leave them. You are a narcissistic, selfish, horrible man with no morals. I don't want you in my life. At all. All you do is bring pain to everyone."

"No, I don't—"

"You do. Every family you have created you have hurt. You have done nothing in your life that is worthwhile. I heard your second set of kids are both on drugs. I met them in Kalulell years ago, remember? They were cute. Your third set is having trouble in school. Both dropped out, right? And now you have a three-year-old with this woman. When will you desert her? You can't seem to stop shattering people's lives. Your children do not deserve it."

He sighed. Pompous. Smug. "You don't understand this situation. You lack maturity and insight. Your mother filled you with hate for me—"

"She never did that. You did, Barney. And I do have maturity and insight. You're simply throwing those words out so you can be condescending and shut me down. You don't even know me. You are not a true man. A true man is a kind father to his children. You are not kind to any of your children or their mothers.

Don't contact me again. Every time you do, I have to go through the hurt and anger again. I don't need it, or you."

"Show some respect to your father and do not talk to me like that, Olivia Rossbach!"

"I am Olivia Martindale Rivera. You are not my father, Barney. Granddad is. I will speak to you how I wish." I hung up.

I don't feel compelled to have a relationship with Barney because he shares the same genetic material as I do. I think sometimes that's where people make a mistake: because we're blood related, because he's our father, or she's our mother, or that's our sister or brother or cousin, or half brother, that we have to have a relationship with that person.

As if it's enshrined in the Constitution, or part of being American.

It isn't.

Toxic is toxic. We cannot choose our family members, and when one of them is only going to bring a wrecking ball of destruction and hurt, I feel no obligation to have a relationship with them. Blood is blood, they say. And usually the person who's saying it is the toxic one and using emotional manipulation to sneak their poisonous self back into your life.

I will not buy into it.

I will, however, buy into cooking.

Cooking and baking are therapy for me. There's no anger, no abandonment. It's peace. It's order. Beautiful food art.

Measure. Mix. Stir. Whip. Bake. Invent. Imagine. Nourish the ones you love, including yourself.

Chapter 6

On Wednesday evening my mother and grandma invited the girls and me to the farmhouse for homemade vanilla ice cream that my grandma made. My mother ended up talking to the girls about how emergency room doctors get to "see everything. I mean, everything. If you want action in your life, girls, become an emergency room doctor. I was in the emergency room in a hospital in New York and let me tell you the types of injuries I saw there . . ."

"Mom, *shhh* . . . they'll have nightmares."

She glared at me. "I'm preparing them for medical school and how to treat emergencies, Rebel Child. This is an age-appropriate lesson."

"I want to know about the action," Stephi said, grabbing my mother's hand.

"What kinds of injuries?" Lucy asked, her face lighting up. "How bad?"

I groaned.

I saw my grandma's leather-bound cookbook later that night. What did the two heart-shaped, gold lockets; the red ribbons; the sun charm; and the white feather mean to her? So many questions, and I knew all the answers would be painful.

Joan the caseworker dropped by. I had no idea she was coming. The girls were in aprons and we were icing a confetti cake

NO PLACE I'D RATHER BE   129

with sprinkles. The scene was so perfect it seemed rigged. She helped eat the cake, then she and I had a glass of wine and made a toast to "Feminism, confetti cake, and wine."

On a snowy morning, Jace walked into Larry's Diner with three of his friends. I knew all of them. They were fishing/hunting/skiing buddies. They had all gone to school with Jace, two years ahead of me, and they'd been friends forever. I liked all of them. They were loud, fun, and respectful to me when Jace and I were married.

Jordan is a screenwriter. He writes romance movies. He and his wife, Maria, have five kids. Michael owns a hardware store, and his wife, Rynnie, is a pediatrician, who my mother respects and likes. They have three kids. Ryan part-owns and manages the largest ski resort in town. His wife, Kelly, owns the city's craft store. They have two kids. Their kids are all unofficial cousins to each other.

We used to hang out with them. When I left Jace I lost contact with the six of them. The wives had all called and e-mailed me. So had Jordan, Michael, and Ryan. Friendly calls, how are you, we sure miss you, Jace misses you. Anything we can do? Are you two thinking about getting back together? Jace is so unhappy.

Now and then I responded, but hardly ever. The friendships eventually fell off. I take full blame. It hurt to talk to Maria, Rynnie, and Kelly. They were with their husbands, their children. I was not.

But the four musketeers were back and in the restaurant: Jace, Jordan, Michael, and Ryan. I knew I would not venture outside of the kitchen, I was not brave enough for that, but I would make sure that what they ordered was perfect.

The restaurant was full and we were flying in the back, but I watched the orders come in and snatched theirs right up. My hands were shaking from lack of sleep as both Lucy and Stephi had had nightmares about living with their parents, in a dark house, and being in a basement alone for days on end. They ate dog food and they could smell cigarette smoke. People were always smoking in their home, which makes Lucy and Stephi feel sick to this day when they smell it.

Let's see...mushroom and goat cheese omelet...French toast with our homemade raspberry syrup...scrambled egg, bacon, and chive western skillet...and Jace's. His was the eggs Benedict with hollandaise sauce with blueberry muffins on the side. He loved my eggs Benedict and my blueberry muffins.

I whipped...I scrambled...I sautéed...I spiced up...I added a dash of this and a shake of that.

I pushed the bell, Dinah hustled over, winked, as she knew why I was hiding in the kitchen like a fool, and delivered their food. I went back to slicing, chopping, and frying and tried to pretend that my soon-to-be-ex, hot husband with the hard eyes that softened up every single time he was around me was not in the restaurant with his loud and funny friends who were married to women whom I had rudely dropped and ignored. I am an awful, awful person.

"They want to compliment the chef," Dinah said about thirty minutes later.

"Who?" But I knew who.

"You know who."

"No. I don't want to be complimented."

"Get out there, Chef Feisty," Larry boomed. "Those guys haven't been in here ever. I want them to come back. They want to tell you that you flipped their eggs like their momma used to do or the bacon made them drool or the pancakes made them hard, then you go listen to it. Now, Olivia. Go. Move that butt."

I took off my apron, which was slathered in egg yolks, blueberry muffin batter, and sugar icing from the cinnamon rolls, then slipped into the bathroom. I groaned. It appeared that death had come and messed with my face. I was white-gray. No makeup. I was, at the same time, flushed from the steam in the kitchen. I resembled a sweating ghost. My hair must have been brushed by mice. I put my hands on the sink and leaned over it. I didn't want to chitchat with Jace and his friends. I had no confidence. None.

Larry pounded on the door. "Out you go, woman. Say hi, try to pretend you're polite, make it snappy, and get your butt back in here."

I washed my hands. I washed my face because I had pancake batter on my chin and my homemade raspberry syrup on my forehead. I leaned in. Egg on my collarbone. I had dark circles under my eyes. What? Was I part raccoon? I took my hair out of the ponytail, and it tumbled over my shoulders. I tried to fluff it up so it wouldn't hang like a brown rag.

I rinsed out my mouth. Dug lipstick out of my purse and put it on. It was the best I could do. I appeared slightly less deathly. One thing I learned from my grandma, though: When you feel you look your worst, be "so friendly they think they've been hit with a friendly hammer, and ask people how *they* are. They'll walk away thinking you looked fantastic because you made them feel cared about."

I opened the bathroom door and headed out to Jace and my ex-friends. I plastered a fake smile on my face.

"Nice fake smile," Larry said.

"Olivia! Give me a hug . . . so good to see you . . . we missed you . . . we heard you were in town . . . Rynnie will be so happy you're back . . . have you talked to Kelly yet? No? Give her a call . . ."

I was enveloped in three hugs by three men. Jace had stood when I came over, let the men out of the booth, and smiled at me. Gentle. Serious. Calm. And . . . blank. He didn't give much away when he didn't want to.

"It's so nice to see all of you." They were all politely covering up the awkwardness of my being back, but not with Jace. They were not intrusive people. "How are you all, how are the kids?"

"Sit down, please . . . please . . ."

"I can't right now, I'm so busy in the back, but tell me."

They told me about their kids, their wives, they laughed and chatted. I knew I had to get back to the kitchen because we were swamped, but also because this conversation was making me feel like I wanted to sprint out of the restaurant and not stop sprinting until I got to the top of a mountain and could scream. I used to be friends with these men. I knew their children. I had held their babies, I had hugged their toddlers, I had cooked with their kids.

They hugged me again before I scooted back to the kitchen. I avoided Jace's eyes when I said, "Nice to see you, Jace."

"And you, too, Olivia."

As I turned toward the kitchen, I heard the abrupt silence at the table.

Then I heard Jordan say, no doubt trying to whisper but he is so naturally loud he doesn't know how to, "Jace, buddy, you two have got to get back together."

"Yeah, man," Michael said. "Do not let that one get away again."

As I have done for years, I cooked to block out what I felt for the rest of the day, but I cried on the way to get the girls that afternoon. Cried like I had two streams pouring out of my eyes. I have to stop crying so much. I pulled myself back together in Portland, but now I was a wet mess again, my emotions a tumbling cacophony of shrieks.

Jace was still so sexy. So huggable. So broad and serious and stable and loyal.

He should hate me. I would hate me if I was him, but he didn't. I could tell. He was a forgiving man, a smart man. I have hated myself, for many things.

My grandma and mother had both asked gently, on several occasions over the last two-plus years, if I wanted to talk about Jace. Gentle is hard for my mother, as she is part bull, so I appreciated her efforts. I said yes, and we did, and we moved on. It is what it is: a wreck that can't be repaired.

"Will you tell me about Ida Zaslavsky, Grandma?" I traced the signature written on the inside cover of the leather cookbook.

"She's my grandmother, Cinnamon, your great-great grand-mother."

We were at the farmhouse, at the table my granddad built, the girls reading by the fire, my mother still at the clinic.

"My great-great grandmother." I studied, in awe, the neat, precise handwriting and the detailed pictures she'd drawn. I looked at the recipes—my grandma translated for me, as they were written in Ukrainian and Yiddish—for beet root soup with pepper and onions. Braided egg bread. Potato pie.

"She was a Jew from Odessa. It was Ida's mother, Sarrah Tol-stonog, who gave her the book. She worked as a house cleaner for a wealthy man who made books." Grandma smiled and flipped through the pages, so old, stains here and there, black burned around the edges. "Sometimes she spoke and wrote in Ukrainian and sometimes in Yiddish. It's how I learned both languages, through my grandma, Ida, and grandfather, Boris. Ah"—she sighed—"it has been so long since I've spoken their names."

"You speak Ukrainian and Yiddish?" I had never known that.

"Yes. Although not well anymore. That's what happens after seventy years. But she and my grandfather spoke to me in those languages when I was growing up in Munich. They started me off with Yiddish because they didn't want me to forget our peo-ple's language, then they started speaking to me in Ukrainian when I was about six."

"So you speak Ukrainian, Yiddish, and German." That ex-plained her accent, or should I say accents. Her English was a blend of British and American, mostly American, with a dose of German and a dash of something else. That something else was the Yiddish and Ukrainian.

"And I do okay with English." She elbowed me and smiled. She took a deep breath when she came to a picture of the family. I knew I was looking at Ida and Boris, their two little boys, one girl, and a baby sitting on Ida's lap. "Ida wrote the recipes in

Yiddish if they were from her mother or grandmother, and she wrote them in Ukrainian if they were hers."

Ida had long, thick dark hair, much like mine, Grandma's, my mother's, and Chloe's. She wore a skirt to her ankles and a buttoned shirt to her neck. Black boots. Her eyes tilted upward at the corners. Cat eyes. Like mine.

"Ida was much more beautiful than this," Grandma said. "She didn't draw herself with all of her beauty, as I understood it from my mother, Esther, her daughter. Her eyes were green, like ours. She was modest. Gentle. Kind. But strong, oh so strong, to have lived through what she did."

She turned the page to a stone and wood home with a brick fireplace.

"This was Ida and Boris's home that was burned to the ground during the pogrom. The men, evil men, came in the night and burned much of the neighborhood down. It was outside of Odessa, on the edges, so it felt like a village to them. My grandma told my mother that it was very quiet that night, too quiet, but that Odessa had been dangerous and tense for a long time. They murdered and raped Jews and destroyed businesses and homes. Their baby"—she tapped the smiling face of the baby in Ida's lap—"died in the flames in the bedroom. They couldn't get to him. That baby would have been my uncle Liev."

I pictured that sickening scene. I put a hand to my heart as it lurched, pounded. I leaned against the table and took a breath. "Grandma, I'm so sorry."

"With their house on fire, they fled into the woods to hide. Boris and Ida couldn't find the boys and my mother for an hour because they pushed the children out first while they tried to save Liev. The black smoke hid them while they ran. Finally they found the children in a log. They didn't go back home for two days, to salvage what they could. Ida found her cookbook. Our cookbook. She told my mother that it had been on the windowsill during the attack. Maybe it was blown out. Who knows? But it survived. They had nothing after the fire, except the clothes they were wearing, the cookbook, the menorah that

Ida found in the dirt that was made by her grandfather, Aron Bezkrovny, and the tools that Boris used to make saddles and harnesses.

"What they did to the Jews during the pogroms was never punished. The government allowed it, encouraged it. Attacks against Jews were accepted." Her mouth tightened, and I saw a flash of true anger from a woman who rarely angered. "Ida was pregnant when they escaped from Odessa. On their way to Germany—it took them fourteen months—she lost her fifth child, a girl. She was going to name her Talia." She turned a page and tapped it. "She had a stillborn birth on the side of a dirt road, at night, and they buried her the next day in the forest. Broke her heart. This forest with the sun shining through the trees and the meadow was the baby girl's burial place. The two deer are for Talia and for Liev."

Ida, my great-great-grandmother, had lost two babies. My whole body hurt for her.

"Grandma." I pointed to the picture of the menorah in the windowsill I'd seen before. "Is that the menorah in the box?"

"Yes, it is."

Incredible. From Odessa to Germany to England to Montana. It had survived all those years, four countries, one ocean between them.

"Ida was not only a cook, who I'm sure did the best she could with what limited ingredients she had, but she was an artist, too," my grandma murmured, running a finger over the drawings.

"I can see that. The drawings remind me of how Kyle draws, intricate, down to the expressions on the people's faces, the hair on the animals, the cuts in the pies."

"Yes, it's uncanny. It's like looking at Kyle's work. There is the same amount of detail, the style is the same, the proportions, the perspective. They each have a flowing hand. It's genetics. It's not only the brown, thick hair and green eyes that have been passed down through our line."

We came to a picture of another home, in the city, elegant,

brick, three story, with a red door and red geraniums in front in flower boxes.

"So it was Ida who started our tradition of planting red geraniums?"

"Yes. She told me it brought a spot of color to her home in Odessa. She and Boris struggled so much as a young couple. When she moved to Munich, as soon as she had a home, she planted red geraniums to celebrate life, her new life, in Germany, in peace and prosperity. So my mother, Esther, planted them at her home to honor Ida, which is why I plant red geraniums every year, to honor Ida, and your mother took up the tradition, not knowing why, as you did, too, as does Chloe."

Amazing. I had red geraniums all over Martindale Ranch. Jace had joked that we should have called it Geranium Ranch instead of Martindale Ranch. I was following a tradition but hadn't known the truth of its beginnings.

"Did she live a long time? Did Boris?"

"They should have lived much longer."

"When did Ida die?"

"She died on January 2, 1942."

"What about . . ." I hesitated. "What about your grandfather Boris?"

"He died on November 14, 1942." She made a raw sound of anguish. So much hurt there.

"How?"

She waved a hand. "Not now, darling Olivia."

"Okay." I put my hand on hers. "I'm sorry."

I drew my finger down the edges of the cookbook, blackened, crisp, a few bits came off. It was a surreal moment. This was the fire that had killed Liev and made my ancestors run for their lives to Germany. It was an overwhelming moment for me. I was touching the cookbook and the recipes and the pictures drawn by my great-great-grandma Ida Zaslavsky, born Jewish in Odessa, in the Russian Empire.

I turned a few more pages. On the left side was a picture of Ida; her husband, Boris, four young boys; and a young girl.

"Ida had two more sons after they fled to Germany," Grandma said. "Their names were Grigori and Solomon. They were my uncles. Grigori was so funny. He played the piano, and Solomon played the guitar. All four of the boys worked for their father, Boris. Harnesses and saddles first..." Her voice faltered. I put an arm around her bent shoulders. "And then he sold women's handbags and wallets. He had a successful business..." Her voice trailed off, and I hugged her. I think I knew what happened.

"Grandma, let's make one of these recipes. Let's make it together. Do you want to?"

My grandma smiled, then the tears came, and she smiled and cried at the same time, so I did, too. "Enough of these silly tears. Yours and mine. Buck up, Olivia. You're too emotional." We both laughed. "And I'll buck up, too. Montana women don't go around whining. Let's not irritate ourselves.

"Ah." She smiled at a recipe. "This pampushky bread with garlic is actually a recipe that Grandma Ida remembered her own grandmother, Tsilia Bezkrovny, making. See? The name Tsilia is here, and this is a picture of her. And her husband, Aron.

"I remember when my Grandma Ida and I made pampushky together, in Munich, in her house. Ida had a huge bakery. It was decorated in pink and white and took up half a city block. My mother worked there, too, as I did when I was a teenager. They specialized in cakes. They loved making cakes."

"Cakes?"

"Yes." She clasped my hands in hers. "Ida and Esther made cakes for their bakery, they loved baking cakes above all else, and we make cakes together, too, the women in our family. And you, my lovely Cinnamon, you love baking cakes more than anything, like me, my mother, and grandmother Ida."

I felt a sudden, intense closeness to Esther and Ida. We were bound by cake baking.

"Let's bake, shall we?" my grandma said, her green eyes shining. "I think we should make Ida's strudel. She learned how to make it in Germany. There is not better strudel in the world than Ida's."

We made strudel. There was a red stain in the corner of the recipe. Could that be wine? A few of the words were smeared, perhaps from water? Or tears?

July 1921
Munich, Germany
Ida Zaslavsky, great-great-grandmother of Olivia Martindale.

Ida Zaslavsky smiled and pushed her brown hair back from her face, only a few streaks of grey in it.

Her red geraniums were blooming in her flower boxes and in her garden in pots. In Odessa she had spent their hard earned money, every year, for two red geraniums. They brought her such happiness, as she loved the color red, and they chased away a tiny bit of the poverty and the danger they were living in. So here, in Munich, in her elegant home, she made sure that she bought at least twenty geraniums a year to celebrate life and to remind herself how far they had come from the deprivations that they had been born into.

When Boris and she arrived with their children years ago, they were exhausted and traumatized. It had taken them four-teen harrowing months to get to Munich, working along the way, trying not to starve or freeze to death. They shared a three-bedroom apartment with two other Jewish families from Odessa. One bedroom per family.

Boris, with the tools he had managed to save after their home was burned to the ground, went to work the morning after they arrived. He got a job in a factory, and they saved their money to buy the supplies for him to make a saddle. It was one of his best saddles ever. He took it door to door, to farmers out in the coun-try, taking orders, and within six months he was able to quit his factory job.

She took her bread-making skills to a bakery. The manager hired her for the night shift. One of the other men they lived with went to work immediately in a textile factory, one in a fac-tory that made machines. One of the wives worked as a maid, the other as a seamstress. Together, with the two other families, they shared childcare and food.

All of their children immediately went to school.

Within a year, all the families had their own apartments in a better part of town, but near each other, then they later bought their own homes, again, within a block of each other. They considered themselves family. The homes all needed work, but the men and the women knew how to fix things, repair, paint. They helped each other. Soon the three homes were tidy and clean. Ida and Boris had two more children, Grigori and Solomon, and they saved their money.

Within two years Ida opened a tiny bakery, hardly bigger than a box, and Boris's business making harnesses and saddles eventually expanded to purses and wallets.

Nothing was easy, they worked all the time, and all five of their children—Esther, Moishe, Zino, Grigori, and Solomon— helped out with the businesses after their studies and school, but they had love. Ida's love for Boris only grew, and he for her. Soon they had a nicer car, nicer furniture, and the children were well dressed. Boris bought this beautiful home for her as a surprise. He had even planted red geraniums in new flower boxes to celebrate life, and he painted the front door red because red meant freedom to Ida. They bought silver Shabbat candlesticks and Kiddush cups, and another menorah.

Their beloved daughter, Esther, ran the bakery with her. They had so much fun together, cooking, trying new recipes, talking to their customers. Their pink and white bakery now took up half a block. Their specialty was cakes. Oh, how they loved to bake cakes together. Black forest gateau with cherries, German apple cake, Kuchen bars with vanilla custard, apple chocolate trifle, Leipzig carrot cake, and cinnamon mousse.

They also loved making raspberry tortes, strawberry cream rolls with powdered sugar, chocolate pecan bars, bee-sting cake, and so many cookies. Ida and Esther's strudel, filled with apples and brown sugar, flew out the door. They could not keep up with the demand. They specialized in bread, too. Hot, crisp, thick bread.

Soon Esther would marry Alexander, the fine son of Aizik and Raisel Gobenko, one of the couples they lived with when they first arrived in Munich, all of the families desperate and destitute. All four parents could not be happier. Esther, her passionate, opinionated, brave daughter who had survived the attack in Odessa, rushing her younger brothers out the door and into the woods, was wildly in love with Alexander, and he with her.

Ida smiled and sat down at her kitchen table with her special cookbook and drew their brick home here in Munich, with the red door, and her lush garden. She added a few more recipes from her mother, Sarrah, and from her grandmother, Tsilia, who were buried long ago in Odessa. She included recipes for pampushky bread with garlic, rich beef stew, dumplings filled with mashed potatoes and chives, yushka soup made with carp, stuffed duck, chicken Kiev, and sauerkraut. She drew pictures of the cakes, cookies, and bread they made, and she drew pictures of her parents and grandparents.

The cookbook would be the perfect wedding gift for Esther. Esther loved the cookbook and she loved her mother's drawings. "You're an artist," Esther told her all the time. "You should paint and let me run the bakery for you."

But Ida loved to bake, loved the bakery, loved her customers and having a job. And she loved being with Esther every day. She had built that bakery herself, she couldn't give it up, no matter how well Boris did with his business.

Tears filled Ida's eyes and she reached for her wineglass. It was a gift to have Esther marrying such a fine man, but it did tug on her heart. The wine spilled on the cookbook, right on her strudel recipe, and she quickly shook it off, then dried the pages. It would stain. The tears rolled off her cheeks and smeared the words. How silly of her!

She turned the pages and looked at the pictures of the children that she had drawn. Esther, Moishe, Zino, Grigori, Solomon. All so sweet. She had drawn them around the recipes as they grew, and had written their names beneath the drawings. On another page, near the front of the cookbook, she looked again at her drawings of baby Liev, burned alive in their home, and she felt her eyes fill. Precious boy, still missed, as was baby Talia.

Ida looked up when she heard laughter. Ah! There they were, coming in for family dinner. Alexander was with Esther, holding her hand. Her brothers were behind her. Yes, she was blessed. Boris waved at her through the window. He was so handsome.

He was still enthusiastic in the bedroom, not quite as enthusiastic as when he was a young man, but my. They loved being in bed together.

"Ida!" he said, arms outstretched, as if he hadn't seen her in days, instead of only a few hours. "My beautiful wife," he whispered in her ear. "Let's go and take a nap shall we, darling?"

She laughed and hugged him back, hugged her sons, then hugged Esther and her fiancé. Esther would love the cookbook. She would treasure it always, she knew it.

When I picked the girls up from their art class on Monday, we had more problems. Lucy whimpered, "Kaila told me I have a nose like a turnip. Do I have a nose like a turnip?"

Stephi said, kneading her fingers into her green frog sweatshirt, "I don't like it here. Too much snow. Too cold. No friends. Megan told me that I'm ugly. Am I ugly?"

Lucy said, "I don't want to go to school anymore."

Stephi said, "I miss Grandma Annabelle." She grabbed a handful of rocks out of her pocket.

Lucy cried. Stephi cried. I missed Annabelle, too.

We made chicken tacos with a dash of paprika and homemade salsa. My mother and grandma came over to eat with us when I called. My mother said, "I need a shower. Dang. Had a bloody one at the office. You know Bangor Reeves? Clean cut off two fingers with an ax. He's never been that smart. I sewed them back on again. He insisted that your grandma be in the room so she could tell him how to, and I quote, 'heal me the natural way, without all these newfangled medicines.'" She swore. "We'll be over after we get our clothes in the wash. Can't have blood stains, makes our patients nervous."

Chloe came over, too. She said, after hugging the girls and watching them scoot off with Kyle to play in their tent, "I need to get laid. I do. It's been a long time. Feels like decades. So I've been thinking about Chase McConnell."

Chase spends part of the year fishing in Alaska and the other part of the year in construction. He's built like a tree. He doesn't say much. I think he might be shy.

"I stalked him accidentally on purpose by driving by his house. Got out of my car this time when I saw him, the last three times I haven't been able to gather up my Montana woman courage, but this time I did and I told him he was a tall and strong son of a gun and he said, 'Thank you, Chloe,' and I said, 'When you need a woman who can handle all of your gun, you can take me to dinner,' and he said, 'Would you like to go to dinner?' and I said, 'Hell yes,' and I told him I'd pick him up Friday at seven o'clock and that I respected his blatant masculinity. He couldn't say anything after that, he blushed, so I patted his arm until he settled down and wasn't so embarrassed about his blatant masculinity and then I wished him a pleasant evening and I left."

"His blatant masculinity?"

"Yes. You should see it." She bashed her fists together. "It practically radiates off him. I told him that, too. I said, 'Your masculinity radiates off of you.'"

"What did he say?" I had never noticed radiating masculinity around shy Chase.

"He said, 'I had no idea,' and I told him, 'It's true, you have an aura.'"

"I cannot wait to hear how his aura and your aura blend," I said.

"Me either. I'm a tough-talkin', hip-rockin' Montana woman. I am. Starting over. I'm a woman. I can do this. I can."

"You betcha." She leaned on me, and I gave her a hug.

"I gotta get my Montana moves back. My groove needs a new beat."

Chloe next raved about the three orangutans at school—Eric,

Jason, and Juan—picking on Kyle and how she told him to "beat the hell out of them with your karate chops, son. Come on. Man up," and how he said, "Intellectual dialogue should solve problems, not violence, Mother."

My mother and Grandma talked about the clinic over tacos. My mother said things to Stephi and Lucy like, "We'll discuss what medical school will be best for what type of medicine you want to specialize in . . . I think surgery would be a strong fit for both of you . . . Yes, cutting into people, taking out what shouldn't be there, sewing them back up and making them healthy again is gratifying . . ."

Kyle has zero interest in being a doctor and has expressed that to my mother, much to her unending disappointment.

Kyle listened to the girls talk about school and how they had no friends and how Lucy thought she had a nose the size of a turnip because of what Kaila said and how Stephi thought she was ugly because of what Megan said. Kyle fiddled with his glasses, leaned toward Lucy, stared closely at her face, and said, "It is false."

"What is?" Lucy said.

"Kaila's declaration of your having a nose like a turnip is false. I would like to prove it to you. May I?" She sniffled, nodded. He took out a tiny tape measure from his shirt pocket and measured her nose. "Your nose is smaller than the average girl your age. It is unfortunate when people make statements that do not have any basis in fact, especially if it brings on negative emotions within the person they are disparaging or ridiculing."

"I don't understand what you said," Lucy said. "But it sounds right."

"I will try a different explanation. Your nose cannot be conclusively labeled as large. Kaila has made an unsubstantiated statement."

Lucy still didn't understand the whole sentence, but she got the first part. "Really?"

"Yes." He turned to Stephi, leaned forward. Stephi eagerly leaned over the table and went almost nose-to-nose with Kyle.

"Stephi. Megan, too, is incorrect. You are not ugly. In fact, based on societal norms of beauty"—he tilted his head—"you are pretty."

"I am?"

"Yes." He did not smile, but his face was not unfriendly. Simply scientific. "Society can often dictate who is pretty. I, personally, believe that that is ridiculous. Nonsense. For example, a woman's BMI in different countries determines her attractiveness. That BMI number is radically different from place to place."

"What is Bees My I?" asked Stephi.

"It's a measure of weight." He shook his head. "More important, Stephi, Megan's statement is erroneous. I don't know how to prove this to you, as you obviously engage in studying yourself in the mirror to prepare yourself for your day. That you do not see that you are pretty is an analytical mistake on your part." Kyle's brow furrowed, and he muttered, "This problem will require proof, as they are both very young and are, currently, judging by the tears, emotional. Mother says when people cry, give them a hug." He stood. Gave them perfunctory hugs. He patted their backs. Three times. He seemed surprised when both girls clung to him. He adjusted his glasses. "I will think of a solution to this problem forthwith."

He got out his Questions Notebook and started writing.

Later we played Scrabble. Of course Kyle won.

In Portland, after I left Montana, I was depressed and a wreck. I had fallen into a pit where I could hardly move, hardly breathe. I thought I was having a nervous breakdown. My chest was tight, my heart raced, and I had trouble swallowing. I felt as if I was choking. All anxiety crap.

Working at Carter's restaurant ended up being my salvation in that it forced me out of my sleeping bag/coffin and out of the apartment in which I was still sleeping on the floor. Carter's restaurant was fast, steamy, all encompassing. Cooking started to heal me, as it had so many other times in my life. Chopping, slicing, sautéing, mixing, stirring, blending, pouring, making food look like art, it took me away from Jace and from a future that seemed hopeless and black.

Annabelle, Lucy, and Stephi lived across the hallway. Annabelle was sixty-one, a nurse in the neonatal unit at the local hospital. She was raising her grandchildren, Stephi and Lucy. Stephi was four and Lucy was five. They had been living with Annabelle for about two weeks by the time I moved in. They were quiet, reserved. They didn't act like normal kids. Both of them had odd, circular scars on their arms that I would later learn were cigarette burns. Stephi had a scar on her left temple, and Lucy had a long scar near her collarbone.

They scared easily. They halfway hid behind Annabelle when we said hello. They did not smile or laugh or jump around. Their blond curls were always brushed, but they were way too thin, their chocolate brown eyes huge and scared.

Annabelle had white hair and a young face. She was friendly, competent, welcoming. I was too withdrawn to make friends with anyone at first, but one night, about four months after I moved in, I met Annabelle in the hallway. We started chatting and she invited me in. She showed me the sweaters she was knitting for the girls. She told me that her daughter and her daughter's husband were drug addicts, in jail, and she was raising the girls. Stephi woke up screaming, followed by Lucy.

"They have nightmares," Annabelle told me, hugging the girls on her lap as they screamed, then cried, then whimpered. I started chatting with the girls when they calmed down, and soon they were on my lap and I read them stories until they fell back asleep.

In the weeks that followed, Annabelle told me how the girls got the scars, the ones I could see and the ones I couldn't, and what else had happened to them when they were in the care of their mother and father.

Annabelle and I became close friends. She was irreverent, hilarious, super smart. The girls grew to love me and I them. They were a second family.

Then something happened to one member of the family, and grief hit like a freight train.

* * *

My pipes froze. My grandma had to go to the hospital because of a urinary tract infection that hit her kidneys. My mother's patients who wanted to see Mrs. Gisela, and get her homespun medical and "natural healing" advice, were particularly upset. Word got out, and meals and desserts were brought to the clinic and to the farmhouse for "Mrs. Gisela and her urinary tract infection," and by the way, will she be healthy enough to be at my appointment on Wednesday, and if not I need to reschedule.

Stephi sprained her arm when she jumped out of a tree, pretending to be "Rock Monster." She was holding rocks in both hands when she jumped. Lucy had a meltdown because of things she remembered in foster care in Idaho and California when she and Stephi were taken from their parents. Chloe called, ecstatic, because Kyle won the school's spelling contest. "He studies dictionaries. He enjoys it. He is so bizarre. I love that freaky kid and his Questions Notebook."

My mother needed me to go with her to pick up a patient out in the country, because the woman was stubborn and said she would come only if I brought her my croissants. She told my mother, "Olivia makes them light and fluffy at Larry's Diner, best croissants ever, and my grandma was French, the old witch, so I know a warm, correctly baked croissant when I taste it."

Some weeks are not very easy, but they can always get worse, that's what I told myself, at least.

Tuesday my attorney called. The week became worse.

Wednesday night I couldn't sleep because I was worrying about what my attorney said. I wandered out to my back deck and saw my grandma in the gazebo. I stayed in the shadows. She was wearing her coat, boots, and blue gladiola scarf. She smiled and tilted her head back toward the moon, raised her hand, and waved to her family on the other side of that endless, dark Montana sky.

* * *

"Aunt Olivia," Lucy said Thursday night, when I was tucking her and Stephi into bed. "Today on the bus Charlie said that his mom said that you're married to Mr. Giant."

Charlie Zimmerman. His mother was Grace Zimmerman, born Grace O'Shea, a longtime, funny friend who came into the restaurant last week to give me a hug and invite me to lunch.

When Grace and I were in high school, at a beer bong party before a choir concert she got so drunk that she fell off the risers in the gym and onto her butt. She climbed back up with my and Chloe's help, then swayed drunkenly, side to side, to the very serious song we were singing in three-part harmony, hands floating in the air above her head like birds, eyes closed. She belted out, "La, la, la! Bong, bong, bong."

I laughed so hard I wet my pants under my red choir gown. Chloe couldn't even sing, because her laughter zapped the words. She stood and snorted, which made me laugh harder. Grace was suspended. Her father is a minister. Praise be to God, it didn't go over well at her house that night.

"Yep," Stephi said. "Charlie said that Mr. Giant is your husband. We said, 'No, he's not.' But are you?"

Why didn't I tell them earlier about Mr. Giant? What was wrong with me? It's a small town. I grew up here. Everyone knew. I plucked at my white, lacy tunic that I'd bought in Guatemala and tapped my black cowgirl boots. It was Guatemala and Montana today for clothing.

"I like him," Lucy said, leaning toward me, her hands on my shoulders. "So it's okay if he's your husband. But our dad hit us on the butt. Does Mr. Giant hit?"

"Mr. Rivera would never hit. Ever." I wanted to hit their jailbird father. "Yes, Jace is my husband."

Lucy's brows scrunched together, then she pointed her finger up. "If he's your husband, why don't we all live together?"

"Because Jace and I had some problems. And we're separated."

"What problems?" Stephi said, wrapping her blue unicorn

nightshirt around her knees. "When I had a problem with Stevie B. the other day, I told him he was a brat." She frowned. "That made him cry. So I drew him a picture of a tiger with a smiley face sitting on some pink rocks, and then he stopped crying. That was nice, right, Aunt Olivia?"

"It was."

"Mr. Giant told us that he has two dogs," Lucy said, her face hopeful. "Their names are Snickers and Garmin. Does that mean his dogs are our dogs if he's your husband?"

Yay! They could have dogs! They liked dogs! Jace had gotten Snickers and Garmin after I left. The two dogs wandered onto his property, half dead, half frozen, that winter. He took them in.

"No, it doesn't mean the dogs are yours."

"Are you sure?" Lucy was quite skeptical. "If he's your husband, don't you get to share the pets?"

"What about the cat, K.C.?" Stephi said, still hopeful. Maybe they could have a cat! They liked cats, too! "Is the cat ours?"

"No."

"This doesn't make sense," Stephi said, shaking her head. "Not at all."

The girls weren't happy. This was a disaster! I had a husband but they couldn't have his dogs or his cat!

"I know!" Stephi waved both hands. "I have it! Mr. Giant should live here and then bring the dogs and cat with him!"

Perfect solution!

"Yes!" Lucy said. "Smart idea, Stephi. You're smart." She hugged her sister, and Stephi hugged her back.

"I like dogs. I like cats," Stephi said. "I like that Mr. Giant, too."

"Me too," Lucy said, bopping on the bed. "If our real dad came and got mad at us, then Mr. Giant could tell him, 'No. Stop yelling. Stop throwing things. Stop punching holes in the walls. Stop getting drunk and mean.' " She stopped bopping and crouched down to go eye-to-eye with me. "That's right, right, Aunt Olivia? He would do that?"

"Yes, that's right."

"Do you know what drunk means, Aunt Olivia?"

"Yes, I do." I wanted to smash their drunken father. And their mother.

Lucy's eyes grew huge. "Do you think he would tell our real dad not to do that drunk stuff?"

"I know he would do that, but remember I told you that your real dad is going to be in jail for a long time."

"I know, but he will get out and then he could come here and do that," Lucy said, her face crumbling. "I didn't like it when he was mad."

"Me either," Stephi said, snuggling into me. "It was scary."

Maybe I would use their father for target practice.

"So let's invite Mr. Giant to come and live with us with the dogs and the kitty cat!" Lucy said, her finger pointed in the air again.

"I'll write him a letter," Stephi said. "It'll be like an invitation. Like some of the girls in my class got an invitation to Ella's birthday party but I didn't." Her face fell.

I hated to do this. They were so excited. "Girls, Mr. Giant is not going to stay here."

"Why? There's room!" Stephi said. "If he's your husband, then you sleep in the same bed. Your bed is plenty big!"

"Because we're not living together right now. He lives on his ranch and he has a lot of work to do there and I have a new job and, like I said, we had problems."

"If you have problems, say sorry, Aunt Olivia. And tell Mr. Giant to say sorry and then give each other a hug," Stephi said.

"That's what me and Stephi do," Lucy said. "Like this." And they hugged each other and smiled encouragingly at me.

"You can do it, Aunt Olivia!" Stephi said. "Just say sorry."

"And hug him!" Lucy said.

I smiled, hugged them, and tucked them into bed.

"I can't wait until the dogs and kitty cat come and live here!" Lucy said.

I went to bed that night with a cold washcloth on my head.

First I thought about what the girls said about having Jace live with us.

Then I thought about Jace.

His smile.

His body.

Then I thought about him naked, in this bed.

Next I thought about why we were separated and why it wouldn't work to get back together because we had an unsolvable problem between us.

Then I couldn't sleep.

My mother picked up the girls from school and took them to the clinic. Over dinner that night they told me all about strange diseases. I could tell that diseases thrilled them. Yep. They might be doctors.

Chapter 7

~

After college I traveled and worked and sampled different types of sweet, sour, spicy, and strange food for three years. I loved cooking, loved traveling, and wanted to experience both.

I traipsed all over western Europe, Turkey, India, Thailand, Laos, and Cambodia, then spent a few months in China and Japan. I worked my way through. I had wanderlust, I had cooking lust. I tasted food completely outside of my experience. My mouth about exploded. I learned about the culture and the people. I tasted the spices, the sauces, the fruits, the meats, the treats.

After the three years, despite my mother's grave disappointment that I wasn't going to become a doctor, I applied to culinary school. I was accepted at a respected school in Portland, Oregon. Two-year program. At the end of it, I was hired at an expensive restaurant in town where I'd done an internship. I loved it. Loved the head chef, Lucinda, loved how we worked together and tried new things. It was on a month-long sabbatical when I returned to Montana that I met Jace at a bar in Kalulell.

The bar was pure Montana. Cowboys and cowgirls. Ranchers and farmers. Doctors and teachers and nurses and motorcycle riders and rebels and intellectuals.

I knew who Jace Rivera was. Everyone knew him. He was two years ahead of me in school, but he was the athlete, he was the student body president, he had all the friends, and the girls loved him. His grandfather had come from Mexico, worked in the mines, then bought land, and kept expanding as his cattle ranch became more successful. Ricardo Rivera married a local girl, Eleanor, and they had Jace's father, Antonio. Antonio married a friend of my mother's, whose name was Clarissa. The ranch stayed in the family. It was now Jace's responsibility.

In high school, Chloe and I played sports hard, we played to win, and we often got in trouble for one prank or another or general wildness. We were outgoing, but I remember being too shy to talk to Jace Rivera. He said hello now and then, and smiled at me, and I smiled back. Everyone knew that Jace was friendly, unless you were a jerk or you were picking on someone, and then there were a few fights that Jace won, and the bully shut up and backed down.

I couldn't believe he remembered me when I saw him in the bar. He introduced himself, and said, "We went to high school together. I remember when you and Chloe made cards that everyone held up at a basketball game that spelled out, 'Whip Their Butts.'"

I laughed and said, "That would be us, practicing our literary skills."

"I also remember when you and Chloe made posters about Bring Your Pet to School Day, which was the next day."

"Ah, yes. We had Lilly and Mr. Bud back then. They missed us when we were at school."

"I brought both my dogs, Rex and Amanda." He smiled. The school had been filled with pets. The principal nearly had a coronary. "And there was also that epic prank with the cow."

"She was a calm cow and wanted to hang out in the school cafeteria and protest the use of meat." I smiled back. "I know who you are, too, Jace." And that was it. We talked and laughed and then danced until two in the morning. I saw him the next day, and the next. Date four we were in bed together at his home, his parents, Antonio and Clarissa, happily retired in California.

We fell in love, so hard, so fast, so fun. We were engaged, we were married on my grandparents' property, in front of the river. Jace's parents were welcoming and happy about the marriage. They knew my mother and grandparents and were friends with all three of them. Jace had agreed that having six kids would be a "fine number. Not enough for a football team, but definitely a basketball team with one to spare."

We used birth control at first. Jace had his family's ranch, and tons of cattle, but decided we should turn part of it into a vacation destination place for families. He had a trusted foreman, Daniel LeSalle, to run the ranch, and this would be a new business, our business.

Families could come and ride horses, hike, fish, boat, ski, snowshoe, play horseshoes, and hang out at the lake. They would stay in private cabins, eat in a dining hall, and there would be sing-alongs at night with guitars and ukuleles, and campfires. There would be a game room with pool and Ping-Pong and board games. We would have excellent food—which is where I came in. The town of Kalulell would attract people, too, as would the annual winter jump into the icy lake, our Bach festival, and a three-day country rock concert.

We planned and constructed and worked and worked and we launched Martindale Ranch and it was a success. Jace had insisted that we call our new venture Martindale Ranch. As a surprise he had a MARTINDALE RANCH wooden sign made to hang from two posts at the entrance. I was flattered, and I showed him how much in bed that night. He said he was going to name our ranch Martindale Ranch every day so he could have the same treat with me again and again.

We had a couple of write-ups in major magazines, and we were soon up and growing. One thing people especially loved was the food. I was delighted. Thrilled. So was Jace. I put meal photos up on a special section of the website called "Olivia's Creations," and I would throw in a recipe now and then.

I cooked. Jace handled the business end of it, the books, marketing, hiring. We greeted all of the guests, made friends, spent time talking with them.

We worked all the time. We loved it. Loved each other.

And then disaster struck too often, and I saw no way out, and I lost my ever lovin' mind.

* * *

"Olivia, phone call." Dinah handed me the restaurant's phone. She had recently cut off the green ends and dyed her hair light pink.

"Hello?" I was making three types of salads—Chinese with scallions and mandarin oranges, chicken Caesar with home-made focaccia croutons, and a vegetable blend with Italian seasoning. We had had more customers than expected, which was encouraging, but I was wiped out.

"Hi, Olivia," Jace said. "I have the girls."

"What?"

"I have the girls."

"What do you mean?" My hand froze above a bowl of chopped vegetables. "They're in school."

"The office called and said they couldn't get ahold of you. The girls are sick . . . no, no, don't worry. I think they have colds. In fact"—he paused, and I could hear the girls chatting and giggling in the background—"they may have already made a miraculous recovery."

"I . . . I . . ." This was so confusing. I dug my phone out of my pocket. Shoot. It was dead. "The school is supposed to call me, then Chloe, then my mother or my grandma when this happens."

"The girls told Sheryl Lalonski to call me as I am your husband."

"Ah. Oh. Ah."

"Sheryl called and said she was so happy we were back together again, and it was the best news she'd had in a long time, and she'd called her parents and told them, and her parents and their best friends, Bud and Alice Jacobi, who were all playing pinochle together, send us their best."

I groaned. Now it was all over town. I could see Stephi's and Lucy's excited faces in my mind. They were probably jumping up and down thinking of a new dad and two new dogs named Garmin and Snickers and a cat named K.C. They would have pets! "Where are you?"

"Your house. Your grandma came by and let us in."

My grandma. Not surprising. The traitor. "I'm coming. I'm almost done with my shift. Thank you, Jace."

"No rush, and you're welcome. My pleasure."

I finished my shift in twenty minutes, then I tried to clean up in the restaurant's bathroom. I unwound my hair, brushed it, washed my face, washed my pits, brushed my teeth—yes, I carry a toothbrush in my bag—put on lotion that smelled like roses that I keep in my bag to hide my usual odor of onions and garlic with a side of meat thrown in, and put on mascara and lipstick. I studied my green cat eyes staring back at me. They looked worried.

I could do nothing about my shirt, which had a marinara stain on it, but luckily my apron had caught most of the mess.

I opened the door.

Dinah said, "Ooh-la-la, Olivia!"

And Justin said, "That's a transformation."

And Earl said, "You look real nice, Olivia."

Larry said, "Got a date?" and leered and did the head-to-toe thing he does that makes me sick.

"Aunt Olivia said that you wouldn't let our real dad yell at us or throw things or punch holes in the walls," Stephi said. "Is that true?"

Thunder. That was the word I thought of when I saw Jace's reaction to what Stephi said. *Thunder.*

I had arrived at my log cabin to find the "sick" girls dancing around the family room holding hands. Stephi was wearing a frog outfit from last Halloween and a cowgirl hat, and Lucy was wearing a dress made from a paper bag that she had decorated herself. On her head she wore a red ski hat with a white owl on top. They were clearly not sick. They were, however, having a fine time with Jace.

"That is true, Stephi." Jace laced his fingers together on the dining room table where we were having Cockadoodle Sugar

Cream cookies and milk. "No man, your father or not, will yell at you, throw things, or punch the walls when I am with you. Ever."

"It was scary." Lucy munched her cookie. Her white owl tipped forward.

"Yeah," Stephi said. She wielded her cookie in the air as if she was swinging a hammer. "And I didn't like Mommy and Daddy's friends. That's not nice to say, but I didn't. They were mean."

"They put needles in their arms," Lucy said, pointing to the inside of her arm. "I hate needles."

I felt slightly ill. Lucy and Stephi's stories came out at odd times. They talked about what they went through, my insides would shrivel, they would cry and need a hug, then they would ask for strawberry pancakes or to go to the park so they could slide down the slide, and they were done talking about it.

"The friends sometimes tried to come in our bedroom at night," Lucy whispered to Jace. "They tried to sneak in, like quiet mice, but me and Stephi put the small white dresser in front of the door. They were bad."

"Bad mens," Stephi said.

"But we had two mice friends," Lucy said.

"Yep!" Stephi said, pushing her cowgirl hat back on her mound of blond curls. "They came out every night and said 'Squeak, squeak.' "

More thunder. "I'm sorry that happened to you," Jace said. "They were bad people."

"One man told us when we went to the kitchen to get food that we had to eat cat food because we were cats and he had eaten everything else," Stephi said.

"And we did a few times, but cat food isn't for kids and it didn't taste good."

Stephi nodded in agreement. "It was yucky."

I had heard this. Jace hadn't. I thought his jaw might snap, he was clenching down so tight.

"And also, Mommy hit Daddy. And Daddy hit Mommy," Stephi said. She sniffled. "Are you going to hit our aunt Olivia?"

"No," Jace said. "I have never, and will never, hit your aunt Olivia. I have never hit a woman in my life."

"Do you hit kids?"

"Never."

Lord. I thought the man might explode.

"We had rats in our room one time. Big ones. They tried to bite our toes." Stephi wrapped her hands around Lucy's feet. "I had to go like this to Lucy."

"We don't like rats. They're scary," Lucy said.

"When we see rats, we scream," Stephi said. "I have rats in my nightmares. That's when I wet the bed."

"And fleas bit, too. We had bites from the itty-bitty fleas," Lucy said. "They itched. We called them biters."

"Kids at school called me Flea Bite. Like it was my name. That's not nice, is it, Mr. Giant?"

"That's extremely mean," Jace said. "They won't call you that here, Stephi."

"One kid called me Dirty Girl." Lucy blinked those huge brown eyes. "Mr. Giant, do you think I'm dirty?"

"No," Jace said. "You are very clean and pretty. More important, I think you have a lot of brains."

She giggled. "You only have one brain."

"I think you two have a lot of brains." Jace smiled, but in it I could see the strain of what he'd heard. He was nauseated by it, as I was. "You're smart. You're tough, too."

"Do you want to play Candy Land, Mr. Giant?"

"I was hoping you would ask."

And they did. We all did. Candy Land drives me crazy. But it was fun with a gentle giant beside me.

"How does it feel to be back, Olivia?"

The girls were in bed. They sleep in the same bed because they get scared at night and have screaming night terrors about things they went through. They had asked Jace to tuck them in and read them stories. They had taken to Jace quickly, which was interesting, and endearing, because they don't trust men. They held his hands until they went to sleep.

"How does it feel?" It feels like I'm sinking. It feels like I'm in danger of throwing myself at you, Jace. It feels like my heart might die of pain. I'm petrified to divorce you, but we have an unsolvable problem, and you wouldn't want to be married to me again anyhow, I mean, who would, to a woman who did what I did to you? Seeing you and that delicious body in your jeans and white thermal shirt and cowboy boots is turning me on. And I'm broke and I might not be able to be the girls' mother for much longer. Other than that, I'm fine and dandy. "It feels fine."

"How's the job?" We were on the couch together, in front of the fire that Jace lit. So close. I had propped a window open so we could hear the Telena River and the wind swooshing through the trees.

"The job is fine." The job was miserable with Larry there. Each day worse. He was condescending and creepy. A man who wanted to control women with barbs and put-downs, disrespect and leers. Last week I'd had it and I wielded a spatula like a weapon as I ordered him out of the kitchen.

"Working for Larry is fine?" He didn't believe it.

"What do you want me to say, Jace? He's a foul-mouthed, knuckle-scraping, whiskey-gargling caveman. But it's a job and I like cooking."

"I still need a chef. I have a temporary one right now. She's pregnant with twins. She's leaving soon."

"No."

"Why not, Olivia?"

"Jace, I'm not working for you again." Why did he have to be so tempting? Why did he have to make my heart cry? I had never been able to stop missing him even after two years. You can't stop missing someone you are still in love with. I knew that, I did.

"What are you talking about? You never worked *for* me. We always worked together. We built Martindale Ranch together, and you should have cashed that check I recently sent you."

I waved a hand, as in "Forget about it, Jace." "That was kind, Jace, but no."

"I'm not being kind. I'm being truthful. We planned it together down to the last deck on the last guest cabin. You cooked our way into excellence. If there weren't cinnamon rolls in the morning, I thought the clients were going to revolt. People arrived a half hour early to dinner. You were constantly asked for your recipes. My tech guy said the most popular part of our website was where you put photos and recipes of the meals you cooked. Come back to the ranch, Olivia. I need you."

"No, but thanks." I need you, too. I so need you. But you need someone else, you need something else, and I am not being an annoying and throat-gagging martyr, it is flat-out true.

One day we'd divorce and then I'd get to see Jace dating someone. Now wouldn't that knock me off my feet and into the pits of jealous ex-wife hell? Talk about a rambling rage. I'd probably start stalking the woman, then I'd be arrested, and that would be embarrassing, and I might have to go to jail, and what would happen to Stephi and Lucy? I'd have to wear orange and I'd look like a giant, temper-tantrum-throwing pumpkin. All for stalking Jace's new wife.

"Please."

"Jace, I'm not here to work for you . . . or with you again. I'm here for a while, then I'll be moving back to Portland." Would I? Yes. No. Maybe. When it felt safe. When I knew the girls would be safe. How could I even live here with Jace around? I couldn't. Could I?

"Why are you here, Olivia? The truth."

I could not tell him the truth yet. I couldn't tell him about the calls. About the threat. "I'm here because I needed a change, and the girls needed a change after their grandma died."

"Nice try. The truth."

"How about another time?"

"Was it a man?"

"No." Never. How could I ever be in love with anyone else besides Jace?

He studied me. I knew he was evaluating the truthfulness of my answer.

"We're separated, Olivia. You can tell me. In fact, I'd like to know."

"You would be okay with it? If I left Portland because of a bad experience with a man?"

"No. I wouldn't be okay with it at all." His face grew hard. He was not happy. "Not at all. Thinking of you being with another man is enough to make me want to hit something. Probably him. It would be like a nightmare that was not a nightmare and my real life."

"Jace, there wasn't another man." Not even close. I had been asked out by several men but had not felt the slightest inclination to go on a date. "None."

He knew I was telling the truth, because he knew me. I could tell he was . . . relieved. Relieved enough to get a little emotional and hang his head, his hands clasped together. That about undid me. Seeing Jace, after all I'd done to him, the pain I'd caused him, getting misty eyed because I told him there had been no other men made me feel all weepy.

"Never." I put my hand out and he held it, then brought it to his lips. He put his other hand on my cheek.

I pulled away before I ripped off his shirt and pulled down his pants. I knew what was underneath those pants . . .

He was hot.

I was not.

I heard the door shut quietly behind him when he left.

I checked my phone on a break at work and felt ill.

The e-mail from my attorney that I had been expecting was bad. Hit me in the face bad.

Oh, my Lord, so bad.

I was pretty sure I stopped breathing for a couple of hours.

On Friday afternoon Larry walked in drunk. This was not the first time he'd had too much to drink. He became more slovenly as the day went on. The staff and I were having a meeting at the time, short and quick. I was discussing menu items, new desserts I was adding, listening to everyone's questions and comments, serving samples.

"Look at this." Larry wobbled in, his stomach coming first. He slammed the newspaper on the center island counter. "It's a review of my restaurant." He smiled and burped, then pounded his chest with a closed fist. "Ha! This rag talks about how things have turned around here, the food is mouth smacking, makes 'em salivate, the atmosphere is 'pure Montana.' What do they mean, atmosphere? This ain't outer space, but whatever. This is freakin' awesome. Glad we worked on those recipes together, Olivia. People are loving the grub."

"We didn't work on them together. I told you what I was going to cook and I made up a new menu."

He waved his hand, as if I were a fly. "We did them together. Ha-ha." He laughed.

Working for Larry was getting harder and harder. He smirked at me. He was gross. He made comments about porn, "wild women, he liked them that way best," how he was a star football player in high school, as if anyone would even mildly care about that, and his new girlfriend, which made me want to dump cracked eggs over his head. "Jealous?" he asked me once.

"Of what?"

"I've got a girlfriend."

"Larry, why would I care?"

"She's not as hot as you—"

I whipped around. "Do not ever talk to me like that."

He put his palms out, a faux innocent expression on his face. So manipulative. "What do you mean? You don't want to be told you're hot?"

"No. Never. It's disgusting. If you do one more obnoxious thing, Larry, I'm calling an attorney and I will sue you for sexual harassment."

"None of that is going on here, darling." I could tell it caught his attention, though. "And watch your mouth. I know you got two kids and you need this job. Not many cooks jobs open in Kalulell."

"One more word." I put my fingers in the shape of a gun and I fired it at him and said, "Boom." He is so stupid he actually flinched. Then he lumbered out, stomach first.

I lay back in my bed at two in the morning on a snowy night.

My financial situation was precarious. I was not making enough money at Larry's. My mother's plea that I stop being "unreasonable and difficult" and quit paying rent fell on my deaf ears. I am a grown-ass woman and I will pay rent. I paid my attorney, I paid the hospital. I bought food with coupons and brought leftovers home from Larry's sometimes, as we all did at the restaurant.

The money math wasn't working. I had eight dollars in my checking account.

I have always wanted to write a cookbook. I wanted to include all the recipes I used at Martindale Ranch.

But there were a million cookbooks on the market. How would mine stand out so I could actually make money off of it? It wouldn't. I don't think a publishing house would want it. I'm not famous. I don't have a following. To put it together myself would be expensive, plus, who would buy it?

Stop with the pity party, I told myself. *You're making me nauseated.*

But at the moment I had a critical problem: Eight dollars.

I am pathetic.

I am desperate.

I am poor. I am racking up my credit card.

Something would have to change.

Immediately.

A week later, Kyle came by. He knocked three times. He had something with him, wrapped in brown paper.

"Kyle, come on in." I hugged him, and he allowed it, then he patted my back three times. He looked into my eyes for about two seconds, then away.

"Good evening, Aunt Olivia. I have come to visit. Mother

says it's best to be invited, but you said to come by at any time, so I have taken your invitation literally."

"I'm so happy to see you, Kyle. I've made chicken cacciatore for dinner. It'll be ready in about thirty minutes. Have dinner with us."

The girls raced out. "Hi, Kyle!" they shouted. They loved Kyle. He played games with them for hours sometimes. Candy Land is enough to make me scream. You're almost at the end, and no. A card sends your sorry self back down the rainbow trail. I've even stopped liking gumdrops because of that game. But Kyle will play it with them, while discussing art or science, of course.

"Kyle," Lucy said, pointing at her chest. "Look. I'm wearing a T-shirt with a spider on it. Tarantula."

"Tarantulas," Kyle said. "Arachnids. They belong to a spider family, the *Theraphosidae*. They are hairy. They can be approximately nine millimeters as measured, or they can grow as large as an average sized human head. Eight legs. Two parts to their bodies: A tarantula has a prosoma and a opisthosoma—"

"They bite!" Lucy said. "Like this." She showed him her teeth. "Sharp teeth!"

Stephi jumped up and down. "I made a cow today at school." She held up her drawing, waved it around, and gave it to him. Kyle studied Stephi's drawing with complete seriousness. He opened his mouth twice to speak, peered down at Stephi through his glasses, then held whatever he was going to say. Finally he said, "The cow's face is symmetrical. The cow's body is the appropriate color, with the exception of the green stripes and pink tulips. I like the cow's smile and his rock collection by his hooves, and I like the hat with the pink flowers. You have personified a cow. This is an artistic accomplishment, Stephi."

She jumped up and down again. "Thanks!"

"What's in the package, Kyle?" Lucy said. "Is it a surprise?"

Kyle set it down on the dining room table, and we crowded around. "I have painted your portraits. I took the liberty of using paints so as to fully capture your coloring."

"You have?" I said. *He painted their portraits?*

"You painted pictures of us?" Stephi said, surprised. Lucy was equally surprised.

"Yes."

"Yaaay!" Stephi and Lucy clapped.

Kyle took his glasses off, then put them back on, his hands flapped, then settled. "During our last visit, Stephi and Lucy, you both said that two unkind girls at school suggested that you were not attractive. I have had the same said of me. Your tears indicated to me that you were upset. This was unfortunate, so after writing the incident down in my Questions Notebook, I went home and discussed this with Mother. Mother said, 'What can you do to make those two girls feel better after what those mean-ass girls said, Smart One?' Her words, not mine. I endeavor not to swear. I thought of what I could do to remedy this situation and reduce the emotional suffering."

"I don't know what you're talking about," Lucy said, pointing her finger in the air, "but okay!"

"I don't understand you right now, Kyle," Stephi said, shaking her head. "But I want to see the paintings!" She jumped up and down again, like a spring. "Cow wants to see it, too." She held up the cow drawing. "Moo!"

"Kyle, this is so kind of you." What a thoughtful young man.

He seemed confused. "I have completed this task so that I can share with Stephi and Lucy an accurate picture of their appearance. Then they will be able to see for themselves that the unkind girls are wrong in their assessment. Sometimes people are not truthful or make irrational statements. This is one of those times, so their opinions must be disregarded. Due to Lucy and Stephi being young, Mother told me that disregarding a false declaration would present some intellectual challenges. Therefore, the paintings should address this issue and provide a positive outcome."

"You're confusing," Stephi said, shaking her head again. "Want a rock?"

"I don't get it. That wasn't in English," Lucy said. "Can we see the paintings, Kyle?"

"These will be our most treasured works of art, Kyle," I said. "I know it."

"Thank you for your confidence, Aunt Olivia." His hands flapped at his sides. Then stopped. "I am feeling some anxiety about the result. Mother told me that the background of the pictures should be a place that Lucy and Stephi enjoy, hence this log cabin with the red door, the sun weather vane, and great granddad's lasso. I added the Dove Mountains and the Telena River in the background for both. Further, I inquired of Lucy and Stephi, individually, what their favorite flower was and included each."

"I understand that part," Stephi said. "I told you it was tulips!"

"And my favorite flowers," Lucy said, "are roses."

"Correct," Kyle said. He took the brown paper off. The paintings had been framed by my sister.

Lord almighty. Lord. Almighty.

The paintings were about twenty-four by eighteen inches, and they were exquisite. The girls were beautiful. Huge smiles, long blond curls blowing slightly in the wind, the log cabin in back of them, the mountains and river beyond that. Stephi was holding a bouquet of red, purple, and yellow tulips in front of her, her red headband on, and Lucy was holding wild red roses, her ponytail high on her head with a pink ribbon.

They were simply stunning.

"Wow," the girls said. "Wow."

Stephi pointed at her picture, her voice hardly above a whisper. "Do I look like that, Kyle?"

"Yes. It is an exact portrait."

"And I look like that, Kyle?" Lucy said, turning to him. "That pretty?"

"Yes. As I said, this is an exact portrait. I simply painted you and added the flowers. Now that you have an accurate picture of your appearance, hopefully you will realize that the girls at school have presented you with a falsehood."

"Kyle." I wiped away tears.

He became alarmed, his face tightening. "I can't read your

expression when you cry, Aunt Olivia. In fact, Mother said I can't read anyone's expression accurately, hence I continue to work on this deficiency with her. Have the paintings caused you sadness? Do you not like them?"

"I love them! They're happy tears, Kyle."

The girls hugged him tight. "I love them, too, Kyle! I love you, Kyle!"

And Lucy said, "Kaila is stupid."

"Megan is mean," Stephi said.

"Kyle, they are perfect. You are a talented artist. Thank you so much. We'll have to hang them up immediately."

He nodded. "I am happy that you're pleased." He turned to the girls. "Kids have been mean, aggressive, and physically hurtful to me in the past, and it's best to know that when they are mean, they are usually telling untruths. Sometimes it is appropriate to explain to them that what they're saying is false or unsubstantiated. Sometimes, depending on how many kids are there at one time, it's best not to say anything at all. I must leave and return home." He checked his watch. "I am now four minutes late."

"But what about dinner and Chutes and Ladders?" Stephi whined.

"Yes, I want to play Chutes and Ladders with you," Lucy said.

He paused. "I can have dinner and play one game of Chutes and Ladders, then I will stay up approximately one hour and thirty minutes later tonight in order to complete Tuesday's study of Michelangelo. Tuesday is also vacuuming night."

We ate while they played Chutes and Ladders, then Kyle left under a chorus of thank-yous and good-bye hugs. He allowed the hugs, his eyes skittering away from ours, then left.

"I love Kyle," Stephi said.

"He's nice and weird," Lucy said.

"Yes. Nice and weird," Stephi agreed. "I love my painting! I'm not ugly!"

"And I don't have a turnip nose," Lucy said, pointing to the nose on the painting. "See?"

*   *   *

"We're going out to see Belinda Bianchi today, Rebel Child," my mother told me.

It was Saturday afternoon. The girls were with my grandma. She wanted to teach them how to make her grandma Ida's apple chocolate trifle. The girls were thrilled. They almost pushed me out the door of the farmhouse and ran back in. They like cake and they like blood. What can I say?

I climbed into my mother's truck. She was on the phone with another doctor about one of their joint patients. "Now, you listen here, Shelby, with both ears. You know as well as I do that Skeeter Lyons is not a compliant patient. He's a son of a gun and he does his own thing, but you are not to treat him with the condescension that you did yesterday, that is not the way to get a patient better. Yes, I heard about your condescension from two nurses."

I lay my head back on the seat as she pulled out of the driveway. It's tiring being stressed out, and I was stressed out. I had gotten a call from the state telling me that my motion to adopt was still on hold. I called my attorney and had a meltdown. Apparently, the girls' mother, still in jail, had an attorney now, too. We were at legal war, and I sure wasn't confident that I'd win.

My mother drove through the snow, coming down harder every minute, through Kalulell, and out to the highway. My personal panic point with blizzards kicked in and my hands shook as I sipped coffee out of a mug. I was on anxiety overload.

"Young woman," my mother snapped to the doctor on the other end of the phone, "you may have a fancy-pants degree from a highfalutin university back east and a student loan the size of my horse's ass, but you have a lot to learn about people. You put on your thinking cap real quick and open your mind so you can better serve your patients. Patients come with all sorts of problems that are not simply physical and treatable with buckets full of medications and operations and extremely poor bedside manners from doctors like yourself.

"They have personalities, problems, and attitudes. You work *with* them. You don't shove your new drugs, your biases about their economic status and intellectual capabilities, and your cold analysis down their throats like bullets down a gun.

"I will call you on Monday, and I hope you'll have done some hard thinking about our mutual patient or you and I are going to butt heads like two bulls and everyone in this state knows who will win. You will work with me cooperatively on our patient, Skeeter, you will be compassionate toward him, and you will not use that patronizing tone of voice again, young woman."

My mother hung up and took a sip of her coffee, completely unfazed after telling someone off. No one messed with her patients. They had top-notch care, or you heard from my mother. And that went for everyone—from the patient who lived outside in a tent during summer and the richest bazillionaires from Silicon Valley who had vacation homes here and had been treated by her and Mrs. Gisela, "who understands the importance of natural healing."

I was with my mother at her clinic when she told one bazillionaire of a high-tech company, "You're rich, but you're stupid, Caleb," because he was making bad decisions that would eventually ruin his health. She told him what he had to change immediately, when to take his medications, and how this was going to go down for him in a bad way if he continued to be a noncompliant patient. "You get your head out of your colon now, young man."

He blinked at her, cowed, then said, "Next time I think I want to be treated by Mrs. Gisela. You're scary." My mother rolled her eyes and said she was going to treat him to a "scary knuckle sandwich" if he didn't follow her directions.

Which made her telling Shelby the doctor off all the more ironic.

"How is Belinda?" I asked.

"I'm concerned about her because she almost cut off her arm with her buzz saw. I forced her to stay for three nights in the hospital so I could keep an eye on her, but then she snuck out. Pulled the IV straight out of her arm, didn't bother to change, and walked out to her car in her hospital gown and boots. I have to make sure that it's not infected."

"So we're going out in a mini snowstorm because Belinda won't come to the clinic?"

"Belinda doesn't like to be away from her cats."

I had a long drink of coffee. I wished I'd added whiskey. "Will the cats be upset if she's gone long?"

"Apparently, yes. They have feelings."

I laughed and spit some coffee out, and my mother laughed, too. "Those darn cats."

We slid in the snow, the truck going to the right. "Dang," she said, when her coffee sloshed.

"We're going to get stuck," I said, my voice wobbling, as my mother straightened the truck back out. "I hope this doesn't turn into a blizzard."

"No, we're not, and no, it won't. Look out the window, Olivia," she said, with some impatience. "Does it look like a blizzard? No. You must overcome your fear of blizzards."

"No. I like my fear of blizzards." I kept drinking my coffee, even when we went sideways again when we turned onto Belinda's road. Belinda's shabby home, with a porch that seemed to be sliding off the house, came into view. "She's a cat hoarder, isn't she?"

"Yes. But I've been here before and, trust me, no cats have ever been treated so royally, so I don't need to call the humane society. Now, you respect those cats, Olivia."

We trudged up to Belinda's door in our thick hats and coats, the snow heavy, my mother carrying my granddad's black medical bag. Today she was wearing brown cowgirl boots with a white lace design on the front. "If we do get stuck going back into town," I said, "I hope you know I get the blue sleeping bag."

"Why don't you quit worrying, Olivia? Put some cement in your spine, some guts in your intestinal tract."

My mother keeps sleeping bags, hand warmers, extra jackets, food and water, flares, a shovel, chains, flashlights, etc., in the back of her truck. She also keeps wine. Says it'll warm the body up in a snowstorm. She does not mess around with the weather out here, neither do I, but she's not scared of it.

Belinda's home was a semi-shack. It was long and low, the

blue paint chipping off. Smoke was coming through a chimney that was missing bricks.

I turned my head to the left. "The house looks better if you tilt your head to the left."

"The house is better inside."

"I'll believe it when I see it." I gently tested the stairs of the porch before putting my full weight on them. My mother knocked and Belinda opened the door, scowling. Belinda was about seventy, could have been eighty. Maybe ninety. Hard to tell, and I forgot to ask my mother. White hair, ponytail. She was wearing a sweater with an embroidered black cat. She has a doctorate in history and used to teach at an Ivy League college.

"Hello, Belinda."

She scowled further. "Hello, Mary Beth, Hello, Olivia. You didn't bring Gisela? That's a shame. She knows all about herbs and how to heal the body naturally. But it's still a pleasure to see you both. It's right kind of you two to come all the way out in this snowstorm. It's almost a blizzard out there, isn't it?" She opened the door and stepped back. "I know you're here to check my arm, Mary Beth, and I'm glad of it. I might be having a small problem with it. However, the larger problem I have is that you made me stay in the hospital. The food was gross and awful.

"The doctors and nurses kept waking me up to check my arm, telling me I was lucky I wasn't dead, blah blah. Using all these medical terms." She scowled even more. "Then they started talking to me in a loud voice, as if I'm deaf. Do I seem deaf? No, I don't. So I shouted back at them, 'I'm not deaf, quit shouting.' I prepared us some lunch. Please sit down."

In we went. My mother had told me years ago that Belinda didn't mean to be so scowly. "It's her face," she told me. "It scowls. I've known her for four decades and it's always been like that."

Cats.

Everywhere. I sneezed. My mother discreetly opened a window. To Belinda's credit, her house was immaculate. My mother was right, the outside and inside were not comparable. The inside had been remodeled. The downstairs was one huge room. Down the hall it appeared there were three bedrooms. Couches with cats. Cat pillows, cat curtains, cat pictures. And everywhere those carpeted cat climbers.

I counted fourteen cats.

"Snuffles and Mr. Temper are in the back room having a nap. Belly and Crackers are talking in my bedroom. But come on in and meet everyone, Olivia, your mother has already met them. Here's Dr. D, and Tulip Rose, and Sir Franklin, and Sophia Loren, and Robert Redford, and the tabby there, that's Frizzy Bear . . ."

We were back in the truck in an hour, the snow coming down like a white blanket. Not a blizzard, but I didn't like it. Belinda had made us lasagna and hot bread and minestrone soup. We ate with only three cats on the table watching us. One was linked around my legs, and another in my mother's lap. At one point a cat jumped on my shoulders.

"Get down, Tiger Lilly!" Belinda swatted at her, scowling.

Belinda's arm was healing nicely. I examined my mother's work. Dang. She was awesome. My mother re-dressed her arm, gave Belinda more instructions about keeping still and made sure she was taking her medications. Belinda said, "I have all the help I need with my cats here. They're healing me." She leaned toward me. "Ruthie told me awhile back that she saw Jace with you at your grandparents' log cabin one night when she was cleaning her gun, so I thought you two got back together, and I was happy about that news. Sheryl Lalonski's parents told my cousin Rowe that you were a couple again, but then I heard you two were living separately from Alina Hines's second cousin, Torey, who lives out your way. I hope things work out for you two. He's a cat lover, in his heart, I can tell." She thumped her chest. "And so are you. Cat lovers should love together."

We got stuck in the snowstorm/blizzard at one point and had to get out of the truck and put on chains.

"Ha, I beat you, Mom." We always raced to see who could put the chains on faster.

"By one second."

At another point we hit ice and white-knuckled a 360-degree turn. "Whoa, horse," my mother said.

"Shoot." Panic point: Blizzard.

We had a hard time seeing the road, but we kept going, with my head out the window guiding my mother. A car had gone off the road into a ditch, and we used a chain to pull them back out. It was a grateful family from town. "Thank you, Mary Beth. Thank you, Olivia," the mother, Orelia, called out.

"I need to come in and see Mrs. Gisela for some advice on herbs to heal my stomach," the father, Morty, said to my mother. "Do you know her schedule for next week?"

"Glad you and Jace are back together!" Orelia shouted at me as they pulled away.

We let them head first back into town, trailing to make sure they got home safely.

Sometimes there is too much excitement when I'm with my mother.

I saw Jace's white fence on the way back down to town. It brought a deluge of memories. I peered up at the hill through the snow. Memories there, too, amidst the magical sunsets.

"Let's make soup," Chloe said. "I need soup with vegetables and broth to build up my hormones."

"Why do you need to build up your hormones?" I handed Chloe a cup of peppermint tea and a plate of tea biscuits dipped in chocolate and sat down with her at my granddad's dining room table. I ran a finger over a few marks and scratches. I remembered him telling me one time that he had sewn up a man who was attacked by a bear in 1955 right on this table. The man lived to 98. My granddad had also taken a bullet out of Sherm Alias's shoulder when he was shot by a cattle rustler right here, too.

"I think hormones running fast through your body gets the ya ya working at fast speed." Chloe dipped her biscuit in the tea. "I need the hormonal boost. I need to speed mine up. I think men can sense it."

"Fast hormones?"

"Yes. You should be chasing after hormones, too, because of your man, Jace. He's a hormone booster, I can tell."

"I'm not with Jace." Only in my daydreams.

My sister banged her fists together. "Not now. You could be soon, sister."

"I don't think so." I didn't want to talk about Jace. I'd talked to my grandma, mother, and Chloe about him since I returned, but it was emotional, there were no answers or solutions, and I didn't want to talk about him again. They had hugged me, and we'd made cakes to heal through Martindale Cake Therapy.

"Let's make a soup recipe out of Grandma's cookbook, Chloe. I saw a recipe in here the other day. Where was it?" I thumbed through the old, dry pages. "Ah. Here it is. Esther's Onion Soup. Munich, Germany, 1938." I went on the Internet to translate the recipe from German into English. "I love how Esther, our very own great-grandmother, made the recipes look so delicious with her drawings. See, she's drawn onions, salt and pepper shakers, and an apple that she used in the soup. Look at that daisy in the corner. The leaves are in the shapes of hearts, and she wrote Esther and Alexander."

"I have a hankering for this onion soup now."

"I wonder what caused that brown stain in the corner here."

"Hmm. I don't know. There are a lot of mysteries in this cookbook. The recipe calls for beef stock. Maybe it's the beef stock?"

I held the cookbook up, and salt fell out of the crease. "Wow. Do you think that was the salt she used?"

"Had to be. No one has used this cookbook besides us in decades."

I had to sit in wonder at that. Salt. From my great-grandma, Esther Gobenko. Right on my granddad's table. "I wonder what happened to Esther. I assumed she died in the concentration camps."

"Probably." Chloe's face was drawn. "She was Jewish. She

lived in Munich, Germany, and the date here is 1938. In fact, there are no recipes written by Esther or Ida after 1940, including the recipes that are taped onto the back pages."

"The Nazis got them."

"Probably."

Chloe and I sat in that unspeakable tragedy. Our own relatives, dying in concentration camps.

We looked at a few of Esther's other recipes, all written carefully, in German, or Yiddish, most with drawings of nature, leaves, herbs, or a garden.

"Let's get cooking," I said, pulling myself away from the horrors of Grandma's past.

"Bring it on, baby. I need to get rid of the sadness sitting on my shoulders from what happened to our relatives."

We made Great-Grandma Esther's Onion Soup.

We talked about Teddy, and how Chloe still missed him but was moving forward, and she said, "Olivia, I know you're hurting. I would be, too. It wasn't fair, what happened to you, but don't let that cowboy go."

We shed a few tears, we laughed, we added beef stock and apple and onions and salt and pepper, as Esther's recipe said to do.

Combine. Stir. Pour. Sprinkle. Slice. Shake. Sautée.

Cooking is healing.

That night we sat down altogether, my grandma, my mother, the girls, Chloe, Kyle, and me at the blue farmhouse. Chloe and I set the table with my grandma's china, a gift from my granddad's parents to her for their wedding. I hoped no one would come through the door needing to be laid flat and treated on the table as it would take us awhile to move the china. We made hot bread and a huge green salad and put both on the china platters.

We put Esther's Onion Soup in a tureen, then Chloe dished it out with a ladle. The first bowl went to Grandma. She was chatting with my mother about one of their patients who came in with an arrow stuck in his arm.

Grandma stopped in midsentence, caught her breath. She bent her head and smelled the soup. She closed her eyes. "That's my mother Esther's onion soup, isn't it?"

"Yes," I said, hoping we'd done the right thing. I was now deeply doubting myself. "We followed it exactly, down to the beer, the marjoram, and the homemade croutons."

My grandma lifted her spoon to her lips. She took a taste, held it in her mouth, closed her eyes. She put the spoon back in the bowl. She bent her head into both hands.

"Oh, man," Chloe whispered. "Grandma, I apologize. I am sorry."

"We didn't mean to hurt you," I said, anguished. "I'm sorry, Grandma."

"You only have to take three bites and if you still don't like it, Grandma Gisela," Lucy said, her brow furrowed with worry, "you don't have to eat it."

"It's okay, Grandma Gisela," Stephi said, leaning over the table toward her. "Spit it out."

Kyle took a bite. "Delicious. Onions. Butter. Flour for thickening. Chives. I am confused. Is there a problem I am unable to discern?"

"Mom?" my mom said to her mother. "Are you all right?" She picked up her wrist, took her pulse.

My grandma stared off into the distance, as if she wasn't with us in our cozy kitchen in the blue farmhouse, next to a kitchen island made from a fallen oak tree, in Montana, the snow lightly falling. Two tears rolled down her cheeks, then another two tears.

Kyle seemed distressed and started writing in his Questions Notebook.

Grandma picked up her cloth napkin and dabbed her cheeks. "It's perfect, Nutmeg and Cinnamon. Exactly as my mother used to make it. I can even taste the Emmental cheese she used." She smiled at both of us. "Thank you. You've brought my mother back to me through her soup." She turned to the kids. "My mother's name was Esther Gobenko. She was a lovely, strong, intelligent woman who went through terrible times, starting when she was little, in Odessa. She was brave. She was smart."

"What happened to her?" Lucy asked.

"Something sad happened to her," Grandma said.

She told us another part of her story. We forgot to eat Esther's onion soup. Horror always takes away the appetite.

Chapter 8

∽

July 1938
Munich, Germany
Esther Gobenko, great-grandmother of Olivia Martindale

The fire tore through the wall of their home. The black, churning smoke clogged her throat, her lungs, stealing her breath away.

Esther could hardly see, but she could hear screaming, yelling and she could hear the baby, Liev, crying in her parents' bedroom. Her brothers woke up beside her on their bed in front of the fireplace and clutched her in fear. Their father yelled at them, "Get out, get out now!" as he tried to run through the wall of fire to the bedroom. She grabbed her brothers and hauled them up. They were terrified, the flames leaping at their backs as the fire streaked across another wall.

"Run for the woods," their mother, Ida, ordered, yanking them toward the door as the fire grew, a monster, the sparks snapping, the roof starting to smolder. "Stay together. Hide. We will come for you. Go Esther, take your brothers. Go!"

Her brothers were hysterical, but the flames were spreading, the smoke burning, searing her flesh, her hair hot.

Their mother shoved them, hard, toward the door. "Now, now!"

Esther saw her father grab her mother, Ida, as she fought to get to the baby. To get little Liev, left behind in the flames. Horrified, she pulled her brothers through the door into the *pitch darkness of the night as the fire roared.*

In their socks they ran toward the forest, away from their burning home, the gunshots blasting through the village, and the screams. They ran and ran until they could run no more, the shouts of the neighbors fading, the shifting shadows of the trees towering above them. They were lost, cold, afraid of wild animals. They climbed into a log, holding each other—

Esther screamed, her eyes flying open.

Instead of the haunting dark forest and the inferno her home in Odessa had become, she saw her bedroom, the walls white, the bedspread white, her husband, Alexander, beside her, holding her, soothing her . . .

It was the same nightmare she always had. It never completely left. It had followed her from Odessa to Munich. Clawlike, it clutched her, as death had clutched Liev, the boy they never stopped missing.

"Shhh, honey, Esther, shhh. It's okay," Alexander soothed. "You're here. At home. In Munich. It's not Odessa, darling. Breathe. Here, drink some water. I filled your cup . . . there, there, let me hold it for you, you're shaking too much . . . Everything is okay, sweetheart."

She pushed back her thick brown hair, sweaty against her forehead, and tried to catch her breath. Esther saw her white nightstand with her white lace kerchief, a gift from her mother. She saw her crystal lamp, her blue wool coat flung over a chair. Alexander's yarmulke, his prayer shawl from his parents, and his prayer book were in the same place, as always. Esther pulled her hands together, her diamond wedding ring heavy on her finger. Alexander had bought her a new ring for their anniversary, sweet husband.

"I'm sorry, Alexander, I didn't mean to wake you."

"Hush, love. I understand, I do." He kissed her, and they made love, always that seemed to settle her down, to remind her that she was no longer living through a pogrom. Afterward he kissed her cheek and went back to sleep.

She and Alexander had come a long way from the poverty both their families had experienced in Odessa. They owned their home in Munich, three stories, on a side street, and a department store, Esther and Alexander's. It had been the most popular store in Munich, their sales high. They sold stylish, modern clothing for men, women, and children. They sold her father's purses, bags, and wallets in the store, and her mother's treats, from Ida's Bakery, in the café on the second floor. Esther advised Alexander on the store, but mostly she worked for her mother in the bakery. She so loved their pink-and-white building; their light, fluffy pastries; the breads and rolls they made.

Mostly, Esther loved baking cakes. Life went away, fear and anger and sadness. It was peaceful, soul enriching. She wanted to turn food into edible art. She loved blending the ingredients, pouring the batter into pans, the scent of the cakes as they cooked. She loved decorating, making each cake special, different, adding humor here and there. Why, the other day she added a real carrot to the middle of a carrot cake and everyone in her family—Alexander, Isaac, Gisela, and Renata—had loved it.

She should have felt safe in their three-story brick home in Munich, but she didn't. No Jew could feel safe.

Their children's lives, with their educations, their music and language lessons, were privileged. Isaac, Gisela, and Renata had had safe lives until the past few years. They hadn't known the pogroms she had known in Odessa as a little girl. She knew the pogroms haunted her mother, Ida, and her father, Boris, too.

The nightmares were coming more frequently now, and Esther knew why: The Nazis. Every day, life was worse for Jews. Esther felt the same danger, the same premonition of more danger to come, that she had felt in Odessa as a little girl. Their department store had been painted with the word Jude, as had their bakery, and her father's shop, Boris's Leather Goods. People were singing anti-Jewish songs and slogans, condoned by the press and the government. The Nazis shouted, "Heil Hitler," the SS terrorized their fellow German Jewish citizens, and the long red flag with the black swastika hanging from buildings flapped in the wind.

The sales in their bakery, their department store, and her father's leather goods were now poor. Their stores had been boy-

cotted by many people because they were Jewish. The Nazis were taking over Jewish businesses. All of their family members had had to register their property and assets with the Nazi government. They were told, as Jews, that they were no longer German citizens. They were all going through their savings, and they had little left.

The Nazis, over the years, had continued to add new anti-Semitic laws. Jews were now second-class citizens. Jews had lost jobs in government, in medicine, in law, in the army, and in education. They had lost jobs as journalists, in the theater, in music, in dance. Jewish students were being barred from school. Some Jews they knew had simply disappeared. Books were being burned. There was talk of a camp for Jews. A camp? A camp where they imprisoned and killed Jews? Surely that wasn't true? Other Jews had left the country altogether, leaving assets here they were not allowed to take.

She and Alexander had talked endlessly, as she had talked to her parents, and to her four brothers and their wives. They all knew that Hitler was a maniac but hoped he would soon be stopped, that other Germans would come to their senses. They hoped that this ugly tone, the threats, the violence, would stop. They thought that sanity would return. It hadn't.

Esther had wanted to leave years ago, but something deep inside her was still shocked. How could this happen again? There were so few voices standing up for the Jews. Millions more were standing up for Hitler, standing up for his hate, his divisiveness, his blame of Jews for all the ills of Germany. He stirred up fear and nationalism and appealed to ignorant people.

"Leave?" Alexander had said to her many times. "This is our home. We have businesses. Family." His father had had pneumonia and was still weak. His mother had had a stroke and was recovering. "It will get better," he told her. "We will wait. If not, we have the money in Switzerland. We can use that and leave at a moment's notice even if the Nazis take everything else."

Alexander and she would have to get both sets of parents out.

They could not, would not, leave them. Her father, Boris, would fight leaving, she knew that. He had run once, from the pogroms in Odessa, and said he would not run again. But her mother . . . Ida knew, she could feel the danger, as Esther could. Ida would agree to leave if Boris would, and if she knew all five of her children, and their families, would leave, too. She would not leave children behind again, dead or alive.

Sometimes, when Esther's fear of the Nazis grew to be too much in the middle of the night, she got up and cooked from her mother's leather-bound cookbook with the pink ribbon, the one her mother had given her for her wedding to Alexander. She would study her mother's recipes, some of which came from her mother, Sarrah Tolstonog, and her mother, Tsilia Bezkrovny.

She would admire her mother's drawings of their poor neighborhood in Odessa, of Boris, of herself and her brothers as they grew, of her mother's parents, Efim and Sarrah, and grandparents, Aron and Tsilia. Ida had drawn pictures of her and her brothers with their new spouses when they were married, the wedding cakes she made them, along with the cake recipe she had used.

Esther had added her own favorite recipes, too. Alexander's Salmon Dinner With Herbs and Shallots. Gisela's Cherry Tart. Renata's Challah Bread. Isaac's Pecan and Brown Sugar Pastry. And a lemon chiffon cake, light and fluffy, which she made when she needed to settle her nerves. The sweet tartness always made her happy.

But instead of drawings of people, which Esther felt she had no talent for, she would draw flowers, herbs, fruits, and vegetables. She would place leaves or flowers or petals, especially herbs, under the paper and use a colored pencil over the top. She had sketched their home in Munich, with its red door, symbolizing freedom, and the red geraniums, celebrating life, according to her mother. This cookbook was their history, after all, going back to Tsilia's recipes.

Esther knew she would not sleep again that night, so she went to the kitchen and opened the cookbook, which sat next to their Seder plate and Kiddush cups. She would make onion soup with a little beer, marjoram, homemade croutons, and Emmental cheese.

She was scared. Her hands trembled as she cooked. Beef stock sloshed out of her measuring cup. She quickly mopped it up, but she knew it would leave a brown stain. She measured the salt into a teaspoon, and some spilled into the crease of the cookbook. She tried to brush it out, but it stayed where it was and she left it.

She would give the cookbook to Gisela and Renata when it was time. It was so precious to her, meant to be passed down the family line. The girls were best friends, and they would share it.

As the onion soup lightly bubbled, she wrote the recipe in the cookbook. She drew the onions, an apple, and the salt and pepper shakers.

She plucked off a daisy from flowers Alexander had brought to her and traced it over the top, in the corner, then wrote their names, Esther and Alexander. She was feeling sentimental so she drew hearts for the leaves and then felt like a little girl.

Esther Gobenko wondered how many more times she would cook in this kitchen.

It wasn't many more, she knew it.

She could feel it.

"Hey. Olivia," Larry said to me as I was leaning over the stove making a marinara sauce, adding parsley and thyme and a smidge of sugar. "What's the special for tomorrow? You better be thinking of something my stomach will like." He burped. Put a fist to his chest.

Oh, gall. I could smell his burp.

Larry's Diner was thriving. I was trying to serve old-fashioned Montana food in the most delicious and gourmet way possible. I had ramped up the dessert menu, too.

The treats were sky high, piled with icing, powdered sugar, and originality. I baked all types of cakes from carrot cake to six-layer chocolate cake to cheesecake chocolate bars, lemon bars, my grandma Ida's strawberry cream rolls, and chocolate chip cookies large enough to fill a plate.

But I always tried to make them different, too—special. The six-layer chocolate cake came with three inches of whip cream. The kids loved it. The lemon bars were stacked up like a mini building with a swirl of lemon frosting outlining the plate. The carrot cake was served, as a joke, with a carrot, which was Esther's idea. The apple pie was served with an apple.

Some people started coming simply for the desserts. We had lines every day.

I hired more line cooks and more waitstaff.

"I always think of good meals, Larry. Like pasta marinara today, served in a swirl with a shake of basil and parmesan cheese flakes on top."

"Yeah, better be finger-lickin' tasty. We've got a party of twenty-five coming in for lunch tomorrow. Got them in the back room. Don't screw this up, hon."

And there it was. He liked to call me hon, and then he pretended to "forget" that I had told him not to call me hon because I hated it.

I was done. Done with hon. "I won't screw it up, tiny dick."

His face flushed. "What the hell?"

"Every time you call me hon, when I have asked you not to call me that, repeatedly, because I am not your hon, I'm going to call you tiny dick."

"I forget! I forget!"

"You never forget. You call me hon and pretend you forget. It's a power struggle. You want me to know that you can call me whatever you want because I work for you. But when you call me hon, which is demeaning and insulting coming from you, I will now call you tiny dick."

And then he did it again. He gave me that look, head to foot, to show me that he could undress me with his eyes and I had to stand there and take it.

I bent down low and stared at his crotch. "Small. Ineffectual. Unused. Old." I stood up.

"Now do you know how it feels?"

He was red, flushed.

"You don't intimidate me, Larry, by staring at every inch of my body. It repels me. Stop doing it."

"You're too sensitive."

"Do not blame me for your disgusting behavior. You're twisting what's happening here." I bent down, stared at his crotch. "Stop doing that, tiny dick."

"This isn't your restaurant, Olivia." He crossed his arms.

"It isn't. And I'll leave."

All around me I heard the waitstaff and cooks stop. I took off my apron and they started taking off theirs.

"What's going on?" Dinah asked, coming through the double doors.

"Olivia is leaving," Justin said. He tossed his apron on the floor.

"If Olivia is gone, I'm gone," Dinah said.

There was general agreement.

That was it. We all walked out. We didn't have to wait ten seconds before Larry was chugging behind us outside on the sidewalk, his stomach coming first. "Olivia, stop. Come on, everybody. I won't do it anymore, I promise. Please."

None of us believed him.

"We all need raises."

He blustered, we walked, he came up with an offer. We accepted and walked back in.

I hated him. I hated working for him. When he lumbered back into the kitchen finally appearing cowed I said, "Get out. Now." He left.

I put my hands heavily on the counter. I could not do this for much longer. Justin, Earl, and Dinah came up and linked their arms around my shoulders.

"He sucks," Dinah said.

"Yes, he does," I said.

"I'm happy to hit him for you, Olivia," Earl said. "Say the word. I enjoyed it last time. My mother told me to tell you hello.

She's hoping you'll get back together with Jace. Hey! Then you could cook with him again out at the ranch."

I saw Jace outside Larry's restaurant after work. He was waiting for me. Black jacket, jeans, cowboy boots.

"Hi, Jace." *Utter relief.* That's how I felt. I had dealt with a classless, disgusting, misogynistic gargoyle, and here was Jace. Total opposite. Classy. Smart. Polite. Caring.

"Hello, Olivia." He smiled, towering over me. His black hair was thick and windblown. His face was adorable and scarred. When he wasn't smiling, he looked like he would enjoy knocking people apart. I knew he was tough but he had a huge heart. "Coffee?"

I was sweaty. I had lemon cheesecake on my boob. I had vinaigrette sauce on my sleeve. I needed a shower. "Sure. Want to come to my house, though? I'm a mess."

I didn't miss the way his face lit up at the invitation.

"You're a pretty mess."

"Thanks. I don't feel pretty."

He stepped in close, cowboy boots to cowgirl boots. "You are always gorgeous, Olivia."

He followed me home. It was comforting to have him behind me.

I was so glad to see the red door, the wagon wheel, the sun weather vane, and my grandparents' cowboy hats on the log cabin. Safety. Warmth. Joy. Jace followed me in, and I smiled at him. He smiled back.

He is my sun.

He slid an envelope across the scratches and dents of our dining room table to me.

"What's this?" I had had a shower and washed my hair with a mango-pineapple-scented shampoo. I used vanilla lotion to smell extra tasty. I pulled on jeans and a red sweater with a deep neckline that maybe, perhaps, was a tad low over my lacy red bra. I dried my hair, put on makeup, and smiled at Jace, waiting for me in the family room in front of the fire. I could tell he liked my cleavage.

I made the coffee while we chatted, then put out sugar cookies the girls and I decorated. I gave him two cats. One cat had three eyes, the other appeared to have a penis. He thanked me, smiled, and said, "I'm eating a cat," and we laughed.

"Open it."

The envelope was decorated with pictures of hearts and flowers and dogs. The dogs might have been stoned, but they were cute. I recognized Stephi's and Lucy's art. It was a one-page letter, also decorated with hearts, flowers, dogs, and one huge cat that resembled a cat vampire.

> *Deer Mr. Giant,*
>
> *Hi! This is Lucy and Stephi. Thank you for picking us up at school when we were very very very bad sick. We liked playing Candy Land next time you might not lose.*
>
> *We no you are not a giant.*
>
> *Right?*
>
> *Charlie told us on the bus that you are Aunt Olivias husband. So we think you should come and live with us in the log house please bring the doggys Snickers and Garmin and K.C. the kitty cat.*
>
> *We like animals.*
>
> *Can you come tommorrrow? Will you play Candy Land with us again?*
>
> *Love Stephi and Lucy*

"Oh, Jace." I didn't even know what to do. "I'm sorry."

"Why?" He grinned. "I thought it was a nice letter."

"They told me that they were going to write you a letter. I didn't know they had. They probably got your address from my mother." I knew it was her. The traitor.

"What did you tell them about us?"

"I told them that we are married but that we live apart because we have problems."

"What did they say?"

"They said that we should hug and say sorry like they do when they have a fight."

"Smart. Let's hug and say sorry."

"Jace." I smiled at him. I can't help it. He was my best friend for a long time. Best in bed, too. He stood up and that giant man reached down and pulled me up and wrapped me in a hug and his mouth came down on mine, and I reacted instinctively because every time I see him I want to get naked with him.

I kissed him right back and soon, with zero thought at all, as my brain was awash in lust, off came my red sweater and that pretty, lacy red bra and I unbuttoned his shirt and I was lost. I unbuckled his belt and pulled down his jeans. My jeans and underwear were already down, his hands on all that nakedness making me groan . . . and then I heard the girls as my grandma dropped them off.

"Oh no, oh my, oh no . . ." I pulled away and yanked up my underwear and jeans, then frantically tried to find my sweater. "Where is my bra? Where is my sweater?"

Jace looked around, totally unruffled, as he pulled up his pants and buckled his belt. My sweater was on the other side of the couch. He leaned over. "Here, baby." I was panicked the girls would come in on a half-naked mother. I pulled it over my head in the nick of time. My bra was on the floor, and I threw it down the hallway. Jace was pulling on his shirt when the girls burst in.

"Hi, Mr. Giant!" Stephi said, smiling.

"Hi, Mr. Giant!" Lucy said. She pointed her finger in the air. "Are you here to play Candy Land?"

"Yes. That's why I came."

"Yay! You want to have cookies first? I found new rocks." Stephi held out her rocks.

"Excellent finds, Stephi. I do want to have cookies. What

kind did you and your aunt Olivia make?" He finished buttoning his shirt, calm and collected.

"We made sugar cookies with love," Lucy said. "I made my cookies in the shapes of dogs and cats like Garmin and Snickers and K.C. And I did Show-and-Share today and I showed everyone an oxygen mask, a shot, a catheter, that's a hard word, I told them where it goes, and I put on the blue gloves so you don't get blood on your hands. Grandma gave them to me to show. I'm going to be a doctor that slices people up and takes out the bad stuff."

Oh, Lord.

"And I made a picture!" Stephi said. She held it up. It was all four of us. Jace was huge, filling up most of the page and smiling in a cowboy hat. The girls were wearing tutus and crowns and carrying swords. There was a pile of gold rocks by Stephi's feet. I had a ton of brown wavy hair and green eyes that took up half my face and a smile that took up the other half. There were two dogs. Lucy held the leash of one, Stephi the other. Both dogs had purple bows and pink smiles. A yellow cat with red stripes was sitting on Lucy's shoulder.

"Wow," Jace said, taking the picture. "You're an artist. Can I have it?"

"Yep, you can."

"Wait. Hold on. Wait." Lucy stopped bopping about, confused. "Why was your shirt off, Mr. Giant, when we came in?"

"I was showing your mom my muscles."

"Oh," Stephi said. "Because you're a giant and your muscles grow quick."

"Exactly. She likes to see them sometimes."

"You've got some black hair on your muscles," Stephi said.

"It's because I eat broccoli."

"I eat broccoli and I don't get black hair on my muscles," Stephi said.

"But you're not a giant," Jace said.

"That's true! You're right! Okay! Let's have cookies and play"—she paused for dramatic effect—"Candy Land!"

Jace was even more adorable playing Candy Land. He winked at me. I tried not to pant at him over the gumdrops.

Lucy and Stephi went to a daycare when Annabelle worked in the neonatal intensive care unit. I worked Wednesday through Sunday at Carter's. Annabelle and I and the girls started having dinner together on Mondays. The girls were nervous, skittish, jumping at any noise and reaching for the other's hand. They would hardly talk and were often unsmiling and withdrawn. If there was a man in the hallway, they hid behind me or Annabelle. Scarred on the inside, scarred on the outside.

But cooking together ended up being healing for us. I showed them how to make manicotti with ricotta cheese, seafood pasta with scallops and shrimp, and homemade peppermint ice cream.

They drew me pictures and I put them on my refrigerator. In one, my brown hair is down to my ankles and I'm wearing a crown. There are butterflies and smiles flying around. In another I'm in a white chef's jacket with red high heels holding a turkey with orange and red feathers in one hand and a cat by the neck in another. (They wanted a cat.)

When Stephi had the flu, she stayed with me on a Monday. Lucy didn't want to go to school, she wanted to stay with me, too, so by nine o'clock the school called and said Lucy said she was sick. Lucy wasn't sick. Annabelle knew it, and so did I. We agreed she could have one day off. We had the best time. I cooked for them and we watched Disney movies and sang all the songs together.

In summer I had the girls every Tuesday, all day. We went to the movies, the zoo, pools, and playgrounds for picnics. Annabelle brought me flowers to thank me. She offered to pay me, but I refused. She knitted me a gorgeous sweater. It is the warmest, comfiest sweater I have. She knitted me a scarf. The girls picked the colors. Best scarf ever. She knitted me socks/booties. Same thing.

The girls let bits of their past slip. "Daddy's friend Craig Zee did that." Lucy pointed to a circular scar on Stephi's arm. "Cigarettes are bad. I said no no no. He pushed me. See?" She pointed to a scar on her hairline. "I bammed into the table. He told the doctor I fell. I didn't fall ... Craig Zee smoked. Now when I smell smoke I throw up."

"Craig Zee is scary. You know needles?" Stephi said. "He put needles in his arm for fun and he put needles in Momma's arm. We saw. She said she liked it. I don't like it.

"Mommy yelled at us because we're bad. One time we got sick but she said she didn't have time to take us to the doctor so when we were at school the school called an ambulance and me and Lucy got to go to the hospital and have Popsicles in bed. Then we went to another lady's house with a bunch of kids and didn't see Mommy for a while."

Annabelle had told me that her daughter, Sarah, had behavioral problems from the time she was three. She had been expelled from preschools and three elementary schools, and had dropped out of high school on the fourth suspension. She attacked teachers, kids, the principal. She hit Annabelle. She tried to burn their house down twice. She ran away and worked as a prostitute. She was into drugs at fifteen.

"My husband and I adored her. She came drunk to her father's funeral, couldn't bother to be sober to say good-bye to Karl. I truly believe that Sarah's problems killed Karl. That's why he had two heart attacks. Third one did him in. We were up all night, so many nights, worried sick.

"Over the years Sarah was diagnosed with oppositional defiant disorder. Intermittent explosive disorder. Narcissism. A general personality disorder. Bipolar. The labels soon meant nothing. She refused to take her medications anyhow. She was an addict and alcoholic. We had her in treatment more times than I can tell you, sometimes for weeks, sometimes for months. She's been to a house full of psychiatrists. Nothing helped. We went through savings, retirement, and equity in our home. I finally sold the home for one more rehab stint off an island in the south. It didn't work.

"She changed her name when she was sixteen to Devlin because it sounded like the devil. She said she liked the devil. She met a real devil. His name was Parker McDaniel and she married him.

"Every morning," Annabelle told me, "I wake up and I have this terrible sense of doom. I love Sarah. I'm so afraid that one day I'll get a call and she'll be dead. I live with this never-ending fear all the time. I try to funnel it into something positive, with my patients, and with the girls. But it doesn't always work. Plus, I live with the fear that when Sarah gets out of jail she'll get the girls back and I won't be able to find them. I won't be able to check on Lucy and Stephi, and horrible things will happen again."

"I am so sorry, Annabelle. I'm so glad you have the girls now. They adore you."

She smiled and we held hands. "You're an outstanding aunt. Thank you for letting them call you Aunt Olivia. They love you. Wait until you see what the girls are making you for Christmas."

The girls and Annabelle made me a Christmas blanket. One side had candy canes on it, the other side had Mrs. Claus.

"Made with love," Lucy said, giving me a hug.

"Like how you cook your food," Stephi said.

The girls hugged me. "We love you, Aunt Olivia."

After work I drove out into the country, past Jace's white fence, and climbed out of my truck where I usually do. The sky was blue, the puffy clouds floating by, as if they had somewhere to be, and way out there was the snow-covered hill and the magical sunsets.

I would go there soon.

"Blow my brain cells from here to kingdom come, Kyle is participating in Kalulell's talent show," Chloe said. She leaned against the refrigerator in my home. I handed her a glass of wine. The girls were upstairs playing in their tent. Both had cried after school because of "no friends. They think we're weird. Are we weird? Katie is having a birthday party this weekend and I didn't get invited."

It is so hard to hear your children's voices filled with loneliness.

My sister drank the wine in one throw-the-head-back move, her ponytail swinging. She, too, struggled with the pain of raising a kid who was different in a society that is often brutal to "different."

"What's his talent?" I poured myself a glass of wine, too. I needed it. Then I tied an apron around the lime green shirt I'd bought in Portugal. It had turtles on it and a drawstring waist. I like turtles.

"He doesn't know. He is, and I quote him, 'assessing my talents to determine which one, if any, I could present in a social setting with the highest chance of success.'"

"You're afraid he's going to get laughed at."

"Yes. Hell, yes." She poured another glass of wine. "When he told me he was entering, I felt my stomach drop through my big-girl panties. I wanted to put my hand under my crotch to catch it. That's how it felt. My stomach was going to slide out of my butterfly."

"I would not want your stomach to slide out of your butterfly." We were indulging in Martindale Cake Therapy and making a lemon chiffon cake out of Grandma's cookbook. It had been written in German. Grandma said it was written by Esther. "She made it when she needed to settle her nerves. She said the sweet tartness always made her happy."

I used the Internet to translate the ingredients into English. It was an honor to be making recipes from Grandma's mother, grandmother, great-grandmother, and great-great-grandmother.

The lemon chiffon cake was our "healing cake," that Chloe and I agreed we would make together. It would be me making the cake. Chloe doesn't have the same passion I do for baking, but she would "help."

"Hey, speaking of my butterfly, let's put the cake in a butterfly pan." Chloe started digging through the cupboards. "Ta-da!" She held up our grandma's two butterfly-shaped cake pans.

"Let's do it. A double-layer butterfly lemon chiffon cake with raspberry filling." For fun I said, "Can you hand me the flour?" Totally distracted by her distress over Kyle, Chloe grabbed a jar of pickles and handed it to me. She took the lid off. "Thank you."

She stuck her fingers in the jar and pulled out a long pickle and waved it around. "I feel like bashing heads together already. I tell you, if I'm at that talent show and I see people with cave-man IQ's making fun of my boy, they will have me and my off-the-leash-temper to deal with." She pointed the wiggling pickle at me, then took a huge bite.

"No one is going to make fun of him at the talent show, Chloe. He'll do something brilliant. Something science-y. An experiment. A model. Or art."

"The boy's odd, like a chicken that thinks in Chinese. Like a bear that tap dances and doesn't realize all the other bears think he's a loon. Like a planet that bounces. The other night he talked to me, at length, about nuclear science. I had to tell him to stop after an hour, and he said, 'Did I speak in an overly lengthy manner?' and I said, 'Yes. Dude. Ask people questions about themselves and listen to their answers.' "

"What did he do?"

"He got out his Questions Notebook and made a notation after asking what kinds of questions he could ask people."

"I'm impressed with how hard he constantly tries to understand people and social dynamics." I couldn't resist. "Can you pass me two lemons?"

"Yes." She passed me a carton of cream. For some reason she shook it up before giving it to me. "He gets so focused on one thing. Right now it's Michelangelo and drawing and painting people. But when his schedule changes, it sets him off like a hot deer strapped to the rack on top of my truck."

I puzzled that one out. A deer on a rack. "Wouldn't the deer be dead?"

"I'd hope so. I wouldn't try to get a live deer on the rack above my car. I only get the dead ones up there. Can't imagine a live deer would cooperate." She stirred the flour, baking soda, salt, and sugar in the bowl I pushed over to her. "Asperger's is a strange-ass problem."

I knew my sister didn't mean it as it sounded. She adored Kyle.

"By the way, Olivia, I have decided that I want to ask Zane out on a date." She grabbed another wiggling pickle out of the jar and waved it around. It was rather phallic.

"Wait. What happened to Chase?"

"I had a date with him. He radiated masculinity, but now I want to ask out Zane. For variety." She ran a hand over her ponytail and zipped her sweatshirt to her chin.

"Zane Corrigan? From high school?"

"Yes. One year older than me. Same class as Jace. They were friends."

Zane owned a lumber yard. Nice smile. Football. "Divorced, right?"

"Yep. He married Marilane Trighty. Remember her?"

"Complete and total snobby priss. Most vain and shallow woman I've ever known."

"She moved to New York. No one liked her. They married right after high school when Zane was in the military."

"I remember. We couldn't believe he'd married her. And no kids."

"No. They didn't have kids. She probably thought kids would mess up her spaghetti hips or her fake boobs. Anyhow, I accidentally on purpose drove by Zane's house the other day, all nonchalant, and I saw him and pulled over. Same as with Chase. It was a drive-by." She took a huge bite out of the pickle.

"Did you get out of your car? You did? What did you say?"

"I said, 'Hello, Zane. Nice to see you.' It's not like he doesn't know me. When we were in high school I followed him around for weeks because I was in love with him and he told me to quit following him."

"I remember. When he didn't ask you to prom, you made me break into his locker and we filled it with empty beer cans. So what did you and Zane talk about?"

"Lots of stuff. I told him that if he was ever lost on a mountain, and hurt, that it might be me picking him up in the helicopter, but I didn't want him to feel emasculated if that happened. I didn't want him to get his pecker out of shape."

"You didn't say that."

"I did. And I told him that I knew he owned a lumber yard and I told him that I could pick up heavy loads, as I was trained as a paramedic, and I was strong, and logs didn't scare me. Long logs, short logs, I could lift them, move them." She took another bite out of the pickle. "Get them in the right place."

One graphic image after another dove through my head. I wanted to laugh. I so did. But it would hurt Chloe's feelings. She would be mortally embarrassed because she clearly did not understand how she sounded about her "logs."

"I told him that I had strong ears, too, and could handle all the noises the saws would make." She flopped the pickle around.

I had taken a sip of wine, and that wine flew clean out of my mouth as I laughed.

She was confounded. "Are you okay, Olivia? Want me to pound your back?" She raised a hand.

"No, thank you." I coughed. "Can you hand me the powdered sugar, and what did he say?"

She handed me an orange and a fork. I didn't laugh. I didn't.

"He said that that was helpful information and he smiled at me, and I smiled back and I told him about how feminism works nowadays."

"How'd he do on the feminism talk?"

"He's a feminist. I told him he was after I quizzed him about his feelings on women. That's important. I'm not dating a man who isn't a feminist. I also told him he was a handsome son of a gun, a man who packed his jeans out, and a man who would be warm at night."

"You didn't."

My sister became cross and pointed the wiggly pickle at me in an accusatory way. "Yes, I did. I told you I did. Did you think I was lying? Anyhow, he blushed and I said, 'Don't worry about blushing, I talk bluntly and it'll take you some time to get used to me.' I think he likes rounded women like me. There's a lot to hold here, and he's a large man and he needs something to fill those large hands of his."

"Please don't tell me you said that to him."

"I didn't. Yet. You have to save something honest for the next encounter, and that's what I'm saving. This man is going to be a panther in bed. You can't tell by looking at him, he's tall and gangly, looks skeletal. I'll have to fatten him up if we get together, but I'm telling you, I see it in his eyes. Panther." She made a growling sound, but then her chin wrinkled up and her eyes filled with tears and she placed the wiggly pickle on the counter and lowered her head.

I put my arm around her.

"I'm trying to be brave about dating." Chloe sucked in a breath. "I'm brave. I'm brave. I'm brave."

"Are you sure you want to date?"

Her lips trembled. "No. Yes. I don't know. I am so scared I can hardly breathe. I like this man, but I'm sure he'll be running for the mountains soon because I have to be the boss, and it's almost impossible to think of being with any man after Teddy, and I still miss him so much, but I'm trying to move on and after eight years I should, but I still feel guilty, and how will it be to have another man in my bed who's not Teddy, the person I thought I'd sleep with forever and then we'd die together holding hands or we'd be ninety and I'd mount that man and we'd both fall dead in the middle of sex and people would find us naked and still attached, but that was not to be. Teddy is dead and I am alive and I'm trying to move on and be normal, and Zane is sexy and I do miss sex but I still want Teddy."

"You were the best wife ever to Teddy and he adored you." I gave her a long hug while she cried. "But maybe you should try this. A few dates."

She said to herself, "Stop crying, Chloe. You are not a baby. You are a paramedic and a search-and-rescue helicopter pilot. You can shoot arrows and bake cakes. You are a tough-talkin', hip-rockin' Montana woman."

"And you're strong and smart, and these dates can go nowhere, by your choice."

She sighed. She breathed. "I'm going to kick butt, Olivia, I am. I'm a Montana woman and a Martindale and a Razolli." She wiped her face. "I'm a butt kicker and I'm not a whiner and I'm going to drive by Zane's house again accidentally on purpose and I'm going to get out of my truck and talk to him about whatever he wants to talk about like engines or football—I know all about that—and skeet shooting."

"I know you're going to kick butt. You always do. You always have." Together we put the double-layer Lemon Chiffon Butterfly Healing Cake in the oven and decorated it later with the girls using the raspberry filling with pink icing and lots of colorful hard candies on top for the wings. It was scrumptious. I think Esther would have been proud.

Sometimes that's all you can do in life. Cry, have a treat, hug someone you love, then get back out there and kick some butt. There's no choice. So you do it.

We brought Grandma and our mother a slice of Lemon Chiffon Butterfly Healing Cake when they got home from a birthday party. Grandma took a bite and said, her voice tearful, "It's perfect. It's tastes exactly like my mother's, Cinnamon and Nutmeg. It's as if she's here with me now."

My mother kissed her on the cheek, a rare tender moment for The Fire Breather, and we all sat in that sweet family moment, our ancestors around us, if only through a lemon chiffon cake, shaped like a butterfly.

I kissed the girls good-bye on their way out of the car, lunch and fudge pinwheel cookies and backpacks in tow. The girls seemed to like school better. "No one has called me frog face in a few days," Lucy said. "I think it's because I socked Brayden in the gut the last time. Now some of the kids call me Fist. You know, because I punched him because he wouldn't stop calling me frog face. Do you think I look like a frog?"

"I had two girls ask me to sit with them at lunch," Stephi said. "And I said yes and we sat together and I shared my fudge pinwheel cookies with them. They liked them!"

Aha! I had a tiny solution to this painful problem. If it helped Stephi to make friends, I would add more cookies to her lunch bag so she could share them. I was learning this about motherhood: You do what it takes to help your kids even if it means you're making special cookies at eleven o'clock every night.

The next night Stephi couldn't sleep because she remembered the times when there was no food in the house and she and Lucy had to go to bed with "tummy aches. Two nights."

Now and then I see Lucy and Stephi opening the refrigerator just because. They're not hungry, but they want to know that there is always food, the fridge full. Sometimes I send them to bed with a snack in a sack.

It's pathetic. No kid should ever have to wonder if they'll eat the next day.

Thursday night I made butterscotch cookies for the girls for their lunches. I would put extra in their baggies for their new friends.

The truth is I love cooking for people I love.

I used to love cooking for Jace. He loved my food. He made me feel appreciated every single time I put a plate in front of him. His response was always the same: "Wow." And "Thank you, Olivia," or "Thank you, baby."

He would study the meal, appreciate the way it was grilled/baked/fried, how I presented it on the plate, how the tomatoes were sliced thin because that's the way he liked them, how the salads had his favorite homemade dressings, and how my bread was sliced thick and hot. There was not a meal I made that that man didn't fall over himself thanking me for.

When we were working together on the ranch he would call to chat during the day, or come by and see me in the kitchen, give me a hug and a kiss and say, "What's for dinner?"

I'd tell him, his eyes would light up, he'd listen so close, and then that guy would look forward all day to what I was making for dinner. After dinner he would say, "Olivia, that is the most delicious meal I've ever eaten," and we would laugh because he had said it the night before, too.

Jace worked long hours, all the time, but he always cleaned up after dinner. He insisted. To give him a break, I always washed up the pans beforehand so he wouldn't have to do much.

He was a kind husband. He was a sexy husband. He was a strong and smart husband. He was ambitious, masculine, protective, and a tiny bit possessive in a seductive 'you are my woman' sort of way.

It about killed me to leave him, but it was leave him or lose my mind.

I chose to save myself. It was better than the alternative.

I still feel so guilty for that, so awful.

It's like the guilt is in my bones and running through my bloodstream.

I held the letter in my hand outside the log cabin, the snow sprinkling down, light and fluffy.

Everything started to spin. The white-tipped Dove Mountains in the distance seemed to blur, then shift, as if they were in the midst of an earthquake. The river expanded, then retracted, then I swear it started flowing backward. Even the snowflakes turned to tiny tunnels, whirling around me, stealing my breath.

I sank down onto my knees, on my driveway, dizzy, sick.

I blinked, rubbed my eyes, took a breath, and started reading the letter again.

It was written partly in legalese, that barely decipherable language that attorneys use to intimidate and demoralize. But I got the meaning.

Sarah Lacey, aka Devlin McDaniel, the name Devlin chose because she liked that it sounded "devilish," was going to get out of jail early because of good behavior. Devlin had called me herself when we were in Portland and told me she would get out early, but at that point she was the only one saying it. Still, it had scared me to the ends of every hair on my head.

Now it was official. There would be a meeting, then a hearing in front of a judge, about the fitness of Devlin's abysmal parenting and steps she would have to take to get the girls back. As if this was a reasonable, possible option.

I was invited to that hearing, as was my attorney, and Devlin's attorney, which Children's Services would hold in downtown Portland, with caseworkers and other concerned parties.

I lay back in the snow, like a dying snow angel, unable to stand upright for one more second.

Chapter 9

❦

"Dang," my mother said, hanging up her phone. "Dorene Morales fell out of her hayloft and says she heard a *click click click*. Thinks her bones snapped."

"Did you call an ambulance?"

"We're going to get her. We're closer and we'll get there faster than they will in the ambulance in this weather."

My grandma put the cream away. We were making cinnamon mousse together at the farmhouse. It was one of Ida's recipes out of the cookbook. Grandma told me she used to make it at her pink and white bakery in Munich. The girls had been invited to Charlie Zimmerman's house, son of Grace Zimmerman, who did not gracefully get drunk at our choir concert. Charlie had an older brother and the four of them were going to play together.

The three of us grabbed our coats, shoved our feet into boots, and flew out the door, into a flurry of wind and snow. We piled into the truck. My mother pulled out as I shut the door.

The snow and wind became thicker as we headed up a hill, then climbed part of a mountain to Dorene's ranch. They had much more snow up here than we did on the floor of Kalulell. I had felt spring coming around the corner a little while ago. I did not feel spring around that corner anymore.

The truck skidded and hit a snowbank. We climbed out of the truck, hoods up, grabbed the chains, and got them on. My mother won this time. I used a shovel to get rid of some of the snow in front of the tires.

Dorene's driveway wasn't plowed, so it took longer than we wanted, but we headed toward the barn.

Dorene is about seventy-five, give or take a couple years.

"Hello, ladies. I have a date tonight." Dorene lay on the floor of her barn. She was clutching her side, her breath catching. Luckily she had had her phone with her. "So, let's get this fixed up quick so I can get ready."

"Don't be delusional. You know you're going to have to go a few days late to your date, Dorene," my mother said, her hands gently examining her.

My grandma examined her, too. "I'll bring you some of my chicken soup with extra onions when you're out of the hospital. It will help you to heal."

"I know it will, Gisela. You've made it for me before, and it healed me so quick I could hardly remember having double pneumonia. Healing done in the natural way, not with all these drugs the pharmaceutical companies gouge us for. Hello, Olivia, wonderful to see you, dear. I heard you're back together with Jace. Good for you two."

"No, I'm not."

"No? I heard you were." She said this as if I might be confused. She had heard it through the Kalulell grapevine, so that made it true. "I heard it from Tobey. He heard it from Melissa St. James."

My mother could tell I was uncomfortable at the mention of Jace, so she got things back on track. "Who do you have a date with, Dorene?"

"Francois, the brother of Antoine. You know Antoine? Cecilia's husband? The French professor at the college? Francois is visiting from France. Doesn't speak much English, but I don't need much English in the bedroom."

Grandma and she chuckled, like schoolgirls. "No conversation needed, Dorene."

"That's right," my mother said. "Turn down the lights, pull

down the sheets, and let your body do the talking, the bed springs do the walkin'. Or something like that."

"You must have learned that phrase in medical school, Mother."

"I'm having Francois over for dinner. I made my ribs. Still in the oven. You know what my ribs do to men."

We all said, "Ahhh . . ."

Dorene's ribs were famous. I'd had them. They were fall-off-the-bone perfect. She'd brought them to my wedding reception with Jace and said, "Have him eat my ribs. He'll stay fired up for hours. If you know what I mean, dear." Jace did not need the help, but still. It was a thoughtful gift.

"Those ribs are from my momma's recipe. It's how she snared my father, at least that's what he said. When they got in one of their fights she always told him, 'None of my ribs for you,' and that usually shut down the fight right quick, I tell you. My father was begging for forgiveness by the second day."

"Okay, Dorene," my mother said. "You really did it to yourself this time, snap, crackle, and pop, and you're going to have to spend some time at Hotel Hospital."

"Oh, hell, no, Mary Beth. You can fix it. I can't leave my ribs." She waved a hand. "Isn't this ironic? I've broken my ribs and I'm making ribs for dinner."

"I'll go and turn off the oven," I said, "and take care of the ribs."

"You have to go to the hospital, lover girl," my mother said. "One of your ribs has flat punctured a lung."

"I am not going to the hospital, Mary Beth. I hate hospitals."

"Yep. You are. Quit arguing, you're giving me a headache. We have a snowstorm and we're getting out of here before it gets worse. Up you go."

"Now, don't you worry," Grandma said. "You'll be pulled back together in no time at all. A hot water bottle and a hot toddy will help heal those ribs, too."

We backed the truck into the barn, gently helped Dorene into the backseat, then I ran into her house, turned everything off, grabbed the ribs with pot holders, put them on a cutting board, locked the doors, and headed back through the snow, trying not to lose the ribs. I put the ribs in the back of the truck and climbed in.

The truck skidded down the driveway, my mother intent on getting to the hospital quickly. The snow was coming down, heavy and thick. I hate blizzards, I do.

"Buck up, Olivia," my mother said, sweet as usual.

"I am bucked up, Mother." I wasn't. She knew it.

Dorene leaned heavily against me in the backseat, pale, her voice raspy, not at all concerned that she had a punctured lung. "This is going to make a mess of my date."

"Tell me what Francois looks like, Dorene."

"Hot," she wheezed. "He's boiling over. Fifteen years younger than me, but I know I can keep up."

"Women always can," my mother drawled. "They always can. Especially those of us born in Montana."

"Ruthie has a boyfriend. Hers is fifteen years younger, too," Dorene said. "That makes us lion cubs!"

"Cougars." My chest was tight. Blizzards equal anxiety attacks.

"Breathe, Olivia," my mother drawled. "You must kick your fears in the butt. You must put steel in your sternum and victory in your vertebrae."

Francois was polite enough to have their date that night in Dorene's hospital room. I cooked the ribs the rest of the way through and brought them up to the hospital that night with the girls.

Francois was a handsome gentleman. He devoured the ribs. I saw him wink at Dorene.

Francois was a man who would come through when the going got tough.

Just like Jace.

"I know you're coming to the meeting," my attorney, Claudine, confirmed.

"Yes." I clutched my phone, the heat from the kitchen in Larry's Diner stifling. The meeting, about the girls, was in April.

"You don't bring the girls to this meeting."

"I know. When I return to Montana after the meeting, that's when I make my plans to leave for Australia."

"You do know that you can't do that, right?"

"I do." Australia beckoned. Australia had beaches. Clean air. And no Devlin.

"Olivia, I don't like the tone you're using. You cannot leave with the girls. Regardless of what happens with this meeting, do not take off with the girls. Do not refuse to give them up. Do not hide the girls. You have to comply with the court's order."

"I know."

"Say you will."

"I will."

"Olivia, when we meet the judge, later, when Devlin is out of jail, she will review everything. The judge could decide to leave the girls with you permanently and allow visitation from Devlin only if she attends parenting classes, stays sober, goes to counseling, and shows that she's complying with the court's orders."

"Or, she could flat-out win, and then the girls will be given back to her. Until some neighbor calls the police because of the neglect, starvation, or rampant drug use, or the schools call another ambulance because the girls are critically ill."

"I think we have a huge chance of success. Devlin's record is alarming."

"And my part in the meeting?"

"You will answer all questions put to you by Devlin's attorney and any other attorney in there and Children's Services and anyone else who asks questions. The meeting is not to decide if you or Devlin would make the better parent. You would win. That's not the question. The question is, is Devlin able to become a reasonably competent parent in future, and what would that involve, and what support does she need."

No! I wanted to scream. *No, she isn't competent.*

We talked further, and Claudine told me her strategy, her arguments.

I was exhausted when we were done. I could not imagine

handing over Lucy and Stephi to Devlin. Anyone who hands over kids to a woman like that should be arrested.

I should arrest myself.

Lucy and Stephi and I talk about their past when they bring it up. They know that I want to raise them, and they know that their mother wants them to live with her when she's out of jail. I will not lie to those children, nor will I divulge every detail of what's going on.

I will not excuse their parents, though, for the hitting, the severe neglect, the drugs, and an unsafe home when they bring it up. I will not gloss over what they experienced, make them feel that their feelings are invalid or incorrect, or that they should simply forget about what happened. I will not minimalize what their parents did to them because it denies the girls the truth and reality of their own lives. They need someone to listen to them and to acknowledge that what happened was wrong and scary.

However, I will balance that truth with love and hugs and their favorite cookies.

"Kyle got in a fight."

"What?" I paused. Chloe loves my Bam Bam Burritos, so I was stirring ground beef on my stove and adding grilled onions and green peppers. The kids were outside on the back deck in coats. Kyle had brought a telescope to show the girls.

"It was the three orangutans. Eric, Jason, and Juan. They pushed him in the hallway, told him he was a dick and a psycho. Kyle tried to change the conversation. He read online that you're supposed to walk away or make a joke or change the conversation when you're being bullied. He didn't want to walk away and he doesn't know how to make a joke, so he tried to change the conversation. He told me he said, 'Instead of talking about how I'm a dick, which is anatomically impossible, or a psycho, which would require a medical diagnosis from a professional, let's discuss the advances at NASA this year. The James Webb telescope is of interest to me because . . .' and he told them how NASA's astronomy and cosmology would advance in the future."

"Those boys would have been clueless." I had to have a little fun with her. "Can you hand me a wooden spoon?"

She opened a drawer and handed me salad tongs, her brown ponytail swinging.

"They didn't even understand what my brainiac was saying. He told me they said, 'What the hell are you talking about, freak boy?' and he said, and this is what made the orangutans truly lose their dumb minds, 'I am correct. You three don't have a broad-enough intellectual platform to understand the advancements that this telescope will bring, nor do you have the capacity to assimilate new scientific information and learn. I am concerned that you are also missing a basic component of curiosity.' It was Kyle's honest assessment."

"What did they do? Can you hand me oregano?"

She grabbed a banana. She peeled it as she talked.

I didn't laugh!

"They're stupid, but they got the gist. They pushed Kyle against the lockers, the three of them, hard."

"And he?"

She raised her fists in victory, the banana high in the air. "He fought back. That's my boy. I have told Kyle, repeatedly over the years, to fight back with his karate skills. The kid's an advanced karate chopper, plus he's over six feet tall. One time he said to me, 'With respect, Mother, karate is peaceful. It is only to be used for self-defense,' and I said, 'Dude, what the heck do you think this is? You're defending yourself from three monsters left over from prehistoric times who trudged across the land underneath our feet,' and he said, 'I, too, am interested in paleontology in Montana and how the weather and topography have changed over billions of years, but I told my karate teacher that I would not use my hands as weapons,' and I said, 'Use them to defend yourself, son, or I will beat you up myself.' "

"So he karate chopped them?" Impressive!

"Yep. Cut. Swish. Kick. Hiya! All the kids on the floor moaning like stuck pigs on a spit. He told me that when they were on the floor, other kids clapped. He said he didn't know what to do, so he bowed, then collected his glasses, his notebooks, and his technology project and went to class. He told me, 'Very unfortunately, and distressingly, I was one minute twelve seconds late, and apologized to the teacher for my lateness. The teacher said, 'You're never late, it's okay, Kyle,' and Kyle said, 'I appreciate your kindness.'"

"I love it. Hopefully that will stop the bullying."

"He had many questions written down in his Questions Notebook that night. Most of them about the morality and ethics of fighting."

"Would you pass me three avocadoes?"

"Sure." Chloe opened the fridge, took out three eggs, cracked them in a bowl, and handed them to me. I said "Thank you," and she said, "You're very welcome, Olivia," and I got the avocadoes.

Watching your kids be hurt, or bullied, like Kyle or, in my case, knowing what was done to my girls when they were younger, stabs a mother's heart. It's a pain that radiates out until you feel like you can't breathe. I hugged my sister. We were breathing easier tonight.

Later that night I tried to think of something Kyle could say, or do, to alleviate some of the isolation he felt at school. His loneliness and aloneness made my stomach churn. I know what loneliness and aloneness feels like, and I so didn't want it for him.

What could he do?

Stephi and Lucy were each invited to birthday parties that weekend.

The invitations came in the mail because no invitations are allowed at school, thank heavens, as it makes things worse for the poor kids who aren't invited.

They brandished them in the air like trophies. Stephi was so excited she cried and clutched her rock collection together with both hands. Lucy said, pointing her finger straight up to the sky,

"We have to go shopping for the presents right now! I'm going to a birthday party! I have a friend! A friend!"

Before I was a mother I never knew how a child's joy could laser focus me in on that one moment, while everything else went away, and I would stand in that joy with them, as if I were in the middle of a golden, happy light.

Larry was intolerable, but I couldn't work for Jace.

How could I be around that hard, tough face with the dark eyes that softened up for me? How could I be around that smile, that quiet, strong, reserved, smart man without jumping on him? We had been best friends. We laughed all the time. Hiked. Skied. Walked. Talked. We read books together, for heaven's sakes. He listened to me as if everything I said was interesting, which it so wasn't.

Did I want to work for him?

I did.

I didn't.

I so did.

Could I do it?

What else did I want from him?

Nothing. Only a job.

That was a lie. I wanted so much. Everything. Hugs. Nakedness.

I couldn't have everything. We had a problem that was not fixable.

I am totally screwed up when it comes to that man.

When my mother read us fairy tales when Chloe and I were little girls, she always changed the endings. Instead of Snow White running off with the prince after a single kiss from her glass coffin in the woods, my mother said, "When Snow White woke up, she saw the prince leaning over her. She smiled at him. He smiled back. She thought he seemed like a friendly, intelligent young man. He helped her up and they visited with the talking animals for a while because they both loved animals.

"They went horseback riding together into the mountains,

which is what you see in this picture here. He was in college studying biology, and she was studying chemistry. They both wanted to become surgeons. They had a lot to talk about because they both loved medicine and nature. They became true friends.

"But they both knew they were way, way too young to get serious about each other so they stayed friends throughout college. Both of them traveled abroad to different countries and volunteered on medical missions. They studied all they could about medicine, operations, diseases, and treatments, and they made other friends. They hiked, canoed, and discovered that they both liked volunteering in their local hospital, rescue puppies, archery, camping, and learning more about becoming doctors. They started dating and went to the same medical school. Both became surgeons who helped the poor. They had four children because they knew their mothers wanted grandchildren.

"But do you see, Olivia and Chloe, they didn't get married right away after that first kiss. How could they? They weren't stupid. They didn't even know each other. Don't believe your other friends when they say that Snow White got married when she went off with the Prince that day to live in the castle. It didn't happen like that at all, lucky for heart surgeon Dr. Snow White."

And she could prove it. The last page of the book was ripped out and she wrote the "real" story on paper and stapled it in.

My mother taught us, through fairy tales, to be independent and strong. To have our own lives and our own jobs, and to rescue ourselves.

So I didn't need Jace rescuing me by taking the job he offered. I didn't.

But was Jace rescuing me if I went and worked at the ranch and made the most yummy food I could imagine?

She called again.

She had found out through her attorney that I was no longer at my apartment in Portland.

"Where the hell are you?" she said, so quietly, softly. Then she giggled, high-pitched. "I'll find you. You stupid bitch. I will find you no matter where you are. You. Will. Lose. See you soon."

I felt ill. Ill because of what could happen, not to me, but to them.

I called my attorney. She did what I paid her to do.

Kyle sat at my dining room table, Stephi and Lucy on either side of him. Kyle did not like to be touched much, but for some reason he allowed the girls to hang on him. I had bought poster board because the girls wanted Kyle to draw them fairies with sparkling wings.

"Smart fairies," Lucy said. "With muscles."

"Brave fairies," Stephi said, "who save men fairies."

"I have never drawn a fairy before," Kyle told the girls. "But I will give this artistic challenge my best effort. I studied fairies for forty-two minutes before coming today after I received your request through Aunt Olivia and Mother." He glanced at his watch. "I have eighty-two minutes. Ninety-seven minutes if I run home instead of walk."

Kyle drew each of the girls a fairy with a face exactly like theirs. They giggled and laughed. Then Lucy and Stephi both wanted their sister's face on another fairy, and he drew that. The two sisters, as fairies. They jumped up and down, then Stephi crawled into his lap.

When the girls were coloring the fairies I said, "Kyle, have you ever thought about asking kids at school if you could draw them?"

"No." He peered at me through his glasses. His hands flapped, then stilled. "That has not occurred to me."

"Think about it."

"I am confounded by your idea, Aunt Olivia. Is this a joke? You know I don't understand humor. Mother says I understand humor 'as well as a cow knows how to salsa dance,' her words, not mine. This means that she doesn't believe I understand humor."

"It's not a joke. It would be a way for you to make kids feel special, to show your talent as an artist but also to have a conversation with the kids you're drawing. They could talk to you, get to know you."

"As far as I can determine, they wish to have little to no contact with me. They do not wish to get to know me. I have been called retard. Spaceman. Freak and Freakoid. Scary kid. Weird One. Frankenstein and Abnormal. No one appears to want to sit by me at lunch, and they often move away when I do sit down with my lunch sack. I am not chosen for teams at PE despite the fact that I run faster than most of them due to the longer than average length of my legs and my lower than average BMI, which allows for speed. I don't think they want me to draw pictures of them." He peered up at the ceiling. "Also, if I drew pictures of them, I would have to look at them in the eye. That's difficult for me." He looked me in the eye, then down, then appeared to reevaluate. "Although, I would not have to look at them in the eye for long, as I have a photographic memory."

"You could use that photographic memory and your drawing skills to talk to people." Kyle broke my heart, he did. Lunch every day alone. No friends at school. Isolated.

"I don't think I was clear, Aunt Olivia." He blinked his eyes many times, took a ragged breath. "My fellow students do not wish to have a conversation with me."

"Kyle, ask one kid, a nice kid, if you can draw them and see what they say."

"I'm confused as to the goal of this project."

"Socializing. Meeting people. Making them happy."

"I'll evaluate your idea further, weighing the negatives and the positives. The negatives being I'm called Frankenstein again, or pervert, the positives being I could talk to one person at school."

That comment put another split in my heart. He wanted to talk to one person. That was it. One.

Stephi said, "I want to play bad dinosaur and brave girls now, Kyle."

"Me too!" Lucy said. "I'm a brave girl. You're the bad dinosaur."

Kyle stood up. "I pretend that I am a Dilophosaurus," he told me. He opened his hands and put them on the side of his head. "This is the best I can do to re-create this dinosaur's interesting physique."

"Have fun."

"Stephi and Lucy seem to find it quite entertaining to have to outrace this reptile." He smiled, ever so slightly. "I do have physics homework to attend to, and a paper on Shakespeare, and tonight the carpets all need to be vacuumed and the garbage must be taken out. I have promised my online chess partner a challenging game. But I believe I have time for one game of Brave Girls versus Dilophosaurus." He turned to the girls, bowed. "Let the game begin," he said, in all seriousness. He paused, and roared, loud and scary. They squealed and ran.

I hugged him. He allowed it, patted my back three times.

Chloe was mentioned in an article in our state's newspaper. She had gone up in a near blizzard to rescue two teenage snowboarding brothers who had gone out of bounds. Dangerous, dangerous, dangerous, but she did it. She was quoted in the article. "Look, folks. Do not go out of bounds on the mountain. These two (expletive) yahoos broke the rules and me, and my copilot, Dunn Silverman, had to go up and rescue their sorry (expletive) and almost died ourselves. Don't do it. Don't tick me off like that again."

Everyone agreed with her.

The brothers' parents' praise was endless. They were seen on TV crying, thanking Chloe and Dunn for "risking their own lives for our sons."

What a hero.

"Let's set a cake on fire."

I smiled at my grandma, sitting beside me on Saturday evening, our family gathered in the log cabin in front of the fire, candles lit. It was cold outside but clear, the stars white and sparkling. I had been daydreaming about Jace naked. The man was lustfully endowed. "Okay. Let's do it." I knew what cake Grandma wanted to set on fire, but the girls didn't. I winked at her.

"What do you mean set a cake on fire?" Lucy said.

"It's symbolic," Chloe said. "I am on fire as a woman, and we'll make a cake that is on fire, too." Chloe put her arms up in a victory pose. "Estrogen power. Feminine fortitude. Unrestrained sexuality."

"What is fem nin fort?" Lucy asked.

"What do you mean Es Trojan power?" Stephi asked.

"It means that women rock this world," Chloe said.

"I like fire," my mother drawled, holding a glass of wine, her feet up on the old black trunk. "If I wasn't a doctor I'd be an arsonist or a firefighter. I'm told that, psychologically, there's a fine line between the two. Probably easier to be a firefighter, though. I don't want to go to jail. I need the wide-open sky of Montana."

"When I think of fire," Kyle said, "for some reason I think of nuclear fusion." He stared into space, lost in complicated nuclear fusion thoughts.

"You mean we're going to light a match?" Stephi said. "But then the cake would be burned."

"We're making a Baked Alaska," my grandma said. She adjusted her scarf. Today it was lavender silk with a dark purple wisteria vine. "It's tricky, girls. But if you like ice cream, meringue, and brandy, it'll do. We'll turn off all the lights and it'll burn."

"Burn, baby, burn," my mother said. She was in her dark blue cowboy boots with the white stars. "I had someone come into the clinic with burns today, girls. I'll tell you how to treat them." She leaned forward. "First, depending on the level of burn, the skin can blister and shed so—"

"Mom!" I said.

"What?" my mother snapped. "They need to know about how to treat burn victims."

"Not now, Mom."

She brushed a hand through her hair, then sighed, so dramatic. "Oh, fine! Let's burn a cake. We'll make it in the shape of a leg, and then I can use it to teach the girls about how to use a scalpel—"

"Mom!"

"And The Fire Breather returns," my grandma said. "Cakes and operations. Who else would combine the two?"

"Do I have to eat the cake when it's on fire?" Lucy asked.

"Does it taste okay on fire?" Stephi asked.

"To be frank," my mother drawled, "legs don't taste good on fire."

"When I'm in my helicopter and I see fire, I know where to go," Chloe said, pointing her fingers up.

I gave Grandma her cookbook, which she had lent me, the leather cover cracked, the pages singed, stains all over, including the stains that appeared to be splattered blood. She undid the ratty pink ribbon. "I remember my mother's recipe. She had heard about Baked Alaska through a friend, an American chef who came into the bakery each day for my mother's croissants. My whole family made it together. What fun my sister, Renata, our brother, Isaac, and I had when she set that cake on fire. Gold, purple, blue flames. I never forgot it."

My jaw dropped. I had seen these names, but that Grandma was willing to talk about them . . .

My mother was silent for once in her life, The Fire Breather's mouth open, gaping as if she were a dying fish.

Chloe said, "I know this is gonna hurt to hear, but I still want to hear it if you want to tell us about it, Grandma. I'm right here for you, right here."

Kyle sat up. "These are two members of your family I am unfamiliar with, Grandma Gisela. Mother previously told me not to inquire about your relatives." He pulled out his Questions Notebook.

"We had a home in Munich. There's a picture of it in the cookbook. It was lovely. Three stories, brick, a black steel stair rail, a red door, and red geraniums. Our home was near our bakery and near my grandfather's store, Boris's Leather Goods, where he sold wallets and handbags. He had started out his working life making saddles and bridles, and his employees still made them, but he found the women's and men's lines much more profitable. Anyhow, it was within walking distance of our department store, too."

Too much to take in . . .

"Your family had a department store?" my mother said, still gaping like a fish.

"Yes. My parents did. Esther and Alexander's. It was the most popular store in Munich. My father ran it as my mother worked in her mother's bakery, although she also advised my father. There are pictures of our businesses in the cookbook, too."

I still couldn't speak.

Chloe said, her voice wobbling, "Yep. I was right. This hurts. So bad. You had a family."

"Yes," my grandma said, so quiet. "I had a family. A very large, loving family. My mother had four brothers. They were all married and had children. My cousins."

I rubbed my face. Too much sadness. She *had* a family. Gone. Long gone. So long gone.

My mother stood up and stared out the windows, but not before I saw her blinking rapidly.

Chloe sniffled. "I'm sorry, Grandma. I feel like my heart is gonna split in two for you." She pounded her chest.

"Thank you, Nutmeg."

Kyle stood up, leaned down, and hugged my grandma. She held him tight. He is a dear boy. He patted her back, three times. Then, quite significantly, which showed his pain for her, he patted her again, three times.

"My mother and grandmother loved to cook. At home, we all cooked together, as a family. Like we do now, the seven of us." She nodded at Kyle. "Isaac was an artist, too, Kyle. And he loved science and math, as you do." Kyle wrote that down in his Questions Notebook.

"Wait!" Lucy pointed her finger in the air and sat up straight.

"Are we, me and Lucy, two of the seven, Grandma Gisela?" Stephi asked, her face lighting up, hopeful.

"You are," my grandma said.

"Really, Grandma Gisela?" Lucy asked.

"Absolutely. We're all family. Forever and ever."

The girls shot up and hugged my grandma. They were so desperate for family, desperate for love and to belong. I thought of my grandma's family. Her sister, Renata; her brother, Isaac; her mother, Esther; her father, Alexander; her grandparents, all named in the cookbook . . . it had to be the camps that killed them.

"This cookbook is our history, our story, our recipes and family drawings, together. It's how we're connected, through all these generations. From Odessa, in what was then the Russian Empire, to Germany to England to Montana. It's our family, all in a cookbook."

By the window my mother bent her head, covered a sob. Then she muttered to herself, "Buck up, you emotional wimp. Get some cement in your spine." She doesn't like to cry.

"Now let's make that Baked Alaska and set it on fire." Grandma tapped the recipe.

We made the Baked Alaska that my grandma made with her mother, Esther, her father, Alexander, her brother, Isaac, and sister, Renata, in Munich, who had all been hidden in my grandma's tragic past.

On the Baked Alaska recipe there were splatters of a dark reddish brown stain and another brown stain in the upper-right-hand corner.

"Do you know what made these stains, Grandma?" I asked.

"Yes, Cinnamon." She pointed to the splatters. "Blood from my father, Alexander." She pointed to the brown stain. "Spilled tea. My father knocked it over after he was beaten."

We couldn't even speak.

She ran a light finger over the faces of three smiling children in front of a three-story, brick, gracious city home with a black steel stair rail, red geraniums in flower boxes, and a red door. Gisela, Isaac, and Renata, drawn by Ida.

"What happened, Grandma?" I asked.

She kissed my cheek. "I will tell you after we have made the Baked Alaska. For now, let's make a cake and let your mother, the arsonist, my own beloved Fire Breather, enjoy herself."

* * *

Later, with the lights off, we watched my grandma pour warmed-up rum over the Baked Alaska. My mother lit the match and the meringue caught on fire, golden and blue flames, dancing and waving.

No one said anything while it burned.

Then my grandma whispered something, in German.

"What did you say, Grandma Gisela?" Lucy asked.

"I said forever and ever our love is everlasting." She wiped a tear, her finger shaking a bit. "I told my family that I loved them, I missed them, that I would see them again."

"Dang it twice. I'm crying again like a baby," Chloe said. "My emotions go deep for you, Grandma."

"Mom," my mother said, holding her mother. "I am so sorry."

I put my arm around my grandma's shoulder, too. "I am, too, Grandma."

We did not bother to wipe the tears from our faces, the room dark, the flames dancing.

Grandma told us her story.

From Odessa to Munich to England to Montana, Grandma's family visited through a Baked Alaska.

January 1939
Munich, Germany
Esther Gobenko, great-grandmother of Olivia Martindale

Esther Gobenko held her husband, Alexander, as he stumbled, bleeding, through the back door of their Munich home at midnight.

Their home was freezing, as they could no longer afford heat. There were blank spaces on the walls where art used to hang. Armoires that held figurines now held nothing, the glass fronts broken. The Nazis had taken everything of value. They had thrown against the walls their Seder plate, the Shabbat candlesticks, the menorah, the Kiddush cups, and had stomped on her husband's prayer shawl.

They had taken the jewelry Esther couldn't hide. One had

knocked her over with his fist when she told him she had no more jewelry. He had even ripped the wedding ring off her finger. She was not about to tell him where the rest of her jewelry was. It was all they had. They would sell it to survive.

The Nazis had also taken their department store, Esther and Alexander's, and Boris's Leather Goods, and they had forced the closure of Ida's Bakery. She had drawn pictures of their businesses in the cookbook so her family would always remember them.

On Kristallnacht, on the ninth of November the previous year, the windows were broken and all of their businesses looted, then firebombed.

Her family was now living off hidden savings, as their bank accounts had been confiscated. Unbelievably, the Jews were told they had to pay for the damage incurred on Kristallnacht.

After Kristallnacht, the truth could no longer be denied: Jews had to leave Germany or die. Alexander's parents, her dear Aizik and Raisel, were ill, and they knew they could not make the journey. "Go, son, leave," they had begged Alexander months ago. "Now. Save Esther. Save Isaac, Gisela, and Renata. Go." Her own parents, Ida and Boris, looking grief stricken but courageous, had told them the same thing, as they had told her brothers, Grigori and Solomon, "We love you. You must leave Germany. Save yourselves and your families."

Alexander and she had not wanted to leave their parents, the thought was abhorrent, but they could get out now or they and their children could all die or disappear, as Esther's brothers Moishe and Zino had disappeared. Moishe and Zino had spoken out against Hitler, now no one had heard from them in months. So many of their Jewish friends, doctors and professors, business owners and musicians, artists and writers, had also disappeared. Some had left Germany earlier, the Nazis stripping them of all their assets, including accounts, businesses, and artwork, before they escaped.

They soon found that they could not get visas, they could not get permission to travel as a family to any country. The paperwork, for them and for a sponsor in a new country, was exten-

*sive, near impossible. No country wanted more Jews, either.
America had closed its doors. They were stuck, and they were
terrified. They had waited too long. They had tried to wait until
the German people came to their senses and kicked Hitler and his
ghouls out. The German people had not come to their senses.
They had embraced a madman. A dictator. A psychopath.*

*Esther's family was starving. They could not get enough food,
as they were restricted on where and when they could shop.
There were curfews for Jews, beatings of Jews on the streets, Jews
moved to ghettos, synagogues burned, and their citizenships revoked.*

*That night, Esther had hoped that her family's cookbook
would calm her as she waited for Alexander. He was so late.
Where was he? What had happened? Would her beloved husband disappear, too? What were they to do? How could they
save the children? Her hands shook as she wrote and drank tea,
her tears falling on the page. She added a recipe for Baked
Alaska, a treat she and her mother had learned about from an
American chef who came to their bakery for croissants.*

*When she heard light knocking on the back door, she stopped
breathing, petrified. She tentatively stepped through the semi-
darkness of her home, clutching a knife.*

*She heard the soft knock again. She wished that Alexander
was home. He would know what to do. He would protect her
and the children. "Who is it?"*

*"It's Alexander, Esther." The voice didn't sound like Alexander's.
It was strangled, panting. "Please. Open the door."*

*She opened it an inch to see him curled up on the back door
step. Alexander had been beaten and robbed of his wallet and
keys by a mob and had escaped only by luck and with the help
of one man, a former customer, who had taken pity. He was
bleeding, blood dripping from a gash in his head, down his
neck, onto his shirt.*

"Alexander," she breathed, trying not to sob.

*She wrapped her arms around him, his weight heavy, and
dragged him into the kitchen, kicking the door shut. She settled*

him in a chair at the kitchen table. He turned his head, blood from the wound splattering across the Baked Alaska recipe. He grabbed, awkwardly, at the table to keep himself from falling, and he spilled her tea onto the upper-right-hand corner.

Gisela, Renata, and Isaac snuck down the stairs, took one peek at their father, bruised, unable to stand, bloodied, and started to cry. They made no sounds. It was one more horror. Gisela held a cloth to her father's head with trembling hands, and the blood soaked through. Isaac, already so tall for a teenager, propped him up, and Renata held her father's head still as it wobbled on his neck.

"We must get the children out, Esther," Alexander rasped, as if they weren't there, all in a miserable huddle in their kitchen, a kitchen stripped of both food and safety. "Immediately."

"How?" Esther said, trying to control her hysteria. "We're too late. We didn't listen. We can't get visas."

"I'm not leaving without you two!" Renata wailed.

Alexander stared at Esther with the one eye that wasn't swollen shut, his head lagging, blood smeared on his face, pale and desolate. "I heard of a way."

"How," Esther pleaded. "What is the way?'

He told her. "We still have the hidden jewelry. We must sell it tomorrow. We must plan."

Gisela and Renata cried. Isaac adjusted his glasses, his hands flapping.

Over spilled tea and splattered blood, the plan took shape.

I hit my last straw at work. The last straw was named Gary. Larry hired him. Gary and Larry. It was poetically gross. Gary had twice served time, once for assaulting his ex-wife, once for assaulting a friend. I was livid. Gary eyeballed me head to foot when he first sauntered in, just like Larry, smirked, laughed in that repulsive way men do when they think women are treats and are valued only for their sex appeal, and said to Larry, "Oh yeah, man. I get to work with that? I'll take her!" They both laughed drizzly, scummy laughs.

"You will not take me, Gary. It's not funny." I had a knife in my hand from slicing chicken. "You talk to me like that again and I will fillet you before I fillet this chicken."

"Tough girl, are ya?" Gary said, leering. "I like 'em that way, but don't fillet me, girl. I have other fun we can get up to."

"I call her Chef Feisty!" Larry said, so proud of his demeaning ingenuity.

I said to Larry, "I don't want him working here."

"Too bad, hon—" He stopped himself, winked at Gary. Boys will be boys, women are toys! "Too bad, Olivia. This is my restaurant."

"I'm the chef."

"And I'm the boss." Larry tried to meet my eyes, tried to be the commanding boss in front of his jailbird friend, but his eyes slid away.

As the days wore on, Gary made my skin shrivel. Larry said, "Ya gotta learn to get along with people, Olivia. Play nice. Be nice to him and he'll be nice back."

Gary was slow. Slovenly. Disrespectful and slimy. One of our waitresses and one of our cooks quit over the next weeks.

One afternoon Gary slithered up behind me when I was bent over a hot stove stirring a gnocchi soup with cream, chicken, garlic, and carrot slices. He said, "How about dinner, sexy momma?"

I jumped. I hadn't heard him. "Back off." I whirled around and faced him, brandishing the wooden spoon.

"Thought I'd ask, baby." His eyes focused on my boobs. Again.

Larry was six feet away, watching. Amused, but wary and angry. Amused because he had a sick control problem with me and liked to see me irritated and powerless. It infuriated him that I wouldn't kowtow to him. But he was wary because he didn't want me to quit, and angry because another man was hitting on me and he's possessive.

"You come near me again, Gary, and I will pull out one of the multiple guns that I have, in my purse, my truck, and at my house, and I will shoot first and ask you questions about your broken kneecaps later. I will then call the chief of police, who has been a close friend of my family for decades, and file charges against you for harassment. Do you need the police, Gary?"

He winked at me. "I've always liked you, Olivia. But you need taming."

I could see the latent fury sparking in his eyes. He was a controlling man, too, like Larry. He hated women because they didn't like him and that threatened his twisted ego. He needed to dominate.

Then Gary made his final mistake. He leaned toward me because he had to show me who was boss, he had to touch me. He put both hands hard on my waist and opened his mouth to say something disgusting. I reacted instinctively, stabbing that wooden spoon straight into his neck, as hard as I could. He staggered back, hit part of a table, and crashed down, clutching his throat, gagging.

When he got up, he swore and charged me, murder on his face, and I picked up a knife and raised it.

Gary paused. He was a possum, but he wasn't a stupid possum and he was having trouble breathing. I advanced.

Justin and Earl yelled and shoved him out the door while Larry swayed. I realized Larry was semi-drunk.

I was so sick of Larry. Him and his lard stomach, the way his eyes watched me, his fleshy lips.

I took a breath. Without this job I would be immediately broke.

I had attorney bills. I had a hospital bill. I had two little girls. I was a single mother fighting for custody and I would be unemployed.

Scary.

But I had a log cabin to live in with a red door, a lasso on the deck, and my grandparents' cowboy hats nailed to the wall. I would find another job. I could work two jobs. I couldn't handle this for another minute.

"I'm done," I said, quiet, calm. "I quit."

"What? No! No!" Larry squawked, coming out of his drunken stupor. "Gary's gone. He's out. I'll fire him."

"It's not only Gary, although you allowed a man to come and work here who was repulsive and offensive. It's you. You're disgusting."

"What?" His voice pitched high. "No, I'm not. I'll change. I've changed. Right here, right now. I've changed." He put his palms out. I could tell he was scared. "You make the rules now, Olivia. You."

"You haven't changed." I was incredibly tired all of a sudden. "I have worked and worked for you for months. Your restaurant was in the gutter when I arrived, now it's the most popular breakfast restaurant in Kalulell and you have thanked me by being a sexist, demeaning, condescending, slobbery, ball-clutching, porn-talking jerk. You are incapable of changing."

"No, no! I'll change." Larry ran in front of me. He gripped both of my arms to stop me. He blocked me from leaving.

"Let go of me before I break all the fingers in your hands."

He let go. "I'll give you a huge raise." He put his face close to mine. "Name a price."

"There is no price, Larry. None. This environment is toxic. I need a job. Desperately. And you played off that desperation, but I don't need one this desperately."

"I'm out, too," Dinah said. Justin and Earl and the other employees took off their aprons. They threw them on the floor. Larry howled, begged, whined.

We left. We hugged each other outside.

I was now both unemployed and broke.

But free. Free of Larry and Gary. I smiled when I climbed into my light blue truck and gunned it.

My mother came over later. She'd had to go to the hospital to check on two of her patients. "I saw Gary Simonson in the emergency room. Next time you're going to attack a flea-bitten criminal in the neck, please let me know. A good daughter lets her mother know when a jackass is going to get what he's got comin' to him."

"Yes, ma'am."

She winked at me and left.

The police chief, Adam Kalama, came to my house the next day in his police car. No lights. No sirens. I gave him a hug, invited him in. He's about sixty. His father is Hawaiian. We ate an apple pie I made that morning. The key is tart apples and half a lemon. "Gary Simonson says you attacked him for no reason, Olivia."

"Self-defense."

"Good enough for me." He took another bite of apple pie. "I love this crisscross crust, Olivia. Can I get the recipe?"

"Sure."

"I heard you and Jace got back together, then I heard that you didn't. Have you worked things out yet?"

"No."

"Sorry to hear that, Olivia. You're two of my favorite people. My wife feels the same."

"Thanks." I added more vanilla ice cream to our pie. So delicious.

Stephi got upset the next afternoon because she missed Annabelle, and she wanted to know if her mom was going to get killed in prison, and she didn't want that to happen, but was it bad to not want to live with her mom because when she was mad she was scary? Did I know that their dad's friend, Ross, killed their cat? He did.

Stephi, Lucy, Annabelle, and I had so much fun together in Portland. We were a family made by choice. We also hung out with other people in our apartment building, including the families from Iran and Ethiopia, often on Monday nights, when I didn't work. We took turns cooking, so we had food from around the world.

Annabelle would sometimes talk to me about her heartbreak over her daughter, Sarah, aka Devlin, how she worried about her in jail but was glad she couldn't get drugs. She told me she had a will, the girls were to go to Annabelle's older sister, in Oklahoma, if anything happened to her and Devlin was still in jail. But then the sister, who was seventy, started having health problems and obviously could not take the girls.

"Would you take Stephi and Lucy, Olivia?" Annabelle asked me one night. We'd been friends for almost a year and a half. "I'm as healthy as an ox and an old warhorse combined, but I like to plan ahead. With the girls, it's even more important. I cannot have them going into foster care again."

I didn't even have to think about it. "Yes. I'll take them. I'll raise them like my own daughters."

"It won't be official. Sarah's and Parker's parental rights haven't been terminated. But it will hold weight, I think, in court, if it came to deciding who the girls should live with if Sarah is still in jail, or refuses to stay clean or commits another crime when she's out."

"I understand."

"I love Sarah. I always will. But I can't have the girls going back to being raised in a drug house." Annabelle hugged me. "I love you, Olivia."

"You too, Annabelle."

And I did. Friends can come at any stage of life. They can be much older or much younger. From a different country, of a different faith, with beliefs like yours or totally opposite. Annabelle was one of those friends. She was, is, one of the best friends of my life.

So Annabelle wrote a letter naming me as her preferred guardian for the girls and attached it to her will. She gave me a copy of the paperwork, and the information for the small college funds she had set up for the girls.

She apologized for not having more money for me to raise the girls if it came to that—much of her life savings had been lost to rehab for Devlin. She apologized for not having life insurance. She had had heart surgery when she was forty-five and since then had not been able to qualify. I told her not to worry about it. Annabelle was only in her early sixties, a healthy nurse who worked fifty hours a week. We never thought about it again, never talked about it. It was only a precaution.

What I learned the hard way? Everyone needs a will.

I untied the pink ribbon and flipped through my grandma's cookbook the next night when I couldn't sleep, too worried about too many things to relax.

I couldn't help wondering about the remnants of the rose, two heart-shaped gold lockets, the two red ribbons, a sun charm, and a white feather tucked into the back pages.

I hoped I would know one day where they came from.

Chapter 10

❧

"Greetings, Aunt Olivia."

"Hi, Kyle." I hugged him, he allowed it. He patted my back three times. "Come on in. The girls and I made Martindale Family Pizza with extra mozzarella cheese, garlic, and artichoke hearts. Want a slice?"

"Thank you. I would appreciate the nourishment." The girls hugged him and made him promise that he would play Darts and Dragons with them later. They dress up like dragons and throw balls at one another. They had told Kyle about it the last time he visited, and he agreed to play today.

"Aunt Olivia, I believe I have had a small, although nonscientific, breakthrough in understanding the social habits and emotional lives of other teenagers."

"How so?" I took a sip of white wine. Wine goes splendidly with Martindale Family Pizza.

"I did what you instructed." His gaze slid away from mine, then back up. "Correction of myself. I wrote down what you said in my Questions Notebook and spent time evaluating your proposal. Then I did what you instructed."

"You mean when I told you to offer to draw other kids at school?"

"Precisely. It was a peculiar suggestion to me, but because I trust you and you have proven in the past to be both sensible and practical, and because you have told me on numerous occasions that you love me, hence you would wish for a positive outcome for me, I embarked upon the experiment."

"And?" I leaned forward, so hopeful. "What happened?"

"I studied all of my peers to determine who might be most receptive to this undertaking. I finally asked a girl in my biology class if I could draw her. She is attractive. Her skin is the color of my mother's coffee with cream in it. She has dark eyes, like one might imagine a black hole, only there is gold and, curiously, both azure and jade. Her hair is an ebony color like the piano key, which is intriguing as she does play the piano. She has a wider than average smile. She said yes to my query, and so I drew her during study hall."

"And?" Please, please, please. Tell me it went well . . .

His hands fluttered, then stopped. "I believe that the session was productive in terms of peer-to-peer relationships, of which I know little."

"Music to my ears, kid. Tell me more. Why do you think that?"

"The young lady's name is Natasha Jefferson, birthday May 14. She smiled and laughed and said, 'Can I keep it?' when I was finished with the drawing, which I found to be a strange question but I did not express that."

"Why did you think it was strange?"

"Because, rightly so, she could keep the drawing. It was of her. She took a picture of it with her phone and sent it to her parents, Zack and Corinne; her grandparents; her aunt Maudie; and her uncle Sam, who is in a mental health institution because he believes he is former President Clinton. She was smiling and thanked me several times and I said, 'You're welcome, Natasha,' each time. I did not comment on the dark color of her eyes with gold, azure, and jade."

"What did the other kids do?"

"That was peculiar to me also." He took his glasses off, then put them back on. "An unpredictable result. When I first began drawing, there was no one around us in study hall. Then one person arrived to my right, behind my elbow, at a thirty-degree angle. Soon another person came and stood to my left, peering over my shoulder, approximately forty-five degrees. Followed by more students. When I was finished and presented the drawing to Natasha, everyone clapped. I then stood and bowed to Natasha."

"Did she like that?"

He was perplexed. "She laughed, but I don't believe it was in a mocking way, though I could be wrong. I thought a gesture of bowing was appropriate. Men used to bow to women in the past when they wanted to impress a lady and show respect. That's when she gave me a hug. She smelled like lemons and jasmine. I told her that."

I smiled.

"A boy named Nathan Beskill, birthday November 29, asked me to draw him, and a girl, Lele Duan, birthday April 2, and another girl, Liisa Elshaund, with two I's, birthday March 12, asked the same question. There was soon a list, I did not start it, Liisa did. Liisa informed me, 'I'll be the organizer.' People signed up if they wanted a portrait. Twenty-seven people wrote their names down. Fortunately, with thirty-seven minutes left in class, I was able to draw LeLe. She seemed equally pleased and felt compelled to hug me also. I bowed. She bowed back. She also took a photo of the drawing and sent it to her mother, her father, her stepfather, another stepfather, and two stepsisters and one half sister."

"How did you feel about the hugs and the attention?" I finished my wine. This was something to celebrate. I poured another glass.

Kyle clasped his hands together, then opened them back up and touched his fingers to his palms and tapped them. "I was uncomfortable with the touching, and it was loud and warm, approximately fifteen degrees warmer than is comfortable for my internal body temperature. My fellow students were crowded around me. These are all triggers for my anxiety and for feeling slightly claustrophobic. However, I determined that to express this, or to leave the room, would only make me seem peculiar. This was not the positive experience I wanted, so I did what my mother said and I breathed deeply, then shallowly, and focused. I remembered her words, 'Don't freak out, Kyle, breathe.' I also used mathematical equations to calm me down as I drew. It did lower my heart rate."

He paused, looked me in the eye, and held my gaze. "I believe it was a pleasant experience. No one wanted to hit me, there was no laughter that I did not understand, and the other students did not appear to be frightened of me or angry."

"They're not frightened of you, Kyle, they need a chance to get to know you."

"I hope that you are correct in that assumption." He sniffled. I saw tears in his eyes. This was a rare, rare occurrence, and I put my arm around him. He allowed it.

"Perhaps this is my chance to get to know them and for them to make my acquaintance. It is better to know people than to always be alone. After study hall there were five people—three girls, two boys—who said, 'Hello, Kyle,' or, 'Hi, Kyle,' in the halls to me later that day. That is five more than normal. I stopped, said hello, and wished them a good day."

"I think you gotta keep drawing, kid."

"It does seem that it might help with my serious deficit in friendships."

I wiped a tear off my cheek.

He wiped tears off of his. "It appears that I'm crying. I feel that my emotions are out of control. Mother says it's puberty. In terms of a teen's biology, she is correct."

"It's okay to cry. You had a huge day. You made people happy."

"I am a human being."

"That has never been in dispute."

His eyes lit up. "I understood that as a joke, Aunt Olivia."

"Excellent."

"Now I shall go and play Darts and Dragons with Stephi and Lucy. I am the dragon." He bent to his backpack and pulled out a papier-mâché dragon mask.

"Did you make that?" It was large and green, with protruding blue eyes and a long tongue.

"Yes. Last week. It's taken some time. I did it after homework and cleaning the house. I believe it will make the playing experience more enjoyable for the girls."

Oh, it did. I heard them squeal and laugh as he roared.

I was putting more and more debt on my credit card. I did the math. It wouldn't be long before the credit card was maxed out. I was done.

I called Jace the next morning. The conversation was brief.

"Hi, Jace. Can I come by the ranch and talk to you?"

"Yes. Anytime. Today?"

"Tomorrow morning?" I needed time to get my courage up.

"I'll look forward to it."

I left Jace a letter on the kitchen table when I left him.

It was a disgraceful way to leave. He deserved more. He deserved a wife who would stay and work things out with him. He deserved a conversation. He deserved a chance to speak and a chance to ask me to change my mind, to make other changes. He deserved a last hug, a good-bye.

I didn't give any of that to him.

I am an awful, awful person.

And now the awful, awful wife is asking the husband for a job.

The next morning I dropped the girls off at school, took a shower with sweet-smelling stuff, washed and dried my hair, and put on makeup. I pulled on my favorite cowgirl boots, the ones with the red cutouts of magnolias, because they gave me courage, and my favorite jeans. They were too loose because I wasn't eating enough because stress makes me feel sick and I can't eat. I pulled on a blue sweater with a ruffled hem I bought in Paris, a scarf I bought in Cambodia with a picture of a blue lagoon, and shiny gold bangles from India.

Ready.

Sort of.

Scared.

Scared of all of the memories that would come at me like a dump truck the second I set foot on Jace's Martindale Ranch. Some of those memories had brought me to my knees, then dragged me through an ocean of pain, and dropped me off a cliff.

"Hello, Jace." I twisted my fingers together. I had not looked up at the hill with the magical sunsets as I drove by the white fence into Martindale Ranch. Still, the memories came rushing in, a gash to my soul, and I'd had to pull over to deal with them. I settled my breathing by saying, "Stop it, Olivia, buck up," then drove on.

"Hello, Olivia." He smiled, welcoming me into his office. "How are you?"

"I'm fine." I'm terrible. *Man, Jace.* Jeans and cowboy boots and a black sweater. You are a sex stud cowboy.

"Please. Have a seat."

We sat at a circular wood table near his windows. On it was a carved, painted picture of Martindale Ranch. Jace had commissioned it from Grenadine Scotch Wild, the same artist in central Oregon we had commissioned to make the paintings of my grandparents' log cabin and our blue farmhouse. It was a work of art, detailed, exquisite, a perfect replica of the ranch, down to the sign.

Jace's office is on the second floor of the dining hall, above the kitchen. It's in the corner, two walls of windows. When I was here he brought in a desk for me. I asked him why, because I was spending all of my time in the kitchen and I actually had a table down there at which to work. He told me it was because we were both in charge and he wanted to work side by side with me. He said he liked my company, too. My desk was now gone.

"I took your desk out, Olivia. Hurt too much to see it."

"Ah. I'm . . . I . . ." I was not prepared for this much honesty and this much pain. "I would have done the same thing."

He smiled again, slow and easy. "Did you come to visit?"

"No. Yes. Uh." I tried to gather up my nerve to talk to him. "No. Jace, I—"

At the same time he said, "You are so beautiful. You walk in and it's like I have sunshine in my life again."

"Oh. Thank you." That was so romantic. And it hurt. "You are, too, Jace. I mean. You are..." Smokin'. Sexy. Huggable. "Healthy." *Healthy? What?* "Like a rancher. A cowboy." *A cowboy and a rancher? Say something normal, please, Olivia. Please.*

He actually winked at me. "Thank you. This cowboy feels healthier now that you're here."

Get it together, Olivia. Get some cement in your spine, some steel in your sternum! "So, Jace. You may know at Larry's. Uh. Hmm. There was a small incident."

"Sounds like Gary Simonson ended up with a neck injury when you defended yourself against him."

"Right."

"I will shoot him if he comes near you again." His face was thunderous.

Would I be a damsel in distress if I let Jace shoot Gary instead of shooting him myself? He looked princely on a horse. I got all confused thinking about Jace riding a horse and forgot what I was going to say next, so I smiled... and kept smiling... "Oh! Right. Because of that unfortunate incident I don't have a job."

"Yes."

"And I was wondering..."

"Yes."

"Yes what?" A yes to work at the ranch?

"Yes, come and work here. My pregnant chef left yesterday."

I about cried. I wanted to cry. My chest got tight. My eyes filled with hot lakes of tears. Was he rescuing me again? Yes. He was. Whatever. I had loved working here.

"Thank you." Whoosh. I could breathe again!

"Thank *you*, Olivia. I'm glad you're coming back. This is a lucky day for me."

My chin quivered. I tried to stop it. *Stop that,* I told myself. *Stop that and be a Montana cowgirl, not a wuss.*

He told me how much he would pay me, so gentle, he saw the tears.

That amount was overboard. "Too much, you know it."

"It's not too much at all. You're worth it and you're a half owner. You bring people to the ranch with your cooking, babe. We were written up several times, in national magazines, because of you. Hasn't happened since you left. The food is not at the level it was when you were here, especially the desserts. You're a world-class chef, and I have truly missed your soups and sauces and those cakes. I have never had a better cake than what you can make. In fact, I don't eat cake anymore because it's not made by you."

"Thank you, but I'm not worth that."

"Comes with health insurance for you and the girls, too. And if you and the girls ever want to stay over, you can stay in one of the guest houses. You can have a guest house if you want as a permanent residence, too. Let me know what works."

"That's very generous." I took a deep breath and focused my eyes on the view of the blue and white mountains out his window. "Thank you, Jace." I cleared my throat. Must change topic or will jump on husband and take off his cowboy clothes. "So, for the dinners here, what do you think of . . ."

And we talked. Like before. About dinner and lunch and breakfast, warm cookies, pasta primavera, onion rings, and cakes that would be rich, fluffy, and delectable.

It was easy to be with him again. It was always so easy to be with Jace.

I smiled at him. He smiled back. I forgot what I was going to say again. He is yummy.

We cannot be together.

My mother picked up the girls from school and took them to the clinic. She had bought them white doctor's coats.

They loved the clinic, but Lucy said, "Grandma Mary Beth talks rough to her patients sometimes. She tells them what to do, and says don't give me a headache, but they still seem to like her because they usually give her a hug." She paused. "I think they might be a teeny-weeny bit scared of her. She told one patient that he was a stubborn old goat."

Stephi said, "But twice the people that Grandma Mary Beth was talking to said, 'Can I talk to Mrs. Gisela and see what she thinks?' So we had to go and get Grandma Gisela."

"And a whole bunch of people come in just to see Grandma Gisela. They said she knew all about healing nature. Did they mean, like, trees, when they're sick?" Lucy said. "Do you know about Saint-John's-wort, Aunt Olivia? I do. Grandma Gisela told me it can help with not being sad. Do you know about marigolds? I do. They help with stomachaches. When I told Grandma Mary Beth that I'm going to be a doctor, she shouted, 'Praise the good Lord.' "

The next afternoon I saw my grandma in the gazebo. She was leaning against the post, her eyes closed, a smile on her face. She was wearing her white scarf with the pink cherry flowers on it. I didn't make a sound as she raised a hand and waved toward Montana's eternal blue sky.

"You can do it. You can, you can, you can." I said this out loud to myself as I drove to Jace's ranch the next morning.

It was snowing lightly, the snowflakes delicate, peaceful. Inside my car I was wrestling with mental chaos.

"You can work with Jace," I murmured, trying to sound Zen-like. "You're at the ranch to cook. And bake. And make everything delicious. You know how to do this. You've been doing it for years." I tried to suck in air. What was wrong with the air in my car? Why was there not enough?

"Don't let Jace make you nervous . . . Why would he make me nervous? Because he's smokin' . . .

"Don't let him make you think about getting naked with him . . . I won't. I can control myself . . . Probably. At least I'll try. But those shoulders, and that butt . . . Don't think of yourself as anything but an employee, not his wife . . . If you feel lustful, shut it down, think about playing chess. If you feel like hugging him, don't. If you feel like reenacting that time on the kitchen table at midnight, don't . . . And please stop talking to yourself. Please, you loon, stop."

Where was the air in this darn car? I rolled down my window and was hit with snowflakes. I kept the window down.

I had deserted Jace. I had abandoned our marriage. We had no future, he and I. Yet here I was, hired by Jace and going back to Martindale Ranch.

My nerves were jangling and jumping.

And I was so happy. Happy to my bones.

It was as if I'd never left Martindale Ranch.

Everything in the kitchen had been left where I'd left it. Mostly. Here and there pots and pans and utensils had been moved, but the kitchen, with its six-burner gas stoves, multiple stainless steel ovens, walk-in refrigerator, and the extra storage we'd designed still felt like my kitchen, it still felt like home. I stood in the middle of it and enjoyed the views of the mountains out a wall of windows.

I had hired Dinah, Earl, and Justin for Jace's ranch. Better salary than at Larry's, plus health insurance. Jace had lost his pregnant chef and two other people. One had decided to go back to college to study chemistry and become a dentist, and the other left because she wanted to trek across America on her bike.

We worked quickly with the other staff members, most of whom I knew. We all introduced ourselves, smiled, laughed. I told them the menu for the day, and we got to work.

I have been in enough kitchens, around the world, with chefs who had all sorts of issues.

One chef, in China, used to throw knives. Honest to God. He never aimed them at anyone. When he wasn't losing his temper he was a kind, compassionate soul, but when one of those knives stabbed the wall three feet from me, when he had another fit, that was it. I walked out that minute, him trailing after me, begging me to stay in Chinese and broken English. I loved learning how to make Chinese food like kung pao chicken, ginger beef, pot stickers, and Chinese fried rice, but it was not enough to make me stay and risk being cut in half by a knife-throwing chef.

I was in another kitchen, in Thailand, a fancy place, with a British chef. He would periodically lose his mind. Truly. He would start to rant and rave, nonsensical stuff. We'd come in and he'd be gone, committed for a couple of weeks, and I would take over. He would come back, steady on, hugging people, we would chug right along, but then he'd hit a bad place again and start crying into the soup, yelling at the soup, and he'd have to be recommitted. He was one of the most introspective, most un-selfish, smartest people I have ever known, and his drunken noodles were spectacular, but the kitchen would be in an uproar, often.

A third chef, in Paris, was a woman named Dominique. My French is conversational only, but I understand enough to cook. She used to sing songs, laden with French swear words. Eating her entrées, especially her coq au vin and her ratatouille, was like eating heaven. But she struggled with obsessive-compulsive disorder. She would take all of our spice jars, which were in al-phabetical order, off the shelves and cooking areas, mess them up, and put them back in alphabetical order again until she felt better.

In my kitchen, it was friendly. I am the boss, but I am a boss who takes suggestions, and I give people a lot of free rein. If Justin wanted to flip our Giddyap Horse Strawberry Crème Crêpes, we made them. If Dinah felt like grilling Gut-Busting Bacon-Wrapped Burgers, we did it. Same with the other em-ployees, if they had a request.

I think cooking should be joyful. It should be near spiritual. It should be done with love and a true desire to nourish and nur-ture other people.

So that's how we cooked at Martindale Ranch. Goal: Make people's lives better, through hearty, tasty food, every time they came in to eat.

It was a fast-paced morning. We whipped and stirred and sautéed and baked. The hours flew by. The dining hall, where the kitchen is located, is rustic, homey, and bright. Jace and I had told the builder what we wanted. It's a Craftsman-style building, with a huge stone fireplace, windows, and French doors all around. Pitched roof, open beams, lighting in the shapes of lanterns. Fishing poles, nets, skis, and ski poles hung on the walls for décor, and a red canoe hung from the ceiling. There were long wooden tables so everyone could eat together, family style, candles down the middle, flowers in the center.

In the middle of breakfast, Jace walked into the kitchen. I didn't see him, but I sensed him at the door, watching me. I finally got my courage up, turned, and smiled at him. He smiled back, tall and handsome in jeans and a blue sweater and a cowboy hat.

A half hour later, Jace gently dragged me into the dining area. "May I have your attention?" All the guests turned toward Jace. Mothers and fathers, singles and dating couples, grandparents, and kids. One man was ninety-four. The youngest was two. We are a family-centered business. "This is your chef, Olivia Martindale. I hope you liked what she made today."

Oh, they did. They truly did. They gave me a standing ovation and cheered. One man held up his cinnamon roll, my grandma's recipe that she got from her grandma, Ida, and yelled, "Best ever, honey. Best ever."

I glanced up at Jace, black-haired and towering over me. I liked his hips. I liked his shoulders. I liked him. He winked at me. I smiled.

It felt like home.

Jace felt like home.

After the lunch shift, with the dinner ready to go for the next shift of people, I left. I stopped on the wraparound deck of the dining hall and told myself I would climb up the hill and watch a magical sunset.

Very soon. I wanted to.

I had to.

The three teenaged thugs at school continued to harass Kyle, despite the principal threatening, and then carrying out, a three-day suspension. Chloe went to the homes of all three boys, even

Jason's, who lived in a scary trailer with a rabid father who openly carried his rifle in town and got drunk.

She told the man to keep Jason away from her son or she would knock him clean out of Montana. Jason Senior showed her his gun, cigarette hanging out of his mouth, gut flowing out of his shirt, dogs chained up beside him barking, and hollered, "Get off my property, Chloe. My son can do whatever he wants to your pansy-ass boy." Chloe kept stomping toward him. Not scared at all.

"Ya wanna piece of me? Do ya? Do ya? Take a shot, Jason. You look like a beaver with those buck teeth, but you will become someone's girlfriend in prison by noon tomorrow. You will have to watch your butt in the shower. You will have to learn how to like laundry duty. You want that? No, didn't think so. Put your gun down, you tiny-balled vermin, and when your brainless son crawls out of his hole, tell him to back the hell off."

During school the next day, Eric, Jason, and Juan pushed Kyle, grabbed his backpack, and dumped out all of his art supplies, which he had been using to draw portraits of other kids. They ran off, probably afraid that he would use his karate on them again.

Over brownies with extra chocolate chips at my house, Kyle told me that when he was on his hands and knees, grabbing for pencils and paper, the revenge plot began. "Intellectual dialogue should solve problems, not violence or vengeance. I want to assure you that I know that, Aunt Olivia. But this time, with my art supplies being scattered, I feel I have no choice. My art supplies allow me to talk to my peers and to build fulfilling social relationships that are not based on confusing mockery and sarcasm that is often incomprehensible." He paused. "Not being called 'freak' or 'shithead' has made school more relaxing. Now my fellow students often call me 'Kyle the Artist.' I prefer that to the profanity."

I patted his back, handed him another brownie, and cursed the kids who were so mean.

"A most surprising thing happened, though. My fellow students helped me pick up my art supplies. Together we returned my pencils back into their organized containers and my drawing paper back into its folder."

"The other kids were nice, then?" Hopeful sign!

"Yes. At study hall I drew two students. They seemed pleased as they said, 'Kyle, I love my drawing. Thank you.' Two people—one boy, one girl—hugged me. Mother said I must allow that, or I will appear to be a 'cold, repressed reptile,' her words, not mine, and so I did and I patted their backs. Three times, to show reciprocal affection. Mother always knows what to do."

Kyle told me about his plan for revenge. I laughed until tears came out of my eyes. "Aunt Olivia, legally speaking, this is breaking and entering, trespassing, and possibly vandalism. You are now associating with a known criminal. I want you to be aware of this."

I told him I was cool with that.

Kyle's creative vengeance began after school closed for the weekend. Kyle propped open the back gym door with cardboard and snuck back in that evening when it was dark.

He had recently begun studying caricature. "Another form of art, although with humor, exaggeration and, often, politics imbedded within."

My sister knew what he was doing. She had helped him with his drafts.

A mother's love is endless.

My mother flipped part of the deer she'd shot last year during hunting season onto our marble island at the farmhouse. Good thing that oak tree island was strong. "One merciless shot." She mimed shooting. "My aim was true."

"I'll make venison stew with bouillon and potatoes and onions."

"That'll warm my bones, Rebel Child. Disappointing you aren't a doctor, but your cooking skills are unparalleled. We'll take some of this to Herbert and Joey Cattlickson. Joey's refusing to come back in for his medical appointment because he has

a paper due for one of those pretentious, snobby research journals that no one reads except the writer and his mommy and he
says he doesn't have time."

"What's wrong with Joey?"

"Joey went to Africa for his work with the university as an
epidemiologist. He picked up all sorts of vermin and bacteria
and yucky stuff from the water out there. Twisted his insides up,
rotted things from the inside out. I've got him on meds, but Herbert called and said he seems sicker, so we have to go out and
see him and make sure he's not being eaten alive by some
African bug or worm."

"And he won't come in to the clinic because he's too busy re-
searching?" I admired my mother's cowgirl boots. Turquoise,
with a silver toe.

"Yep. Stubborn son of a gun. Won't come to see me even when
I said that his symptoms indicated his condition was worsening.
He said he was on the verge of a breakthrough, and I said, 'Look,
Jingle Bell Joey, do you not see the irony here? You have a disease. You are sick. You need a doctor, you may need hospitaliza-
tion, but you're so weirdly interested in writing about diseases
you're dumping your own health in the bucket as if you're your
own petri dish,' and he said, 'Mary Beth, I cannot possibly stop
now,' and on and on. He's obsessively nerdy. So is his brother.
They have nerdiness seeping out of them. I've told them that,
too. 'Joey and Herbert, you two are the crack bomb biggest
nerds I've ever met in all of Montana.' "

"You're so friendly to your patients, Mom. Your sensitivity is
touching."

"It sure as hell is." She believed that "being sensitive" meant
that she should be blunt with her patients and not coddle them,
especially when they said, "Now, Mary Beth. What does Mrs.
Gisela think about all this?"

"Let's get going to Joey and Herbert's. Your grandma will be
back with the girls from the movies in a couple of hours and I
want to talk to Lucy and Stephi about not fearing the cadavers
they'll be working on in medical school. I have a plastic human
body I want to show them."

"Cadavers, Mom? They're young children." At the same time, I thought: My mother is the best. Her love is true for her new grandchildren.

She shrugged. "It's part of their training."

"Let's stop by my house. I'll grab Joey and Herbert some of my cinnamon sugar cookies. They love those."

The Cattlickson brothers are longtime friends of my mother's. They spend evenings together playing Scrabble and watching the History Channel. I'd played with them a few times and was boggled by those brainiacs. A few of the words those two came up with during our last Scrabble game, two plus years ago? Hypoxic. Lockjaw. Jackpot.

As an epidemiologist, Joey likes studying diseases. Ask him any question about any sort of disease, and he knows it all from elephantiasis to fop to kuru disease.

He loves talking about it. It gives me the creeps. He's been all over the world. "When you study diseases, when you track them, when you know their origins, how they spread, how they manifest, you can help people."

Herbert is his brother. Herbert has a doctorate in archaeology. He loves ancient ruins. They are both out of town a lot, and sometimes their paths won't cross for months. They're both in their sixties, never married. They have a brick home twenty minutes outside of town on a hundred acres. When they're not in the trenches, in obscure locations, they like peace. Their home is unusual in that it has a main room and kitchen, tall windows, exposed wood beams, and a brick fireplace, but then branching off from the main room are two wings. Each brother has his own family room, bedroom, bathroom, and office.

It's perfectly suited for them. I think it could work perfectly for a lot of people, including married couples. Meet in the middle, then you go your separate ways.

"Hello, Olivia. Hello, Mary Beth," Herbert whispered, smiling, waving us in, giving us warm hugs. He was wearing an outfit that could only be described as an Indiana Jones costume. I wondered if he, too, had an extreme aversion to snakes. "You didn't bring Mrs. Gisela?" Herbert was clearly disappointed.

"Sorry, no," my mother whispered back. "You're stuck with me, Dr. I Don't Know Anything."

"That's too bad. She knows how to fight disease the natural way."

"And I know how to fight disease with a shot and drugs."

"Okay, here we go," Herbert whispered, then raised his voice to a semi-shout. "Hello, Mary Beth and Olivia! What a miraculous surprise!"

Herbert had made my mother swear she wouldn't tell Joey that he called her and begged her to come out because "Joey will be so displeased. He won't take a minute away from his research at the moment, I'm afraid. He does get rather obsessed. He's hardly sleeping. Manic stage, if one can have a manic stage working as an epidemiologist."

"Greetings," my mother called out in an even louder voice, so Joey could hear. "Sorry we didn't call ahead. Gee-whiz. I forgot. We were in the neighborhood."

I coughed over a laugh. We were not in the neighborhood. Joey and Herbert lived in the boondocks.

"We've come to examine Joey and make sure that he is not being devoured by an African worm or a strange beetle," my mother shouted.

"I don't think he'll like that," Herbert yelled, looking at us apologetically. "He's very busy. But since you're here, Mary Beth and Olivia, but not Mrs. Gisela, come and see him so your trip is not wasted." Herbert held his hands out, as in, "Can you believe this," and rolled his eyes. He whispered, "He's talking to Stepan. I know you both know Stepan."

Stepan was a university professor, too, and a friend of my mother's.

Herbert led us down to Joey's wing. I could hear Joey on the phone. He was in his king-sized bed, and the bed was covered with papers, books, his computer, graphs, and drawings.

"Listen, Stepan. We have got to get this research done immediately . . ."

Joey smiled and waved, indicated for us to sit down next to the bed in chairs. He was pale, too thin. My mother waited for about twelve seconds, patience being nonexistent in her personality, then took the phone.

"Hey, Stepan, this is Mary Beth. How are you? Yeah? Is that right? When are you home from Morocco? Sure. We can play Scrabble. No, you may not use Arabic words. Okay, we gotta go. I have to examine Joey. He brought a bunch of gifts of the bad variety home with him from Africa . . . You want me to examine his ass?" She eyed Joey, who shook his head, and Herbert laughed. "That would be fun. Holy cow, I didn't realize I was going to have so much fun today. If only I could have pictured this when I woke up this morning . . . You want me to give him an enema? Hey, Stepan, why don't I let you give Joey an enema yourself? You think we doctors like giving enemas? We don't. We don't have morning coffee and think, 'Hey, swell. I get the pleasure of flipping someone over and sticking an enema up his rectum.' Yeah, you too. I'll drop an enema in your beer next time I see you . . . You tell Phyllis I said hi and ask her why she stays with you. Tell her I said that. Good-bye."

My mother hung up.

"I should have married you," Joey said. "I'm in awe of you, Mary Beth." His brow furrowed. "But you also scare the heck out of me."

"I would never have married you, Joey, unless I'd had a lobotomy. Or your brother." My mother started taking supplies out of her black bag.

"What? Why not?" Joey mock-whined. He turned to me. "It is a gift to see you Olivia, but your mother is an ax-wielding warrior woman." He seemed puzzled. "There's something very attractive about that."

"You wouldn't have married me without a lobotomy?" Herbert said. He clutched his chest. "Now that wounds, Mary Beth. Wounds. Like a spear on fire."

"Oh, hell, no. Neither one of you. I'd run you both over. You intellectual, germ-studying, dead-people-hunting, odd donkey men. So, Joey. Tell me your symptoms."

"Once again, Mom, it is a privilege to witness your gentle care of your patients. Kind. Sweet. Accommodating."

"Please, Olivia," she corrected me. "I need to figure out what bug has invaded this man's body and possibly reproduced."

"Olivia," Herbert said, his face now creased in a huge smile. "Maybe you can clear something up we've been wondering about. We heard from Ruthie Teal that she saw Jace at your house months ago when she was cleaning her gun. We heard you two might be getting back together."

"Right," Joey said, sitting up, eager to find out the real truth. "Then we heard you weren't getting back together from Martha."

"Then we heard you were back together from Chuck Chen, who heard it from friends of Sheryl Lalonski's second cousin, Tabitha."

"Then we heard you two aren't back together from Apurna and Celise."

"We aren't together," I said.

Their faces fell, shoulders slumped. "Very sad . . . Wish you were . . . We like both of you . . . Any hope?"

My mother saved me. She threw her hands up. "Are we done talking about Olivia's love life?"

"I'd like to know more, but okay." Joey leaned back on his pillows. "It's unfortunate that Mrs. Gisela isn't here."

"Sorry." My mother dug in her doctor's bag. "Poor you, you miserable, African-bug-infected man."

"Mrs. Gisela knows how to cure diseases in the natural way."

"She can't cure a worm, or a bowl full of bacteria swimming around in your gut, Joey, so out with it. What are your symptoms, and don't be shy."

Joey told her. It was rather graphic, I thought, until my mother started asking more questions and it got more graphic. She examined him, head to foot, took blood, gave him medicine, told him when to take it. I turned my back a couple of times to give Joey privacy.

"Hey!" Herbert protested as we got up to go. "I wanted Joey to get an enema! Make my day, Mary Beth. Stick him with an enema."

"What? Why me?" Joey protested. "I have an as yet unidentified African disease. I have suffered intestinally enough. Give Herbert an enema. He hasn't been the same since he got back from Egypt last month. I think he brought home the ghost of an Egyptian princess. I think that Egyptian princess is fiddling with his intestines."

"I'd like an Egyptian princess fiddling with my intestines. I haven't had a date in two years. You can't get picky when you look like this." Herbert pointed to his face. "My face is a domino. All dots. Big eyes. Big nose. Big mouth."

"She probably wouldn't take you," Joey said, shaking his head slowly. "You have gas problems. You don't swallow right, and you have to thump your chest. You have abnormally large feet."

"You do, Herbert," my mother said. "You do have abnormally large feet. And your gas is lethal."

"What about Joey?" Herbert protested. "Look at him. The man has a head the size of a cantaloupe. He has enough hair to cover a chimpanzee. I don't know why the women go for him."

"Joey talks them to death," my mother said, putting her medical paraphernalia back in Granddad's black bag. "They give in so he'll be quiet. Plus, some women like chimpanzees." She glared down at Joey. "I will call you when I get the blood tests back, Joey. I'm having them test you again for all sorts of odd and wondrous things. You're going to live, though."

"Damn," Herbert said. "As soon as Joey cuts out, I'm taking all of his epidemiology books. I can't wait to have them for myself for ever and ever. My life will be so much more fulfilled when I can study the history of obscure diseases."

"And I can't wait to get ahold of all those bizarre things you've got stuffed with formaldehyde in jars in your office," Joey shot back. "It looks like you've murdered several people, animals, and insects. I'm glad the police have never been here, because you would have some explaining to do. I mean, who formaldehydes body parts?"

"They're ancient body parts."

"So you say. But do we know?"

"I'm so glad I came," I said. "You two are better entertainment than anything on TV."

They liked that!

I pulled a plastic container with the venison out of my bag. "Venison. I spiced it up for you."

"You didn't!" Joey exclaimed, grinning. "Thank you, Olivia, thank you."

"And"—I paused, for dramatic effect—"I brought you some of my cinnamon sugar cookies."

"My day is made," Joey said, collapsing against the pillows. "I dream of those cookies, Olivia. Dream of them."

"He dreams about your cookies and diseases," Herbert said. "My life is now perfect. These are my favorites. You are the best, Olivia."

I laughed.

We gave them hugs and turned to leave.

"Next time bring Mrs. Gisela!" they both called out.

Chapter 11

∽

On Monday, when Kyle and his classmates all filed into school, they were greeted with a spectacular, colorful new mural over Eric, Jason, and Juan's lockers, all conveniently grouped in the same hallway.

My sister took pictures of it and showed me later. "I hardly saw him this weekend. What a hard worker. This is a boy who was willing to commit crimes, including breaking and entering, trespassing, and possibly vandalism, to extract creative revenge after relentless bullying. So proud of him. He talks like he's the spawn of a sixteenth-century prince and Marie Curie, with a twist of Vincent van Gogh, but you gotta love the work ethic."

I laughed. It was the perfect revenge. "It's a mural that should live on the walls of that school forever. The details, the size, the humor. My mind is blown."

"It's a testimony for all bullied kids," Chloe said. "A monument. An artistic example of individual power against evilness. This is what you, too, can do to get back at kids who bang you up and bring you down, curse them and their muskrat faces forever, may they grow fangs and a tail. I love that son of mine."

The mural was about twelve feet long. Eric, Jason, and Juan were so cleverly drawn and painted. Eric's hawkish face was enhanced. He looked demented and was wearing a diaper. Jason was drawn with buck teeth, a bandanna around his head, and a stunned expression, tongue out. Juan was long and skinny, snake-like, with a black cape. The facial likenesses were incredible. Kyle had enhanced their faults.

Chloe later learned from Kyle and other students and their parents what happened at school when the kids came back on Monday morning.

Eric, Jason, and Juan were furious, and Juan started to cry and left school. None of the kids took any pity on them. These three were bullies who had taunted, mocked, and beat up kids for years, and no one liked them. Eric started hollering, "That bat crazy freak retard Kyle. Where the hell is he?" And Jason yelled at the janitor, "Why are you standing there, you idiot? Paint this off."

And the janitor, Bill DeNota, a Vietnam vet who worked as a janitor only because it funded his summer-long journeys to different continents each year, stood within three inches of Jason and growled, "Don't you talk to me like that, Jason. I won't sit and listen to that foul mouth of yours. No one wants to listen to it. Do you understand me? Now you shut your trap."

The kids clapped, and Jason snuck off after muttering, "I'll get paint from home." Eric ran out behind him, those weasels, swearing to get "revenge on Kyle, the OCD scum."

But bringing paint in didn't work, either. When Jason and Eric returned with paint and brushes to cover up the drawings, the principal was waiting for them, hiding around the corner.

"Destruction of school property!" she shouted as soon as they opened the paint and whipped out paintbrushes. "You should be ashamed of yourselves. This is attempted vandalism and destruction of school property! Put those paintbrushes down immediately and go to my office. Now!"

She hauled them off, *by their ears*. This might not be tolerated in other districts, but we're Montana. Both boys were suspended, along with Juan, who had declined to come back to school anyhow. He moved the next week to Great Falls.

Jason's parents and Eric's mother came to get them. My sister was there, too, as the principal had requested to meet with her. Chloe said the mothers looked exhausted. Jason was smacked on the butt, three times, by his mother. Eric's mother yelled,

"You stupid egghead chicken shit," which gives you an idea of what Eric was dealing with at home, but my sister could not summon up any pity after the years of bullying that Kyle had had to put up with and how the parents had not even tried to get their kids to stop.

Jason's dad, Jason Senior, came in a tequila T-shirt that almost covered his gut, smelling like smoke. He crossed his arms and glared and my sister said, "What? Hungry? You couldn't find a possum to eat this morning? No chipmunks and syrup for breakfast?"

Jason whined to his mother, pointing at the principal, "She dragged me down the hallway by my ear!" And Jason's mother, in a state, said, "Which ear?" He cried, "My left one. It hurt."

She grabbed him by his right ear and said, "Well, hell. Now we'll make it even," and dragged him out.

Unfortunately, as Bill, the Vietnam vet, told my sister, there was "absolutely no time" in his schedule to paint out the mural for weeks. Maybe months. Could be next year. "No time at all. I have to sweep the floor of the utility closet, visit with the kids during my cafeteria duty, and the principal's office needs a thorough winter dusting." He then told her, "Art school for your son, Chloe. Kyle will make a fortune. The mural is magnificent."

The magnificent mural stayed. The kids loved it. The local press came and took photos of it, and it was on the front page of the newspaper. In three weeks, when Eric and Jason returned from their suspension, they were changed people. They never teased, beat up, or shoved anyone ever again, especially Kyle. The mural stayed there to remind them of who they used to be.

"Hello, Olivia."

"Hi, Jace."

We were in the kitchen, the breakfast/lunch employees gone, the dinner crew to be in soon. We would be having fried buttermilk chicken, which I had named Saddle-Up Fried Buttermilk Chicken. We would also be having double-stuffed baked potatoes with sour cream and bacon called Double Spuds and Bacon, and caramel apples on sticks called Caramel Fruit Sticks. There were still salads and a squash soup to prepare.

At the moment, Jace and I were alone, our view, private and expansive, out the back at the mountains. On the other side of the building, one family was having a snowball fight. They were from Los Angeles. Their kids could not contain their excitement, as it was the first time they'd seen snow. Several families were in the game room. Some people were skiing or snowboarding, and about ten had gone off on a guided snowshoe walk.

"Do you want some coffee, Jace? I made toffee squares with melted chocolate." I had made them because we always served cookies in the afternoon to the guests, but I also knew they were some of his favorites.

"Yes and yes." He grinned, and we sat down at the table near the windows.

"Thank you, Olivia."

"You are very welcome." I set the coffee and cookies in front of him.

He raised his mug and we clinked them together. I tried not to get too emotional. We had done that every morning at breakfast.

"I'm so glad to have you back."

"It's . . ." I paused, admiring that white beauty outside, the handsome man inside. "It's . . . I'm happy to be back, too."

Every day he came in and smiled at me in the kitchen, chatted. It was as if I'd never left Martindale Ranch, except I did not snuggle up to him at night after having multi-orgasm sex.

"We're better already with you, Olivia. Everyone loves the food."

And I love you. The words, in my head, echoed along, true and strong. I couldn't believe I hadn't said them out loud.

"Everyone loves . . ." I started, then stopped. Why were those dark eyes always so comforting to me? ". . . loves the . . . uh . . ." And that black hair! I could hardly keep myself from running my hands through it and pulling his mouth to mine. "And, uh . . . the ranch is, uh, in love . . ." and his body. Rangy. Powerful. Mostly his brain attracted me, though. Jace was razor sharp. Witty. He grasped everything quickly, way before I could. He had majored in math and finance in college.

"The ranch is in love?" Jace smiled.

And those teeth! And that smile! I couldn't figure out what he was talking about. "The snow here . . . it's I love . . . white."

"I love white snow, too."

"What?" What did he mean he "loved white snow"? So confusing. I loved the way Jace listened to me, eyes straight on mine, and how he always regarded me with humor and indulgence and kindness. When I had made suggestions about how to run the ranch in the past, he treated me like a business partner and implemented my ideas. "Everyone loves . . ." What else about love? I couldn't think with him and his sexiness around. Oh yes! "The horses and . . . rabbits and . . ."

"The rabbits?"

Why was he laughing? I smiled back. We had actually had sex, here, in the kitchen many times, late at night . . . "And cats and dogs. Stephi and Lucy love cats and dogs."

I remembered all the times when that smile was kissing my smile, and we were soon naked . . . I shouldn't have done it, but I leaned over, put my hand on Jace's shoulder, put my smile on his smile, and kissed him.

He took things from there right quick. He was always one to take charge. He put a hand behind my head and guided that kiss, then with both hands he lifted me straight up, and I was straddling his lap.

I had my arms around him, my mouth on his, and I thought I was melting, like marshmallows on a fire pit. I heard myself groan, and breathe way too heavily, and I was shaking, a smidge, because being back in Jace's arms was scrumptious and seductive at the same time.

The kitchen door opened, and I flew right off that cowboy and flung myself back in my chair. The chair started to flip back, my legs flying up in the air, and Jace caught it and righted me in the nick of time.

"Hello, Olivia. Hi, Jace." Dinah shifted her flowered bag.

"Hi, Dinah!" I was way too perky.

"Okay, Olivia. I have to tell you about this recipe my grandma sent over from Trinidad. You're going to love it."

I stood up and hurried over to the kitchen island, my whole body on fire and frustrated. I snuck a peek at Jace as he left the kitchen, and that man actually had the audacity to wink at me.

This work environment might be too much for my heart.

Before I went to sleep on Thursday night I thought of Jace, because I always think of Jace, but instead of forcing him from my mind because it hurt too much, I rested right there. I thought of the happy memories. The laughing, making love in his truck, cooking for him, riding horses, making love in front of his fireplace, skiing fast, hiking, making love in the woods, hugging him on his ranch as we watched the sun go down and pitching a tent in his backyard and roasting marshmallows at the fire pit and then making love yet again.

I got up and ate some strudel, filled with apples and brown sugar, made by my great-great-grandma Ida. I would have to make her chocolate pecan bars soon.

I finally went to sleep.

Joan, the case worker, came by my log cabin. My whole family was over. We were having a contest to see who could catch the most popcorn in their mouth. Joan got last place. She was bad at it. I knew it wouldn't affect her review of my parenting.

Annabelle always dropped the girls off at daycare or school in her car, parked, then detached her bike from the rack and rode to work. There's a lot of rain in Portland. It gets slippery and gray. She was hit by a bus. The driver didn't see her. People on the sidewalk and on the bus rushed to help. Too late. Impossible.

The funeral was filled with hundreds of people, many parents and grandparents whom she had comforted when she was taking care of their babies in the neonatal ward.

The most important children in the church, Stephi and Lucy, stayed dry eyed, clutching my hands in the first pew.

It was one more unspeakable loss for two children who deserved only peace.

I became a mother, but not the way I wanted to become one.

After Annabelle died, they went silent again, as they had when they'd been removed from their parents' chaotic home. They withdrew. They cried. They stared vacantly. They couldn't sleep, they had nightmares, they were anxious and worried.

They are better now. We still miss Annabelle, every day. She was a compassionate, insightful, caring woman. My gift to her is to be the best mother I can possibly be to Lucy and Stephi, her beloved grandchildren, and to keep her memory alive with the girls.

Annabelle, always, will be their Grandma Annabelle. Remembered and loved.

The girls were making friends at school. Lucy had won an award for jump roping—best in her grade. Stephi had won an art contest. She drew our log cabin, with six cats and two dogs on the front deck, all wearing red ribbons. She had even included the sun weather vane, my grandparents' hats, the old wheel from the wagon train, and Granddad's lasso. They were getting invited to other kids' houses, and we had kids over to our log cabin to play, too.

Seeing them smile, seeing how much fun they had with other kids, seeing them playing dress up and running around, made me so happy. They had been through more than many people will go through in a lifetime, but they were resilient, they were strong, they were learning to be happy again, and to be courageous Montana women.

Then their mother called me and told me she couldn't wait to see her girls again and have them live with her, you bitch, Olivia, and my attorney called and told me that Devlin would probably get out of jail soon and told me the legal reasons she might be able to get her children back, as outlined and argued by her court-appointed attorney. "I'm sorry, Olivia."

I think I felt my soul shrivel in fear.

*   *   *

"When I was here before, Jace . . ." I stopped as a truckload of memories hit, happy and horrible. He leaned back in his chair at the circular table, in his office, his face hardening up. I breathed, stared out his office windows at a bright, blue Montana day, and tried to find the right words.

"You mean, when we lived here on the ranch together as a married couple?"

"Yes. Uh. Yes." I tried to gather my jangled nerves together. Jace was wearing a flannel shirt and a white thermal underneath. He was so manly it should be illegal. "Anyhow. I wanted to write a cookbook."

He nodded. I had told him I had always wanted to write a cookbook, and he had encouraged me to do so. We had been so busy setting up Martindale Ranch, advertising, hiring, etc., that I hadn't had the time.

"The cookbook could be filled with all the recipes that we use here. I could write them up, and use your camera, you have that fancy one, to take photos of everything I cooked and baked. I could also take photos of the animals, the pets and the wild ones that come through here sometimes, the guest cabins, the game room, the dining hall, and the kitchen. I'd take photos of the views, the mountains, the sunsets. I would take photos of our guests around the campfire, snowshoeing, making snowmen, playing in the lake in summer, jumping off the rafts. We could have a recipe on one side and the cake or the entrée or salad or soup on the other, and then intersperse the cookbook with the other photos. It would be a whole picture of Martindale Ranch."

He leaned forward and clasped his hands on his desk. "I still love the idea. Let's do it."

"You think so?"

"Yes. It's brilliant. I'll fund it. We'll pay whoever to put the book together. You sell it and take the money."

"Ah, Jace." I shook my head at him and smiled. "No. You know I'm going to say no to that. We'll split the costs, split the profits."

"No."

"Yep." I smiled again. He is easy to smile at.

"No. Selling the cookbook will be helpful marketing for our ranch."

"Your ranch. I don't know if anyone will even buy the cookbook . . ."

"But we won't know unless we try," Jace said. "And I think they will."

"That's what we said about the ranch, too."

"Right. And I had faith in our abilities to launch the ranch, faith in your cooking abilities, and I have faith in this venture, too. We'll sell them online, through our website, and here at the ranch. I think people would love to have a souvenir of their time here. Right now we have the T-shirts and sweatshirts you designed, which people love, but we need more. What's the title?"

"I tried to think of something more clever, but I thought it should stay simple. *Cooking on Martindale Ranch.*"

"How about *Cooking with Olivia on Martindale Ranch in Montana*? More personal."

"I, uh . . . Wow. You're quick, Jace."

"Let's do it."

Why does he make me smile so much? He's not a smiley sort of man. He looks like he could bash someone in the face. He's tough. But I had to smile at him. His toughness made me smile. And the cookbook was exciting to me. It would be fun. I would love it. "Thanks, Jace."

"No, thank you, smart one. Don't work too hard, Olivia. You've got the kitchen, the girls, and now this."

"I love this, though." I tapped my fingers together. I was so happy about this project. "I love cooking and baking and recipes. I'd love to have all my recipes from here together, along with the photos of the ranch. But I have another idea."

"Let's hear it, babe."

"I thought I would also make some cooking videos, with my recipes that will be in the cookbook, and put them on the website. Hopefully it will make people more interested both in the ranch and in the cookbook. We can even put them on YouTube."

"Both ideas are perfect. Go for it. Tell me what you need me to do and it'll be done."

"Okay." I waited a sec because I wanted him to brace himself. "What I'd like is for you to come in to assist me in cooking for the videos. You own the ranch—"

"As do you."

"No, I don't." I so didn't. "I'd like you, my mother, my grandma, the girls, Kyle, and my sister to be in the videos. We'd make some of the recipes together. A family thing. It'll be personal then."

"I'm a lousy chef and you know it."

"I'll show you exactly what to do." He was hilarious when we cooked together. He truly didn't know what to do, but it was endearing.

"I'm not wearing a pink apron. Or a flowered one."

"I'll make sure you have a masculine apron."

"Then I might do it."

"You look hot in aprons." Shoot. Had I said that?

He smiled. "Nowhere near as hot as you, babe."

Shoot. Had he said that?

He smiled. He looked lusty.

I smiled back. I couldn't help it. I felt lusty.

Then he stood up, cupped the back of my head, and kissed me. "Why don't you and I get naked, except for our aprons, and cook dinner together. Alone. At my house. How does that sound?"

I couldn't even meet those dark eyes.

"Are you going to look at me, Olivia?"

"Nope." I felt myself blush. I couldn't believe I could still blush in front of my own husband.

I heard his low rumble of laughter, then he pulled me up close and kissed me again. He growled like a bear, to make me laugh, and kissed my neck and collarbone, then things went all sizzly from there. He was so quick at unsnapping my bra and going where he wanted those warm hands to go.

I could have an orgasm in Jace's arms without sex. I could. I had done it before, many times. He had magic hands. I'd probably do it again.

I pulled away. I had to. Nakedness was coming next and we were at work. But I smiled when I did it because I have to smile at that man.

On the way home I reminded myself of this fact: Nothing would come of making love with Jace but more shearing, face-planting pain.

Nothing. A crushing amount of despair hit like a truck.

That night I didn't sleep much because Lucy had a nightmare about her life before she went to live with Annabelle. "The mens were scary. They yelled, like Mommy and Daddy yelled at each other. One, Boom Boom, he hit my butt, and Mommy laughed. She thought it was funny. It wasn't funny." After I got Lucy back to sleep, her sobbing gone, Stephi told me, "The police came to our house and Boom Boom fought with them with a knife. There was blood. Lotta blood."

"Who was Boom Boom?"

"I don't know. Not Daddy." She leaned toward me and whispered, "But I saw Mommy naked with him in the shower."

I had to chuckle the next morning. Larry's Diner had gone out of business.

"Let's make something from Grandma's cookbook," I said. "One of Esther's recipes."

Chloe leaned over my shoulder as I flipped through the pages and said, "Fire away, sister."

My mother and grandma were on the other side of the butcher block kitchen island in our log cabin drinking scotch. The girls were laughing in the loft with Kyle. He was teaching them to play chess. It wasn't working out, because Lucy wanted to make the queen "magic" and Stephi wanted the king to be "locked up in jail," but he was trying.

"Grandma, this recipe has bananas in it, right?" There were bananas, spice jars, and what looked like a sugar container drawn on the pages.

My grandma put her shot glass down. She never had more than one shot. She said she always wanted a "clear brain, just in case something bad happens."

"That's banana bread, Cinnamon."

She ran her fingers down the ingredients, written in German, then traced the spices and a purple wisteria vine that was wrapped around the edges. "It's my mother, Esther's, banana bread recipe. She made the best banana bread in all of Munich. We always sold out at the bakery." Her voice cracked and she put her hands to her eyes.

"Mom," my mother said, linking an arm around her waist, her brown and gray hair to my grandma's white.

"I'm all right, Fire Breather. Don't worry. My mother wrote this recipe when she was teaching us at home because Isaac, Renata, and I were not allowed to go to school anymore. We were not allowed to go in swimming pools, the theater, or the parks. Jews were not allowed to vote. Two of my uncles had disappeared. Our assets were gone, as were our bank accounts, our art, and the gold my parents had hidden and saved. Everything. We had nothing. Our passports were stamped with a red J for Jew. On Kristallnacht, our businesses were looted and fire-bombed. Synagogues were burned to the ground, and the truth was clear to all of us by then. Germany had gone mad, as mad as Hitler was, and Jews wanted out."

"Grandma, that sucks," my sister said. It might have sounded flip, but Chloe had tears pouring down her face, her voice wobbling. "I'm sorry. Those pissant Germans. Those mother bad word Nazis. Those sick devils. I hope they're rotting in hell, their balls on fire."

"Outstanding vision, Chloe," my mother said in all seriousness. "A Nazi with his balls on fire. Dying."

"You're welcome." Chloe wiped her eyes.

"This." Grandma tapped a brown stain. "That's vanilla. I remember my mother telling me the morning that Renata and I had to leave, the last day of our lives that we saw her and my father and Isaac, that she'd accidentally spilled vanilla on it. She said the cookbook would always smell good. We loved her banana bread, which is why she made it for us that day."

I touched the vanilla and became so choked up. The vanilla was spilled by the mother of two daughters whom she would not see again in her lifetime. She had made her children a last loaf of their favorite bread before saying good-bye. I closed my eyes as we all sat in the black, excruciating pit of my grandma's tragedy, her family's tragedy.

We made her mother, Esther's, banana bread.

When we were done, my grandma said something in Yiddish. "What did you say?" I asked.

"I said, 'I love you, I miss you. I will see you again.'" Then she told us about the Kindertransport.

February 1939
Munich, Germany
Gisela Gobenko, grandmother of Olivia Martindale

Gisela gripped her sister's hand, fear flying up and down her spine like an electrical current. When her father had stumbled home beaten and bloodied and told her mother that they had to get the children out, Gisela had been scared. Now she was petrified.

The scene around her, at the train station, was controlled chaos. Parents and children, all desperate Jews, were crammed together in a large room. They were not allowed onto the platform, so they were all waiting, waiting for an agonizing good-bye that would rip their families apart, most forever, and send children off to strangers in another country. The fear and grief was like a noose around them all, tightening each minute.

"We must get the girls out," Gisela heard her father say to her mother behind the closed door of their bedroom where her father was recovering from the beating that had nearly killed him. "We can't with Isaac. He is eighteen. Too old. But we have one chance for the girls. We have to take it."

What were they talking about? Isaac, Gisela, and Renata put their ears closer to their parents' door. Isaac tapped his finger-

tips against his palms, then flapped his hands. The three siblings heard the word train. Kindertransport. Jewish children. Escape. Now. They must go.

And that's what today was. Today was the chance. Their one chance. Her parents had sold the jewelry they had hidden. It was all they had.

Before they left that morning, she and Renata had decided to hide some of their favorite things under a floorboard in their bedroom, as they were only allowed one bag on the train. They would add something from each member of their family. Inside a tin box, the top imprinted with women dancing in lacy, ruffled, fancy ball gowns from long ago, they placed two red and purple butterfly clips they had given each other; their charm bracelets, each with a red pomegranate, a Star of David, a faux blue stone heart, a lion, a tree of life inside a circle, a four-leaf clover, a cat, a dog, and a key, which were gifts from their parents; and colored pencils that Isaac gave them, such a talented artist he was. They also saved photographs of their family.

"For safekeeping," she and Renata said, then hugged each other, Renata's green, tilted cat eyes stricken. When they returned to Germany, they knew their favorite treasures would still be here, hidden from the Nazis.

Gisela and Renata stood close to their family in the train station as their parents told them, again, how they had to work hard in school, be well behaved, do what they were told, that they would see them again when things were better in Germany. Her brother, always reserved, who spoke so properly, like an old-fashioned scientist, and who compulsively studied math and physics and drawing and art, and was rather odd, but kind, hugged them tight, and said, "I love you." He looked them in the eyes, then away. Isaac could never hold anyone's gaze very long. His hands flapped at his sides.

Gisela tried to be brave, but she started to cry. Renata cried. Isaac cried, agitated, disturbed. Their parents cried. They all hugged one another again.

When it was time, when a man yelled that all children were to board the train in an orderly and quiet fashion, no parents on the platform, they went together, the two sisters, Gisela seventeen, Renata sixteen. Their passports, stamped with a red J, as ordered by the Nazis, were in their bags.

Midway across the platform, Gisela turned to go back, but she was pushed forward by the other children, many of whom were crying, all who were scared witless. They had no choice but to continue toward the train, numbers draped around their necks. Gisela had one bag in her hand, stuffed with clothes and food for the journey, including her favorite banana bread that her mother had made for them that morning.

Her cousins had not been able to get on the train with her and Renata, and she was already grieving. She feared for them. She had heard her parents whispering to each other, crying for their nieces and nephews. "They will have to fight to get their children on it. Orphans and homeless children, children with both parents in the camps, they have gone first. There is a limited amount of space . . ." She knew her parents had sold all of the hidden jewelry, that they had even had to pay a bond for Gisela and Renata's future care in England, for them to board this train. It was the last-chance train.

Her mother had put their family's leather-bound cookbook with the pink ribbon in her bag that morning and had taped photos of their relatives to the last pages. "Take it, Gisela," she said. "Don't lose it. You will be taking our family with you on this journey." She had also given them the small, silver menorah they had seen in their grandparents' window since they were children.

"This is a gift from your grandma Ida and granddad Boris. They wanted you two to have it, to remember their love, to remember your faith." The menorah had been made by Ida's grandfather, Aron Bezkrovny, who made it for Ida and Boris as a wedding gift. It was the only item to survive when Ida's home was set on fire during the pogrom in Odessa, besides the cookbook and Boris's tools.

She and Renata stumbled into seats on the train and tried to wave to their parents, to Isaac, but they couldn't see them, they were lost. They waved anyhow. Then they cried, along with many of the other children, their loss unbearable, their world shattered.

Later, the train whizzing through the night toward a boat that would take them to England, Gisela held the cookbook. She touched the leather cover and the pink ribbon. Inside her grandma Ida had added more recipes, from herself, her mother, Sarrah Tolstonog, and her grandma, Tsilia Bezkrovny, and had drawn her own home in Munich in summertime, and their home, too, both with red doors and red geraniums.

Her mother had also added more recipes, many for desserts and cakes they used in Ida's Bakery, with drawings and imprints of leaves, flowers, and herbs. And there were stains—tea, wine, blood, tears. Gisela knew what they were, where they were from. She knew why some pages were damaged by water and fire. Her mother and Grandma Ida had told her.

"Girls, use the cookbook, use our family's recipes, and think of how much we all love you," their mother had said to them, hugging them one more time. "Our love will come to you through the recipes."

Gisela studied the banana bread recipe. Her mother had drawn a banana, a sugar container, and nutmeg and cinnamon jars. She had drawn a purple wisteria vine around the edges. Her mother loved wisteria. Her mother had accidentally spilled vanilla on the corner. She could smell it. There was also some cinnamon between the pages. She smelled that, too. She wanted to cry again, but she didn't. She would be brave. She had to be brave.

Renata took her hand in that crowded, cramped train car, filled with hundreds of suddenly orphaned children, all with numbers around their necks, all holding suitcases and bags, all with their passports marked J for Jew.

"Gisela?" Renata said. "I'm so scared . . ."

"Me too, Renata, me too."

They ate two slices of banana bread and shared the rest with two brothers who had no food.

The girls wouldn't know for years, but the fear they felt then *was nothing compared to the terror they would have felt had they stayed in Munich, Germany.*

They would have ended up in the camps: Dachau. Buchenwald. Auschwitz.

They were the lucky ones.

They were on the Kindertransport.

The sisters were going to England.

I gathered all of my recipes that I'd used at Martindale Ranch and started typing them into a document. I also started taking photographs of the meals we were making, the fancy appetizers and layered desserts, the colorful salads and thick soups.

I took photos of the horses, the dogs, the cat, the ranch itself. I took photos of the sunsets and sunrises, the bunkhouse for the employees, and the employees themselves as they worked. I took photos of the dining hall, set for dinner with our heavy white dishes and candlelight, the log cabins, the wild animals, the mountains, the river, the hills. I took photos of Jace.

I loved those photos the best.

I asked Jace to write the introduction, about himself and his family, starting with his grandfather, Ricardo Rivera; the cattle ranch, which he still ran; and the inspiration to open Martindale Ranch.

I wrote a few paragraphs introducing myself, how I started cooking as a girl in our blue farmhouse and my grandparents' log cabin here in Montana. I wrote about baking cakes with my family during Martindale Cake Therapy, the countries I'd traveled to and cooked in, the culinary school I'd attended, and what we liked to serve at Martindale Ranch. I encouraged them to come and visit us at the ranch.

I certainly couldn't write a *truthful* introduction, as it would have to go something like this: Now, folks, here is a husband and wife team running Martindale Ranch, but they're separated, and the wife is a head case. She is so turned on by her husband she loses track of what she's saying, but they can't get back together because their problem can't be fixed. There are also two almost-adopted daughters in the picture, but the bio mother is a dangerous drug addict about to be sprung from jail and the girls might be placed back into her morally corrupt hands.

I have realized, as I have gotten older, that the beaming, smiling faces in the photograph with the perfect family can be the cover for a deeply troubled life.

What a mess we often hide behind our beaming smiles.

My phone rang.

I saw the number and didn't answer it, once again. I wished that she would never call. I wished that she would leave us alone, but I had to have these recordings.

When she was done leaving her vitriol, her hatred, on my voice mail, I listened.

This time, she was conciliatory. Apologetic. Her voice sweet. Reasonable. Calm.

That scared me more than the screaming and swearing.

I had Dinah help me with the first video. She had dyed her hair with pretty purple streaks, so first we had to talk about that, but then we got on with it. She held the camera.

I had decided to make a dark chocolate, four-layer truffle cake for the video. I figured I would go for delicious, and fairly simple, first. It wouldn't be a normal chocolate truffle cake, though. I was going to add chocolate meringue logs and chocolate shavings two inches high on top, with a ring of raspberries around the outside.

I was nervous. I don't like cameras, or photos of myself, or feeling like I'm being watched. And, gee-whiz, the dang camera does that.

Dinah laughed. "Okay, Olivia. Shake it off. Be you. You know, the tough Montana woman who tells Larry off, whacks Gary in the neck with a wooden spoon, and shoots at bears coming too close to her property. Ready? Go!"

I smiled at the camera in my white chef's jacket. I tried to appear calm and serene. "Hello, everyone. I'm Olivia Martindale.

Welcome to *Cooking with Olivia on Martindale Ranch in Montana*.

"I live in Kalulell, Montana; I'm the head chef at Martindale Ranch; and I love to cook and bake. Measuring. Mixing. Stirring. Simmering. Sautéing. It all brings me joy.

"I absolutely love to bake cakes. I was brought up baking cakes with my sister, mother, and grandma, so that's what we're going to do today. I'm going to show you how to make a dark chocolate, four-layer truffle cake. Ever wonder how pastry chefs make their cakes look so fancy? We're going to get fancy today, too."

I went through the ingredients they would need, then I started combining them. I tried to smile at the camera and look like a natural and normal woman, not one with a whole host of demons in her head who didn't like cameras pointed at her pointy face. It was when we got to the mixing part that I had a problem.

I have never had problems with hand mixers. Never. But my hand was shaking the slightest bit as I gripped the mixer. I was trying to bake "the old-fashioned way." Also, I know that many people don't have expensive kitchen gadgets, but they would have hand mixers. I smiled into the camera and said, "It's important to whip the ingredients together until they're completely mixed. I can only compare the importance of completely mixing ingredients to shooting cans off a log here in Montana. You have to aim, hold it, shoot. It's the same with baking. You have to have a goal in sight that you're aiming for. Hold the vision of what you're making and . . . don't shoot"—I smiled, finally feeling more comfortable—"but mix it and take your time. Remember, cooking should be soothing. It's cooking therapy."

That's when it happened. I turned the mixer on high and somehow that sucker flew right out of my hand, spun around the bowl, then shot out of the bowl and onto the counter, upside down, spurting batter everywhere. I put up a hand as chocolate batter splattered my face. The mixer took off as if it were trying to escape from the counter and whirl itself out of the kitchen.

"Oh, my gosh," I said. I lunged for the devilish mixer and knocked over the vanilla. The vanilla spilled. I got the handle of the mixer, brought it back, and then hit a bowl of cream. The bowl whooshed across the counter, careened off the edge, and broke on the floor.

Dinah was cracking up, but she had not let go of the camera, and it was still pointed right at me. My vision was blocked by a glob of chocolate batter. I pulled it from my hair, then ran a hand over my cheek.

Then I laughed. I laughed and laughed. "I caught the devil mixer," I said, holding up the mixer in victory, now turned off. "Remember, friends. Sometimes your utensils, your kitchen gadgets, even your oven, they're going to turn on you. It'll be like they have a life of their own. Sort of like the black bears we have up here in Montana. Most of the time they're nice, and they leave you alone. Sometimes, they're not so nice and they want to eat you. This here mixer was having a black bear grumpy day. Let's try this again."

We did. I went back to the lesson. I wiped the chocolate batter off my face, cleaned up the vanilla, and the mixer behaved like a haloed angel the next time around.

Later Dinah and I watched the video, including the grand finale, which showed a tasty end result: a perfectly formed dark chocolate, four-layer truffle cake, with the chocolate meringue logs wrapped around the cake and the dark chocolate shavings piled up on top with the raspberries. I showed my sister, my grandma, my mother, the girls, and Kyle the video when they were over at my house for a simple beef stroganoff that night.

We laughed until we hurt.

"Put it up on the Martindale Ranch website," my mother said. "This is proof that hand mixers can be dangerous and might land you in the ER. Also another reason for me not to cook. A mixer might attack me."

"We all need laughter in our lives," my grandma said, flipping her pink carnation scarf back. "Share it to share the joy."

"Women will relate," Chloe said. "In it you said something

like, 'Life is a mess and so is cooking' and 'Never try to be perfect, ladies, it will give you a migraine.'" She banged her fists together. "They'll get it. We women understand messes, the messes we make and the messes in our lives that are made by others."

Kyle said, "I thought the presentation was quite amusing and entertaining, Aunt Olivia. I understood the humor."

Stephi said, "I think that mixer was having a temper tantrum. When I feel like doing that, I grab my rocks and squeeze them, like this!" And Lucy said, her finger pointed in the air, "It's okay to make a mess in the kitchen, Aunt Olivia, as long as it's yum yum for my tum tum. Can I have some of that cake?"

I showed Jace the video the next day. He laughed so hard he almost cried. Earl and Justin saw it, too. They bent over double laughing. I posted it. I forgot all about it.

"I have continued to take into account your sage advice, Aunt Olivia."

"With the portraits you're making of the kids at school?" I pushed a plate of cheese and crackers toward Kyle across my granddad's dining room table. The one that my grandma told me he'd laid a pregnant Martha Schumann on during a blizzard when her twins decided to come early.

"Yes. I have continued to draw my peers."

"They love it, don't they?"

"I would say yes, affirmative." His hands fluttered, then he held them together. "When I arrive at study hall, the people whose portraits I am to draw that day, who have signed up on the list, have increased their attention to their personal hygiene. For example, Jacob Nashiro, birthday April 4, wears one of three pairs of blue jeans. Two have significant holes in the left side, and one has a frayed hem on the right side. His T-shirts say "Eat Me" or "Stay Alive, Baby" or "Mangoes Are Like Breasts," which forced the principal to send him home from school on November third at 9:14 in the morning. But on the day when his portrait was to be drawn he wore a plaid shirt, blue and white, beige pants with a brown belt, silver buckle, and he brushed his hair. He also sat very still for the portrait instead of gyrating his body in jerky movements as is normally the case."

"Did he like the portrait?"

"When I was done he held it in his hands and didn't say a word, and I thought he was displeased. I said, 'Are you displeased?' And he said, 'No, man. I love it. My parents are gonna love it, too. Thanks, Kyle.' Please note, he said 'gonna.' That was not my word, Aunt Olivia. I do not use the word 'gonna.'"

"So noted. You're making each one of them a gift, Kyle."

"I believe—" He stopped, stared out the window, blinked rapidly, and cleared his throat. "I believe that the students no longer think that I am an oddity, a pervert, or a dick. As you proposed, this has given them a chance to know me. When I sit in the cafeteria with my lunch sack, people come to sit with me. They talk to me. Mother told me to ask people questions of themselves, so this is what I do. I use the questions from my Questions Notebook. Now they tell me their problems. I asked Mother what to say when I hear a problem, and she said, 'Tell them you're very sorry, and listen closely and try not to let your eyes skedaddle off like a raccoon hiding in the bushes. You have to look them in the eye, Kyle, or they'll think you don't give a rat's ass about them.'"

I was delighted. "It sounds like things are much better."

"Yes." He sniffled. "Although my emotions are less controlled recently."

"Kyle, you are a brilliant artist. You have the gift to make people happy."

"Thank you, Aunt Olivia. I believe you are brilliant, too. In cooking." His face drew together in concentration. "But you and my mother are brilliant with people. Something I am a failure at."

"You are one of the kindest people I know, Kyle."

"It does not come naturally to me, but I endeavor to be better, with the help and wise counsel from Mother. She said to me yesterday, 'Kyle, you are coming in from outer space and becoming a normal human.' I took that as a wonderful compliment. May I draw you soon, Aunt Olivia?"

"Yes. I would love that."

"We have an agreement then."

"We do." I ruffled his hair, then I hugged him. He allowed it. He patted my back. Three times.

That night the girls and I went to the farmhouse and had tea and chocolate pecan bars with my grandma and mother. My grandma made them from Ida's recipe. I saw her leather-bound, pink-ribboned cookbook on the counter. I thought of the remnants of that pressed pink rose, the lockets, the red ribbons, the sun charm, and the white feather. I thought of what I already knew, the tragedies and traumas that my relatives had gone through, what my grandma had gone through. They had gone through far, far more than me. They had shown strength and courage when they had been hit with disaster.

Had I? Had I shown strength and courage?

That question kept me up for hours that night.

Chapter 12

"Did you see this, Olivia?" Dinah asked me at the ranch four days after the demon mixer showed me who was boss. She had added a blue streak to her hair.

"What?" I was flying, making Pancakes Bigger Than Your Head on the griddle, which would be served with a ring of bananas and strawberries around the top, and Big Bear French Toast with powdered sugar.

"Ya gotta stop and get over here, Olivia." Dinah pointed to her laptop screen.

"I can't right now. Where is the buttermilk? Shoot. Are we out of buttermilk? No, it's right here. Where's the—"

"Olivia!" She laughed. "Come on!"

"Later, Dinah. Do you have the omelet ingredients together? We're having the Montana-Mexican omelets today, did you remember—"

"Olivia!"

"What?" She held the laptop up in front of me. "What?"

"It's the hits on the website for the last few days."

"I know that. But why are you holding it in front of my face? Did you get the oranges squeezed?"

"Yes. Please. One second."

I finally focused. What? Were those... "What happened?" The numbers were way, way up. About 7,500 more hits than normal per day.

"It's your video, Olivia. The one when the mixer takes on a life of her own and rebels."

"Oh, my gosh."

"And look at your e-mail in-box."

Filled. Tons of e-mails.

"I think they want your recipes, minus the devil demon mixer. See this comment? Does Martindale Ranch have a cookbook?"

Wow. Oh, wow.

I showed Jace the hits for the website in his office upstairs. He grinned and wrapped his muscled arms around me and gave me a whirl. "Great job, Olivia. Make another video. I have not stopped laughing over the possessed hand mixer."

He dropped me back down and, smashed up against his chest, I couldn't resist him and we had a long and seductive kiss. He picked me up, my legs around his hips, and leaned me against the wall. I thought I was going to lose it in a sensual and sexy way right there, but I didn't because I heard our guests laughing outside and said, "Jace, we cannot do this," and he said, "How about coming to my house," and I said, "No," and he smiled and I smiled and I said, "You are irresistible," and he said, "I have felt the same about you since we met. You are driving me out of my mind, babe."

What to do?

I kissed him again.

I loved how the Martindale Ranch cookbook project was coming along.

I had no idea how to put a book together, so I started making a very primitive, fake cookbook in a three-ring binder with the recipe on the right side and a suggestion for a photo on the other.

I would photograph Jace holding a platter of ribs made from his grandfather Ricardo's recipe, called Rockin' Rivera's Ribs.

I would have Dinah, Justin, and Earl hold out bowls of Super

Delicious Spaghetti with Ox-Sized Meatballs while sitting on the white fence. I'd make our Sky-High Lemon Cake with lemon slices piled on top and photograph it outside on a picnic table, the mountains a blurry image in the distance. I'd take photos of our staff, cowboy hats on, eating Manly-Man Burgers in front of the campfire, and I would have Lucy and Stephi hold out Crazy Coconut Cream Pie while perched on hay bales. I would have my mother, in her cowgirl boots, hold fancy cocktails next to the red barn, and I would have my grandma hold a silver tureen of her mother's onion soup on the wood deck. Kyle would hold a cinnamon roll in one hand and a handful of colored pencils in the other hand, and I'd have my sister balance a platter of stacked onion rings on her head. She would love that goofiness.

In my heart, I finally felt it, after years of heaviness and darkness: Light.

"Mom," I said, "want to join me as a guest cook for a video I'm making?"

"A guest cook?" She turned and glared at me, as if to say, "What is this nonsense!?" We were out on my deck watching the Telena River run by. It was warmer than usual, and there were pinkish buds on the trees. "That's a ridiculous idea. You know I bake cakes but I don't cook. It nauseates me. All that measuring and slicing and burning food. The smoke."

"But you're funny."

"Funny? No, I'm not. Don't flatter me, it's irritating, Rebel Child. I'm not funny at all. I deal with blood and guts, and diseases and accidents, and hysterical and scared people. Nothing funny about that."

"You're funny in the way you talk. How blunt you are."

"Blunt is best. I am so sick of people tiptoeing around each other. My philosophy is: Say it and then shut your mouth."

"That's what I'm talking about."

"What?" She pulled her thick brown and gray hair back into her no-nonsense bun. "You want me to get on your video and tell people, 'Dump this much sugar in and not more, but I don't cook because it bores me straight out of my skull, but if you do, make sure you add a tablespoon of vanilla, and for those of you who don't want to cook, go and get takeout and wine?' "

"I want you to help me cook something. Something tasty."

"And you want me to pretend I'm excited about turning a blender on or cracking eggs or measuring flour? What am I supposed to say about that? Boring. I'd rather talk about infectious diseases."

"Please don't. Diseases and dinner aren't yummy together."

She rolled her eyes. "Fine. I'll do it. You homemaking freak."

"Thanks, Mom. Love you, too."

"Love you, Olivia." She pushed my hair back from my face and kissed my cheek. "I wanted you to be a doctor, but you turned into a dang-fine chef, dang fine."

"I try."

"Don't be modest, young woman. You're irritating me again, and that's the second time during this conversation. Don't do it again."

I laughed. Under my mother's brusqueness, I have always known she loves me.

The governor had a heart attack in his vacation home here. Chloe was first on scene. She provided the care, got him breathing again, pumped his chest, etc. The governor is not popular. He invited Chloe to Helena so he could publicly thank her in his office at the state capitol, the press present. "Anything to get more attention for himself. 'I had a heart attack and I came back from the dead, whooeee, vote for me!' " Chloe told me. "The man is a cold, slithering snake under that sneaky smile."

When asked by the press for a comment, after the governor thanked her at the capitol, wrapping it around a cheesy but hopefully vote-getting speech, Chloe said this, which was broadcast in full on the news that night.

"Look. I'll save anyone's life, no matter if they have sound and sane political opinions or if their opinions are archaic, sexist, discriminatory, or ridiculous." She turned to stare at the governor, whose face had gone slack. "That's my job. But Governor Balio, you need to stop being a misogynistic Neanderthal.

You cut funding for women's health care. You voted against raising the minimum wage, which hurts women and leaves them in poverty. You're against family leave and equal pay for women. You want to cut funding for birth control, but you're against abortion. How does that make sense, you idiot? You have chosen no women for the highest levels in this state. You pretend that you care about women, but you don't, and a woman saved your life. Hopefully you'll make some changes and start respecting people who aren't white males. Now I gotta go. I have to go back to work and save someone else's life—even if their opinions are based in caveman thinking, like yours."

Governor Balio, shown on TV, opened his mouth, shut it, opened his mouth, shut it. Hard to criticize the woman who saved you.

Chloe is extremely popular in Kalulell.

As I left the ranch on Monday afternoon I stared up at the snowy hill with the view of the magical sunsets. I would go up there soon no matter how hard it would be. I thought again of my grandma and my ancestors and what they had been through.

This time, I would do it.

"Hello, everyone." I smiled as serenely as I could at Dinah, who was holding the camera for another cooking lesson that we would upload to the Martindale Ranch website, along with the recipe. I was wearing my white chef's jacket. "I'm Olivia Martindale. Welcome to *Cooking with Olivia on Martindale Ranch in Montana.* Today I'm cooking with my mother, Dr. Mary Beth Martindale."

My mother, who was still wearing a white doctor's coat and a stethoscope, waved in the direction of Dinah, on the other side of our long island. I opened my mouth to talk again, when my mother interrupted me.

"I am not a competent cook," she said, her tone impatient, sharp. "In fact, I'm a lousy cook. When my daughters were growing up, Olivia and Chloe, both wild girls, I am being honest here, they were out of control in high school, I was a working, single mother seeing patients all day. Their rat-ass father left with his girlfriend—she was from Vegas. I've always wondered if Barney's girlfriend was a hooker—anyhow, I was busy. This is Montana. We get a lot of accidents out here with yahoos heading out to the wilderness from New York and California who don't know what the hell they're doing. They think they're gonna play cowboy and cowgirl. They ski too fast. Shoot each other hunting. Get lost and fall down ravines on trails." She rolled her eyes. Those yahoos!

What? What was all this? My mother was facing the camera. We were side by side. I thought we were there to make a chicken taco soup together.

I kept trying to smile calmly and serenely.

"Anyhow, as a doctor I was too busy sewing people back together and taking care of sick patients to cook. My own mother, she calls me Fire Breather, cooks like a professional chef, but my girls grew up on the basics. Spaghetti. Tacos. Hamburgers. I can grill almost anything, but that's because I like flames and fires. Personal preference. My girls also had cereal a lot, and they had popcorn for dinner when I was wiped out from working all day. Hey. Popcorn is made from corn kernels. Corn is a vegetable. Therefore, their dinner consisted of vegetables. So to all of you moms out there who can't get a nutritious dinner on the table. Hell." She waved a hand in the air. "Don't you worry and don't you feel guilty. Say no to guilt. My daughters grew up and they're healthy and strong bull-whipping, target-shooting women." She turned to me. "Okay, are we ready?"

I stood there, openmouthed.

"Are we going to cook, Olivia," she snapped, "or are you going to stand there with your mouth hanging open, trying to catch flies?" She looked at Dinah, holding the camera and laughing. "Not that there are flies in Olivia's kitchen. It's clean." My mother's face scrunched a bit, as if she was thinking. "Not like my kitchen, which isn't always sterile clean like this." She spread her arms out, indicating my stainless steel kitchen.

"Who has time to clean their kitchen at home constantly? Women who don't have enough going on in their lives have a perfectly clean kitchen, that's who. Don't be that woman. *Pfft.*"

Pfft? What was *pfft?*

"I don't have time to make sure that there is not a sliver of bacteria doing a dance on my kitchen counters, and you don't have time, either. You could end up in the hospital tomorrow, trust me it happens every day, so don't waste your life cleaning away. I've always said that a too-clean house will cause kids to get sick because their immune systems aren't used to fighting germs."

Oh. My. Goodness.

"Now, in my medical clinic, everything is sterile. Let me tell you, the diseases that walk through our doors every day. Today we had a man, he returned from Africa weeks ago, he had contracted this rare—"

"Thank you, Mom," I interrupted, still smiling. I kicked my mother behind the island, and she said, "Ouch, Olivia."

"Today Mom and I are going to make one of my favorite recipes. Everyone loves soup, and here at Martindale Ranch we are no different. Soup warms the bones, is what I say. We're going to make chicken taco soup. Perfect after a day of work—"

"Perfect after a day where you have to do three prostate checks for three brothers who come to see me on the same day, once a year, for their checkups—"

"Mom!" I kicked her again, and she said, "Ouch, Olivia!"

"The ingredients are . . ." I hurriedly listed the ingredients.

My mother interrupted. "I want to say, before I forget, or in case I get a call to run back to the clinic, two words." She held up her fingers. "Red wine. Listen, ladies, when you're cooking, don't hesitate to have a glass of wine and have another one during the meal. Unless you have to drive the kids to soccer, or some such drivel. Or, if you have a night shift working at a hospital and you might have to cut someone open and move his organs around, don't be slamming wine down like a drunk coyote. No one wants a drunk doctor, but if not, drink red wine. It's a health bump for you and your heart. That's all."

"Thank you, Mom, again," I said. "The next step is..." I went through the process, adding ingredients, my mother "helping," by making comments like, "If you want to be a feminist, you must include vegetables in your diet. They'll give you strength." And "Fresh deer is delicious. Kill it in the morning, eat it over a fire at night." And "Broccoli. It'll clean the colon. Shut your eyes, swallow it."

I smiled at the camera, Dinah trying not to laugh so that the viewers wouldn't hear her, but it wasn't working, and I said, with as much composure as I could manage, "We're almost done, Mom. For the final touch, remember to add shredded cheddar cheese and—"

"Eat it with tequila," my mother said, with authority. "It'll taste better. Nothin' like chicken tortilla soup and tequila."

"Thank you for joining us today on *Cooking with Olivia on Martindale Ranch in Montana*."

"And remember that wine, everyone."

I watched the video with Dinah, Justin, Earl, and Jace.

"Put it up," Jace said, laughing. "No one has seen a cooking show quite like this one."

I posted it.

Two days later, Dinah came up to me, laptop open, giggling. "You did it again, Olivia. Look at these numbers!"

The cooking video with my deer-shooting, blunt-talking momma had gone viral. More people on our website wanted to know if we had a cookbook.

I wanted to say, "*Yes!* The cookbook is coming!"

I hugged my mother that night.

"What's that for?" she snapped.

"It's because I love you." She hugged me back. "Love you too, Olivia."

I wrapped myself in a jacket and brought a blanket out to the gazebo after I put the girls to bed that night. Crocuses were coming up, purple and white, all over our property. The wind puffed through. It didn't wail, as it had been. The sun stayed and visited during the day. At the picnic table in the gazebo, which my granddad built for my grandma so she would have a peaceful place to think and be and wrestle with her grief and a hideous past, I thought about how I was still in love with Jace.

I always would be.

But there was no future, so why was I here? We would never nail our old cowboy hats to the wall of his house like my grandparents had done.

Why did I smile at him?

Why was he my best friend again?

And why was my lust so out of control?

There was not a happy ending here.

I am a fool. I know that, I do.

I also know that I can't leave him again. I can't.

But what was I supposed to do?

In my grandma's gazebo, I found no answers, or peace.

On Wednesday afternoon, on a clear blue day, the snow melting, I called Jace from the kitchen after the clients at the ranch finished lunch. A bunch of them had gone off skiing, as there was still snow on the mountain. Another group was in town at a festival, and some were hiking around the lake.

"Hi, Jace. Do you have a second? I wanted to talk to you about the cookbook I'm making."

"I'm working at the house right now. Come on out."

No.

Not to his house.

No.

I couldn't. Too many scraping memories. It was a sad place that would take me back to a swamp of sadness that I had worked hard to crawl out of. "How about we talk on the phone?"

"Today is not a talking-on-the-phone day."

"What?"

He laughed and said, "Come on out to the house, Olivia. Please. I'll give you directions."

"What do you mean you'll give me directions? I believe I know how to get to your house, as I did live in it for years."

"Follow the road off the ranch, turn left, but then when you come to the fork, don't go left, as you normally would to get to the house. Go right, toward town. It'll take about fifteen minutes. I'm on the left."

"I don't get it—"

"Left outside of the ranch. At the fork, go right. I'm on the left. Look for my truck."

He hung up. I was left staring at my phone. Jace never hung up on me. Ever.

What was he talking about?

I turned left outside of Martindale Ranch and drove to the fork. I knew I should go left to Jace's family's home, but he had said go right, toward town. That did not make sense, but I did it. I drove for fifteen minutes.

There was a new Craftsman home built about a quarter mile off the street. But . . . this was Jace's property. His land. Whose house was that?

Had I taken a wrong turn? How could I have taken a wrong turn? But the white fence was Jace's fence, which encircled part of his property.

I peered down the driveway toward the home. There were windows everywhere. Stone steps up to the house. Wooden pillars, and a wide deck all around with a steel black rail. A new red barn sat out in the pasture, as if it were part of a postcard.

There was a red door. *A red door.* Just like the red doors on our blue farmhouse, my grandparents' log cabin, and Esther's and Ida's homes in Munich.

And what the heck? That was Jace's black truck in front of the house.

He came out onto the deck and waved. He put both hands on the rail. The wind ruffled that black hair. He stood there like he owned the place. And then I realized: He did own the place. That was his home.

Jace had moved.

*   *   *

"This is your home."

Jace's home was large, but not too large. It wasn't a Mc-Mansion. It was warm and cozy. High ceilings, wood floors, exposed rafters and beams, a river rock fireplace to the second floor. The whole downstairs opened up—family room, kitchen, dining room, a breakfast nook, with a separate den off to the side. It was light, windows framing views of the craggy mountains, that ever changing Montana sky, and any wildlife that wandered through. There was a hot tub out back on the deck facing the mountains.

"Yes."

"When did you build it?"

"The planning started about three months after you left."

Three months after I'd left? "Why? Why did you leave your family's home? You love it there." I put my coffee mug down on his kitchen table, where we were sitting, after I'd walked around the first floor.

"I left because it was time, Olivia. Past time. You were right. It was dark. The logs were dark, there weren't enough windows, as there are in your grandparents' log cabin. It was too old, freezing and drafty in winter. It was too isolated, especially in bad weather. Too far from town."

I studied my coffee. He was right about the house. I had totally loved Jace, loved being there with him, but I found that home depressing. It was even more depressing after what happened.

"I left, Olivia, because I knew you would never live in that house again."

My eyes flew back up to his. "You moved because of me?"

"Yes. I should have moved earlier, with you. I'm sorry I didn't. I failed you, babe. You told me you thought it was dark, you told me you felt isolated, and then it got worse for you. I should have moved us. Again, I'm sorry."

"Jace, you don't owe me an apology. You offered to move when we were still living together."

"When you told me how unhappy you were in that house, how hard it was for you to be there, I should have had us out of there within days. We could have rented another house, moved into one of the guest houses at the ranch, anything. I didn't do that for you. You never complained about anything, Olivia. Ever. So when you told me how you felt, I should have fixed that problem right away. That day. We were slammed with the business and the ranch, and I put it off. I told myself I'd get to it, I'd build, or we'd buy a new house, in the future. That was an extremely bad decision on my part. I have lived with how I failed you as a husband since you left."

"Jace, you didn't fail me at all. Not for a minute. I flipped out." My voice was muffled by my inelegant sniffling. His apology was turning me into a teary mess, and I told myself to get some cement in my spine.

"I did. I hope you can forgive me, Olivia."

"Jace, there is nothing to forgive, not a dang thing." I sniffled again. "But I love this house. It's the most incredible home I've ever seen." As a chef, the kitchen alone was enough to make me start salivating. Long, wide island painted a dark blue, with its own sink and drawers beneath. Tons of storage in cabinets stained a natural wood color, a copper vent hood, six-burner gas stove, double ovens. He even had an antique armoire built into the kitchen. I love armoires in kitchens, and he knew it. He had open shelving, which I also love. "This kitchen is the best kitchen I've ever seen. You designed it?"

"I told a kitchen designer exactly what I wanted. What *you* wanted. He threw it together."

"That window seat is wide enough to fall asleep on." I had told him, one time, when we were dating, that one day I wanted a window seat wide enough to fall asleep on. And there it was.

"I believed you mentioned wanting one."

"And your views, all around." We were up on a slight hill, and I could see the town. At night the lights would sparkle, it would be a friendly view. There was privacy out here, but it wasn't isolating. In ten minutes, you could be in town, having coffee or dinner.

"Want to see the upstairs?"

"Yes, definitely." Upstairs there were three bedrooms. Those extra bedrooms hit like bricks being throw at my face and made me unbearably, rippingly sad.

Jace would eventually meet someone, probably blond and small and perfect, not tall and rangy with messy brown hair with egg yolk and spices and olive oil all over the place. He would fall in love, and they would reproduce. They would have offspring. Kids would drop out of that woman as fast as apples fall off a tree.

They could call their kids Apple and Orange.

I already disliked his future skinny wife.

The kids' bedrooms were empty, no furniture, and I walked out quick. We didn't say anything to each other. That tight silence said it all. I caught my breath, made a sad squeaking sound, and he put his hand in the middle of my back as we headed down the hall.

The master had his king-sized bed in it and the bedding I'd bought for it. The bedding was all white.

That bed! The bed I slept in, that's where Jace and Bimbo Wife would make more babies. They could call one kid White Comforter and the other kid Pillow Sham.

I tried to pull myself together before I said something snappish and unhinged. "You still have the comforter."

"It's still comfortable."

Despite the deep pain in my heart looking at those bedrooms, Jace The Man could still make me laugh.

There was a huge soaker tub, for two, in the bathroom. So this is where he and Big-Boobed Wife would make a couple more babies. They could call those babies Bubbles and Soap.

I'd had enough. I took my almost-unhinged self back downstairs to the kitchen. He followed me, the silence heavy, rife with a mess of cauldron-sized emotions.

My eye caught on that granite kitchen counter. Heck, it was long enough and strong enough so that Jace and Witchy Wife could make babies there, too, and name them Carrot Peeler and Blender, and outside was the hot tub where more babies could be made, and they'd probably even do it in the red barn. So many places in this house for Jace to mate and spawn. I felt dizzy and sick thinking about all the mini Jaces running around town.

I would not, *could not*, stay in Kalulell once Jace was married and his wife was breeding. No way. Pain cut through me, chop, slice, dash.

I shifted my gaze to the view because suddenly water was in my eyes, drowning them. Drowning me.

"You want to talk about this, Olivia?"

"It's nothing." *Buck up, Olivia, now.* "I was thinking that every detail in this house is exquisite."

"No, you weren't."

"Stop trying to read my mind, Jace. You think you're some sort of male psychic?"

"Not at all, but your face is transparent, so I know you're not thinking of architectural details."

"What did you think I was thinking of?" Your children named Carrot Peeler and Blender and Pillow Sham? Ha. You'd never guess that one, cowboy.

And, like that, amidst my ridiculous vengefulness, my anger evaporated. Jace was the best man I'd ever met. He deserved a sweet wife and a pile of kids. He did. I still didn't like Miss Perfect, but he deserved her. I closed my eyes against that rush of hurt and upcoming loss.

He knew what I was thinking about, and we locked gazes, then he smiled, soft and slow, and the mood changed. Sometimes I can feel myself having sex with Jace even when I'm not touching him. How can he do that to me? We had sex all the time when we were married. It's a wonder I could walk. But I did. I walked. Felt like skipping sometimes.

And here it was again. This tight, rapidly spiraling, steaming passion where I could hardly breathe. I heard myself take a breath that was way too loud.

He lifted up a strand of my hair and wrapped it around his fingers. I sucked in another breath. This one sounded like a mini hurricane. I wished my heart would stop pounding.

He put an arm around me and pulled me close. Body to body, and my body was suddenly on fire. I kept my head down because if I tilted my head up, he would put his head down and I'd be lip-locked with the cowboy god.

"Give me one kiss, Olivia."

"You're making this hard."

"You're making me hard."

"I know."

Jace cupped my face with his hand, then let his hand drop to my neck, my chest, then my breast. Now I really couldn't breathe in a soft, rolling, amazing way.

"Jace—"

"Olivia."

"You're too close."

"And you are not close enough."

His finger traced my nipple through my burgundy sweater and my red bra. "I think I'm going to have a standing orgasm against you." Oh no! I had said that out loud.

Jace laughed, low and deep, and bent his head, his lips to mine. He knows how to kiss me until I'm half out of my mind.

And it was when I was half out of my mind, but still half in it, that I pulled an inch away.

"Jace, this isn't helping things."

"What is there to help?" He pulled me in closer. I put my hands on his chest. What I wanted to do was run my hands over his chest and then move lower.

"Us."

"Let's help us in bed."

I couldn't look away from him or those dark eyes. I had missed him. Missed him every day. But I am screwed up. I am a mess. I am a wreck. I am trying to get myself together, and I can't be with him and get myself together, and we had that mega problem between us. Unworkable, mega problem.

So there was no rational reason to step closer, wrap my arms around him, and kiss him until I couldn't think. I simply couldn't resist the cowboy any longer. It wasn't long before our clothes were off and we were on the couch, and Jace was doing what he does best to me.

I pulled away at the last second, a strangled cry in my throat.

I snatched up my clothes and rushed to the door. I stuffed my legs into my jeans.

"Olivia, wait," he said, following me. "Come on. Please, sweetheart."

I shoved my feet into my cowgirl boots, threw my sweater over myself, held my jacket in my hand, and grabbed my purse. I ran to the truck and locked the doors.

Shoot. I'd forgotten my red bra. And my purple lace underwear. I shoved the keys in and sent my light blue, old, and rumbling truck back down the driveway. In my rearview mirror I could see Jace on the deck, in his boxers, hands on his black steel railing, head down.

He does not deserve to be hurt anymore, and I'd hurt him again. I am an awful person and I am so screwed up.

After a week, on a sunny day, I finally got myself together and did what I knew I needed to do. I drove the back way through Jace's ranch, where the buttercups lie like a golden blanket in summer. I hiked up a hill to an old, craggy oak tree with a labyrinth of branches that had seen many generations come and go.

I dropped my red picnic blanket and sat down by three white crosses, each two feet high. The view went on forever, soft hills and soaring mountains, towering trees and a glistening lake, a meadow only half filled with snow, a winding stream in the distance. This is the prettiest graveyard in the world. I wrapped my arms around myself, rocking back and forth.

I had always wanted children. I played with dolls and baby dolls for hours and hours when I was a child. I also ran around outside, explored nature, climbed rocks, galloped on horses, skied fast, lassoed cows, hiked, and boated in the lake. Chloe and I drove our Jet Skis fast and our trucks faster. We were headstrong, we were on the edge, we were trouble.

But I always, always wanted to be a mother. I had a wild streak, and a maternal streak. Both equally strong. I had picked out names for my children when I was a child. I wanted to name them after flowers when I was seven: Rose. Petunia. Marigold. Daisy. Honeysuckle. Wisteria.

When I was ten I decided I would name them after neat places in Montana: Glacier. Helena. Bozeman. Gallatin. Madison. Ruby.

When I was fifteen, I decided I would go traditional: Victoria. Emma. Grace. Jack. Johnny. Tommy.

I was so relieved when I fell in love with Jace to find that he wanted kids, too, and he happily agreed to six. It made me love him even more.

A year after opening Martindale Ranch we decided we couldn't wait any longer, though we were both working long hours. It was a delight to make a baby with Jace. It was fun, it was exciting. We were thrilled. I could not wait to get pregnant.

We got pregnant the first month. I made a tiny white cake in the shape of yellow baby booties, thick with lemon frosting. Inside, between the three layers, I used light pink and light blue frosting. Girl? Boy? Did not matter to us. We were so happy our tears mixed together when we hugged.

I had hardly any morning sickness. We painted the baby's room, next to ours, a light yellow and switched out the darker trim for white. We had an animal theme. We bought the crib together, after Jace had endlessly researched which one to buy. It had been so sweet watching him, printing out possible cribs, asking my opinion, studying any and all research on safety. We bought a changing table, again researched diligently by Jace. We bought a rocking chair. I brought my childhood books over to the house, we went to a bookstore to buy our favorite childhood books together, we laughed.

Our sex life was hot. Being pregnant turned both of us on even higher. We went to sleep with Jace's hand over the baby. We rocked in the rocking chair.

At three months, I started bleeding, on the ranch, and we raced to the hospital. It was too late.

The grief was overwhelming. I could hardly get out of bed. I lay in it and cried, and so did Jace.

We climbed the hill, above Jace's family's property, and put the white cross down in front of the oak. The cross faced the sunset. We shut the door to the nursery.

Within two weeks we were making love again. We used birth

control so I could heal physically and in our heads. In three months we tried again. My mother and my OB-GYN assured us that miscarriages were so common, my future in birthing many children was bright, nothing was physically wrong with me, go make another baby.

We were pregnant immediately. I made a tiny white cake in the shape of a heart with white icing. Thrilled again, but muted. Smiling, but tearful. Hopeful, but wary. We opened the door to the nursery, aired it out, dusted. We rocked in the rocking chair. I got to four months that time. All was fine, and we breathed. The next day I bled, gushing. We rushed to the hospital. I cried the whole way. I knew we were too late.

We climbed the hill. We put a second white cross by the first, so, in our heads, our second baby could watch the sunset with our first. We shut the door of the nursery once again.

We waited a year the next time. We couldn't do it sooner, couldn't face the loss, the grief. Our sex life returned to what it was, we adored each other, but we were older, we'd been hurt, we had aged.

We got pregnant. I did not make a cake this time.

We opened the door to the nursery, aired it out, dusted. We rocked in the rocking chair. We got to four and a half months this time and we started to breathe, to hope. I bled again.

The baby did not make it.

We climbed the hill. We put a third cross in. Our third baby could watch the sunset with our other two babies. We lay down by those crosses and cried until we couldn't move.

The door to the nursery stayed shut until I lost it one night and kicked holes in it with my cowgirl boots. Jace wrapped me in his arms.

A month later, my grief turned me into someone I didn't recognize, someone near comatose, emotionally dead, yet one who exploded, too. Jace and I had a huge fight. It was as if I finally woke up and had to scream, had to emit my rage and loss, had to lose it.

I was done, no more pregnancies, I told Jace. Though the specialists could find nothing wrong with me, I knew that my body was flawed. I could not bear to lose another child, another beloved and wanted and precious child. I could not bear to do it to the baby. Warm and living one moment, gone the next. Did the baby hurt when he or she was dying? Did he or she suffocate? Was my son or my daughter scared? Crying? Oh no oh no oh no, I would not hurt another baby in my life. I would not allow another baby to die inside of me.

Jace was kind and understanding, but he couldn't commit to no more pregnancies, he wouldn't. He didn't say, "No, I can't agree to that, Olivia," he said, "Let's wait. Let's go and see another specialist. Let's not make a decision now. Not today."

I screamed at him, glad we were so far away from our visitors at the ranch. Told him it wasn't *his* body that couldn't handle a pregnancy, that killed a baby, that failed, it was mine. How could he ask me to do it again? To endure this racking pain and guilt? Didn't he get it? I could hardly breathe it hurt so much.

He got it, he said. He loved me, he loved our babies. He tried to hug me, and I pushed him away with both hands and screamed at him again. *No more babies, Jace. None.*

And in the midst of my sheer grief and ever rising fury, I told him other things, too, things that had bothered me, things I couldn't speak of before. I hated this stupid log cabin, his family's home, I told him. It was dark. It was depressing. It was old, creaking, cavelike. There weren't enough windows. The ceilings were so low it made me feel smothered and claustrophobic.

I hated being so isolated, away from town, away from my sister and Kyle, my mother and grandparents, especially in winter. My granddad, the man who acted as my father from day one, protective and loving, had died three months before and I hadn't been able to see him as much as I wanted because I was stuck out here in this "godforsaken brown cave under a truckload of stupid snow." I was lost in that river of guilt, lost in the thunder of my unending grief for my granddad.

"I'm in a log cage, not a cabin, Jace. This is your house, your parents' house, your grandparents' house, this is not *our* house, and our babies probably wouldn't even want to live here, and I don't want to live here anymore at all. Not for one more day."

It was his boyhood home, he loved it. It was his history, his family. What I said went to the core of him.

We had wild, up-against-the-wall sex that night. There was anger in it, a rawness we hadn't had before. Afterward he held me close and an hour later we gently, so caringly, with such love, made love again. With protection, both times.

I was exhausted, more exhausted than I'd ever been. My body had broken. My mind had snapped. I could not live in this stress or relentless grief, in this log cabin out in the middle of nowhere, snow piled up in winter like a trap. I was having trouble eating, I lost twenty pounds. I had nightmares about babies dying whom I couldn't save. I relived my miscarriages, each one, the loss and the blood. My mind would get stuck in a loop of despair.

I would often go out to the barn, up to the hayloft, and cry. I'd cry on a hike, sitting on a rock. I'd cry horseback riding. I'd cry making up grocery orders for the ranch. I'd cry while I cooked and baked for our clients in the dining hall. I hid much of what I felt from Jace, so he only saw what I let him see.

I was having a nervous breakdown. A true, utter, anxiety-provoking, can't breathe, crying-all-the-time nervous breakdown. I started having trouble swallowing. Food made me feel like choking. My mother wanted to medicate me.

Jace hugged me more. He spent more time with me. We played cards. We played horseshoes. My tears fell on his chest and cheeks, but I was a broken, cracked, emotionally disintegrating, tearful, hopeless wife. Every time I raged I knew I was failing him as a wife. I said mean things. I shut down. I was moody and temperamental, and I began to hate myself for how I was and who I was.

I wanted to be alone.

My leaving was not the stuff of martyrs. Jace wanted kids, I was unwilling to try again. I knew he thought I would eventually change my mind, that we would go to another specialist and we would get pregnant. I didn't have the strength to fight with him about it, and the thought of fighting with him about it in the future, for the rest of our marriage, was something I could not do.

He needed, he *deserved* children, a family. He wanted kids so much. I would not be giving him that family. So we had an unsolvable problem.

It was at the end of fall that I left. Jace went to town. He would be gone for a few hours. I packed up. I didn't take anything I bought the babies. Nothing. I didn't bring much with me at all. I wrote the note with shaking hands. My hands had hardly stopped shaking since the third baby died. I told him the truth, but it was short. I would not be getting pregnant again, he deserved kids, I was depressed, and I couldn't be his wife anymore. I wished him the best. I put the note on our kitchen table along with my wedding ring.

I don't think I stopped crying until I got to Coeur d'Alene. Jace called, several times, and I finally called him back. I could hardly talk. He said, "Olivia, please, sweetheart . . . come home. Or tell me where you are, I'll come to you. We can talk. I love you, babe . . ."

I told him I didn't want to talk about it anymore. I was done.

I didn't call Jace back for a week, though he called every day, twice a day. Our conversation was short. I told him the same thing I said in the note. I could tell he was crying. He said we did not have to have kids. He was happy with it being only him and me. He loved me. He missed me. He asked if he could come to me, where was I? I told him I was going to get a job outside of Montana, I didn't say where. He guessed Portland.

I hung up on him. I didn't return his e-mails or take his calls for another two weeks. I picked up the phone in a moment of weakness when he called at ten one night. I cried. He wanted to come see me. I said no.

He arrived on my doorstep about a week later. He'd hired a private detective. He was pale, thinner, seemed ill. Those dark eyes of his filled with tears, but I refused to return to Montana. He didn't push. He didn't argue with me. He pulled me into a hug and I made the mistake of tilting my head up, and that was all it took. We were naked and on my sleeping bag within minutes, but then I stopped him because he did not have a condom and I knew I'd probably get pregnant and I could not take that.

It was soul destroying to roll off of him. He lay there with his hands over his face. I told him, quietly, gently, to leave. We argued, he pleaded, I told him again, please go. And he did.

He returned to Montana, but the calls and e-mails came less frequently.

Jace came to see me a month later. That time he brought condoms, and I gave in because I loved him with all my heart. It was wrong to do so. What was I doing? I was not intending to get back together with him. I hated myself. He wanted to stay, to talk, to work things out. I told him to leave. I thought my heart would stop, watching those broad shoulders retreat right out my front door.

He visited two months later, same thing happened. He told me, again, that we didn't need to have kids. But he did. Jace needed a wife who could have kids. He would deeply miss not having children. He would resent me, resent us. It wasn't fair to him. I told him not to come again. It was too hard, we needed to move on.

Leaving Jace was shattering. It is hard to make rational decisions when you are where I was: devastated from three miscarriages and losing my granddad. Probably hormonally screwed up. Exhausted from crying. Grieving a life without children. Plagued with anxiety, panic attacks, trouble swallowing, insomnia, and a huge weight loss.

Was my decision to leave Jace rational? It seemed so at the time. I had lost my mind. I needed my mind back.

In the lonely months that followed, he would call now and then, send flowers for my birthday, send flowers because it was a Tuesday. He sent me Christmas presents. He e-mailed and texted sometimes. It wasn't clingy or creepy, but an open door to start a friendly conversation about anything.

By the time I returned to Montana with the girls, I hadn't heard from him in six months.

I have never stopped missing Jace, never. But in the two-plus years in Portland, I'd put myself back together again. I'd gotten some of my confidence back, some of *me* back. I was stronger than when I left. I felt older, too. Grief does that, it ages a person.

And I was a mother. A mother to two thoughtful, smart, sweet girls who had been through one terrible time after another.

Jace and I still had that unsolvable problem.

Didn't we?

The girls were busy memorizing the organs and bones of the body with my mother. She had photos and diagrams. "It's important they get a head start for medical school," my mother said.

"Now I know where my liver is," Stephi said, pointing to it.

"And I know where my colon is," Lucy said, pointing to it.

"Do you know where your fallopian tubes are, Aunt Olivia?"

Oh, yes, I did.

"And this is my uterus!" Stephi announced.

I had one of those, too. It didn't work. It was broken.

My mother had a quiz for them. If they got everything right she would take them to get hot fudge sundaes.

It worked.

Chapter 13

My sister became more and more nervous as Kalulell's annual talent contest drew closer.

"My son is going to get up in front of hundreds of people, many of whom think he's the weirdest thing since Edward Scissorhands, and do something." She threw up her hands, then poured herself a straight shot of scotch. She handed me a shot, too.

I glanced at a recipe for Bubble and Squeak Cake in my grandma's cookbook. It was not a sugary cake, it was a cake made from potatoes, Brussels sprouts, onions, cabbage, carrots, peas, beans, salt and pepper, a little cheese, and flour. Eggs would be added later, on top of the patties, when it was done. It was written in English. I recognized my grandma's writing. In the notes she had written things like, "If you cannot find onions, don't worry." And "If you cannot find eggs, or egg powder, add more beans." And "You can use almost any vegetables you can find." It was war time, I understood. With rations, they had to do the best they could.

There was an oily stain in the upper right-hand corner. I wondered what had made it.

To add a touch of humor to my life, I said, "Chloe, can you hand me the cheddar cheese?"

"Yes." She opened my fridge and gave me a gallon of milk. Ah! Both milk products. Close. I tried not to laugh. When Chloe is in the kitchen and distracted, she simply can't think.

"So Kyle won't tell you what he's doing for his talent?"

"Nope. I've told him he doesn't get a long time up there on stage. He says he's"—she made air quotes—" 'timing it to the second so the presentation fits within the parameters of the stated rules.' " She had another shot of scotch. When we were younger she could sling back multiple shots successively and still walk a straight line, ride a horse, or shoot cans off logs.

"Things have been way better at school since he drew the mural of the bully whackers, and because he's still drawing kids' portraits, but still. What if they laugh at him? At my son?" She put her hands on the counter, her head down. "I can't stand the thought of people laughing at my son up on stage. I'm a tough-talkin', hip-rockin' Montana woman, but I can't take my son getting humiliated like that."

"They won't laugh. They'll be stunned watching his talent. Whatever it is." I gave her a hug; she sniffled. "Okay, Olivia. I gotta straighten my spine. My son is being brave, so I gotta be brave. Let's cook this sucker." We turned to the cookbook.

Tucked into the pages following the recipe for Bubble and Squeak cake were the two red ribbons and a picture, drawn in pencil, of an extended family, grandparents to babies, a menorah in a windowsill. The artist was Isaac Gobenko.

There was another drawing, tucked into the next page, of Isaac alone holding colored pencils, the resemblance to Kyle uncanny. When Chloe saw it she said, "That's a self-portrait that Isaac made of himself, Grandma told me. Kyle has a twin born decades apart. I'll have to ask her if Isaac was as obsessed with science and math as Kyle. They have the same artistic talent; you can see the similarities in their artwork. I wonder if Isaac was an Edward Scissorhands kind of kid, too."

I studied the pictures again and was overwhelmed with sadness for Grandma. How do you live through losing your whole family? How do you go on? How do you breathe?

But Grandma had gone on. She had breathed. She had started a new life. She had not let her grief stop her. I thought about that. I had let my grief stop me.

Chloe pounded her closed fist on the cutting board and let

out a mini Tarzan scream. It scared me, and I dropped a cube of butter on the floor.

"I am so worried that I'm going to have to beat up a whole bunch of people at the talent show when they laugh at my son."

"They won't laugh. They won't. We'll all be there together. We'll cheer. No one will need to be beat up. And you're a paramedic. Don't cause blood."

"I don't want to cause blood. I like to clean it up and get people patched together again, blood and guts back in the right place." She put her hands on her back. "This body makes the men lose their minds. I am a curvy woman and proud of it, but my watermelons are killing my back."

"Then I think you need smaller watermelons. Can you hand me three carrots?" Chloe opened the fridge and gave me the mustard. Almost the same color! "Thank you." I put the mustard back and grabbed the carrots.

I could call it Having Fun Cooking With Chloe.

Later, when the Bubble and Squeak patties were done and we were waiting for my mother, Grandma, Kyle, and the girls to sit down for dinner, Chloe and I flipped through the cookbook again. We studied handwritten recipes that had been taped into the pages of the cookbook, some written by Ida, others by Esther. A few of the recipes, signed by Ida, also had the names Sarrah Tolstonog and Tsilia Bezkrovny on them.

Ida had drawn her daughter, Esther, and four sons, Moishe, Zino, Grigori, and Solomon, on their wedding days with their new spouses, along with the wedding cake and the recipe. Other recipes, signed by Esther, were surrounded by drawings of red geraniums, tulips, roses, daisies, and herbs. There was also a picture of two girls—Grandma and her sister, Renata, I guessed—in what looked to be a subway, sitting together, the people around them knitting, reading, chatting, praying.

Tucked in between more pages were a few poems and letters, written in different hands, in Ukrainian, Yiddish, and German to Gisela and Renata Gobenko, in London, England.

"I would love to know what these letters say," I said.

"Me too."

"Maybe she'll translate them for us."

"Hopefully she'll want to."

That night, Grandma told us more of her story.

September 1940
London, England
Gisela Gobenko, grandmother of Olivia Martindale

The Germans came like hellfire to London on September 7, 1940, bombs torpedoing through the sky and exploding buildings, industrial sites, neighborhoods, churches, ports, and businesses. Destruction, death, war. The Blitz had started.

Gisela and Renata thought the world might be ending in the hurricane of Hitler's hate and violence, but each day they would get back up, like everyone else in England, and carry on.

Gisela was training to be a nurse at the hospital, and the training immediately began with hands-on work, as the hospital was in dire need of nurses. Renata was in school, and after school worked at a garment factory, awaiting the time when she, too, could go to nursing school.

Their destiny, to become nurses, had been set soon after they arrived from Munich, scared and exhausted, at Liverpool Station in London, with the rest of the children on the Kindertransport. All of the children and teens on their train debarked and waited in the cavernous station for their names to be called. Renata and Gisela were two of the last people to be called, their name tags around their necks, their bags on the floor beside them.

"Renata and Gisela Gobenko?" They heard a man call out.

They walked over to a cheerful, harried, bald man with a clipboard. "Hello, girls. I am Mr. William Danafort. The two of you will be going to live in a group home with other teenage girls your age. This is Mrs. Lowenstein. She will be taking care of you."

Mrs. Lowenstein was a white-haired, smiling, strong-willed woman in her seventies. She was calm and competent. She had been a nurse for decades.

And so it was. They went to live in a group home for girls run by Mrs. Lowenstein. They had a room with two other Jewish girls, sisters named Keila and Naomi, from the town of Kassel in Germany. The four became best friends. Renata and Gisela put their family's cookbook on their nightstand next to the silver menorah. They were fed, they went to school, and then they went to work at the garment factory and tried not to lose their minds to fear and grief. They wrote to their family, told them their new address, cried, hugged each other, and hoped.

In the first months the girls received letters from their family members once they received their address in London. Their mother sent recipes with hand drawn pictures of red geraniums, tulips, roses, daisies, and herbs, along with her letters. Their father sent poems he had written about a father's love for his beloved daughters.

Their brother, Isaac, sent letters discussing his favorite science topics, and he sent two red ribbons that they had left behind. "Make sure you remember to brush your hair," he had joked. He drew an exact likeness of himself, colored pencils in his hands. Renata's green eyes, tilted like a cat's, lit up with joy when she saw Isaac's self-portrait. Isaac also sent a picture, drawn in pencil, of their entire extended family, from babies to grandparents, with their menorah in the windowsill.

Their grandfather, Boris, sent letters of love and good wishes. Grandma Ida sent along new recipes for their cookbook, from her, and a recipe each from her late mother, Sarrah Tolstonog, and grandmother, Tsilia Bezkrovny. She wrote their names under the recipes. She again told Gisela and Renata to cook the recipes and remember their love. The girls taped the recipes into the cookbook for safe keeping, tucked a few of the letters into the back, the rest of the letters into a drawer in their nightstand, and tied the cookbook with the pink ribbon to keep the whole thing together.

Their four aunts and two uncles also wrote—Uncle Moishe

*and Uncle Zino still missing—as did their cousins and their fa-
ther's parents, Aizik and Raisel Gobenko.*

*When Mrs. Lowenstein saw Gisela's and Renata's school re-
ports she decided that they should be nurses and that was that.
"You'll always be able to support yourself, girls, and the world
will always need nurses."*

*Gisela applied for a program. Mrs. Lowenstein called one of
her many friends, her late husband a reputable doctor, and she
was in. Surprisingly, Gisela loved nursing school. Loved caring
for others, learning, working with the doctors, and meeting the
other young women. In the hospital she could put aside her own
problems, her deep and endless worry about her family, and
bring peace and healing, a kind hand, to someone else who was
suffering.*

*After work and school the girls tried to use the cookbook as
often as they could. Their family seemed closer to them when
they cooked their recipes. It was almost impossible, because of
rationing, to find the ingredients they needed. Onions were hard
to come by, bananas impossible, and they had to scrounge and
trade and save their rations for sugar, eggs, flour, and butter, but
they tried. They had to resort to using dried egg powder when
real eggs were not available, and they started using carrots for
sweeteners.*

*They soon added their favorite British recipes to the cook-
book, including shortbread, cottage pie, and Bubble and Squeak
Cake. They liked Bubble and Squeak Cake because they could
often find potatoes and cabbage, a few vegetables, and, if they
were lucky, a tiny bit of chicken. Fried in butter, salt, and pepper, it tasted warm and hearty. This was wartime eating, after
all, and everyone was making sacrifices.*

*The last time they'd made Bubble and Squeak Cake, Renata
had accidentally smeared some of their precious butter in the
top right-hand corner of the page. They'd both laughed about
wanting to lick the cookbook clean.*

*When the Nazis came to London, flying overhead in their
death machines, and when the air raid sirens went off, Gisela
and Renata brought the cookbook with them to the bomb shel-*

ter, or to the Tube, for safekeeping, just in case their home was bombed. It also brought them comfort to look at the recipes, and their family.

When the bombs thundered, the dust fell, and the sirens screamed, Gisela and Renata sat close together, in the pitch black of the bomb shelter, holding hands, praying a bomb would not hit them, tearing them apart, limb by limb, burying them alive.

They also wrote recipes in the cookbook in the bomb shelter, old recipes from Germany and new recipes from London. They liked shepherd's pie, English crumpets and scones, and Battenberg cake with white marzipan and apricot jam. Renata wrote a recipe for cauliflower cheese quiche and drew the London Bridge around it. They would never eat haggis, they decided. Ever. They drew pictures, together, of the people in the shelter who talked, knitted, sewed, darned socks, prayed, and hoped to live until the next day.

When they emerged from the shelters when the bombings ceased, often the buildings around them had been leveled. It was like walking out into a new world. One walked down into the Tube and there was a neighborhood with sidewalks, trees, and homes, then one walked out and the neighborhood was obliterated. The streets were clogged with debris. Fires burned, people were helped out of tons of concrete, crying or in shock, or digging frantically for family and friends who were buried in the tombs of toppled homes that they had not escaped in time.

Ports and ships were blown out of the water, schools destroyed, and churches turned to ash as the Nazis pursued their relentless quest for world domination.

The letters and recipes from their family abruptly stopped coming.

Gisela and Renata wrote and wrote. To everyone.

They heard nothing. The letters came back to them, one by one. "Does not live here anymore," "Return to sender," "Incorrect address."

Every returned letter brought a new wave of utter despair and throat-choking fear.

*   *   *

I wrapped myself in two coats and headed out to my grandma's gazebo late on Thursday night, the stars a bright, sometimes smeared, glowing picture. I sat down at the picnic table and watched the Telena River. I needed to calm my nerves.

Devlin, the girls' mother, hated me. One time, on a prison visitation day, Annabelle told me that the girls talked about me. They talked about Aunt Olivia. It enraged Devlin, and she shouted at her mother for allowing another woman, me, to "take my place." Annabelle assured Devlin that she had not, that I was a friend in the apartment complex, to which Lucy popped up and said, "We spend all day with her on Tuesdays! She's teaching us how to make cakes!" And Stephi said, "She took us to the zoo and the beach to find shells."

Annabelle said that Devlin was so angry she kicked a chair over, and the visit immediately ended when a guard rushed over. Annabelle told the girls not to talk to their mother about me again, which they agreed to because Devlin's anger scared them. But when Devlin pushed, during the next visit, about whether they spent time with me and what we had done, the girls, intimidated, whispered, "Yes." Devlin was livid.

Annabelle threatened not to bring the girls if Devlin was going to bully them, which enflamed Devlin more. She called her mother a "bitch" and "stupid whore." The girls and Annabelle left as Devlin stood up and screamed at them, the guards again moving in. The girls were still shaking when I went over that night for turkey sandwiches and ice cream.

Devlin called me from prison. "Stay away from my girls… They don't need you in their lives… I am their mother, not you… Don't try to replace me… You're trying to be my mother's daughter, my daughters' mother, you are after my mother's money…" She called me the same names she called her mother, only she added the words "ugly dog bitch."

I knew she was mentally ill. She had displayed that as early as three years old. She was born with it. I tried to feel sorry for her, but I couldn't get there. Mentally ill is one thing. Mentally ill and abusive and neglectful to children is another matter entirely.

I put my head on the picnic table in the gazebo that my granddad built my grandma so she could find some peace from her past. Again, I found no peace at all.

Lucy and Stephi were whispering on the couch. I smiled at them, then stopped. "What's wrong?"

"We want you to be the mom, Aunt Olivia. Forever. Okay?"

What could I tell them? I was trying, couldn't guarantee it?

"That's what I want, too. But your mom wants you, too. We've talked about this together, a lot. You know I love you two."

"We love you, too. And we love Mom, too," Lucy said.

"But we don't like being scared," Stephi said. "Or sleeping on the floor, or rat bites, or when they left for a long time and we thought, are we alone forever now?"

I hugged them tight. If the girls were taken from me, I would feel alone forever, too.

I smiled into the camera that Dinah held, ready to make another cooking video in the kitchen of Martindale Ranch. I had made several on my own, showing how to make stuffed mushrooms, shrimp and crab pasta, grilled crostini, chocolate croissants, and tortellini soup.

I invited Chloe to make a video of the two of us making cauliflower cheese quiche, a recipe we found in Grandma's cookbook, written by her sister, Renata, in London. Across the quiche recipe was a sketch of the London Bridge.

"Hello, everyone." I always tried to be smiling and serene when shooting these videos for our website. Calm. As if I know what I'm doing and my head doesn't have a tornado in it. "I'm Olivia Martindale. Welcome to *Cooking with Olivia on Martindale Ranch in Montana*. Today I'm with my sister, Chloe. Chloe is a paramedic and a search and rescue helicopter pilot. So if you have an accident up here in Kalulell, up in the mountains, or out in some remote area, look twice, because it might be Chloe piloting the helicopter. In addition, Chloe served in the army for six years—"

"So I can kick almost anyone's butt, just sayin'," Chloe interrupted, banging her fists together, her brown ponytail swinging. "You know what I excelled at in the army? Two things: One"— she pointed one finger in the air, not the middle finger—"hand-to-hand combat. No kidding. I took karate all the way through school, was number two in the state. I'm still pissed that Jimmy Thomas beat me in that final round. Jimmy"—she pointed at the camera—"any time, any place, I will whip your ass. And, two, what I also excelled at was sharpshooting. I was awesome at it. Still am. I can shoot a flea off a dog, an eyeball off a spider."

Dinah laughed, the camera shaking in her hand.

"Yes." I smiled at the camera, still trying to be serene. "Chloe has many skills. One of them is cooking."

"Oh, heck, no, but thank you, Olivia." Her voice lowered, the tone sweeter, her hand on my arm. "That's awfully nice of you to say." She turned to the camera. "Olivia, she's the kindest person. Now don't let me blow smoke up your ass, she's tough, too. She's one of the bravest women I've ever met. One day I'll tell you the story of how she scared a bear back into the forest when we were teenagers.

"Now me, I'll take you flat out if you look cross-eyed at me in a bar or if I see any of that judgment on your face because I'm not the size of a pinhead and I got boobs the size of watermelons on me right here"—she lifted her boobs and they bounced when she let go—"but Olivia, she has a warm heart." She thumped her heart, then thumped mine. Too hard!

"Olivia can make food so delicious, you'll orgasm. You think I'm kidding? I'm not. You wait until this is done and you'll see what I mean. You won't have your panties in a twist anymore if you had a bad day at work. You will eat this sucker and you will think, 'I am going to have an orgasm,' and you will." She turned to me. "We should rename this Orgasm Cauliflower Cheese Quiche. Let's rename it folks. So, first step." Chloe took out a handful of shredded cheese that I had in a bowl. "Don't ever skimp on cheese, folks. I'm telling you. You could die tomorrow, and if you died and you didn't put enough cheese into this breakfast delight you'd regret it. I mean, you'd be heading up to heaven, or down to hell, I don't know how you've lived your life, and you'd be thinkin' I wish I'd had more cheese, so do yourself a favor and get this cheese in there . . ."

"Exactly," I said. "Cheese is the—"

"The thing with cheese is that it'll make your, you know"— Chloe paused, glanced down—"it'll keep everything down there moist. Everyone knows that. It's the calcium."

"Uh, I don't think—"

"You don't need to think here, Olivia, it's plain truth. Cheese is like an aphrodisiac for a woman's personal butterfly. Also, folks, when you're making an Orgasm Cauliflower Cheese Quiche you have to add a shake of mustard powder and a shake of paprika. If you have a date and you're hoping to get lucky, add a pinch more like this," she demonstrated. "I don't know how it works, but somehow it heats things up in the bedroom."

"Right, Chloe. Thank you—"

"You're welcome. Anything I can do to help women have more oomph and ahhh in the bedroom, I'm gonna be sharing that information. I have had a lot of experience in that regard, and I think we women got to stay together. As I tell my personal butterfly, 'It's you and me, baby,' and I think we should say that here, too, on your show, Olivia, 'It's you and me, baby.' " She smiled at the camera. Banged her fists together again. "Boom, boom."

What in the world? Why was I allowing guests on my videos?

"Oh," Chloe said. "And to the men out there. I'm single. Yeah. I am. I know, hard to believe, but my husband died eight years ago, and if you like a woman who knows how to love and who will hug you in a way that makes you feel all tight and wrapped up, warm and snuggly, that's me. If you want a woman the size of a stick, who resembles a skeleton with skin, don't call. I am not that woman. Also, you gotta be okay with all of this." She tapped her temples. "Smart. Tough. I will beat you in shooting matches and arm wrestling and karate. You got an ego that can't handle that"—she picked up a knife and stabbed it into the cutting board—"don't you bother calling me. I'm not here to pander to your little whing whang and your tiny balls and your pride on overdrive."

Whew! "So, friends," I said, "this recipe was written by our grandma's sister, Renata, in London during the Blitz in World War Two. Everyone in England had a ration book, and ingredients were hard to come by, but Renata and our grandma, Gisela, were able to make this dish because cauliflower was plentiful in England. As you can see, Renata drew a picture of the London Bridge around it. You can see a close-up of this recipe, and the drawing, on our website. Now, let's talk about the ingredients for this incredibly simple dish . . ."

No surprise.

The video with Chloe was watched thousands and thousands of times.

She was inundated with e-mails on our website and on her Facebook page from men who knew they could handle a large woman who could beat them in shooting matches and arm wrestling and karate. Apparently a lot of men out there don't need to have their whing whangs or tiny balls or egos pandered to and like a woman who is tougher than they are.

We had a zillion hits, and many people asked, "Do you have a cookbook we can buy?"

My mother pulled up outside my house on Sunday afternoon. She interrupted a daydream I was having of a hot romp with Jace, but I was still glad to see her. "Hello, Rebel Child. I've got to go and check on LizAnne Hammerstead. She's having a bad time, losing her marbles again. Your grandma said she'll pick up the girls from Chloe's. I'd like you to come and help."

"Sure." I climbed in to her truck and we drove off. "What's happening with LizAnne?" I knew most of it, but something new was up.

"Her momma called me." I noticed my mother was wearing her black cowgirl boots with silver stars. I marvel at her collection. "She's refusing to take her meds. Again."

LizAnne and I were friends in high school, but the friendship started to crumble because of LizAnne's bipolar disorder, which hadn't been diagnosed then. Sometimes she was LizAnne—interesting, captivating, wild, funny, impulsive, almost hyper. And other times, she'd explode in a rage and raze anyone in her way, including me. She would target your weak spot—your weight, clothes, lack of a boyfriend, your face or your hair, your family if they were different in any way, and attack. She'd bring up imaginary offenses that took place months or years ago, twist them around, and harangue you to apologize.

There were mood swings and some delusional thinking about herself and her abilities, which led to bragging, which was hard to take when you're a teenager and feel like you resemble a limp spaghetti noodle.

"She'll talk to you, Olivia. She doesn't always open up to me. Last time I was at her house she called me an overbearing witch, then she called me a blood-sucking vampiress. Feminine."

"At least it's creative. Are there female vampires?"

"She's always been creative. I think vampires can be female, but they didn't address it in medical school. By the way, she's in one of her manic episodes."

"And here comes the crash." Creativity abounded when LizAnne was manic, but the crash came after that. We headed out of town. LizAnne lived about five miles west.

"I want to check on her and make sure she hasn't crashed already and is not suicidal. You know how she gets."

I did. When LizAnne was manic, what she accomplished was miraculous. Awe-inspiring. She's an internationally famous glass artist, popular among collectors, museums, and cities across the country for her brave, wacky, free-flowing art. Everything she makes is an artistic wonder. Six-foot-tall glass flowers that line pathways in a formal, public garden in Canada. Luminescent glass ocean waves, rainbow fish included, that now hang suspended from an aquarium's ceiling in New Zealand. Sparkling glass butterflies in elongated shapes that were bought by a children's museum in Portland.

LizAnne has remodeled her barn into a studio. There are wood floors, high ceilings, and an abundance of French doors, skylights, and windows so the light shines through.

"You haven't seen her recently?" I asked.

"No. She usually comes in once a month or so. I called her and she said she didn't have time to see me. Said something about fruit, glorious fruit. So my noggin's worried." She tapped her head.

"I heard she was hospitalized six months ago."

My mother nodded. "She stood on a table at Beatrice's Restaurant and told people that this was her last week and then she was going to use her grandpa's gun on her head. I was flooded with calls. They didn't let her leave the restaurant. Chief Kalama got there when I did. Your grandma came when LizAnne insisted on 'Mrs. Gisela,' because I, apparently, that day, was a 'pushy warlock,' and my mother knew how to heal her the 'gentle, natural, old-school way.' " My mother made air quotes. "I had her forcibly committed. The doctors there had her for about two months, got her stabilized."

"But the medication. It dulls her out, doesn't it? It makes her feel drugged and dead and sick, right?"

"It does," my mother said. "Without it she swings up and down and gets suicidal and cuts herself sometimes. But with the medication she wants to die because she doesn't feel like herself, she can't do her art, she can hardly move."

LizAnne's house is cottage style. White. Light blue door. Lavender front porch. In better weather, white wicker furniture with pink cushions welcomes you to her home. In spring and summer the property around her house is near covered in wildflowers, flowering trees, bulbs, roses, and plants I've never seen before. She gardens all day, most days, unless she has to work. She has a long trellis that holds climbing roses, and honeysuckle pours over an arch that leads to a vegetable garden.

She told me that gardening is her therapy.

We knocked on the door, but LizAnne didn't answer, so we headed to the barn and opened the doors. The rock music was blaring, and LizAnne didn't see us for a while. She was in front of the kiln, spinning a long stick with molten glass on the end of it. In front of us were four tables full of huge glass fruit—oversized, incandescent, glowing.

"Wow," my mother whispered.

"Wow and wow," I said.

LizAnne was singing. When she was finished with the molten glass, we waved and she turned.

"Hello!" she shouted at us, taking off her protective glasses. "Hello Mary Beth and Olivia Martindale!" She ran/skipped over and hugged us, rocking us back and forth. Aha! LizAnne was in one of her effusive manic moods. She smelled like sweat, cigarette smoke, alcohol, unwashed body, and strawberries—maybe lotion? She had a thing for lotion. Her red curly hair was sticking out all over her head. She looked like she'd lost weight, too much weight. She had circles under her eyes. "I'm making fruit. Fruit after fruit after fruit. See it? Bananas, apples, cranberries, blueberries, raspberries, melons, kiwi. I am obsessed with fruit lately. It's all I eat, too."

We could tell.

"It's magic, this fruit," she gushed, running her hands over a pomegranate, each seed a shiny red oval. She put her head on it. "Glorious fruit! I can *feel* it. I can taste it. I am one with the pomegranate. I am a fruit. Hey now, I have a question!" she popped her head up. "Are you back together with Jace, Olivia? I heard a long time ago that Ruthie said she saw him at your house when she was cleaning her gun, but then I heard you weren't together from Kai, then Dirk's best friend, Renee, she said you were and now you're working with him again, so are you? I hope so."

"No."

"Aw. That's sad. What happened to you is sad. I cried for you." She burst into tears and hugged me tight. "I love you, Olivia."

"Love you, too, LizAnne."

"How long has it been since you've slept, LizAnne?" my mother asked, deftly changing the subject.

"What is today? Did you see this orange?" She let me go and hugged the giant orange. "It needs a hug."

"The orange is spectacular, and it's Sunday," I said.

"I slept on Friday." She stroked a three-foot-tall green apple. LizAnne was puzzled. "Or Thursday. What is today again? I can't stop working. I keep hearing this voice in my head telling me to finish, to get all my glorious fruit done. A museum wants it. In Boston. Boston fruit." She shook her head. Her red hair flew about at the ends, but some of it was stuck to her head because she hadn't washed it. "So here I am! I am, I am!" She raised her arms and twirled around. "I'm a pineapple. You're a crabapple, Mary Beth, because you get so cranky sometimes, and you're a watermelon, Olivia. Tough outside, soft inside. Did you bring Mrs. Gisela? No? That's too bad. She knows all about natural medicine. Does she know about natural marijuana?"

LizAnne laughed, she sang, she chattered super fast. She was on something, I could tell. I could hardly blame her. I couldn't judge. Bipolar is vicious. It's a sanity-stealing, emotion-yanking, normalcy-shattering bear. She told me once that she'd been self-medicating the delusions and mood swings and rage since high school with pot and mushrooms and a hit now and then of acid. Alcohol ran through her bloodstream like water, too. Who knew what she'd taken today.

We held her ten minutes later when she collapsed, sobbing, hysterical, crushed. She was skin and bones. We took her to Serene Hands. She refused to get out of the truck, yelled for Mrs. Gisela, instead of "You, Mary Beth, the pushy vampire lady doctor," then gave in. "I'm toast, aren't I?" she asked me.

"Right now you are," I said. "You know how this works. You stay, you get better, you get settled, and then you're home."

She hugged my mother and me. Yes, we would come and visit her. And yes, we promised that Mrs. Gisela would come and talk to the doctors here about giving her "natural medicine."

"How about a beer?" I asked my mom on the way home.

"Yes to that."

"I saw you kissing Aunt Olivia," Lucy said to Jace, her blond curls back in a ponytail.

The four of us were in the stables at the ranch, "visiting" the horses.

"You saw me kissing Aunt Olivia?" Jace said. "Hmmm." He crossed his arms. "Did I do that? Let me think . . ." He peered up at the ceiling, as if trying to remember. I tried not to laugh. He had kissed me when I drove the girls up in my truck twenty minutes ago.

"You did it when we got out of the truck. You grabbed her and gave her a lot of kisses," Lucy said, with some accusation, that finger of hers pointed straight into the air.

"I saw it, too," Stephi said, fiddling with her rocks in her pocket. "You're kissing."

"Charlie Zimmerman told me that you're Aunt Olivia's husband, and I went home and I said, 'Is Jace the Giant your husband?' and Aunt Olivia said yes, so does that make you our uncle?"

"Yes."

Whoa. I whipped my head around to Jace.

"So we call you Uncle Jace?" Lucy asked.

"Yes."

"I'm confused up here." Stephi tapped her head, those brown eyes baffled. "You're married to Aunt Olivia but you don't live with us."

"That's weird." Lucy shook her head. "Weird. If you're married you live together and you sleep in the same bed."

"It is weird," Jace said. "Maybe you all can come over to my house and have a spend-the-night party."

"Oh! Oh! I want to do that." Lucy's face lit up. "I want to play with Garmin and Snickers, too."

"And I want to play with K.C. the kitty cat and look for rocks for my rock collection." Stephi clapped. "And Lucy and I will sleep together because we get scared at night, and will Aunt Olivia sleep with you? Because you're married, you know."

"I hope so," Jace said. "I'll say please."

"Oh, for goodness' sakes," I muttered.

"Aunt Olivia says that you can't eat cookies in bed because of the crumbs, Uncle Jace," Stephi said. "So no cookies in bed."

"It's a smart rule. I won't let Aunt Olivia eat cookies in our bed."

"And she also says no drinking in bed because it could spill," Lucy said.

"I won't let her drink in bed," Jace said.

I coughed and raised my eyebrows at him. I tried to appear stern. Didn't work. I smiled.

"You two want to go and find Garmin and Snickers?" Jace asked.

They did. I rolled my eyes at Jace. He winked back. "Can't wait for the sleepover. How about tonight?"

To work on Kyle's empathy for others, Chloe told Kyle to draw people in town who seemed like they were having a bad day. "Give them a better day," my sister told him in front of me. "We all get crap thrown at us. When you see someone who has had a lot of crap thrown at them, give them the gift of one of your portraits and de-crap their lives for a while."

Kyle said, "Thank you, Mother, for that advice." He wrote the advice in his Questions Notebook. "I'll follow it. The word 'de-crap' is not in the dictionary, but I understand the meaning."

So that was how a number of people in Kalulell, who were having a bad day, came to be sitting quite still, on a chair, while Kyle drew their portraits.

"I drew a Vietnam veteran at Beatrice's Restaurant," he told me one evening. "His name was Rodney. Birthday April 16. I deduced that he was unhappy based on the fact that he wiped tears away with a napkin. He told me about crawling down holes in the ground to get to the Viet Cong and how they would shoot at him. He said he was 'screwed up in the head for about twenty years,' his words, not mine, Olivia. He said he tried to forget what happened through 'those damn drugs and alcohol but that made it worse,' so he got himself cleaned up and now he's a trucker. At first I laughed when he told me about the drugs and alcohol, which is an inappropriate reaction that I am working on. Mother is helping me with this problem. I drew his portrait. Afterward he tried to pay me, because he said he had a work of art, but I remembered what Mother said, 'Do good for other people with your art, Kyle. De-crap their day. You've got some strange kinks in that personality of yours, and this will show people that behind the strange kinks you are one cool kid.' Mother's advice is always helpful."

I laughed. Chloe is so blunt. "Your mom told me that you drew a picture of Harry, too."

"Yes. Harry, birthday March 21, was having a bad day indicated by him shouting at himself in downtown Kalulell. I watched him shout at himself and I remembered what Grandma told me about him. Harry has schizophrenia.

"I relate to Harry because of my challenges with Asperger's, though his challenges are exponentially greater than mine. Harry was yelling at voices to get the hell away, pardon the word 'hell,' and he was going to kill them and he had a knife and was going to use it on them. I approached him when he held the knife up in the air, and said, 'Harry, are you having a bad day? May I draw your portrait?' and he said, 'What did you say, you little shit?' Again, Aunt Olivia, I apologize for the poor language that is not in the dictionary.

"I said to Harry, 'I would like to draw your portrait,' and he said, 'I know what a portrait is. I know Van Gogh. You can draw me a Van Gogh but don't draw the voices in, I don't want the voices in the picture.' I assured him I would not draw the voices as I could not see or hear them. He said, 'And don't cut off my ear like Van Gogh did.' I assured him that cutting off an ear wouldn't happen and he said, 'I'll sit down and you can draw me but don't use a pen that's got a gun in it.' I again assured him that nothing like that would happen, that our guns are all locked in a safe in the basement and are taken out only for hunting season, which I do not partake in because I cannot stand to see an animal hurt.

"By the time I was done, I believe that Harry was having a better day. His brother, Marvin, birthday March 21, as they are twins, but Marvin does not have an affliction of schizophrenia, came down and sat with Harry while I was drawing. Someone, apparently, told Marvin that Harry was in town. Harry said, 'Don't worry, Marvin, this kid's not drawing the voices in the picture. He told me he'd leave them out.'

"Because Marvin was then sitting by Harry, I drew them together. You can definitely tell that they share common genetics, though Marvin was in a suit and has trimmed hair, and Harry's hair is long and straggling and his face is creased with lines and wrinkles. I gave the portrait to Harry and Marvin and they sat and stared at it for a long time and Marvin had to be handed a handkerchief by a man nearby who had watched the process because Marvin was crying. I have learned that tears over my portraits do not mean that I have hurt someone. So I kept quiet and refrained from inappropriate laughing.

"Then Marvin said to Harry, 'Hey, Harry. How about you come home with me, we'll try it again, and I'll hang this picture in your bedroom.' And Harry said, 'I'm not going to your house unless all the snakes under the bed are gone,' and Marvin said that all the snakes were gone, and he said, 'We can eat pizza and watch a game,' and Harry said, 'I'll do it, but I don't want any scissors in the house,' and Marvin said, 'All the scissors are gone.'

"Marvin hugged me and said, 'Thank you so much, Kyle. Thank you.' And Harry said to me, 'I think you beat back the voices for a couple hours, kid. I hate those damn voices. Driving me out of my mind,' he said the f-word here."

"You reunited the brothers," I said, sniffling.

"For the moment." His brow furrowed. "That would be a positive outcome."

"You are a positive outcome."

"Now I'm confused, Aunt Olivia."

"It simply means you are a gift because you make other people happy."

He didn't look me in the eye and his hands flapped, then settled. "Thank you, Aunt Olivia. Birthday February 27."

I told my sister about the drawings later. "He has the social instincts of a polar bear, but he's teachable."

I could tell she was proud of him. As she should be.

As the meeting with my attorney, Devlin's attorney, and Children's Services in Oregon loomed closer, like a devil with a switchblade, my nerves shattered at the ends and split. To calm my shot nerves, I made my great-grandmother Esther's twisted bread rolls after I put Lucy and Stephi to bed that night. Flour, salt, yeast . . .

I could lose my girls.

I love Stephi and Lucy with all my heart. I have not had the honor and joy of raising them their whole lives, but they are my daughters.

Mix the ingredients . . .

They could be sent back to live with their drug-addicted mother.

And if that happened, we would leave the country.

We would get in my truck and fly out of here into the wild blue yonder.

Knead the dough . . .

My shoulders slumped. I couldn't do that.

You can't hide anymore in this world. You can't get a job without paperwork, a social security number, references. What would we live off of? I'm a decent shot. I can kill deer. I can fly-fish with the best of them.

But that wasn't enough. The girls would need to go to school. We would need money.

I would be found. I would be jailed.

Knead the dough, knead the dough . . .

The girls would go back to their mother and I wouldn't even be given visitation. You cannot be given visitation in jail with the girls you kidnapped.

But how could I let them go? How could I let them go back to Devlin, who would only neglect and abuse them again and hook up with some other drug-addicted freak?

I kneaded the dough harder, then I gave up, sank down in my kitchen, leaned against the cabinets, and had a good cry.

When I was done, I brushed off the tears and kept kneading.

I did not have time for these breakdowns anymore. I needed cement in my spine.

I sniffled.

Sometimes cooking is the best therapy for the bricks that life throws at your head.

Measure. Mix. Stir. Whip. Bake.

I kept taking photos of the hearty, ranch-style entrées, appetizers, desserts, salads, breads, and soups that we made at the ranch, including Grandma's recipe for Battenberg cake with white marzipan and apricot jam that she wrote down in a bomb shelter in London during the Blitz.

"Let me take photos of you," Jace said one afternoon as we had what was becoming our usual coffee break in a quiet kitchen. I had not forgotten whipping my clothes off with him at his house. He hadn't, either. We had silently decided not to discuss it. But I could see it in the way he smiled at me, kissed my neck, and hugged me. He is too, too much, and my resistance was wearing down.

"Oh, ugh. No photos of me."

"Not ugh." He laughed and took the camera. And that's where we became the old Jace and Olivia who goofed off *a lot.*

I posed with my favorite red mixing bowl...on my head, covering my eyes. I posed holding a whole bunch of bottled spices, as many as I could hold, with a bottle of nutmeg in my mouth. I posed lying on top of the island counter, trying on my sexy expression, with an apple in my mouth like a stuffed pig. I posed with two wine bottles in each hand and a pile of bananas stacked on my head.

"Your turn," I told Jace, as we laughed.

I took photos of him holding two uncooked chickens in both hands, by the legs, his jean shirt making him look all the more masculine. I gave him a huge, five-layer white coconut cheesecake to hold, and pushed it down so he was holding it straight on his crotch.

I wrapped a flowered apron around him, put flowered hot mitts on his hands, and shot away. He was so sexy.

We did selfies together and made such weird, scrunched funny faces we laughed until I thought I might wet my pants. Goofing off is like food for the soul.

Ah, Jace. He kissed me before he left, an up-against-the-wall, full body-to-body kiss, and I let him because I couldn't resist him, I can't resist him. And I didn't know what I was doing here, as his chef, and I didn't know why I was letting myself slide into a relationship with Jace, because the ending wasn't pretty last time and it wouldn't be this time, and it would slice my heart in half.

Again.

Yet there I was, working on the ranch, kissing Jace.

I laughed when I thought of Jace holding two wine bottles straight out on his chest as if he had wine bottle boobs.

I sat in the gazebo that night by the river after I got the girls in bed. The sky was clear, stars so white, as if someone had picked up white jewels of different sizes and brightness and threw them into the sky. I thought of Jace in his flowered apron and how I'd missed him the last two years.

I realize now that part of the reason I left Jace was because I didn't feel like I, alone, was enough for him. I had to have children, the children we agreed upon, to be worth enough. I know now it had a lot to do with how I felt when my father abandoned me. I wasn't enough for him, so he left.

Making that leap, rationally, doesn't make sense. My father was a selfish, cold, faithless, irresponsible, unloving, immature man. He left because he's a failure as a man. But my self-worth, as a child, was damaged by my father's rejection when he walked out on our family, and his continual rejection and absence over the years did further destruction. He didn't love me. He didn't want me. I was not important to my father. I was a rejected daughter. It was like taking a razor to my soul.

I carried that lack of love, those feelings of unworthiness, that I alone was not enough, that I wasn't lovable enough, as part of my being. I hadn't been able to see it for what it was, and then throw that damage out of my life forever. Unfortunately, so unfairly, I threw some of that emotional mess on my relationship with Jace.

It was one more thing that cowboy did not deserve.

*   *   *

On Thursday afternoon I left to go to the meeting in Portland. The girls would stay with my mom and grandma. The girls thought I was going to a cooking class. I asked Jace two weeks before if I could have that Friday off. I knew he would say yes. I told him I had to go to a meeting about the girls. I smiled brightly, told him it was a formality. He already knew that Joan, through Montana's Children's Services, regularly came by to check on the girls.

"Sure," he said. "You don't have to ask. Want company?" He grinned.

Oh, I so wanted his company. He would be a comfort. He would prop me up. He would calm me down when my insides shook with the fear of losing the girls. But I hadn't told him about how serious the situation was getting for the girls with Devlin getting out of jail soon, having an attorney, demanding her parental rights back, etc. I hadn't wanted to involve him in my fight. "No, thanks. I'm going in and out."

"Okay." His brow creased. "Is there something wrong? Anything else?"

Dang. My bright smile did not deflect his curiosity, his sense that something was off. "No. Everything's fine."

I could tell he sort of believed me. Somewhat. Maybe. Not really.

Twice more he asked me, before I left for the meeting, if something was wrong. That man can see right inside me, I swear.

Chapter 14

~

"I don't understand."

Everyone in the conference room, in a squat building in downtown Portland, turned to stare at me. My attorney, Claudine, raised her eyebrows at me, as in, *Do not blow up, Olivia. Do not.*

"I don't understand why we're even here. Devlin is not a fit mother. She is in jail. She committed a robbery. Before that she was a neglectful mother and a drug addict. Annabelle Lacey, her mother, had custody of Stephi and Lucy. When she died, with the full support of Children's Services, the children came to live with me. And now, because Devlin is pretending to be a model prisoner and will be released soon, you are actually considering giving Stephi and Lucy back to her? How is that a safe placement for them?"

Claudine kicked me under the table. I was in a blue suit, and she whacked me in the middle of my shin. A bad word almost slipped out.

The meeting had not started off on a positive note. The room was stuffy and suffocating, the table full.

Besides Claudine and me, there was a court-appointed attorney for Lucy and Stephi's mother. His name was Anthony Bastfield III. He emphasized III. When he shook my hand it was clammy. Anthony III had a reddish beard, a skinny build, and was in his late twenties.

There were also three people from Children's Services, two

women and a man, including Dameon, the caseworker with no personality and no smile, who wrote me excellent reviews, and another attorney from the state named Zoe Something. I couldn't remember her last name.

Anthony III announced, early on in the meeting, "I am here to protect the mother's rights to her children. I will reiterate that Sarah's parental rights have not been terminated. Again, jail does not necessarily terminate a parent's rights to his or her children. Sarah has been a model inmate. She has been in counseling, she goes to Bible study once a week in the jail, and she works in the cafeteria helping to fccd and nourish her fellow inmates. She is sober and has turned a corner. When she is released early for good behavior, she will be a completely different person than when she went in. She is on the road to success."

"You have used a lot of clichéd phrases to lift your client to sainthood," I said, "but it's not working. How about going over her past?"

"Olivia," my attorney warned.

"Sarah was abused by her husband," Anthony III droned on, as if I hadn't spoken. Of course he would not call his client Devlin. Too devilish. "Parker McDaniel threatened her life and, worse, the lives of her children, if she did not participate in the robbery. Sarah felt pressure to stay with him, to do what he told her to do, to save her own life and those of her children. She suffered from battered women's syndrome. Her actions as a mother were heroic. She is proud to be drug free."

"Give me a break," I said. "Parker did not force her into the robbery. That never came out in the trial, or in any investigation, and you know it. Look at the security footage of the robbery. She was clearly the leader. She broke the window herself with a bat, then turned and yelled at Parker and told him what to do while she went through the cash register. It sounded like the robbery was Devlin's idea. She's lying to you about Parker."

"I agree," Zoe Something said. "I've looked at the trial transcripts and there was nothing in the trial to indicate that Sarah was forced into the robbery at all." She tilted her head at Anthony III. "Where did you get this information?"

He cleared his throat, twitched. "From Sarah. She felt comfortable opening up to me and being honest about her life and her marriage, now that she's away from the dangers that Parker presented."

I laughed. "She's lying."

"We need to stick with the established facts, Anthony," Claudine said. "We're not going to create a new story here, one that hasn't been presented before, and run with it."

"Sarah is—" Anthony III went on after an awkward pause.

"Devlin," I corrected. "The reason Sarah changed her name to Devlin, Anthony the third, is because the name reminded her of the devil. Devlin has no addiction problems at the moment because she is locked up behind bars. They don't sell cocaine in the vending machines. She has been an addict since she was a teenager."

"Sarah adores her children." Anthony III talked over me. "She tried as best she could to take care of them with love, but Parker was abusive and she felt like a trapped prisoner in her own home."

"That is not true," I said. "Annabelle told me that Devlin, her own daughter, was a neglectful, abusive mother. Didn't you read the Children's Services reports not only from Oregon but also from Idaho and California? She was a hellacious mother."

"I object to your tone and to your argument." Anthony III stroked his red beard.

"And I object to your lies. Devlin's desperate. Devlin thinks that her mother left money for the girls and she wants it. The only money is in college funds. The girls told me, many times, how life was with Devlin. Lucy talked about being hungry all the time. They both have a horrible fear of rats. They have scars from the cigarette burns. They call fleas 'biters.' They remember being scared and alone. They are still not comfortable around men and loud noises. They both told me about how they couldn't sleep at night because of the fighting, and they talked about the scary people in their home, some of whom tried to get in their bedroom at night, and they talked about the needles and the trash and the mice they made friends with—"

"You weren't there, now, were you, Ms. Martindale?" Anthony III said. "Or is it Miss? Or Mrs.? I am confused about your marital status."

"I am their Aunt Olivia."

"But your marital status?"

"We are not here to talk about Olivia's marital status," Claudine said. "We are here to talk about why these children, who were abused and neglected by Devlin, would go back to her when she gets out of prison."

"Ms. Martindale," Anthony III prodded again. "What is your marital status? I believe we need to know that, as we need to know who the children are living with."

"The children are living with me."

"Are you married?"

"Legally, yes. I'm separated."

"And where is your husband?"

"He lives about twenty minutes away from me in Kalulell. I work for him."

"And how does he feel about the children?"

"He thinks they're terrific."

"I care about the girls, too," Anthony III said, his tone pious. "I want what's best for them."

"You care about them?" I leaned toward him across the table.

"Yes. Very much. I am here to do what's right for those girls, which is to reunite them with their loving mother, who is starting a new life."

"What are their names?"

"What?"

"You care about the girls. What are their names?"

"I . . . uh . . . not relevant . . . er . . ."

Two of the women in that room sighed. Dameon, who usually has no facial expression, frowned. Zoe Something said, "If you care about the girls, you should know their names."

Later, two of the people from Children's Services spoke to discuss Devlin's parenting and her alarming past. Their folder on her was thick. Dameon, back to no facial expression, said that I was an outstanding mother to the girls, that I was loving and caring and made sure that the girls were on track in school. The girls' teachers also felt that I was outstanding as a parent, as did the neighbors he talked to. He said that I took the girls on many outings, which he listed, and taught them to cook. The girls, in the many individual interviews he had had with them, said that they "loved their Aunt Olivia."

He also read aloud, in a monotone, the report from Joan, in which she gave me an A-plus.

"Anthony the third, you are trying to give these innocent children back to a mother who will abuse and neglect them again, as she has done since they were born. She is a drug addict with a long criminal record and a personality disorder. I know she's beautiful, but get past the blond hair and falsely innocent blue eyes and see the truth."

Anthony III actually blushed. I'd hit a nerve. Devlin was beautiful. A beautiful sociopath.

"She is their mother. It is my aim to reunite the girls with their mother. And I don't appreciate your insinuations, Ms. Martindale."

"But it's true, isn't it?"

He blushed again. Coughed. "No. Not at all. Not for a minute."

I leaned toward him again. "She's got you wrapped around her finger, Anthony the third, and she will drop you as soon as she gets what she wants, do not delude yourself."

Zoe Something said, "Let's move on."

The meeting continued. Things did not end on a bright note, an hour later, when I told Anthony III, in a shouting type of voice, that if he returned my girls to their biological mother I would hold him personally responsible when she starved and hit them again, and when rats bit, and fleas crawled, and scary men brought their needles into the home.

I also accused him of being an "uncaring, ridiculously stupid, reckless asshole." And topped it off with, "And I don't care if you appreciate my insinuations or not. You are one more man Devlin is manipulating with the tears, and the lies. You are very young, and you have no idea what she's doing to you."

Anthony III blushed again. "I know what she's doing to me." He coughed. "I mean, I know what I am doing to her." Coughed again. "I know that I am Sarah's attorney doing her, doing her . . . her work."

Children's Services chimed in, as did my attorney, and I spent the rest of the meeting glaring at Anthony III, who tried as hard as he could, without blushing *too* much, to hide his burgeoning feelings for Devlin, resident sociopath.

"The most important thing you must remember when cooking for other people is that you want to bring them love and peace," my grandma said, staring straight into the camera that Dinah held in the ranch's kitchen, her smile angelic, as always.

I stood beside my grandma in my white chef's jacket. I smiled, too. It was easier to be serene and calm with Grandma by my side. At her request, we were going to make shepherd's pie, a recipe she wrote down in the bomb shelter with Renata during the Blitz in London. "It will warm my soul," Grandma had told me. "And it will make me feel closer to Renata."

My grandma's white hair was pulled back into a bun, and she was wearing a turquoise scarf with yellow daffodils on it. She was bringing beauty to the world. "May I tell you about this shepherd's pie recipe? My parents, Esther and Alexander Gobenko, put my sister and me on the Kindertransport in Munich in 1939. We had to leave them, and my brother, Isaac, who was too old for the train, behind in Germany. They knew it was our only chance at living, at escaping the Nazis who were rounding up Jews. Our family businesses had been looted and firebombed, and the Nazis had robbed our homes and bank accounts. Two of my uncles had disappeared.

"We escaped to England, and Renata and I soon trained to become nurses. When the Nazis came to London and the Blitz started, the bombs relentless, my sister and I had to go down into air raid shelters or the Tube to survive. That was where we wrote down this particular recipe for shepherd's pie. I hope you enjoy it, and I hope that the people you cook it for find peace and your love within it. Let's begin, shall we?"

We began.

So many, many, many hits on the ranch's website. We received a ton of e-mail. People wanted to know when Mrs. Gisela was going to be on again, they wanted to hear more about her life in Germany and England, they wanted to know what happened to her family, they wanted to see the shepherd's pie recipe in its original handwritten form, and they wanted to know if Martindale Ranch had a cookbook.

"That was fun, Olivia!" my grandma said. "May I visit again?"

Oh, she absolutely could.

On Tuesday evening, with the girls out with my mother for ice-cream sundaes because they'd memorized ten facts about the body's immune system and five facts about cells, my grandma and I sat in front of the fireplace at the blue farmhouse.

She held the old cookbook in her hands, the pink ribbon stained, the pages burned around the edges, water damage, blood splatters, and tears telling our family's history. The upper-right-hand corner of the back cover was slightly torn. We looked through the pages together as the fire crackled. There was a drawing of a park in Munich, Germany, the city rising behind it. There was a drawing of Ida's Bakery, pink and white, and the desserts, cakes, and breads Ida and Esther used to make. There was a picture of Boris's Leather Goods and Esther and Alexander's, the department store Grandma's parents owned.

Inside the cookbook were the last remnants of a pink rose, the two heart-shaped gold lockets, two red ribbons, the sun charm, and a white feather.

She said something in German.

"What did you say, Grandma?"

"I love you, Renata." She kissed my cheek. "Let's make a

Danube Wave Cake. I have the recipe right here. I think we need Martindale Cake Therapy."

While we baked, she talked. She told me the story of her and her sister, Renata, the pink rose, two heart-shaped lockets, two red ribbons, the sun charm, the white feather, and the poems.

May 1941
London, England
Gisela Gobenko, grandmother of Olivia Martindale

The bombs started dropping through the pitch-black night over London, bringing the usual chaos and annihilation. Gisela heard the sirens and the explosions, but she, and the surgeon she was working with, didn't leave their patient. They couldn't run to a safe shelter, they couldn't hustle underground to the Tube. If they did, the British pilot, whose leg had been nearly entirely cut off when he crash-landed his plane after a bombing mission over Germany, would die. He had risked his life to save England, and they would risk their lives to save his.

Gisela and the exhausted surgeon were doing the best they could to put the young man back together again, working in an underground ward below the hospital.

They heard the sirens, warning of the Luftwaffe flying in to pound the British people into submission. Then they heard the doodlebug, like a hive of angry bees, then silence. They knew what was coming next: A building exploded on their block and the surgeon, two other nurses, and she instinctively flinched. They worked on.

Later, they sewed a woman up who was covered in blood and unconscious. Her building had collapsed when a bomb hit it. Though she had sheltered in the basement, half her ribs were broken, she had a terrible concussion, and her left ankle snapped. After that victim, they sewed up another victim, who had multiple gaping wounds from shattering glass. All from those beastly Nazis.

After twelve hours of the cacophony in the hospital, Gisela returned to the girls' group home she lived in with Renata. It was six in the morning, the golden light barely over the horizon. Some of the streets she walked on were mostly intact, others weren't, the bombs from those damn Nazis taking out buildings, churches, another hospital, and blocks of neighborhoods. Her rage rose at Hitler and the German people who had allowed this monster to erupt, who supported him. Injured and traumatized people were being loaded into cars, undoubtedly to be taken to the hospital she just left.

There were children crying, mothers consoling, and some people were going about their day, as if the British were not fighting for their very survival. What else could one do? Help others, be brave, and continue life. There was no choice. They would never give in or give up. Never. Carry on.

Gisela turned the last corner and was confused at first. Had she taken the wrong street, the wrong turn? Surely she had ... but there was the butcher's, albeit damaged, there was the school, there was the grocer's. And ... and ... oh no oh no oh no!

Gisela's high-pitched scream, raw and echoing, was a piercing cry of disbelief as she sprinted to what was left of the home she and Renata lived in with their beloved Mrs. Lowenstein; their best friends, sisters Keila and Naomi; and other young women. Their neighbors and strangers were pulling away the rubble, the front door, and the bricks that had made up their home, as if there was someone buried beneath it.

A bobby she knew tried to stop her, "Wait now, Gisela, let us work here," but she shrugged him off and ran toward the home. Surely Renata was fine. She would have been in a shelter, right? She would have been in the Tube, the Underground, when the bombs came down. She was asleep somewhere. Gisela only had to find her, find Renata.

She saw Mrs. Lowenstein, Keila, and Naomi digging through the rubble, covered in debris, trembling and crying. "Where is Renata? Where is Renata?"

They didn't know. They didn't want to tell Gisela what they feared, didn't want to tell her they were frantically digging through the rubble with the neighbors for Renata. The four of them had headed to the bomb shelter when they heard the sirens, but Renata told them she was going back for something she forgot and they hadn't seen her since.

"Renata!" Gisela yelled. "Renata!"

A firefighter came around from the back of the building, holding someone with long, thick dark brown hair, covered in dirt and dust.

It wasn't her sister.

It couldn't be. Her sister, her very best friend, didn't have dirt in her hair. She was never covered in gray dust. She was clean and cheerful and had lovely green eyes tilted like a cat's. She had been working in the hospital with her, training these last eighteen months. They had had lunch together yesterday in the cafeteria. They had escaped from Germany together on the Kindertransport, and they would find their family again after the war. They would be in each other's weddings, and they would raise their children together. They would grow old and hug each other's grandchildren.

No, that girl, that limp and unmoving girl in the firefighter's arms, wasn't her sister. It couldn't be.

Gisela ran over with Mrs. Lowenstein, Naomi, and Keila, stumbling, crying, reaching out to touch the long, dark hair.

The screaming started again.

Gisela accompanied Renata to the morgue. She did not want her to be alone. She filled out paperwork, her tears sopping the paper as she shook. Mrs. Lowenstein, Keila, and Naomi came with her, their clothes gray and dirty from digging for Renata. When they were done, Gisela insisted on going back home to find what she could. The four of them, all of whom had seen way too much tragedy, dug through the disaster again.

Gisela found the leather-bound cookbook fifteen feet from the wrecked home. It was half buried in dirt, the back cover torn in the upper-right-hand corner, the pink ribbon now brownish, but still tied tight around it. How it wasn't burned to bits when the bomb exploded, she couldn't fathom. It should have been buried under the rubble, like the body of her sister.

Gisela knelt in the dirt, trying to calm her hysteria, her insid-

ious grief, her rage, clutching the cookbook to her chest. She rocked back and forth, Mrs. Lowenstein, Keila, and Naomi not leaving her side. Three nights ago, sitting in the Tube underground, she and Renata had written a recipe for Danube Wave Cake. Their grandma Ida had made it for the bakery and had taught them. Gisela knew the cookbook was what Renata had gone back for. She knew it. And now her sister was dead.

Her sister was dead.

Her sister was dead.

How could that be?

She undid the ribbon and opened the cookbook, as if she could find Renata there. Inside was a pressed pink rose that Renata had dried out between napkins and heavy books. She had found it last October and said that it resembled hope. There were two gold, heart-shaped lockets that Renata had bought at a secondhand shop, one for her, one for Gisela, to show their love for each other. There was a charm, in the shape of a sun, that their mother had given Gisela as a birthday gift, tucked inside a letter.

There were two poems that Renata had written, one on friendship and one on sisters and everlasting love, and their father's poems. There was the white feather that they had found on a walk through Hyde Park, so pure and magical that they'd kept it, and the red ribbons their brother had sent. There were the photographs and mailed recipes from their family that they had taped to the back pages. These were their treasures.

Renata had rushed back during the bombing raid for the cookbook, for their family's history, their stories, their recipes, the hand-drawn pictures. She had gone back for Tsilia and Aron Bezkrovny, Sarrah and Efim Tolstonog, Ida and Boris Zaslavsky, Esther and Alexander Gobenko, and all of their children and grandchildren. She had gone back for the recipes she and Gisela had written together and for Isaac's pictures and red ribbons. And now she was gone.

Gisela lay down, amidst the destruction, and cried until her heart felt it would break if one more tear fell out. Mrs. Lowenstein, Keila, and Naomi didn't even try to move her. They simply sat in the rubble with her, all too exhausted and stricken to move. They had loved Renata, too. Damn the bloody Germans. Damn the Nazis to hell.

When Gisela finally stood up, Keila and Naomi holding her, she saw something shimmering amidst what had been their home. Something silver. She stumbled toward it, sank to her knees in the rubble, and held her family's menorah in her trembling hands. The menorah that had been made by Aron Bezkrovny and given to his granddaughter, Ida, for her wedding to Boris Zaslavsky in Odessa. Decades later, Ida tearfully gave it to Esther, to give to her and Renata when they were escaping on the Kindertransport out of Munich. Gisela clutched it to her chest. The menorah had now survived two attacks—one in Odessa, one in London.

That night, when the Germans came again, Gisela stood in the middle of the street, clutching the cookbook and holding the menorah high, swearing at them, using every swear word she knew. She swore in German and in English. She swore in Yiddish. People tried to get her to go underground, but it wasn't until three men dragged her off—"Come along now, lass. You'll do no good out here, we have to carry on"—that she was forced away from cursing the Nazis for what they had done to her family.

She hated them.

There were rumors of camps. Concentration camps. Where Jews and gypsies and foreigners and enemies of the state were being held and killed. Burned in gas chambers. Starved. Worked to death. That couldn't be true, could it?

Her sister was dead, she couldn't locate her family, and London was being bombed and obliterated from above. Was she all alone?

Gisela wanted to die.

The girls had another day off of school for a teacher work day, and I couldn't miss work. I bundled them up in their coats and we headed out. My grandma said she would pick them up by two. She had appointments that morning, people who would come into the clinic only to see Mrs. Gisela, "who knew how to naturally heal people without all this modern bullarcky and who wouldn't charge a fortune for fake medicines that make the pharmaceutical executives rich!"

"We're going to work," Stephi declared. "I'll bring my rocks."

"I'm going to help you, Aunt Olivia," Lucy said.

"I'm going to help, too, right, Aunt Olivia?"

"Yes. Both of you are going to work and help me out."

Two little girls. In the kitchen. With my full staff flying around in orchestrated chaos.

Sheesh.

It was in the middle of flipping huge slices of cinnamon and nutmeg Big Bear French Toast that Jace walked in and saw Stephi and Lucy. Both of them wore white aprons. They were at the island "helping" Dinah make lemon muffins. He had known they were coming, as I had asked if I could bring them. His response was, "Anytime, Olivia."

"Hi, Uncle Jace," they both said, flour on their sweet, smiling faces, their blond curls back in ponytails.

Lucy was wearing her purple and blue butterfly wings and a blue T-shirt with a green lizard on it along with her red cowgirl boots, and Stephi had on a pink tutu and a pink shirt with a furry mutt. Her cowgirl boots were light blue. The boots were from my mother to "start their collection."

"Hello, Stephi. Hello, Lucy." He smiled, seemed happy to see them. Tough Montana cowboy had a soft spot.

"We're helping." Stephi waved a wooden spoon around, batter flying.

"I put the flour in." Lucy pointed her finger in the air.

"I put the vanilla in," Stephi said.

Jace peered into the bowl. "I think I see a tiny fairy in there."

The girls gasped and yanked the bowl closer. "You do?"

"Yes, she's in there. Tiny wings. Glitter."

The girls' heads conked together as they searched for the glittering fairy. "I got a fork!" Lucy said. "I'll move the flour around. I bet she's hiding."

"No, you might poke the fairy!" Stephi admonished her sister.

"I won't poke her." Lucy frowned. "I'll be very very very careful."

"Wait a minute!" Stephi's head whipped up. "Are you kidding us?"

"Would I do that?"

"Yes!" they said together, and grinned.

Jace chatted with them, made them giggle, then wandered over to me and slung an arm around my waist. "You've made my favorite chocolate breakfast mousse."

"I renamed it." I loved my chocolate mousse recipe. And yes, it was for breakfast. What was wrong with a dollop of cold chocolate before starting your day? I put the mousse in elegant wineglasses.

"What did you name it?"

"Chocolate Mousse Moose."

He laughed. The corners of his eyes crinkled. "I'm looking forward to eating my chocolate mousse moose." He kissed me on the temple. It made me want to whip open my white chef's jacket and get naked.

Stephi said, "I saw that. Gross." She smiled.

Lucy said, "I saw it, too. But I guess it's okay because you're married." She put a finger up. "But it's still gross!"

Jace greeted the rest of the staff, then he left to say good morning to the clients, and I cooked.

Blue skies, no snow coming down, spring tumbling in, the air warmer, the snow melting, the bulbs peeking through the soil, the girls still surreptitiously searching for a glittery fairy in the pan, and Jace.

I didn't let my mind go any further than that for once. I simply thought: This is what I've always wanted.

Including the glittery fairy.

Dinah, engineering student turned my right-hand woman in the kitchen, held the camera as the girls and I cooked that afternoon. Dinah's hair was pink tipped today. One more video for our website. Who knew what would happen this time?

"Hello, everyone. I'm Olivia Martindale. Welcome to *Cook-*

ing with Olivia on Martindale Ranch in Montana. These are my girls, Lucy and Stephi."

Lucy and Stephi waved in their white aprons. They were wearing cowgirl hats that Jace gave them that afternoon. They had both been so excited when he put them on their heads. They were real cowgirl kid hats, leather with silver medallions in front.

Lucy was still wearing her purple and blue butterfly wings, and Stephi was wearing her pink tutu.

"Today I want to show you how to make a special, healthy, and delicious macaroni and cheese that your kids will love. It's called Double Delicious Mac and Cheese Noodles—"

"Yep. They'll love it!" Lucy said. She was sitting on a stool at the island next to Stephi, who was next to me. "They'll eat it up like a lizard. Like this lizard." She pointed at her T-shirt, then yelled, "Lizard power!"

"Unless they burn it," Stephi said. "That's happened at our house before." She pointed at me, her pink tutu bopping. "One time she burned spaghetti noodles. They turned all black. Like dead black worms."

"Right," I said, maintaining my smile and trying to appear, yet again, calm and serene. "Sometimes cooking disasters do happen. To make the macaroni and cheese you need—"

"What? Now, wait a minute." Lucy turned to me, her butterfly wings flapping. "I don't want to make macaroni and cheese. I want to make a pizza. I thought we were making the pizza called We Are All Crazy Ladies Pizza."

"Not today—"

"I thought we were going to make a pie today," Stephi said. "Grandma Gisela's pie? From her cookbook from her grandma Ida. I love that pie. Chocolate pie. It looks like dog poop." She giggled at the camera and pointed at Dinah. "Don't eat dog poop!"

Dinah laughed.

"Stephi." I tried to say it in a soft voice. "We don't need comments like that. We're cooking. That's gross."

"I'm sorry, sorry, sorry. Ding dong, ding dong, I'm sorry."

Ding dong? "Thank you. Okay." Back to the camera! "This is the kind of noodle you need for the macaroni and cheese—"

"Aw, man! Not macaroni and cheese! Not that!" Lucy put her head on the counter and conked it a few times, as if life was so frustrating she simply couldn't stand it.

"I got a new cowgirl hat!" Stephi took the hat off her head and swung it around to show Dinah. "See? I'm a tough-talkin', hip-rockin' Montana woman!"

What?

Lucy conked her head another time and sighed dramatically, her butterfly wings straight up.

"Here we go." I began the cooking lesson. *Think serene!* I gave Lucy the cheese to grate. She scrunched up her face so that it was all sulky and mad. I told Stephi to measure out the butter. She bopped up and down, the stool fell out beneath her, and I caught her around the waist before she fell, her pink tutu flying up, cowgirl boots in the air. "Thanks, Aunt Olivia. I almost fell on my ass."

On her ass? "Stephi," I admonished, dumping her back on the stool. Where in the heck had she heard that? I do not swear around the girls. *Rarely.* Hardly ever. Only now and then when the moon is blue. "Don't say that word."

"Okay. It's a bad word. Hey!" She turned to Dinah. "Look at this damn tutu." She pointed to her butt.

"Stephi," I snapped. "Stop."

"I wear my tutu at recess when I'm running so fast I beat the boys. They're slow. Girl power!" She raised her fists in the air, and her cowgirl hat fell off her head. "Girl power!"

"I want to put the milk in," Lucy said. "Milk is from a cow." She still had her grumpy face on. "That's kind of yucky. I mean, you pull on the cow's"—she paused—"*thingies* and then milk comes out. I wouldn't want someone pulling on me like that."

What was wrong with them? They never acted like this.

"Cows like it," I said, then I rolled my eyes. Why had I said that? "I don't know why I said that. Anyhow." The noodles were boiling, the cheese shredded. "Now, while you're waiting for the macaroni to cook, make a smoothie for your kids. Blueberries are delicious to add to a smoothie because—"

"Uncle Jace says that he's a giant, Dinah," Stephi said. "Do you think he's a giant? You do?" Her eyes became huge as Dinah nodded behind the camera. "He is big. Aunt Olivia says he's big, too. She says that Uncle Jace is really, really big, yes, you did, Aunt Olivia, I heard you say that he's big. One time you said Uncle Jace was too big. Why are you telling me to shush? Shush! Shush! I know you said it. I heard you. Why do you say he's too big?"

Oh. My. Lord. I felt myself blush. "Girls, let's get back to the smoothie recipe." Smile! Choose serenity! We went through the motions of making a smoothie. Lucy started throwing blueberries up into the air to catch them with her mouth. Stephi put three strawberries in her mouth and smiled, the berries sticking out like teeth. Lucy said she wanted to grow up to be a leprechaun one day, and Stephi put two blueberries up her nose and grinned. I pulled the blueberries out of her nose and threw them away.

Honestly. What had happened to my sweet girls? Do other parents deal with Jekyll and Hyde children?

"Now, girls, hold the lid and turn the blender on." I smiled at the camera. Be calm! "Cooking with kids can be fun—"

Lucy held the lid, and Stephi turned the blender on.

Then Lucy was distracted. She announced, "I'm a fairy queen! I own the world!" and put both hands in the air, taking the lid with her. The entire blueberry, strawberry, raspberry smoothie erupted, splattering everywhere.

Stephi screamed, excited. Lucy screamed, surprised.

I said, "Damn it," and pulled the plug on the blender. Dinah laughed so hard she snorted, the camera still on.

Lucy and Stephi were covered in smoothie. It was on my face and in my hair.

"And that, everyone," I said, smiling through the goo because what else could I do, "is how fun cooking with your kids can be."

"I want to be a lizard," Lucy said. "And a doctor. I want to cut people up and take out the bad stuff."

"I want to be a frog ballerina!" Stephi said.

Dinah's laughter filled that kitchen.

I couldn't help it. I laughed, too. Then I took the smoothie on my hands and ran it over the girls' faces. They giggled and laughed and did the same to me.

The video was seen thousands of times.

I showed the girls.

"Now I'm a famous butterfly," Lucy said.

"And I'm a tough-talkin', hip-rockin' Montana woman!" Stephi said, spinning around.

Mr. Giant had never been too big. He had always been the perfect size.

"She's been released."

I gripped the handle of a wooden spoon with one hand and my cell phone with the other as I listened to Claudine, my attorney, who had seriously bad news.

"I'm sorry, Olivia, but Devlin's out. She's on parole. She'll have to participate in parenting classes, drug tests, counseling, she'll have to find a place to live that's safe, and a job. She'll probably fail at all of this, so getting the girls back may not even be a possibility. A judge will decide, at least about the girls' current placement, at the hearing."

"Devlin's record as a lousy, neglectful mother is hardly going to count, is it?"

"The courts hate severing parental rights, you know this. But listen, you have almost a three-year relationship with the girls. You were close to their grandmother, who wrote a letter indicating she wanted you as the girls' guardian. The caseworkers have all loved you. That will count with the judge."

"Will it count enough?"

She paused. "I don't know. She is their biological mother, and Devlin is a master manipulator."

I was past tears. I wanted to cry, but I couldn't. Panic can do that. You panic so quickly, it's like your tears freeze. They're on hold because you are not in a normal state of life. You can't breathe, you can't think, you are seeing devastation coming at you at the speed of a Mack truck and you cannot move out of the way. You're stuck. And you don't know what to do.

The Mack truck was coming for the girls.

I didn't sleep all night.

First thing in the morning Devlin called. I let it go to voice mail as I lay in bed and clenched my teeth. I listened later.

She whispered, "I'm out, Olivia."

She laughed and laughed, then she screamed that I was a "stupid bitch" and she would get the girls back and I would "never, ever see them again, you demented asshole," and hung up.

"What's wrong, Olivia?"

I busied myself at the sink. Breakfast was over. We had served ham and bacon crêpes, our usual omelets that are individually made for our clients by Justin, and cinnamon rolls.

"Olivia?" Jace came up beside me. I was glad that the staff was in the other room, sharing a late breakfast and coffee.

"I'm fine, Jace, everything's fine, everything's good. It'll all be fine and good." I sucked in a breath. I was having trouble breathing, my chest tightening. I was even having trouble swallowing again. It felt as if I was choking.

"Everything is not fine, I can tell, babe. You're pale, you're almost hyperventilating. Come on, Olivia, what is it?"

I kept scrubbing a pot. Rather vigorously. I wanted to keep moving because I was trying to outrace the panic attack. Sometimes, if I can change course in my head, I can beat it back or lessen the impact.

"Can you give me a hint about what's wrong?"

I couldn't give him a hint, because my tears were falling into the pot.

"Aw, geez, Olivia. Whatever it is, I'm sorry."

He put a hand around my waist and that made my tears slip

out faster and harder. I scrubbed the pan with all I had, then I shoved it back into the hot water and gave up. I muffled a sob.

"Olivia, let me help you." He turned off the water, grabbed a towel, and dried my hands. "Please talk to me."

Jace was strong and smart. He could help. He could listen. I felt dizzy.

"It's Stephi and Lucy."

"What's wrong?" His voice sharpened, tightened. "What is it? Are they sick, are they hurt?"

"Their mother is out of jail. She is petitioning for full custody of the girls. She has an attorney."

"Are you kidding me? I thought this was all hammered out. Why didn't you tell me?"

"Because I didn't want to involve you, Jace. I didn't want my problem to be your problem."

"If you have a problem, I have a problem, Olivia. You should have told me. I can't help you if I don't know. Damn, Olivia."

"Jace, there's nothing you can do anyhow."

"I can get you an attorney in five minutes."

I told him about Claudine. "Devlin apparently has been well behaved in jail and she says she is no longer addicted to drugs and has found God." I rubbed my face with my hands. "Found God. A mother who semi-starved and severely neglected her kids claims to have found God, and the court might believe her and return the girls to her."

"All criminals claim they have found God when they want something, and some people are stupid enough to believe them," Jace muttered. "So what happens next?"

"I have to go to court. A hearing. We're fighting over the girls."

He pulled me into his arms, and I cried on that huge and strong chest while he said soft and gentle and reassuring things. "I'll help you, Olivia. I will do whatever I can to help you."

I nodded, cried more, and he pulled me in tighter.

"In fact," he pulled back. "Move back in with me."

"What?"

"The judge will like it. Married mother. Father in the picture. Stable home life."

"No." I stared into those dark eyes through a wash of tears. Oh, my gosh. "Yes. Thank you, Jace." I sagged in relief against him. Total, complete relief. This would help. I was not a separated mother anymore, who might have, in the state's mind, family issues, domestic issues, broken home issues, and an upcoming contentious divorce. Anthony Bastfield III was already making spiteful, gargling noises about it.

"Do you want to move in here, or do you want me to move into your house?" he asked.

I thought of the girls. They loved it here, loved the animals, especially the dogs and cat. Plus Jace and I worked at the ranch. His new home was close to the ranch and ten minutes from town. "Here. If you'd like. It's easier." I smiled. My smile wobbled. I felt weak and jiggly inside. "Shorter commute."

"Fifteen minutes from my house to here."

Living with Jace again. Living with the stud in front of me. I wondered how long I could go without jumping that body like a warrior woman.

"I'll come help you all move. When is good for you? How about today?"

I laughed through tears. "Today?"

He didn't laugh. "Would you like to go now?"

Wow. He's fast. But it worked. "After I get lunch going?"

"Sure." He nodded.

"Thanks so much, Jace."

He smiled. That smile lit up his hard-jawed, weathered face. "No, thank you, Olivia." He winked. "I know you're doing this for the girls, and for the custody issue you're dealing with, but I could not be happier to have all of you living here with me. This is one of the best days of my life."

"It is?"

"Yes." He was completely serious. "Best days? When I met the love of my life in a bar. The day we got engaged. The day we got married. All of the days that we were married were my best days. And now, another best day."

"You are a kind man, Jace."

"I want you here. I want the girls here. You make me happy, Olivia, so do they. I want you to be happy. More than anything, that's what I want."

I sniffled. Why can't I have a tiny, sweet, soft sniffle instead of a big, honking one? And why did Jace make me cry so much? "Three women, Jace." I smiled up at him. "Are you ready for it?"

"I've been ready for it forever."

And that was that.

Jace and I drove to my house, my grandparents' log cabin, early that afternoon. We loaded up. I didn't have that much stuff. I could tell that Jace was surprised. Being broke is quite limiting in what you can buy.

Jace wrapped me in a bear hug, kissed me, then drove to his house while I cleaned the cabin. Afterward, I stood on the front porch. I had found peace in this home my whole life. I put my hand on the red door, the lasso, the wagon wheel that brought my granddad's ancestors west, then my grandparents' cowboy hats nailed to the house. I loved the weather vane with the sun, because my grandma was my granddad's sun.

Now I would be going to live with my sun.

The question was: Could I handle it this time?

Chapter 15

I picked up the girls at school after their art class. I took them for ice cream cones. "You girls like Uncle Jace, right?"

"Oh yeah." Lucy licked her cone. "He's nice. He's going to teach me how to ride a horsey."

"Uncle Jace is funny. But there wasn't a fairy in the batter." Stephi's brow furrowed. "I don't think."

"So, Lucy and Stephi." I took a deep breath. "We're going to go and live with Uncle Jace. At his house."

They both stopped eating.

"What?" Lucy shrieked, smiling, standing up, her ice-cream cone in the air.

"We're going to live with Uncle Jace?" Stephi started jumping up and down. Her ice cream fell off her cone. It didn't faze her. "When, when, when?"

"We're going to live with him starting today."

"Oh yay!" The girls hugged each other and jumped. Lucy's ice cream fell off her cone. It didn't faze her, either.

"We love Uncle Jace! And the dogs and the kitty cat," Stephi said.

"Now we have a dad," Lucy said.

"A giant dad!" Stephi said.

"A big dad," Lucy said. "Uncle Jace can beat up the bad mens anytime."

"Yep," Stephi said. "Bad daddy can't get us. Uncle Jace is our dad now. And the dogs are our brothers."

"And the horses are our sisters," Lucy said.

Perfect, I thought. Animals for siblings for the girls.

And a hunk of a cowboy wandering around who will be impossible for me to resist.

The girls were offered their own rooms at Jace's house, but they didn't want to be separated. They chose the bedroom with a view of the mountains, and we moved their new twin beds and new pink comforters in. After dinner I helped them unpack. Jace helped, too.

"I think I see a glittery fairy behind this dresser . . ." Jace said. The girls rushed to see her.

I did not stay in Jace's bedroom. He said, "I'll sleep on the couch," I said, "No, it's okay. I will." We argued. Neither one of us would give in, so we ended up sleeping together, on the carpet, under a pile of blankets, in front of the fireplace, the flames dancing. We laughed. He kissed me, and we somehow became semi-naked and I pulled away, because I don't know what to do with our problem, and he groaned and said, "You're killing me, Olivia."

My grandma and I made her family's peach pie out of the old cookbook. Then she told me another wrenching story about the cooks.

May 1941
London, England
Gisela Gobenko, grandmother of Olivia Martindale

Two weeks after Renata died, one of the doctors from the hospital came by the new apartment Gisela was sharing with Keila and Naomi and begged her to come back.

"Gisela, please," he pleaded, bags under his eyes, his white hair standing on end. It was usually impeccably brushed. "I am so sorry about Renata, about your family." He took her hand.

"But there are people at the hospital who need help. We are shorthanded, you know this. Please. Please come back."

Gisela wanted to die. Grief was sealing up her throat like a coffin. Hope had drained out of her. She couldn't reach any member of her extended family in Munich. She had met a man in the hospital last month. He was Jewish. He was emaciated, diseased, and had escaped from Germany, after hiding in a warehouse, the foreman a friend. He told her what she'd already been told: The Nazis were burning and gassing Jews.

Why live anymore? What was there to live for? The world was on fire. It was being bombed to annihilation. The Jews were being hunted down and persecuted. If England fell, the Nazis would kill her, too.

She wanted to lie on her cot in this bleak apartment and let one of the Nazi's bombs obliterate her. It would take away this searing pain. She wanted to stop eating, stop drinking. For some reason she couldn't get her mother's peach pie recipe out of her head. It was as if the pie were home. But she had no home, not anymore, because she had no family.

"Gisela. Dear. Please. The people we are treating, the people we operate on, they are someone's sister, too. They are someone's brother, someone's son, someone's father, their mother, their aunt. They are part of a family. Help me. Help me save other people's family members." His voice broke on that last word. She liked and respected Dr. Hirschfield.

"Please, Gisela." He actually teared up. Controlled, calm Dr. Hirschfield. "I need you to help me. Help them."

She closed her eyes. Pain ran like a waterfall down her whole body, drowning her.

She got up. She went to the hospital with Dr. Hirschfield. She saved other people's family members.

For years.

In April of 1944, Dr. Hirschfield yelled to her, "Help me, Gisela. In here. Room nine. Downed American pilot."

She was exhausted. She had not been home in three days,

sleeping here and there at the hospital. Members of the military, Americans and British primarily, were coming in, often flown in, with grievous, critical injuries from the battlefield and the air. Some they could save, some they couldn't.

"Come along now, lass," Dr. Hirschfield said. "We'll both get home one of these nights. We've got to carry on."

And carry on she did.

There was nothing else to do, and people needed help. They were members of other people's families.

Today she would assist in the operation on the American pilot, covered in blood, who promptly passed out from his injuries when they lifted him onto the operating table.

But Gisela could swear, she could, that before he passed out he stared right at her and winked. She was right.

He winked.

Gisela assisted in three other operations that day with Dr. Hirschfield. They had done their best, but they would lose one patient, a young woman, a victim of a car accident. A lieutenant driving a jeep hadn't seen her in the rain. Another sister had lost a sister. She swiped at her eyes. She had stayed late again before going home and collapsing on her bed.

The next morning, her relentless routine began again. The American fighter pilot was sitting up in bed and smiled at her. His smile was wide and friendly. He had blond hair. She had heard his story through another doctor, who heard it through this man's British and American air force buddies who had stopped by the hospital.

He had dropped bombs on Germany, then had gotten into a firefight with a German pilot. He shot that plane clean out of the sky, but not before he had been wounded in the shoulder, his plane hit. His plane, barely flying, crash landed on the British air strip, injuring his leg, too.

"Hello," he said. "I remember you from yesterday. Thank you for what you did to help me."

"You're quite welcome. I'm surprised you remember. You weren't in the best shape."

"*I winked at you. Didn't you see my wink?*"

For the first time in a long time, Gisela Gobenko laughed. "*I did see it. I didn't think it was a wink, though, I thought it was accidental.*"

"*No, ma'am. I saw you and all that pretty brown hair and those green cat eyes and I said to myself, 'That is the most beautiful woman I have ever seen on Earth,' so I winked at you before I went and had myself a nice, long Montana nap.*"

"*A Montana nap?*"

"*That's what we call it back home.*"

Back home. That hurt. She thought of her home. How was their elegant brick home with the red door in Munich that the Nazis had looted? How and where were the people who had lived in that home? She choked back a sob. "*I need to examine your leg and your shoulder.*"

"*Thank you. My name is Oliver Martindale. May I have the pleasure of knowing your name?*" He shook her hand.

"*Gisela Gobenko.*" She went to work. Checking his wounds, cleaning them.

"*You're from Germany.*"

Her hands stilled. "*Yes.*" She waited for the negative comments, sometimes hateful, about the Germans. She had tried as hard as she could to rid herself of her German accent but hadn't fully succeeded. Dirty Germans. Nazi dogs. Heil Hitler, my ass. We'll bomb those dogs down to the ground.

"*You ran from them, didn't you?*"

Her green eyes flew to his blue ones. "*Yes, I did.*"

"*How?*"

She didn't want to think about this. She was so busy. She had other patients. Maybe it was because Renata's death had shredded her and left her hopeless, or maybe it was because she sensed a gentleness in him, a kindness, but Gisela found herself talking to Oliver Martindale, sitting beside him on the bed. At one point he took her hand and held it, his eyes so wise, compassionate.

"*You haven't heard at all from your family in almost four years?*"

"No."

He squeezed her hand. "I'm so sorry."

She went to see her other patients, but over the next couple of weeks she dropped by Oliver Martindale's room several times a day, to chat, even now and then to laugh. He had sustained shoulder, leg, rib, and lung damage on his crash landing. There was also an infection that raged after his operation.

But Oliver Martindale healed. He was a doctor himself, he had finished his medical residency, and had enlisted to fight for "America's, and the world's, freedom from tyranny, danger, and Hitler himself. I cannot, I will not, sit back and let other men fight while I stay home." He would return to Montana and work as a doctor in his hometown as soon as the war was won. "You must come and see Montana, Gisela."

Ah. That would never happen.

Soon the American was ready to leave the hospital. By then, he was promising to come back for her after the war to take her to a "proper dinner with a man from Montana."

She doubted she would see him again. He was a fighter pilot. He could die on his next sortie over Germany. In fact, he probably would.

"Good luck, Oliver," she said, softly.

"And to you, Gisela. I will be back for you. I promise. The doctor will come for a date with his nurse."

He kissed her then, on the mouth, and all the passion they had stored up for one another, all the pent-up emotions from a war that was cremating the world, their own grief, fear, and loss, and their budding, romantic love, came forth.

He hugged her close and whispered, "You're my soul mate, Gisela. Please wait for me." He walked out, friends of his, other fighter pilots, waiting for him in the crowded corridor. They laughed and slapped him on the back. "Ready to fly again, old man?" they asked. "Let's go get those Nazi bastards."

Gisela blinked back tears as he walked down the hospital's hallway. He turned once and blew her a kiss, then disappeared.

She did what she always did: She went to work, healing and helping and saving other people's family members. She survived.
She, along with all of the other British people, carried on. They had no choice.

The girls went to the clinic again with my mother and grandma and wore their white coats.

"Lotta sick people today," Lucy said. "I like that Grandma and Grandma Gisela make them healthy again. They put 'em back together. Hey! Like a human puzzle, but the puzzle's sick."

"Grandma Mary Beth," Stephi whispered to me, even though we were miles from my mother, "told one of her patients that he needed to take his medicine or else he would die like a gutter rat. He said to her, 'What does Mrs. Gisela think about this stuff, Mary Beth? I want her herbs.' We had to go and get Grandma Gisela, and Grandma Mary Beth said, 'Get some cement in your spine and take your medicine, Willy.'"

"He didn't want to be a dead gutter rat." Lucy pointed her finger in the air. "No one does."

"I think that Grandma Mary Beth is going to let me sew people up soon," Stephi said.

"Me too," Lucy said. "I can't wait. It's like sewing a dress, except it's skin, right, Aunt Olivia?"

Chloe was on the news again. She's incredible. She was first on the scene of a house fire in her ambulance, a fire truck stuck in the snow. She climbed up the outside of the house, partly via a tree, then climbed in a window and threw three kids out the window to waiting neighbors, black smoke and flames pouring out. No kidding. I mean, how much more heroic can you get? If it hadn't happened for real, people would assume it was on some cheesy, unbelievable movie.

She then shimmied back down the tree as part of the roof caved in. The house fire was caused by cigarette smoking. Chloe said to a news reporter, "And tell me again why we allow a product to be made in America that causes millions of Americans to die prematurely and sets houses on fire? Tell me that, would you? That man! Mother's boyfriend. Smoking in a house with children. What a selfish dumb-ass."

Chloe is so popular in Kalulell.

I made my grandma crumpets and scones at our blue farmhouse from the recipes that she and Renata wrote in the cookbook when they were in the shelter during the blitz in London.

I made chamomile tea for her, too.

"Cinnamon," she said to me, her voice trembling. "You are a gift."

"I love you, Grandma."

"And I love you, my darling Olivia."

Later she wandered out to the gazebo, wearing her blue silk scarf with the white daisies on it. She tilted her head up to that Montana sky, then she raised a hand up and waved.

"Thank you, Jace," I said as he handed me a toasted cheese sandwich with a smear of garlic butter and mayo on my thick, homemade grain bread. We'd put the girls to bed, turned off the lights, and he'd lit a fire in the family room. "You make the best cheese sandwiches."

"Taught by you."

"You make them better than I do."

"I aim to please." He sat beside me on the couch and we watched the flames leaping, the shadows dancing on the walls while we finished our sandwiches.

"I love your house, Jace."

"I built it with you in mind."

"Don't say that."

"Why? It's true."

"Because you shouldn't have built this house with me in mind."

"I wanted you to be happy here."

I could be happy here. But I could not be happy here if I kept getting pregnant and losing babies. I swallowed hard. I try not to cry about losing the babies so much, but sometimes that loss sneaks up on me and clutches my heart with sharp talons.

"What is it, Olivia?"

"Oh," I waved my hand. "I was thinking about . . ."

"Our babies?"

"Yes." Our babies. His and mine. Jace had grieved, too. He had cried. Every time, with me. He was better at controlling himself, but I was not the only one in a tornado of pain, I knew that. "I'm sorry about how I handled it, Jace."

"Please, Olivia." He lifted my hand and kissed it. "Don't be. You have nothing to be sorry for. It was a terrible time. The worst."

"I shut down on you. I shut down on us. I felt like I couldn't move, couldn't breathe, couldn't think. All I wanted to do was cry, and sometimes . . ." I took a shuddery breath. "I didn't even want to live anymore, Jace. I had lost the babies, I had lost my granddad. We would never have children. It was too much loss. I didn't see any light."

He closed his eyes for a second and bent his head, the impact of my words so painful. He pulled me in close, and I hugged him. "I understand, baby. I do."

"And it was my body," I said, the flashbacks of my miscarriages graphic and soul sucking, "that kept screwing up, kept losing our babies."

"Don't take that on, please, Olivia."

"I am sorry, Jace, that I couldn't stay pregnant with our babies. I'm sorry I wrote a note and left you the way I did. I wanted out. I couldn't handle my grief and living in the house with all those memories, the nursery, the children's books we bought, the rocking chair, the toys. I lost my mind. I did."

"Olivia," he said, kissing my forehead, "we both lost our minds. It was devastating to lose our babies. Every time. But I was not the mother of those babies. You were. And I know it was worse for you. I watched you after we lost our first baby, then the second, then the third. It was like watching someone disintegrate. I couldn't help you. You were lost in that grief. You couldn't even get out of bed." He teared up and so did I. "After you left, I kicked myself every single day. Every. Single. Day. I should have done more for you. I hope you can forgive me for that."

"Jace, you were the perfect husband to me. I should have talked to you more. I couldn't. I felt dead. I didn't have any more fight in me, any more energy, any more of anything, but I knew I couldn't get pregnant again, so I left."

"I think life gets too hard for couples sometimes," he said. "It's not anyone's fault, there isn't any blame to be laid, and that's what happened to us. Let's let it go and be together again. Please. I want to be together with you again, Olivia, more than I want anything else."

"But I can't give you kids, Jace." I choked on a sob. "I can't give you the life you want."

"You are the life I want, honey. That has not changed."

"I'm a wreck."

"You are not a wreck." He kissed me and whispered, "I love you, Olivia. I always have, I always will, for my entire life."

He loved me. Still. "I love you, too, Jace. I have missed you so much. I have never stopped loving you, and I know I will love you until... until... until..." Oh my. I could hardly talk through the emotion. "I am old and cranky."

He smiled. "We'll be old and cranky together."

Jace was such a man. Strong and smart and confident and loving and forgiving. And amazing in bed. Sex on a stick. I couldn't resist him. He bent his head and I gave in because he lights me on fire. I fell right into that kiss, and it felt like heaven with a hard-on. Our clothes went flying, our breathing was heavy, we smiled at each other, he lifted me up, and I was straddling him on the couch, totally naked.

Then I froze. I couldn't help it. I saw myself pregnant. Damn. We still had the same problem. Huge, huge problem. "Jace, we need a condom."

"No, babe, we don't."

"I can't get pregnant again, it'll kill me, Jace. I can't do it."
My voice caught, and a rush of searing anger stole through me,
taking away all the warmth and love. *Why didn't Jace get this?*
Why didn't he understand me? Why was he pushing me to have
sex and get pregnant when he knew what it had done to me? He
had been there. I had just told him how I felt. He was okay with
my losing another baby and losing my mind? Wasn't he listening
to me at all? I tried to get off of him, feeling like I'd been kicked
in the stomach, but he held my face gently with one huge, warm
hand, my waist with another, and said, "Sweetheart, you will
not get pregnant, because I had a vasectomy."

"You what?" I settled back onto him. *He what?*

"I had a vasectomy. You never wanted to get pregnant again.
I know you, and I knew you would not change your mind. I
don't blame you at all. I also knew that you and I would never
be able to be together if you thought I would pressure you to get
pregnant again in the future."

"Why didn't you tell me you had a vasectomy earlier?"

"I didn't want you to feel that you had to come back to me
because I'd had a vasectomy and had given up the possibility of
having kids for you. You don't owe me that. I wanted you back
because you loved me and wanted to be married again."

I was stunned. "But you could have had kids with someone
else."

"There is never going to be anyone else, babe. It's always
been you. Without you, my whole life is nothing. Ever since you
left I have felt this huge, gaping hole. I have never felt so alone,
or so lonely, ever. You are my whole life, Olivia. I love you, I
want you, I want us."

"Oh, Jace." I was overwhelmed, naked, and straddling him.
"I can't believe you did that."

"I can. It made complete sense. And we already have two
daughters. Lucy and Stephi."

I nodded. Sniffled. Not so graciously.

"And if you want to adopt more, we will." He kissed me.
"What do you want? Do you want to adopt?"

"I thought we agreed on six kids." He smiled. "So we're four away from that number."

I laughed. "You want to adopt four more kids?"

"Why not? We have a lot of love here, and I can always add on more bedrooms to the house."

"Jace Rivera, you are the best man in the world. There is no place I'd rather be than right here, with you."

"Forever?"

"Forever."

I leaned against him, chest to chest, and kissed him. The kiss got better and hotter and wilder, and I looked him in the eye and said, "I love you, baby."

"Love you, too, Olivia. Always."

"Hi, Uncle Jace. Hi, Aunt Olivia."

I sat straight up in Jace's bed, absolutely aghast, clutching the sheet to my naked chest when I heard the girls' voices. *Oh, my God.* They eyed Jace and me from the foot of the bed. They were wearing their pink bunny pajamas.

"Hello, Lucy," Jace said, shirtless, and as calm as if this happened every day. "Hello, Stephi."

"Uh. Oh. Hell . . ." I scrunched down in the blankets. "Hello, Lucy and Stephi."

"Did you and Aunt Olivia have a sleepover, Uncle Jace?" Lucy asked.

"Yes, we did. We had popcorn and then we went to sleep."

I blushed. Couldn't help it. That was not exactly how it happened. After sex in front of the fire, we came up to Jace's bedroom and had popcorn and a shower, then we had up-against-the-wall sex. Then more popcorn. I ate it off his stomach.

"How come you don't have a pajama shirt on?" Stephi asked him, her eyes narrowed.

"I took off my shirt because during the night my muscles grow extra large and I need more room."

Stephi studied him. Was that true? Then she said, happily, "You do have a lot of muscles."

"But wait." Lucy stuck that finger in the air. "How come Aunt Olivia doesn't have a shirt on?"

Oh. Goodness. Gracious. Argh. I scrunched down farther.

"She got hot."

I blushed again. Oh boy, did I get hot.

They tried to climb up on the bed.

"I want to do a sleepover!" Stephi said. "All four of us in the bed. I'll get some of my rocks, too."

"I get the middle," Lucy said. "I'm a Lucy sandwich."

"Not yet," Jace said, holding an arm out, completely naked under the blankets. "Your aunt Olivia needs to go back to sleep because she didn't sleep much last night, and I'll get up and make you pancakes in a minute. Who wants a pancake in the shape of the sun?"

"I do! I do!" the girls shouted.

"Okay. Run on out, shut the doors, and turn on cartoons and I'll be out there in a minute when my muscles stop growing."

"I think you're being silly," Lucy said, but she was skeptical. Maybe Jace's muscles did grow during the night.

"He's a giant," Stephi whispered to Lucy, her hand in front of her mouth so Jace wouldn't hear. "Don't you remember when I asked him? He said he's a giant."

They climbed off the bed, arguing about Uncle Jace, the giant.

Jace The Giant kissed me, then got up and locked the doors. My. He was fun to watch in motion.

"Jace The Giant wants his woman to climb on top of him again." He kissed me, pulled me up on top of him.

The pancakes in the shape of the sun would have to wait.

Later, Jace opened a drawer in the table next to his side of the bed. "Sweetheart, I love you. Will you do me the great honor of wearing your wedding ring again?"

"Yes. Oh, yes." I sure would. He put it on my ring finger and kissed it. I slipped his ring back on his finger again, too, which had been in a box with mine.

Jace was seduction on legs. Bliss on two feet. He was extraordinary in bed because he was loving and caring and creative and fun and intense and serious and funny out of bed.

He was the only man I have ever been in love with, and I know that he is the only man I will ever be in love with.

"I love you, Jace." I flipped on top of him and gave him a big smackeroo.

"And I you, Olivia. Always have, always will, babe."

"I think I'm ready to get naked with a man."

"Cheers to that, Nutmeg." My grandma kissed Chloe's cheek, then my grandma, mother, Chloe, and I clinked wineglasses.

"I think it's time," my mother said, leaning against her kitchen island, made from her favorite old oak tree. "You've got your Martindale woman power back. Go forth and mate."

"Yep. I'm a tough-talkin', hip-rockin' Montana woman."

"Which lucky man will you choose?" I asked. I had a lucky man. Tonight I hoped he would pull off my blue-green skirt from India with sequins and tiny mirrors. I'd flip off my black cowgirl boots and we'd be set.

"Choose the man who acts like a man, Nutmeg," my grandma said. Her pink scarf had red tulips on it. "Protective. Smart. Calm. Loving. Caring."

"Choose the man who won't let you run over him like a tractor on high speed, like a charging grizzly, like a tsunami of woman," my mother said. "You need to choose a man who can remain standing under the hurricane force of your personality, or you won't be attracted to him."

"Choose someone who won't freak out when you're in the helicopter under gale force winds and snow getting someone off a mountain," I said. "That's part of who you are."

"That's right," my mother said. "He can't restrict you or what you need to do in any way. He accepts what you're doing, respects it, or haul his butt out."

"I am going to choose Zane Corrigan," Chloe said.

"Excellent choice, but why is he the lucky man?" I asked.

"Because I like his shoulders." Chloe crossed her own arms and patted her shoulders.

"Oh, *pfft,*" my mother said, tapping her black cowboy boots with red trim. She called them her Devil Boots. "You're going to judge a man on his shoulders? Why don't you judge him on his capillaries or his heart or his blood pressure? All better predictors of health and lifestyle."

"Listen to your daughter, Fire Breather," my grandma said. "Wait."

My mother squirmed. But she did as told.

"I like his shoulders," Chloe said. "He stands straight, that says something. When I reached up to kiss him, his arms went right around me and I felt protected by those shoulders. When I was upset about a patient who we rushed to the hospital, and I put my head on his shoulder, he was comforting, like a teddy bear. When I laughed with him the other day, I saw his shoulders shaking, like he thought what I was saying was super dang funny. When I told him that I worried about Kyle a lot, he put an arm around my shoulder to make me feel better, and when I was tired after a trip up the mountain in the big bird and I fell asleep on his couch, he didn't move his shoulder away because he was afraid it would wake me up and he knew I was wiped out."

"Wow, Chloe. I think this man's shoulders sound about perfect," I said.

She nodded. "And he lights my personal butterfly on fire." She pointed at her boobs. "Lights these girls on fire, too. That's important. Without that chemistry you don't have anything. We have it. I told him I'm getting these girls reduced and he said he'd like them any size at all. I need a man like that. Accepting. I don't need anyone judging my love machine."

"Get him tested for diseases before you engage in intercourse," my mother said. "Chlamydia. Gonorrhea. AIDS, herpes, the works."

"Mom. Duh. I already sent him to the doctors for a test, and he went. A woman has to protect herself. No test for bugs and bacteria, no bang bang. No condom, no cutesy. No lab tests, no nakedness."

"He's kind, then," I said. "He wants to protect you, wants to make you feel reassured that you're going to be healthy with him in bed."

"Zane is so kind he could melt your insides with a smile. He's warm and ready to go, ready to rock, ready to roll and schmoll and bowl."

"You're going to bowl with him?"

"Sure," Chloe said, shrugging. "I love bowling. Throwing balls is my thing."

We laughed. I had a vision. I laughed again.

"I think you know what you need to know, Nutmeg." My grandma gave her a hug.

"Yeah, me too. So that's why I think I'm going to get naked with him, soon. I think he can handle all of this. A big woman like me."

"A beautiful woman like you, Nutmeg," my grandma said.

"You are the bravest woman I know, Chloe." She was. Army. Paramedic. Search and rescue helicopter pilot. Fearless mother to Kyle.

"You're not a doctor," my mother said, "but I'm still proud of you, kid."

"I want to take a moment and tell all of you that I love you with all that I am," my grandma said, "with my heart and soul forever and ever."

"We love you, too, Grandma."

Chloe called me a few days later. She said, "Zippy zap Zane." And laughed. A happy laugh. I happy laughed back at her.

"Hello, everyone." I smiled into the camera from behind the island at Martindale Ranch. Today Dinah's hair was her natural brown but she was wearing a silver sequined headband.

"I'm Olivia Martindale. Welcome to *Cooking with Olivia on*

Martindale Ranch in Montana. Today I have a guest with me, my nephew, Kyle. I asked him what kind of recipe he wanted to whip up, and he said that the most important thing about cooking is for everyone out there to understand the importance of baking soda and why we use it in so many recipes. So, because Kyle loves science and experiments, today we're going to do something different. Kyle, what are you going to teach us about baking soda today?"

He fiddled with his glasses, then put his hands down at his side. They flapped, then stopped.

"Greetings. Let's discuss baking soda. Baking soda is sodium bicarbonate. It releases carbon dioxide—which, as you know, is an odorless and colorless gas—when it mixes with acidic ingredients. It makes tons of gas bubbles.

"For example, you use baking soda to make breads, or buttermilk pancakes or cakes, which is what my family likes to make together. We call it Martindale Cake Therapy. The baking soda makes the cookies and cakes rise. The chemical formula for baking soda is, and you probably want to write this down, $NaHCO_3$. It has a crystal structure."

I nodded at him, twice. That was our silent communication for him not to go on and on about baking soda because he was fascinated by it.

"Let me show you an experiment with baking soda."

Kyle showed everyone the experiment. He had made a two-foot-tall German chocolate cake. Not a real one—it was made from papier-mâché, with ruffled brown and beige tissue icing—but it looked delicious. Tucked inside was a plastic bottle in which he had combined baking soda, vinegar, warm water, and a pink drink mix. The cake erupted and started fizzing out "icing." It was quite cool. Dinah cheered, as did I.

"You see, baking soda has many uses," Kyle said. "Now we're going to make a real German chocolate cake from my great-grandma Gisela's cookbook." He smiled, tapping his fingertips against his palms. "Mother told me to smile. She says if I don't I come off rather robotic. Obviously, I am not a robot." He paused. "For the record here, that was a joke. I am learning about humor."

I held up the ingredients. "Chocolate. Pecans. Coconut. Baking soda. Now we're going to have some fun."

Needless to say, the viewers loved Kyle. We got many, many requests for more science experiments on the cooking show. As one young reader wrote to me in an e-mail, "I am seven and I love watching things explode like that. When is Kyle on again?"

And "Do you have a cookbook, Olivia? I would like to try your recipes..."

Chloe said to me, after seeing the video, "He's got a bit of the Mad Hatter in him, don't you think, Olivia? I seriously believe he might also be channeling both Julia Child and Charles Darwin."

On Sunday evening, one set of guests gone, another set arriving tomorrow, Jace and I took a drive. We drove across the land that would soon be covered in buttercups like a golden blanket, to the hill where the white crosses stood tall. We sat behind the babies, me in front of Jace, his arms wrapped around me, as we watched a magical purple, blue, and pink sunset. The glowing sun hung from an invisible string from the sky, the clouds opened, and white lights tunneled down from heaven.

On the way back, in his truck, my hand in his, I felt something I hadn't felt in a long time: Peace.

I made my grandma chicken Kiev using her cookbook. I translated it from Ukrainian. I also made dumplings filled with mashed potatoes and chives, and sauerkraut, translated from German. She said to me, when our whole family sat down to dinner, "Cinnamon, you have brought my family home to me."

My grandma touches my heart every single time I see her.

The courtroom was small but intimidating.

Devlin sat at the front with her attorney, red-haired Anthony Bastfield III, who was in love with her and her blond hair, blue eyes, flirty personality, and victim aura. He didn't understand what lurked beneath like a human scythe. Devlin was wearing a pink blouse, buttoned almost to her neck, a dull beige skirt to her knees, and beige flats. She wore the largest silver cross I have ever seen on a necklace. Her hair was nice and neat, perfectly combed, and she wore little makeup. Mascara and pink lipstick.

She resembled annoying Pollyanna.

I wrapped my arms around my stomach and swayed on the hard bench, in my black suit and heels. Jace held my hand, and Claudine, ready to swing and fight for us, was at the table at the front of the courtroom.

We rose for the judge. She was African American with black braids. About sixty.

We began.

"I love my girls. I have always loved my girls." Devlin sniffed as the proceeding got under way and she addressed the judge. She held a tissue. "I have made bad choices. I started using drugs when I was fifteen because of the abuse and meanness I was suffering at home from my mother, which I could tell no one about because I was scared. I'm sure, with the better knowledge that I have now, that she was double polar. Loving one minute, slapping me the next."

What? *Double polar?* Devlin was actually going to lie about Annabelle? I sucked in my breath.

"My father was a freezing cold man who did nothing to protect me. Plus he had a temper tantrum. I mean, a temper. I think he was double polar, too."

I had never met Devlin's father, but Annabelle adored him. Said he was the kindest man she ever knew and he loved Devlin. They went through almost their entire life's savings trying to help her.

"I made bad decisions for myself because of my parents. I made bad decisions with men and with Stephi and Lucy's father, who beat me and beat me, but I am so glad that I have them."

She grabbed the huge cross on her necklace. "I love my girls. I was so scared living with Parker. He became violent and controlling and jealous of how men found me so beautiful."

Her hands shook as if she'd been electrocuted when she swiped the tissue across her nose, then they abruptly stopped. She was faking the shaking.

"I committed a robbery. I regret it every second of the day, but I didn't know what else to do. Parker said he would hurt or kill me and the girls if I didn't do it. I did it to save them. I don't think I'm a hero. I did what any mother would do."

I saw Anthony III stare down at his papers. He knew Devlin was lying through her teeth to the judge.

"Going to jail was a blessed thing for me because it got me sober, it got me away from Parker, and it brought me close to God and Jesus." The waterworks started up again. "I spent all my free time with my Bible."

I rolled my eyes. I'm surprised they didn't drop into the back of my head.

"Please. Please. Let me have my girls. I will be a better mother to them. I will be the best mother to them. My mother is dead and she can't take care of the girls anymore. The girls should be with me, not"—she turned and glared at me, the victim mentality gone for a second—"*with her*. Not with a stranger. She is not family. I am their mother."

The proceeding went on. Anthony III spoke. He blushed when he stared down at Devlin, who smiled up at him. I saw her lick her lower lip one time. Jace saw it, too, and shook his head in disgust. Anthony III blushed again, stuttered.

Sarah was a loving and devoted mother! She had changed! Sarah said that Jesus was in charge of her life now! She was sober!

My lawyer stood and spoke to the judge. The caseworkers spoke in favor of me. They outlined their concerns with Devlin in detail and reviewed her extensive file.

I spoke about how I met Annabelle and the girls, our friendship, how Jace and I loved the girls. I talked about the ranch and the activities that we did together as a family. I sat back down and clutched Jace's hand. I felt ill at one moment, tearful the next, furious again, and back around to flat-out panicked.

Finally, the judge said, closing a folder in front of her. "I've heard enough. Sarah, or, is it Devlin?"

"Sarah, please," Devlin said, her blue eyes as big as she could make them. She stood up. "I gave up Devlin after I was imprisoned. I spoke with God about it, and he told me to change my name to my given name. Sarah is from the Bible."

The judge studied her, unsmiling, then pushed her braids back. "So you know the Bible now?"

"Yes. It's been my salvation." She held up her cross as proof. Boy, those hands shook!

"What is your favorite verse?"

"My what?"

"Your favorite verse in the Bible?"

Devlin dropped the cross. "I...I...love that one verse about forgiveness."

"Ah." The judge raised her eyebrows. "The one verse about forgiveness. What is your favorite book in the Bible?"

"Uh," Devlin said, confused but struggling to come up with something. "Uh. I love the book written by Mary Christ, mother of Jesus, because I'm a mother, too. She told all mothers how to be Christian mothers with her...list."

"Right. Mary Christ's list on being a Christian mother." The judge frowned. "You say you have found God."

Devlin piously raised her palms upward, as if in supplication. She shook them hard, as if she was trembling. "Glory be to God, Your Honor. He has saved me. I am in prayer many times a day. I know that the Lord has forgiven me, and I pray that you can forgive me, too."

"You have talked at length about how you have changed in jail."

Devlin nodded. "I have, Your Honor. I am a new woman. I am strong. I am learning who I am all about. I have thought about my sins and my past and how I will express myself and share myself with the world when I'm out so people can feel my light."

"You have talked about how you are no longer an addict, due to being locked in jail, and how you know that you will stay clean."

"As God as my witness, I will not do drugs. Or drink. Never again. I was numbing my pain from the abuse I suffered from my mother, who was double polar and depressed and...and... abusive with her polar... with her double polar, and I had to get rid of that pain. From my mother. And how my father was gone all the time. With. Uh. His coldness."

The judge tapped a pen. "You have talked about how you're going to change this time around if your daughters are returned to you."

"My children are the world to me. I love them. I miss them." Devlin started making crying sounds, but no tears filled those blue eyes. "Every day I ache for my children. I want to hold them in my arms and give them a hug." She put her arms out in a circle, as if she was hugging them. She forgot to shake her hands that time. She glanced back and sent me a murderous look. I wanted to scream.

"I have studied this case from one end to the next, Sarah, because I take terminating parental rights very, very seriously," the judge said. "I have listened to everything said, by everyone, today."

I waited, Jace holding my hand. I could hardly breathe, my heart racing.

"I don't believe a word that has come out of your mouth, Sarah. Not one word."

Devlin stopped mid-sniffle.

I sat up straight. *What?*

"I have analyzed the reports that Children's Services made in Oregon, Idaho, and California, and I was appalled by your neglect, disregard, and abuse of your daughters. I read about the conditions the girls were living in with you and Parker, in all three states, and I am aware of your past arrests and your drug history."

Devlin was not sniffling. She was not holding her arms out in a hug anymore. Gee-whiz. Her hands had stopped shaking, too.

Her face was red, she was twitching, and her mouth was in a screwed-up line. Yes, Devlin was livid.

"I see nothing in your past that indicates that you will be a competent, caring mother to these girls. Nothing. Lucy and Stephi are currently living with Olivia Martindale and her husband, Jace Rivera, in Kalulell, Montana. Olivia is the woman who volunteered to be the girls' guardian if something should happen to Annabelle Lacey, your mother, who had temporary custody of the girls when you went to jail. Annabelle, a nurse in the neonatal intensive care unit at the hospital, did not have bipolar, or depression, nor was she abusive to you, was she? Your father wasn't a cold man and he didn't abuse you, either, did he? But, like your mother, he is dead and can't defend himself. For two parents who, you say, were awful, they sure spent an enormous amount of money on multiple trips to rehab, counselors, psychologists, and special schools for you.

"Sarah, custody of the girls was taken from you in Idaho, Oregon, and California because you are an unfit mother. You lost custody in Oregon when you robbed a store. This court, I, will not give those girls back to you and wait until they are half dead again to take them away from you. They deserve better. The girls will remain, from this day forward, with Olivia Martindale."

"Damn it. You can't do that!" Devlin yelled. "Those are my kids. Mine."

"I can. I have," the judge snapped. "You should have treated them better when they lived with you. You should have fed them so they would not be emaciated. You didn't. You should have kept rats away from them, and fleas, and drug addicts. You didn't.

"You should have had a clean home without drugs and drug paraphernalia lying around, and you should have gotten them medical care when they needed it. Especially when Stephi had double pneumonia and almost died, and would have died had CSD not been called by a neighbor. Lucy fainted from *malnutrition* and the school had to have her taken away in an ambulance."

The judge's voice rose in anger. "You should not have been a drug addict and living with another addict. You should have protected them. I am not fooled by the pink blouse, the cross, the talk of Jesus, and the innocent mother act. I've been doing this for too long and you, Sarah, are a poor excuse for a mother. Your parental rights will be terminated. If you comply with all of the rules of the court, in one year I will allow limited, supervised visitation."

I leaned back on the bench and closed my eyes. I felt the tears burn. I thought I was past tears, but I wasn't. The girls would be safe. They would be with Jace and me. Loved and cared for. My daughters. Our daughters.

Devlin turned to me, raving. Across the courtroom she yelled, "Olivia Martindale, you stupid bitch. You will never, ever be a mother to my girls. Never."

"By the way," the judge said. "Your calls to Olivia were recorded from jail, Sarah. I listened to every one of them. You are to stay away from Olivia Martindale and the girls. Are we clear on that?"

Devlin didn't even hear her, her voice rising three octaves. "I swear, Olivia, I will have those girls. You took them from me. You stole my girls from me. They are not yours. They will never be yours. If I can't have them, you can't have them!"

The judge nodded at the bailiff. "Ms. McDaniel is done here." Devlin swore and swore as the bailiff dragged her out, then she laughed. High-pitched, giggly. She yelled, "Never, bitch," to me before she was yanked out of the courtroom. "Never, bitch."

The judge looked at me. "I have entrusted you with the lives of these precious children. I will recommend that the adoption papers be put through immediately."

I stood up, wobbled. Jace stood with me. "Thank you, Your Honor. I love them. I promise you I will be the best mother I can be."

"I know you will be. You have already proven that. Obviously, you read the book in the Bible written by Mary Christ, mother of Jesus, where she wrote a list on how to be a proper mother." I laughed. She winked at me, rapped the gavel. "Adjoined."

If I thought that Devlin had a heart, I would feel bad for her for losing her children. If she hadn't been neglectful and abusive, I would feel bad for her. If she hadn't allowed her children to be starved, and left alone for days on end, and if she hadn't put them in the way of scary, dangerous men, I would feel bad. Of course, if she hadn't done all that she wouldn't have lost her children in the first place.

I felt sweet relief as I turned to Jace and held him close. Our tears ran together. Claudine stood up, cheered, climbed over the barrier, *in her skirt,* and hugged us both.

Chapter 16

I wanted to celebrate that the adoption of Stephi and Lucy would now go through. I wanted to celebrate that they would be safe forever, that they would be my and Jace's daughters.

But how do you celebrate that?

Their father, an addict and criminal, would be in jail for years. Their mother, an addict and criminal, had lost custody permanently.

We would be essentially celebrating that two people, their own mommy and daddy, had failed as parents and their parental rights were terminated. So what to do?

The girls figured it out for me. "Now we're your daughters forever, right, Aunt Olivia?" Lucy asked.

"Yes." I hugged her and Stephi.

"And we're not going to live with Mommy?" Stephi said.

"No. But you'll probably be able to see her again, after a while."

They looked worried. "But you or Uncle Jace will stay with us when we see her again, right?"

"Yes."

They sniffled, their eyes filled. "It's not that I want to live with Mommy," Stephi said.

"No, we want to live with you, our real mommy, Aunt Olivia," Lucy said.

"But it's sad, too, isn't it?" I said, and they nodded and they cried, their small bodies shaking, and then I said, "Why don't we invite everyone to meet us at the roller rink tonight and we'll have pizza."

Their eyes lit up.

"Go roller-skating?"

"Yes."

"I'm going to wear my tutu!"

"I'm wearing my butterfly wings and the cowgirl hat that Uncle Jace gave me!"

So that's what we did. We roller-skated. I fell. Jace fell. Once I accidentally skated smack into Jace and we both fell. My mother face-planted, and my grandma fell on her rear. Kyle was terrible, clinging to the side of the rink the whole time, determined to master roller-skating, to no avail. The girls were quick, daring.

Chloe was the star. I think Zane was impressed. She glided. She skated backward. She skated fast, she twirled, she spun. "Big, fat girls know how to do it on skates," she yelled out. "I'm a tough-talkin', hip-rockin' Montana woman."

And that was our adoption celebration. Family. Pizza. Roller-skating.

Kyle presented the four of us with a special gift at Jace's, at *our,* house two weeks later.

He had drawn Jace, me, Stephi, and Lucy, sitting on our front steps, the house behind us, the mountains behind the house. We were smiling, Jace had his arm around me, and the girls were in front of us. Stephi was wearing her fake raccoon hat and her pink tutu over her red jeans. Lucy was wearing a flowered dress, her butterfly wings, and red boots. Kyle drew the dogs, Snickers and Garmin, and the cat, K.C. Both girls were holding chocolate chip cookies.

We framed that family picture.

Were we actually doing this? We were having sex in Jace's truck, down a deserted street.

"Are we not too old for this?" I panted. I had been sitting by him on the way home from town. Then I felt like kissing him, so I did. Then I felt like letting my hands wander, so I did. Then I felt like opening up his shirt and seeing all that muscle. So I did. And we had to pull over outside of town, where I showed off my flexibility in a truck.

"I know you're not too old, so I'm not, either." He pulled off my shirt. I pulled off his.

It is amazing what you can do in a big truck with the seats leaned back ever so slightly.

Awesome.

The school bus picked the girls up in the morning and I waved them off. It had been two weeks since the trial, and I was starting to breathe again like a normal person.

That morning, over eggs, Stephi told me, in all seriousness, "Aunt Olivia, we have made our decision."

"And that decision is?"

Lucy said, "We're going to be surgeons."

"Super. You can fix people up and make them happy."

"Yep," Stephi said. "We'll be fixers."

"And they'll say, 'Thank you,' and we'll always have candy for our patients, like Grandma Mary Beth and Grandma Gisela do," Lucy said.

Dinah, Justin, Earl, and I and the morning staff whipped up a delicious breakfast for the clients who oohed and aahed over the Buckin' Bronco Breakfast Burritos, then I called Jace.

"Hey, Jace. If you can get home soon I'll be in a red negligee in our bedroom. Do you need a morning nap?"

He did.

Spring brought a soft beauty. It tossed down golden buttercups, white columbine, and light pink bitterroot blossoms. It brought the sun, warmer winds, green leaves, and endless postcard-like views.

The school bus rumbled down the road toward the ranch and

I smiled, knowing the girls could see me, even if I couldn't see them. They were always waving by the time they arrived. I had made them gingersnap orange cookies, which would sandwich a layer of vanilla ice cream.

The bus stopped in front of me.

"Stephi and Lucy aren't on the bus, Olivia," Mickey, the bus driver, called down.

"What? Do you know why not?"

"I don't know. But they did not get on. I waited for ten minutes."

"Huh. Okay. Thanks, Mickey." I called the school as I walked back to the house. Something . . . something scary, something unknown, started to rattle me. "Hi, Mattie. It's Olivia. Lucy and Stephi didn't get off the bus. Mickey said they never got on. Do you know if they stayed after school? They didn't have an after-school class today."

"Hang on. Let me call down to their teachers."

I waited, my stomach starting to hurt.

"Olivia? Their teachers said they walked the girls outside to the front of the school with the rest of the class to the buses. Do you think they went home with a friend?"

I tried to think around my taut nerves. Had the girls said they were going home with friends today? "No. Not unless they decided to go without asking, which isn't like them."

"Let me check outside. Maybe the little rascals are playing on the equipment."

I started to feel sick.

I waited and waited.

"Olivia, they're not out there. I went out with Jefferson and Leroy. Sheryl's looking in the music room and the gym."

"Let me call a few friends."

"Okay. Call me back. We'll keep looking here."

I called three of their friends. The friends were not with the girls. I called my mother and grandma at the clinic, on the impossibility that they had picked the girls up. I knew they would never do that without telling me, but I was grasping at straws. I called my sister, who was at work, driving an ambulance, and I called Kyle.

"I have not seen the girls." Kyle asked for more information, and I told him. He took a shaky breath. "I'm uncomfortable with this situation. I will call Mother."

I called Jace. He heard my worry. I raced up to the school with him. Together with Sheryl, Mattie, and several teachers, we went through the school.

No girls.

My mother and grandma and sister texted me, asking if I'd found the girls.

"I'm sure we'll find them." Jace hugged me.

I received a call from one of Lucy's friend's mother and put her on speakerphone. "Harper just told me that she saw Lucy and Stephi get in a car with a woman with blond hair."

The school tipped and spun, the floor fell out. Jace wrapped his arms around me. "Shit," Jace muttered. "Oh, shit."

"Oh no. Oh no. Oh no, no, no." I cried. "Oh, my God, no."

"It's okay, Olivia. We'll call the police." Jace took the phone and spoke to the mother. "Ask Harper what color the car was . . . it was blue? Does she remember anything else about it? The back had been hit? Okay, thank you."

He dialed the police and told Chief Kalama about Devlin, while Sheryl and Mattie propped me up.

Chief Adam Kalama and his police force were immediately looking for the girls, for a blue car with damage to the back, a blond woman driving. Soon it wasn't only the Kalulell police but state and county. An Amber Alert went out. The police tried to contact Devlin, and when they couldn't reach her, they put out an APB and tried to trace her. My sister went up in a helicopter with a copilot to look for the car.

The police questioned us, as they should. We went to the station, and we took lie detector tests and passed. W knew it was a formality.

Police officers questioned the staff at the school and our staff on the ranch. The ranch, every building, all barns, and our homes, the old home and the new, were searched. We handed over our phones and computers. An hour went by, a second hour, a third. Police and FBI filled the house, men and women in and out. I took a photo I had of the girls, gave it to Dinah, Justin, and Earl, and they made thousands of copies. They started distributing them in town. Our guests helped, too, which was very touching, and when our friends found out, including Michael, Ryan, and Jordan, and their wives, they raced to the house and we handed them flyers, too.

Two of our guests, social media experts, immediately set up a Facebook page to get the word out. Grandma and my mother came over immediately, and my mother jumped in with the FBI and police as if she was employed with them.

Jace and I rushed to his truck. As we left, I looked up at the hill. Underneath that craggy oak tree were the three white crosses. I could not lose more children, I couldn't. I couldn't, I couldn't. I made a strangled sound, shut the door, and we started driving country roads in the dark.

Soon the girls were on the news, along with Devlin's photo, and on the next news cycle, and the one after that.

"How in the world could two little girls disappear?" I wailed, holding Jace, his arms tight around me when we finally arrived home at three in the morning. My mother put her arms around both of us and said, "We will find them. We will." Her arms trembled. My grandma said, tears in her eyes, but her chin up, "Courage. Hold yourself together, my love. You must be strong."

Kyle stared at his computer, the loud buzz around him of the police and FBI not distracting him. His Questions Notebook was open in front of him. There were many new notes in there.

"I'm searching for them, Aunt Olivia, birthday February 27. I feel confident that when I collate all of the information that I'm hearing here, as the police and FBI communicate, I will be able to solve the puzzle of their abduction." His hands jiggled. He tapped his palms. He twitched. "I am uncomfortable. I believe it is fear that I am feeling. Mother has ordered me to remain calm, to not, in her words, 'lose my freakin' marbles,' and I am striving to attain that goal, but when I think of Stephi and Lucy my agitation begins once again."

My sister landed the helicopter after hours of searching and drove out to the house. "Olivia, I have made a decision. I'm going to kill Devlin for you." She patted my arm. "Kyle's older than the girls and the girls need you more, so I'll go to jail. I'll take the hit. My sharpshooting skills are excellent."

She was completely serious. I knew it. That made me cry.

The rest of the night brought more hopeless, mind-numbing fear.

Morning came, cloudy, rainy, bleak. Then afternoon. Then night again. We searched for them continuously. I made a plea for the girls through the media. We had made more flyers to take out of state, including flyers with Devlin's photo on them from the police.

I was having trouble breathing again, my chest tight, swallowing almost impossible. I felt as if I was choking on fear. Devlin would disappear with them for as long as she could.

Why couldn't the police find them? Where were they? *Where are you, Stephi? Where are you, Lucy? Where?* Jace held me when we cried in our bedroom that night at four in the morning. Jace was white, strained. Not eating, not sleeping.

Day three came and went, and I felt myself shutting down. More police and FBI came through the house, the girls were on the news all the time, the flyers were all over five states, and social media was saturated.

Day four came, and no sign of them. Together Jace and I were in hell. But this time, in bed, where neither Jace nor I could sleep, I turned to him and said, "Jace. I love you. I will not leave you again. No matter what."

I hadn't realized how worried he'd been. His expression was one of ragged relief as he pulled me close and kissed me. "Thank you, baby. I love you, too. We'll find them. We will."

Where are you, Stephi? Where are you, Lucy? I love you, I love you, I love you.

July 1945
London, England
Gisela Gobenko, grandmother of Olivia Martindale

When the war in Europe finally ended, London pulverized but victorious, tens of millions of people dead all over the world, the atrocities only beginning to be known, Oliver Martindale, Gisela Gobenko's Montana Man, came back for her. He arrived at the hospital and found her, bending over a patient. She took one look at him, her handsome American air force pilot, and he swept her up in his arms and kissed her.

Oliver Martindale took her to dinner, though in war-torn London they had to step over rubble and rock to get there. He said, "The doctor has come to take his nurse to dinner." Gisela had two dresses. She wore the brown one first.

They went to another dinner, the next night, at a café with only minor damage, almost all of the buildings around them having been cratered by the Nazis. She wore the blue dress with the blue flowered hat and a white ribbon. Gisela knew she was in love with her Montana Man.

In one month, in the aftermath of a nation torn to pieces, they were engaged. Married the month after that. Gisela wore a white lace wedding gown she found at a secondhand shop. Naomi and Keila took it in for her, and they both served as bridesmaids. Mrs. Lowenstein brought her bridal bouquet. Dr. Hirschfield and his wife came, as did other doctors and nurses at the hospital.

Gisela was haunted, though. She had to find out what happened to her family back in Munich. She had already tried, contacting everyone she could, but her continual, frantic efforts had been in vain. Europe was in chaos. Millions of people were on the move, including emaciated and traumatized concentration camp survivors, guilty Nazis and SS trying to escape and hide from their crimes, and Jews headed to Palestine, giving up on life in Europe after their near annihilation.

Germans were fleeing west to safety from the Russians who were taking revenge for Germany's brutal attack on the Soviet Union, for the tens of millions of their people killed by the Nazis, for their military men frozen to death on the battlefield, tortured and slain, and for their civilians who were starved to death during the relentless siege of Leningrad. Some of the Russians, infuriated, vengeful, were robbing, beating, shooting, and pillaging in Germany. They were raping women and girls.

Still others in Europe were on the move, hoping to immigrate to the United States, Canada, and South America to start life over.

It was difficult to travel, it was difficult to find passage, but Montana Man arranged it. They went to Munich, sometimes with other American troops on U.S. transportation. It took long days, longer nights, as the international community had moved in by force and Germany was being divided and partitioned off, as punishment and consequence for starting World War II.

Munich had been bombed during the war more than seventy times by the Allies in air raids. It had been one of Hitler's bases of operations. The city had been pummeled into submission.

When Oliver and Gisela arrived in Munich, she often could not figure out where she was, where to go, as familiar landmarks and buildings were gone, eerie skeletal frames or concrete and metal rubble the only things remaining.

People were wandering, hungry, scared. Gisela tried to feel sorry for her fellow Germans, but she simply couldn't. How many of these people had embraced Hitler and his ideas, his murderous rule? How many had turned away when another Jewish family was dragged off in the middle of the night? How many had looted Jewish homes or thrown rocks and firebombs through their businesses? How many had burned synagogues down to nothing? Which ones had worked in concentration camps? As Nazis, as members of the SS? Who had helped round up the Jews? Who had tortured and shot them?

When Gisela and Oliver found her family's three-story brick home, the damage to the east side of the house extensive, another family was living in it. She tried to open the red door with her key, but the lock wouldn't budge. A woman she didn't recognize with a sharp face and a bony body answered the door. Gisela said, "What are you doing in my home?"

The woman, alarmed, guilty, tried to shut the door, but Oliver wouldn't let her, holding the door open with one hand. "Now, ma'am. We're here to talk to you. We need to know who you are and why you're living in my wife's family home."

Gisela translated what Oliver said. The bony woman tried to slam the door, but her husband, a much more compassionate man, invited them in. The Nazis had looted the house, and then it had stood empty before this family moved in three years ago. There was nothing of value left. The husband told Gisela, "I'm so sorry."

They had known, as millions of other Germans had known, that the reason he was able to buy this elegant home in a fashionable part of Munich for much less than market price was because the Nazis had taken all the homes owned by Jewish families and thrown them on the market as they had thrown the Jews into the concentration camps.

In fact, he and his wife had known that this home had been owned by the daughter of the owners of Ida's Bakery and Boris's Leather Goods, Esther Gobenko. They had known, too, that she was Esther of Esther and Alexander's Department Store. They also knew that the couple had had two daughters and a son, as the girls' rooms still had their pink bedspreads when they moved in, and the son's was blue. And now, here was one of the daughters, in a dark blue dress and blue hat with a white ribbon with an American military man.

Gisela hardly recognized her home. It had been cheerful, filled with love and laughter. There was none of that now. It was dull, lifeless.

She could fight for her home. Demand it be returned, but already she hated being in Munich again. Hated it, hated the memories of people's harshness, their evilness toward her family. She hated what the Germans had done, eagerly joining the

SS, the Nazis, cheering Hitler on for the Jews' destruction and his plan for world domination.

She could almost hear the Nazis' boots clomping on the cobblestones, the Heil Hitler salutes, the screams of her neighbors as they were hauled off in the night. She remembered the long, red Nazi flags and her father coming home, beaten to a pulp. She remembered when two of her uncles had disappeared, never to be heard from again. She remembered Kristallnacht, when their family's businesses had been firebombed and looted, synagogues destroyed, Jews attacked and jailed, then sent to camps.

"May I check one place for our belongings?" Gisela asked, heartbroken beyond belief. She had hoped for a miracle. Hoped that her family was here, that they had found their way back home, that they had survived the war.

The man was puzzled. He had been through the house. Hardly anything had been left when they moved in, aside from odd furniture pieces and the children's beds. "Yes, please."

Gisela went up to her bedroom. She did not enter any other room. The pain would have killed her.

With her Montana Man and the husband and wife behind her, Gisela lifted up a floorboard in her bedroom, where Renata and she had hid their treasures. She pulled out the tin box with old-fashioned ladies dancing at a ball, their dresses filled with lace, buttons, and ruffles.

The husband sucked in his breath, as did his wife. His wife covered her face with her hands and Gisela saw that she was crying. "We're very sorry," the man stuttered out, tearful.

"I'm so sorry, dear," the woman said.

Her Montana Man supported her as they left, the tin box clutched in her hands. The treasures inside were priceless to her.

Gisela and Oliver went to Ida's Bakery. The pink and white building had been bombed. She went to her grandfather's shop, Boris's Leather Goods. The roof and a wall were missing. She went to her parents' department store, Esther and Alexander's. It was locked up, in shambles.

Gone.

Everything, everyone was gone.

*   *   *

Gisela and Oliver searched the lists coming out of the camps, with help from U.S. and British military friends of Oliver's.

Their searches, the phone calls, the visits to the Red Cross, their letters, yielded nothing initially.

Finally, there were the names she didn't want to see on lists coming out of the concentration camps.

Bergen-Belsen. Dachau. Buchenwald.

Each day Gisela found more names on the list. Each day she collapsed, Oliver holding her tight.

Esther Gobenko
Alexander Gobenko
Isaac Gobenko
Ida Zaslavsky
Boris Zaslavsky
Grigori Zaslavsky
Solomon Zaslavsky
Devoran Zaslavsky
Aviva Zaslavsky
Miriam Zaslavsky
Deena Zaslavsky
Johan Zaslavsky
Rafael Zaslavsky
Alim Zaslavsky
Aizik Gobenko
Raisel Gobenko

Gone. All gone. She was alone.

Gisela thought she would lose her mind. She thought the grief would kill her. If the grief didn't kill her, perhaps she would kill herself. Why live anymore, why live? But then she felt Oliver's hand in hers, warm and loving.

Oliver Martindale was why Gisela Gobenko Martindale did not hang herself from the rafters from one of the many buildings in Munich that had been bombed by Allied forces.

*   *   *

Later, from Montana, with Oliver's help, by writing letter after letter to various organizations, they found many, but not all, of the names of the rest of Gisela's family. On her mother's side, she had four uncles and four aunts and sixteen cousins. She could never find the names of Moishe and Zino, her two uncles who had disappeared, taken in the night by the Nazis before she left on the Kindertransport. But she knew the truth: Their bodies had not been found, their names had not been recorded, they had not lived.

Gisela's family never left her heart, not one of them. She knew she would never be, truly, happy. How could she? It was foolish to think so, to hope so. But she started over in Montana with Oliver, who she loved with every breath she took.

She began a new life and put her past in a cardboard box in the attic, including the dark blue dress she would never wear again, her wedding dress, and her white nurse's uniform, to remind her of what she had been. Inside the tin box with the dancing ladies were Isaac's colored pencils, the red and purple butterfly clips she and Renata had given each other as girls, the charm bracelets from their parents, the menorah that had survived two attacks, lost letters written by lost people, and photographs. She tucked the battered and burned cookbook in the box, too, making sure the pink ribbon was tied so the treasures inside would not fall out.

Gisela told her Montana Man that she needed windows all around in their new log cabin to feel safe, so she could see everywhere. When she was younger and the Nazis barged into their home and took their furniture, their art, their jewelry, she hadn't seen them coming. She had felt trapped. She didn't ever want to feel trapped again. She told him she needed a red door, like her mother, Esther, and grandmother, Ida, to symbolize freedom, and she needed red geraniums each summer to celebrate a new life. He gave her everything she asked for.

Gisela had trouble getting pregnant, had one miscarriage, then Mary Beth arrived. There were no more babies after that, but Gisela and Oliver adored Mary Beth. She would teach her how to cook, but they would not use the recipes in the cook-

*book from Odessa, Munich, or London. Those recipes would
stay in the attic, hidden. How could she make the recipes written by the women in her family whom she would now have to
live without forever? It was too much.*

*Gisela left her faith behind, too. She had seen too much suf-
fering. She doubted there was a God at all. And, if there was,
He had chosen not to intervene. He had chosen not to stop the
killing. But what kind of God refuses to intervene in a
Holocaust? Why had He let the Jews suffer? Why hadn't He
helped other innocent people in a world war that killed tens of
millions? She couldn't follow a God like that. And yet she believed in an afterlife. She believed in heaven. She knew it didn't
make sense. So maybe, somewhere in her soul, she still believed
in God. Maybe.*

*Oliver built her a gazebo. "For when your memories are too
much to bear, my love. You can sit in the gazebo, watch the
river, stare at the mountains, and hopefully find some peace."*

And that's what she did.

It was all she could hope for.

On the fifth morning of Lucy and Stephi's abduction, still
pacing, hardly eating, our house filled with law enforcement
people, news reporters bunched outside, I tried to think through
the bubbling panic in my head. Devlin must have stopped somewhere after she picked up the girls. She had to be nearby and
hidden. If not, with the Amber Alert, wouldn't someone have
seen her car, reported her? But how would she know where to
go? She was from Portland, not Montana. She didn't know anyone here, did she?

And then I remembered a tiny, tiny fact. Annabelle had told
me when I first met her that Devlin had run away from home
when she was seventeen, to go back to a boy she'd met in Montana on a family vacation. Devlin was furious when the vacation
was over and Annabelle said she had to go back to school. Devlin
actually hit Annabelle, then stormed out and went back to Montana on a bus . . . the town was named . . . named . . . argh!

And then I knew. It was the town of Bellington. The boyfriend's name was Hatch. Annabelle and I had chuckled at that. *Hatch*. Was his real name Howard? Harry? Henry? It was Henry. I remembered. Could Devlin be with him?

"Kyle." I whipped around and told him what I knew. I told the police officers and FBI in our living room, then Jace and I ran out to his truck, followed by the police and FBI. Bellington was a half hour away.

Within ten minutes Kyle called. "Aunt Olivia. In regards to the situation of your missing daughters, and in conjunction with the information that you provided me about Sarah Lacey, aka Devlin McDaniel, birthday June 16, I have located eight Henrys in Bellington. I decided, for expediency's sake, to remove all minors and men who would be too old for Sarah, aka Devlin, to be attracted to them. I now have four Henrys.

"The first Henry is forty-eight, probably too old for Devlin. I have ascertained that he is a principal at the local high school with five children. Birthday December 14. The second Henry is a priest. Age thirty-six. Unlikely that he had a romantic affair years ago with Devlin, but still quite possible. He can be located at St. Andrews Church on the corner of Main and Hubbard Streets. Birthday November 12. The third Henry is a woman. Real name, Henrietta. Birthday October 31. Age twenty-six. As you gave me no reason to suspect that Devlin is a homosexual, I believe we have to cross her off our list."

"And the fourth?" My voice wavered, my throat tight, strangling me. Jace was flying as we shot down the road. In front and back of us were other police cars.

"The fourth Henry is thirty years old. A mechanic. Birthday April 16. He also has the nickname of Hatch. I have cross-referenced his Facebook page. He is not unattractive. He is single. He likes hunting, cockfights, which is illegal and abusive, marijuana—"

"What's his address?"

"One moment, please." He told me.

"Thank you, Kyle. Thank you."

"A thank-you is unnecessary." I could tell Kyle was crying. "I feel extremely unsettled with the girls missing. I am trying to control myself so that emotion does not cloud my thinking in my quest to rescue Stephi and Lucy and return them safely home in the most expedient manner."

We hung up and then I called the police, gave them the address.

We headed to Henry's, aka Hatch's, home. It was outside of Bellington, down a gravel road, way back in the hills. It was a rusting double-wide that had seen better days. Law enforcement stealthily surrounded it, and we were told to stay back. They knocked. Identified themselves. Hatch answered, gut sagging, shirt off. Devlin sprinted out the back. The police on that side of the trailer easily caught her. She swung at them and swore. She was facedown on the ground in seconds.

The police yelled at Hatch to put his hands up, *now,* guns pointed at him. He did so and yelled, "What the hell? I ain't done nothin'. If this is about the cockfight, it wasn't my idea!"

When he was down, I sprinted to the trailer with Jace, following the police inside. We found our daughters cowering in a dirty, shadowed corner, dazed. They were emotionally gone. I could tell. They had their arms around each other, but their eyes were blank. They were still. They were filthy. They were thinner and wearing the same clothes they'd gone to school in days ago. They had been crying, I could see the streaks down the dirt on their cheeks. They were pale and had dark circles under their eyes.

"Stephi." I held their limp hands. "Lucy."

They did not respond, hardly moving. Jace kneeled and leaned toward them. "Girls. Everything is okay now."

They turned to him, blinked, turned to me, blinked again, but I could tell they didn't see us. They were shut down.

"Hi, darlings," I said, my voice catching on tears. "It's Aunt Olivia."

They still didn't move.

"Your giant is here," Jace said, his voice choked. "Waiting to play Candy Land with you."

And that did it. It was as if they finally woke up. Returned to the world. They blinked again and I could see them focusing, seeing us, for the first time. Their faces crumbled, and they fell into our arms, their bodies shaking with sobs.

After a check at the hospital, which found no sexual abuse but did find them dehydrated, starving, traumatized, and hardly able to talk, Jace and I took the girls home and made them macaroni and cheese. They ate and ate, then cried and cried.

They took showers, and Jace and I brushed out their hair. The police talked to them when they were in their pink bunny pajamas, oh so gently, and we heard things we didn't want to hear, but at least we knew, then we tucked the girls into bed, and thanked, once again, the FBI and the police as they left. My mother handled the media with her usual efficiency and ended with, "Now off you all go. No more talking tonight. You leave these people alone. Don't make me get a tractor out to shovel you off this property."

Jace and I took a shower together. I leaned against him and cried. That tough guy cried, too. We toweled off, put on sweats, and went to lie on the floor in the girls' room. An hour later we fell into bed, holding each other. So grateful. Eternally grateful.

The next morning I thought the girls would want a day off of school, but they didn't.

They wanted normal. They wanted to go to school and do math and writing, skip to music class, and play with their new friends.

But underneath the courage and bravado was a deep sadness, a jagged brokenness. It was their mother who came to get them at school and invited them to ice cream. They love their mother. They will always love their mother. Even though Devlin was a crappy mother, she was still their mother. Parker was still their father.

That's why they got in the car. Devlin was Mommy.

Their tie to her, and their father, who both failed them, will cause a cascading amount of pain in their lives for years to come, and we will hug them and help them through it as best we can.

Devlin was arrested and charged with kidnapping, custodial interference, endangering minors, assaulting a police officer, etc. She was high on cocaine and meth.

Henry, aka Hatch, said he didn't know Devlin had kidnapped the girls and said he didn't watch the news. "It don't got nothing to do with me." The police were inclined to believe him. One of them told me, "I've met raccoons smarter than him."

Devlin is now going to jail. I don't know for how long, I don't care. By the time she's out, the girls will be older and can figure out what kind of relationship they want with her, if any.

Jace and I hugged Lucy and Stephi after we walked them to the bus stop outside the ranch. We waved. They waved back, their faces worried at first, but then they turned to their friends.

When the bus turned the corner I said to the cowboy, "I'm ready to go back to bed."

"So am I, baby. Lead the way."

On Saturday afternoon we gathered at the blue farmhouse, the whole family passing through the red door, the color Ida chose to symbolize freedom. In the summer we all—my mother, my grandma, me, Chloe—would plant red geraniums to celebrate life.

We had each decided to make a treat from a recipe in Grandma's battered cookbook, tied together with a stained pink ribbon, in honor of her family, our family.

Chloe and Kyle were making a black forest gâteau with cherries.

My mother and grandma were making a German apple cake.

The girls and I were making Kuchen bars with vanilla custard.

It was Martindale Cake Therapy. We laughed and chatted.

Jace, Zane, and other friends, including Michael, Ryan, and Jordan, and their wives and kids, would come over when we were done to eat.

My grandma held the cookbook to her chest, the leather beaten, the pages burned by fire, the words smeared by the tears and blood of our ancestors, before we started. She spoke in Yiddish, Ukrainian, then German.

"What did you say, Grandma Gisela?" Stephi asked.

"I told my family I missed them. I would see them again. And I said the same thing I'm going to say to all of you. I love you. You are my heart. You are my life." We told her we loved her, too, then we were silent while Grandma gathered herself back together. "Now let's bake. In honor of my mother, Esther, oh, how wonderful it feels to say her name again, for my sister, Renata, my grandmother, Ida, my great-grandmother, Sarrah, and my great-great-grandmother Tsilia, who all have recipes in this book."

As we baked, Grandma told us one more chapter of her story.

When my grandma arrived in Montana in 1945 she did not feel welcome by the people here.

Though she had been taught English, with a British accent, in Germany, and was completely fluent in English before she left on the Kindertransport, and further corrected her German accent in the years she was in London working as a nurse, a bit of that German accent still rang through.

The United States had been through war. Many had lost sons in Germany. They, rightly so, blamed the Germans for the war and, by extension and by mistake, my grandma. The people in Kalulell could not believe that my granddad would marry a German woman, no matter how precise her English, no matter how pretty her face. He had been a soldier himself, attacking the evil Germans as a fighter pilot! And here was the enemy!

"Your granddad heard the talk in town about me, none of it flattering," Grandma told us, "and so did his parents. People were angry, they were grieving. They were furious that their country had been bombed in Pearl Harbor, that their loved ones were locked up, tortured, and starved in prisoner of war camps, that their family members were coming home in coffins or with lifelong injuries.

"And there I was. A woman from Germany. They didn't know my story, they didn't know me. They didn't know that I was Jewish and escaped Germany, that my entire family had been gassed, tortured, and starved in concentration camps. They didn't know my sister had died, bombed by the Nazis. They didn't know that I had tended to American and British sons and daughters, as a nurse, in a hospital, for years, part of that during the Blitz.

"I remember being in many an operating room with critically injured boys from Montana, often in the basement to protect ourselves from bombing raids. They had been evacuated to London from the front. Some didn't make it, calling for their mothers at the end. I had their blood all over me. I sewed them up. I assisted doctors who dug deep into their bodies and pulled out bullets. I took the leg, or the arm that was amputated. I held their hands. I listened to them, made sure an infection didn't kill them.

"Then I came to America, in love and married to your granddad. I was soon in love with his parents, who were always loving to me, but I faced hatred here. Part of me was so hurt, so furious that they judged me to be like the Germans, the Nazis, who had started the war. I was German, I was Jewish, and I was on their side. But the other part of me understood why they hated me.

"I, however, had no energy for hate. I had lost everything. I had lost everyone." Her voice wavered. "I decided to be kind, not bitter, helpful, not angry. Hatred had almost killed the world. I decided to stand for my family and honor them. To be strong and courageous. I felt such guilt for surviving. Why me? It should not have been me, but it was. There was no undoing it. I wanted to make my family proud of me, and I was determined to make the life that I lived, that they should have lived, worthwhile. How to make it worthwhile? I would continue being a nurse. I would heal."

People here started treating her differently. It was hard to be hostile to a woman who sewed up Uncle Rigert's leg after it was shot in a hunting accident. It was hard to be angry at a woman who so diligently cared for the Millers' son, Tye, when he caught double pneumonia. It was difficult to be resentful of a woman who handled the care of three members of the same family who were in a mangled car accident on the highway, right in front of her, two of whom would have died had she not been there to render emergency aid and tell others there what to do to help.

Plus, my grandma started cooking for others. Uncle Rigert was gifted with a blackberry pie. Tye got his favorite—lemon meringue pie. The family in the car accident received a salmon dinner.

It took time. Years, my grandma said, for some, who had lost sons and daughters in the war. But time moved on, and Grandma's gentle hands, her natural remedies, and generous soul brought peace and healing.

"It is fine to be accepted," my grandma told us, "but the most important person who needs to accept you is *you*. Don't ever forget I told you that. If you don't like yourself, it doesn't matter what others think. Be a person who *you* like."

It is hard to find a more beloved person than my grandma in all of Kalulell.

The annual Kalulell talent show is a popular town event. Everyone goes unless you're passing kidney stones. After the talent show we all have dessert together, waiting for the winners to be announced. My family always donates cakes. This year we made a fluffy four-layer coconut cake with pink buttercream icing, apple pie cupcakes, and a peppermint ice cream frozen pie with a cookie crust.

The talent show is held in an old armory that's been remodeled and cleaned up. The walls are brick, the floor is cement, lights hang from the rafters. A stage has been built from wood, complete with burgundy velvet curtains.

I sat with Jace, my hand in his. Lucy was next to him, showing him how to draw "nice monsters, not bad monsters," as she felt that the monster Jace drew was too scary, therefore, a "bad monster." She added a smile to Jace's bad monster's frightening face. My grandma was beside me in a white silk scarf with blue irises, my mother beside her in silver cowgirl boots, with Stephi on her lap, then Chloe and Zane with the fine, manly shoulders.

I usually love the talent show. It is truly amazing what people in our town can do. Some people don't compete, or they would win every year. For example, members of our small symphony, many who have played in prestigious national symphonies, don't compete, although they do open up the competition. Christina Angelli doesn't compete, either, as an ex-opera star, but she does sing the "Star-Spangled Banner." And Gregory Sochia doesn't compete, as a famous rock star, either, but he'll sing a song.

But we still had a bunch of talent. That night there was a bluegrass band made up of high school teachers who sang a song about a man named Kit who drank too much and "fell down the ditch, darn him, yes, he did." There was a talented teenage ballerina, a trumpet player who had spent years in New Orleans, a juggler who juggled fire (the minister), several one-act plays, a six-year-old who played Beethoven on the piano, two comedy skits that were hilarious, and a group of moms who dressed up like showgirls and performed admirably as the Rockettes, among others.

Kyle was last.

Yolanda Marquez was the emcee and she finally called his name. "Next up, we have Kyle Razolli. Kyle's talent is drawing." We all clapped and screamed like crazy, but we stopped when Grandma got up and walked to the stage.

"What's she doing?" I asked my mother.

"I have no idea. None. She confounds me, that secretive woman, even after all these years."

Grandma climbed the stairs and stood tall beside Kyle and smiled. People started yelling, "Mrs. Gisela! Mrs. Gisela!" She waved.

Kyle pushed his glasses back up his nose, then held his hands straight down by his sides, which for him was impressive. There was no flapping.

"Good evening. My name is Kyle Razolli. You all know my great-grandma, Gisela Martindale. Tonight she is going to tell you her story, which she has not talked about until recently. She has kept her past private. While she is telling her story, I am going to draw a picture of her."

My mother held my hand and I held Jace's. I heard her suck in her breath and say, "My mother is a woman above all other women, and that is the truth."

Chloe said, "Glory hell's bees. I didn't know this was going to happen."

Kyle sat down in front of an easel and began to draw. My grandma, so elegant and dignified, told her story, quickly. There was one spotlight on each of them.

My grandma talked about how her relatives fled Odessa in the Russian Empire because they were Jewish and the pogroms were a threat to their lives, how their home was burned and a baby was lost, and then another after that. She talked about their escape to Germany, and how they started businesses, a leather goods store, a bakery, a department store. She talked about the hate that brought Hitler to power and how Hitler began exterminating the Jews.

She talked about her two uncles disappearing, her father being beaten, and how she and Renata had escaped via the Kindertransport to England. She talked about the Blitz, working as a nurse in a hospital, and a bomb from the Nazis hitting her home and taking Renata's life. She talked about returning to Germany and losing her home, and knowing her family was all gone.

"This is what hate can do," she said. "This is what racism can do. I couldn't speak of what happened to my family for decades because I didn't want to bring the darkness in. I couldn't bring it in. I was afraid of it, afraid of what it would do to me. Now, as I am very old, I know I must speak of it. My family deserves to know what happened. You all deserve to know what

happens when evil wins, or when a group of people turns against
their own, or when the wrong person comes to power."

Crying. All around us. I could hear people sniffling, muffling
sobs.

"Sometimes life is so painful you think it will kill you."
Grandma paused, and those weighted words flew around the
armory. "It was for me. I fought through it, not because I
wanted to but because I had to. I had to live in honor of my
family. They had lost their lives. I could not take mine. I wanted
to help others, to heal, so that my life would mean something,
to them and to me. I found love with Oliver, and we had our
beloved Fire Breather, Dr. Mary Beth, and she had Chloe and
Olivia, my Cinnamon and Nutmeg, and they had Kyle, Stephi,
and Lucy. Teddy, Jace, and Zane joined our family. My family
continued on. There was light after the darkness. And there is so
much love here. So much love, right here, in Kalulell."

My mother, tough woman, was crying. "Momma," she whispered. "Oh, Momma."

Chloe said, "I'm crying. Like a dang baby. Help me. I'm crying. Help."

I cried, too. Jace put an arm around me.

"I want to tell all of you"—my grandma's smile was radi-
ant—"that it has been my pleasure to be a nurse here in Kalulell
for sixty-five years. It has been my honor to serve you and your
families. Most important, I want you to know one thing: I love
you. I do. I love all of you."

All around us we heard people calling out, "We love you,
too, Mrs. Gisela . . . I love you, too!"

The lights went out. Total darkness, and we sat and waited,
the crying magnified in the silence. Then one spotlight came on.
It shone on Kyle and my grandma, standing together. She was
proudly holding the drawing that her great-grandson had made
of her. It was remarkable. It was perfect. It showed my grandma's
strength and courage, her wisdom, her beauty, and her elegance.

We all stood up and cheered. My mother kept crying, saying,
"She is my thundering hero." My sister shouted out, "Way to

go, Kyle! Way to go, Grandma!" Jace wiped his eyes, so did Zane. Tough men know they can cry. It was a long, long ovation. A whole bunch of people climbed the stairs to the stage and hugged my grandma and Kyle. She hugged them back, smiling. Kyle allowed the hugs and patted their backs. Three times.

Later that night, after dessert, the award ceremony began. The bluegrass band came in third. A ballerina came in second.
Kyle came in first.
This time, it was my grandma who cried.

Winning the talent competition, along with my grandma, for Kyle, was huge. Kyle knew that he didn't fit in. He felt it. He felt the loneliness. He had often been teased and bullied. But to be up in front of the town, to have them clapping for him, cheering, did wonders for his self-esteem.

He kept drawing people in town, especially people who "appeared to be having a bad day." He was offered money, but he declined. "Mother said I must bring joy to people with my drawings, without compensation, so people can make my acquaintance and I can get to know them. I will continue as instructed. Mother's advice is always correct."

When an eighty-nine-year-old neighbor lost her ninety-five-year-old husband, Kyle walked to her home and drew a picture of them together, from a photograph, their red barn in the distance. When a firefighter broke his leg when he fell out of a burning home, Kyle went to his house and drew a picture of him, his wife, their five children, two bunnies, three horses, and four dogs to bring "goodwill." "That one took a long time because the animals refused to sit still for long."

Kyle will have a bright future. More important, Kyle has a place where he has a home.

It's all most of us want. A place, people, we call home.

Dinah nodded at me, camera at the ready. She had wrapped her pink hair up in a purple-flowered headband today.

"Hello, everyone. My name is Olivia Martindale. Welcome to *Cooking with Olivia on Martindale Ranch in Montana*. Beside me is my husband, Jace. I had to bribe him to come on the show." I smiled. My bribe was that I would stay in bed with him all day on Saturday while my mother and grandma took the girls horseback riding. "Today we're making ribs, but we're using a special sauce. This sauce was developed by Jace's grandfather, Ricardo Rivera. Jace, tell us about your grandfather and the sauce."

Jace talked about Ricardo, how he'd grown up poor in Mexico, one of ten kids, how he'd worked in the mines for years, saved his money, became a citizen, and bought the land we're on today. He talked about how Ricardo worked as a farmer and a rancher, was married for fifty-one years to a local Kalulell woman—his grandma, Eleanor—and they had his father, Antonio. Ricardo gave the recipe to his son, and Antonio gave it to Jace. "This is Ricardo's recipe we'll be using today. It's called Ricardo Rivera's Ribs."

He was so handsome I wanted to eat him up.

We made the rib sauce together. We brushed the sauce on the ribs, and we chatted about the ranch, what our clients love to do here, the campfires and snowshoeing, the lake and the game room, the afternoon cookies and wine during dinner.

I smiled serenely. Jace smiled like a cowboy. The man was simmering hot. Dinah turned the camera off, we put the ribs in the oven, Jace and I went home for a couple of romps in bed, and I told him I loved him. We came back for the rest of the show when the ribs were done, Dinah holding the camera, and we showed everyone what the ribs looked like cooked, which was totally scrumptious.

Funny thing, though. Jace had not told me that my hair was a wreck when we went back to the kitchen to do the second taping. Maybe he didn't notice. It was quite clear by my pinkish flush, silly smile, no lipstick, and my mascara slightly smeared that we'd been messing around. I looked like I'd just gotten out of bed. Which I had. If that didn't seal the deal, when we watched the video later, after it was already up on our website, Jace had lipstick on the left side of his mouth and a full kiss on his right cheek, and my blue blouse had been rebuttoned wrong. I also forgot to put my white chef's jacket back on.

When we were done, I said, "Thanks for watching *Cooking with Olivia and Jace at Martindale Ranch in Montana!*" I smiled into the camera, trying to be serene and calm, poorly buttoned shirt and all.

"You all have to write your favorite recipes in our family cookbook," Grandma said, her hands on the leather cover. "See all these blank pages? They're for you to fill, Mary Beth, Olivia, Jace, you put your grandfather's rib sauce recipe in here, Chloe, Kyle, Stephi, and Lucy."

Grandma turned and glared at my mother. "I don't want you to use that chicken scratch you usually write in either, Fire Breather. No one can read your writing. It looks like a drunk bear picked up a pen and tried to kill the paper. You write neatly, Mary Beth."

"I'll be sure not to write like a drunk bear," my mother drawled, taking another sip of wine. "Unless I'm drunk. I love this wine."

"And you, Cinnamon"—she turned to me—"don't put your most complicated recipes in, the ones with a hundred different ingredients from all over the world where you have to cook for three days straight and not sleep. Put in your favorite recipes that a normal woman could cook. And, you, Nutmeg"—she stabbed her finger at my sister—"you don't cook much, so you're going to have to make something up."

"I cook," my sister said, but it was weak. She bakes cakes, but dinner? Eh. She slammed a hand on the table. "Sometimes. I shoot better than I cook. I fly a helicopter better than I cook. I stick IV lines in better than I cook, and I'm proud of that. But I do cook." Her voice fell off.

Kyle wrote something in his Questions Notebook.

NO PLACE I'D RATHER BE 393

"You reheat, Chloe," my mother said. "You get food from the store that's frozen in bags and you throw it in a pan with olive oil and turn on the gas. An attempt is made not to burn it."

"I don't think *you* should be accusing *me* of not cooking dinner, Mother, as you often fed us hot dogs and Popsicles and popcorn for dinner when we were younger."

My mother waved her hand as in, "I did not."

We all laughed. She had served us hot dogs and popcorn and Popsicles for dinner often.

Kyle said, "Nourishment is important for the brain. May I tell you about the brain?"

Lucy said, pointing her finger up, "I want to be nourished with a hot dog."

Stephi said, "Can we get a llama for a pet, Jace? I could make him a rock necklace with my collection."

Jace said, "How about a bat monster instead?"

My grandma spoke, soft, sure, her voice filled with love. "I love to cook because it's what my mother, Esther, did. It's what her mother, Ida, did, and her mother, Sarrah, and her mother, Tsilia. It's why our family cookbook is my most precious possession. It links us all, as a family, one to another, generation to generation. Through love and joy and heartbreak and loss. We're all here. In this cookbook."

Wow.

"One more thing," she said to us. "I love you all. You are everything to me."

Measure. Mix. Stir. Whip. Bake. I love my family. I love Jace.

Later, we ate dinner together. Jace bought takeout Japanese food, and we ate with chopsticks. It was noisy. It was funny, fun, relaxed. I kissed Jace and held his hand. The girls crawled on his lap.

At the end of the night I watched my grandma walk out the front door, the moon high, a warm breeze flowing through. Her scarf, with scarlet roses on it, fluttered in the wind. Soon we would all be able to plant our red geraniums, honoring Ida and Esther. I watched her walk toward her log cabin, then she veered toward the gazebo.

She tilted her head back and brought a hand to the sky. She waved.

Chapter 17

～

June 12, 2011
Kalulell, Montana
Gisela Gobenko Martindale, grandmother of Olivia
Martindale

Gisela Gobenko Martindale curled up in bed on a clear, warm night in the blue farmhouse and held her family's cookbook in her hands. Earlier that day she had planted red geraniums in the flower boxes at the farmhouse and at her log cabin. She had run her hand over her husband's lasso on the deck, then kissed his cowboy hat, nailed above hers. She put her hand on the red door, remembering. She smiled at the wagon wheel, then stared up at the weather vane in the shape of the sun because her Montana Man, Oliver, told her she was his sun.

She sat in the gazebo and watched the Telena River run by, the magnificent Dove Mountains in the distance. Oliver had known she would need this gazebo to save her sanity.

In bed that evening, Gisela wore a light blue silk scarf she had bought in 1945, here in Kalulell. It had red geraniums on it. She had not worn it until today.

Propped up against the pillows, she held her special cookbook in her hands. She was now at peace.

Everyone in her family had written their favorite recipes in the cookbook.

Her daughter, loyal and strong Mary Beth, her Fire Breather, had written a recipe for chicken soup called Don't Be a Sickie, Be Healthy Chicken Soup. This was not surprising, as chicken soup did aid in making people well. As Mary Beth was a doctor, on the opposite page she had written down instructions for CPR, how to wrap a tourniquet, and symptoms not to ignore.

Olivia's recipe was for bouillabaisse with lobster, clams, and halibut. She titled it Seafood Delight. She had included ten rules that a chef should always remember, including, "Never skimp on butter."

Chloe's recipe was for steak. "A real woman eats steak," she wrote, "and this is how to make it so delicious you'll moan." Which is why she named it Moaning Martindale Razolli Steak. She wrote a passage about loving yourself for who you are and never buying into what society says is beautiful and what society says you should do. "Be your own brawling babe," she wrote, "and never let a man railroad you off of your dreams." She drew a picture of a curvy woman in a bikini.

Kyle's recipe was for chicken cordon bleu. He said that the blend of chicken and cheese reminded him of the blend of math and science. He drew a picture, across two pages, of their family—she and Oliver, Mary Beth, Chloe, Teddy, Zane, himself, Olivia, Jace, Stephi, and Lucy. It was down to the finest detail, and it was one of his best pictures ever. Every inch of it reminded Gisela of Isaac's drawing of her own family in Munich that he mailed to her and Renata in London.

Jace had added his grandfather's rib recipe. He had shown Kyle a picture of his grandparents, Ricardo and Eleanor, and his parents, Antonio and Clarissa, and Kyle had drawn them all.

Stephi had written a recipe for peppermint brownies. She drew butterflies in the corners eating the brownies and colorful rocks along the edges.

Lucy had written a recipe for cheese sandwiches. She drew a purple monster with a smile. Not a scary one.

Gisela touched the recipes that her grandma, Ida, had written down that were from Sarrah and Tsilia. She reread her mother,

Esther's, recipes, especially the recipes for cakes, and the recipes that her best friend, her sister, Renata, had written when they were in London together. She drew a gentle finger across the pictures of her ancestors, old and young, some who had lived a long time and some who had not, their deaths a crime.

There were pictures of a village in a far-off land, people on horseback, donkeys pulling carts, women with kerchiefs and shawls in the middle of a town square, lush gardens, homes with red doors, herbs and vegetables, red geraniums, sumptuous cakes and cookies. There were recipes written in the midst of tragedy and stifling fear, and recipes written with a light and joyous heart.

She touched the flakes of what had been a pink rose and blew them into the room. She held the two thin, heart-shaped gold lockets that Renata had bought for them to show their sisterly love; touched the white feather to her cheek they'd found in Hyde Park; and she held the red ribbons from Isaac and the sun charm from her mother. She reread the poems by her father and Renata.

The tin box with an old-fashioned picture of ladies in ruffled dresses dancing at a ball that had been hidden beneath the floorboards in their home in Munich was beside the bed. Gisela opened it and touched the two red and purple butterfly clips and the two charm bracelets that their parents had given her and Renata. She ran her fingers over the red pomegranate, a Star of David, a faux blue stone heart, a lion, a tree of life inside a circle, a four-leaf clover, a cat, a dog, and a key. Each charm given to them with love.

She held Isaac's colored pencils. What an artist he was! And yet he studied math and science constantly and always spoke formally. He was so like Kyle.

Gisela kissed the small pile of lost letters from lost family members she had brought from London to Montana that had been kept in the back of the cookbook. Letters from loved ones who were soon dead or dying, burned, gassed, tortured, starved, critically ill and withering away in concentration camps.

Gisela had let her family read these letters and the poems, from her parents, brother, grandparents, uncles and aunts and cousins. Even tough Mary Beth, her Fire Breather, had sobbed. But now they knew. Her family knew her truth.

She had shown her family the photographs that she and Renata had saved in the treasure box and in the cookbook, pointing out who was who. Everyone remarked at how much Renata resembled Olivia with their thick brown hair and green, tilted cat eyes.

Gisela held the small silver menorah in her hand for a moment, the menorah that had survived a firebombing in Odessa and a bombing in London, then picked up the cookbook again, the pages singed around the edges, and blood and tear splattered, yet filled with history, love, and devotion to family.

Gisela's heart skipped a beat, then another. It was time, she knew it. She had done what she had thought impossible all those decades ago: She had survived. She had lived. She had loved. She had, she hoped, made her family back in Munich proud, by loving and caring for others. She would miss her beloved family here, but she longed to see the family that had gone before her.

Gisela could see a light, golden and warm, in the corner of her bedroom. It grew and grew until she saw the outlines of people. She heard talk, laughter. A few notes of a song. Yiddish. Ukrainian. German. English. The people were hazy at first, then she saw who they were. She smiled, she stretched out her hands, laughing, crying, overcome. She climbed out of bed, leaving the cookbook, the menorah, the photographs, the lockets, behind.

She was hugged and kissed by her sweet parents, Esther and Alexander; her brave sister, Renata; her brilliant brother, Isaac. She was hugged by her grandparents, Ida and Boris Zaslavsky, and Aizik and Raisel Gobenko, her aunts and uncles, Moishe and Zino found now, and all her cousins. Teddy, Chloe's husband, hugged her tight.

Gisela had once heard that family members come and get you to bring you up to heaven. Now she knew it to be true.

Her family parted and she saw Oliver, her beloved husband, her Montana Man, tall and strong and young again, smiling. He wrapped her up in a hug and kissed her. Her heart skipped a few more beats. He could still do that to her! Her heart skipped again. And again. She loved him so. She gaped down at herself. Why, she was in her pretty dark blue dress with the blue hat and white ribbon. She tucked her thick brown hair behind her ear. How young she felt!

"I have missed you so much, Gisela." Oliver kissed her hand, "The love of my life. Are you ready?"

Gisela Gobenko Martindale nodded. She tipped her head back and laughed. "I am, Oliver. I am."

And she was.

It seemed that everyone in Kalulell was at my grandma's funeral. People walked in crying and did not stop.

We held it at the armory. We made cakes that we thought Grandma would appreciate: a cake in the shape of the log cabin she had built with my granddad. With fondant we added the lasso on the front deck, a sun weather vane on top, their cowboy hats, the wagon wheel, lots of windows made out of spun sugar, a red door, and red geraniums.

We made a cake with red geraniums made from icing, and we made Ida and Esther's black forest gâteau with cherries, German apple cake, Kuchen bars with vanilla custard, and raspberry tortes. We made a white sheet cake and then used icing to re-create five of her flowered scarves, to bring beauty in. We cried while we baked. It was Martindale Cake Therapy, our tears becoming salt in the recipes.

My mother, my sister, and I spoke at the service about her dignity, her grace, her love, and the enormous courage it took to continue living after she had lost her entire family to the Holocaust and a bombing in London. We told many funny stories, too, because people needed to be reminded of her humor and her laughter. I had a hole in my heart when I spoke about her. I knew that hole would be with me for life, but I also knew it would be filled with my grandma's love and wisdom, too. She was the guiding light of our whole family.

Mrs. Gisela would always, always be missed.

She knew how to heal people in the natural way.

Epilogue

August 2015
Kalulell, Montana
Olivia Martindale

Chloe married Zane. She lost sixty pounds. "Grief pounds gone," she said. She also got the "boob reduction job so the girls won't get in the way of target practice." Then she had twin girls. "They're trouble. Pure trouble. And I like 'em that way."

Kyle graduated from high school early and attended art school. He now has a popular studio and gallery in town. He lets people come and watch him while he works so they can "make my acquaintance and I can get to know them." He still draws people having bad days. He is dating Natasha Jefferson, the girl he first drew at school with eyes like a black hole with azure and jade. She understands, respects, and loves Kyle. "Natasha is enlightenment," he told me. "I respect her brain."

My mother is dating a man named Martin O'Lear. He owns an Internet company, but lives here. He has asked her many times to marry him. "Give me a lobotomy before giving me another husband" is her motto.

Jace and I were off by one.

We did not have six kids.

We have seven.

Lucy, Stephi, Elijah, Zack, Brandon, Savannah, and Ellie Martindale Rivera. We have adopted all of them. Elijah and

Zack are brothers. Brandon and Savannah are sister and brother. Ellie came to us because we saw her photo in the newspaper as a child who was available for adoption and we loved that kid on sight. They're all within three years of age of each other and are very close.

They come from troubled backgrounds, all of them. I will not pretend that our lives are full of sweet pink blossoms all the time, or that raising kids is easy, especially with what our kids have had to deal with in their jagged pasts. But Jace and I, we love 'em, and they love each other. The horses have helped for therapy, our three dogs and four cats have helped, too. Fishing helps. Cooking with me in the kitchen and working with Jace on the ranch helps, too, as do the wide-open, blue and green spaces of Montana, the buttercups that lie like a golden blanket, and the magical sunsets seen from the top of the hill.

My mother has decided it is her life's mission to dedicate seven new doctors to the world, so all of the kids happily spend time at the clinic, study anatomy and biology, and watch medical videos of operations, etc. The videos do not give them nightmares.

Family comes to us in different ways. Some people are born as family to one another and some choose to become family. I love my Martindale family, and I love the family that Jace and I, and our kids, have become.

We are the Martindale Riveras. We have seven kids. We are loud and like to laugh. We ride horses and swim in the lake. We eat pies and pizza. We are not perfect and the house is often a wreck, but we love each other, we do.

And the cowboy still makes my heart race.

NO PLACE I'D RATHER BE

Cathy Lamb

ABOUT THIS GUIDE

The suggested questions are included
to enhance your group's reading of
Cathy Lamb's *No Place I'd Rather Be*.

DISCUSSION QUESTIONS

1. Who was your favorite character and why? Were there any characters whom you didn't like? Was there any part of Olivia's journey, or another character's journey, that you could relate to?

2. Olivia said, "I had a moment of blackness. I did not want to come back to my hometown and work in a dive. I didn't want to come back here after my mother and grandma told everyone I was a chef in a 'fancy-pancy' place in Portland and start flipping burgers. I didn't want to work for Larry, whom no one liked, in his grease-filled slop of a kitchen and have people I've known since I was a baby see me in the back of this squalid, virus-laden hole. I didn't want Jace to see me here most of all. Not Jace . . . My shoulders sunk. I was broke, but my pride was gone in favor of two little girls with blond curls and beautiful smiles whom I loved and adored. *Buck up, Olivia,* I told myself. *You are making me ill with your pity party. No whining. No complaining, you pathetic, wretched creature. Get to work.*"

   Can you relate to Olivia's humiliation? Has anything like this happened to you?

3. Chloe said, on Olivia's cooking show, "And to the men out there. I'm single. Yeah. I am. I know, hard to believe, but my husband died eight years ago, and if you like a woman who knows how to love and who will hug you in a way that makes you feel all tight and wrapped up, warm and snuggly, that's me . . . If you want a woman the size of a stick, who resembles a skeleton with skin, don't call. I am not that woman. Also, you gotta be okay with all of this." She tapped her temples. "Smart. Tough. I will beat you in shooting matches and arm wrestling

and karate. You got an ego that can't handle that"—she picked up a knife and stabbed it into the cutting board— "don't you bother calling me. I'm not here to pander to your little whing whang and your tiny balls and your pride on overdrive."

What did you think of Chloe? Would you be friends with her?

4. Olivia said, "When my mother read us fairy tales when Chloe and I were little girls, she always changed the endings. Instead of Snow White running off with the prince after a single kiss from her glass coffin in the woods, my mother said, 'When Snow White woke up, she saw the prince leaning over her. She smiled at him. He smiled back. She thought he seemed like a friendly, intelligent young man. He helped her up and they visited with the talking animals for a while because they both loved animals. They went horseback riding together into the mountains, which is what you see in this picture here. He was in college studying biology, and she was studying chemistry. They both wanted to become surgeons. They had a lot to talk about because they both loved medicine and nature. They became true friends...' "

What did you think of Dr. Mary Beth Martindale? Would you like to have her as your doctor? What did you think of how she changed the fairy tales? How do you feel about fairy tales and reading them to children, especially to girls?

5. This book took the reader from Odessa in the Russian Empire, to Germany, to London, to Montana, across a hundred-plus years, to tell the stories of Olivia's ancestors. Did you like the historical background in the book and the structure in which the ancestors' stories were

told? Have you studied your family's ancestral history? What did you find out?

6. "Gisela left her faith behind, too. She had seen too much suffering. She doubted there was a God at all. And, if there was, He had chosen not to intervene. He had chosen not to stop the killing. But what kind of God refuses to intervene in a Holocaust? Why had He let the Jews suffer? Why hadn't He helped other innocent people in a world war that killed tens of millions? She couldn't follow a God like that. And yet she believed in an afterlife. She believed in heaven. She knew it didn't make sense. So maybe, somewhere in her soul, she still believed in God. Maybe." Can you relate to Gisela's religious struggle? At the end, did she believe in God?

7. Did you have empathy for Devlin, Stephi and Lucy's mother? Did you think she should get her children back or have them for visitation? Was it right for Olivia to become, legally and forever, their mother? Do you agree or disagree that parental rights should rarely be revoked?

8. Was there a scene(s) that made you laugh? Was there a scene that made you cry?

9. Is this book fiction? Historical fiction? Women's fiction? Romance? Literary? Why?

10. Would you rather live in the log cabin, the blue farmhouse, or in Jace's new house? Why?

Connect with

U(s)

Visit us online at
KensingtonBooks.com
to read more from your favorite authors, see books
by series, view reading group guides, and more.

Join us on social media

for sneak peeks, chances to win books and prize packs,
and to share your thoughts with other readers.

facebook.com/kensingtonpublishing
twitter.com/kensingtonbooks

Tell us what you think!

To share your thoughts, submit a review,
or sign up for our eNewsletters, please visit:
KensingtonBooks.com/TellUs.